Sharon Butala is a leading Canadian author whose most recent book, a memoir called *The Perfection of the Morning*, was a number one bestseller in Canada. For most of her life she has lived in Saskatchewan, which forms the backdrop to a large part of *The Garden of Eden*.

the garden *of* eden

sharon butala

(In writing about Ethiopia I have followed established conventions for the English spelling of Amharic words.)

A *Virago* Book

First published by Virago Press 2000

First published in Canada by HarperCollins Publishers Ltd 1998

Copyright © Sharon Butala 1998

The moral right of the author has been asserted.

A CIP catalogue record for this book
is available from the British Library.

ISBN 1 86049 765 9

Printed and bound in Great Britain
by Clays Ltd, St Ives plc

Virago
A Division of
Little, Brown and Company (UK)
Brettenham House
Lancaster Place
London WC2E 7EN

This book is dedicated to the memory of my mother.

the garden

of eden

PART ONE

—⟨∾⟩—

Seeding

Ethiopia

January 1985

When the muezzin calls faintly from the mosque in town it is still dark, but Lannie is awake, listening to the mournful notes floating, dreamlike, through the silence. Even though she knows the country is still more Christian than Muslim, the sound is, for her, an incarnation of all the sorrows of its people, a fitting way to announce another day with its endless, stale afflictions. Each morning when she hears it, not knowing even what the words mean, the disembodied voice drifting woefully across the rooftops and dusty fields, she listens as closely as any of the faithful. It is the only moment close to prayer in her life, the only moment in which she allows herself to grieve, although for what she hardly knows: for the centuries of suffering these people have endured, for the daily multitude of pointless, cruel deaths, for the countless injustices. If, in these few weeks she has been here, she has been schooled in nothing else, she has learned humility.

The muezzin, having altered the silence, is quiet, and Lannie begins her daily task of girding herself to face whatever this day will bring. She will look only at what she must look at, she will keep silent, she will make herself as useful as possible. She will be willing and quick, gentle and firm. She will be grateful to be here, never forgetting that this is life — what she would go home to is not life at all.

Thus fortified, Lannie gets out of bed. Her bedroom contains only her narrow bed, a small table, and a closet. She washes perfunctorily with water she pours into a basin from the jug she has filled the night before — if she wants to, she can shower later at the hospital — pulls on her worn jeans, her baggy blue T-shirt, her scuffed white runners. She remembers first that Sarah is off for two weeks' rest in Addis. She runs a brush through her fine red-blonde hair, pulls it back from her face and fastens it with a rubber band into a low pony-tail. She has been getting more and more run-down, what with the long hours and the trauma they all live with every day. Some of the nurses stand it better than the others — there doesn't seem to be any way to tell in advance who will have the hard struggle and who will go on evenly day after day, no matter what happens. But Sarah has turned out to be one of the weak. Or maybe it was the innocence Lannie saw shining out of her eyes that had defeated her. Already, after only a month here, she has had to take time off. It's possible, Lannie thinks, that she won't be back at all, that her agency will thank her and send her home. To come all this way, prepared to give a couple of years of your life to good works, determined to live and work steadily in the midst of horrors, only to be defeated in a month by the trivial: fleas, lice, rats, exhaustion from overwork, and the lack of the comforts of home.

As she dresses, she reflects on what has happened to Sarah, how there is a parallel, maybe, with the people who come here to the famine camp. It was a seasoned nurse's observation: *Strange how some nothing will kill, while others cannot survive even with food. As if they lack something,* she'd said, *some . . . integrity of character maybe.* Lannie had thought it a harsh judgement, believing it instead to have something to do with refusal, with some kind of private decision. For herself, she is grimly pleased by the absence of frills; how could she bear a soft couch, a footstool, when outside her door children sleep without even a blanket on the hard ground?

In the kitchen she finds Caroline, the head nurse, pouring herself a cup of coffee from the pot she's made herself, since the kitchen staff doesn't arrive for another hour.

"'Morning," she says, and yawns, pressing the back of her hand to her mouth. Lannie replies, "'Morning," and accepts the mug of coffee Caroline, without asking, pours for her. It is just as she likes it, Canadian-style but strong, too hot to drink. She cups the pottery mug in both hands and blows on it before she sips. Caroline points to the slice of buttered bread on the plate sitting on the table beside them, but Lannie shakes her head no.

"Big day today," Caroline remarks, looking across the long, nearly empty room now and not at Lannie, and sighing. She's about fifty, slender, although not as thin as Lannie, and taller than Lannie who at five seven is not considered short. Even in her dressing gown Caroline exudes the calm that at work transforms itself into authority.

"Yes," Lannie agrees. She clears her throat. "It'll be big." The house is quiet, the others not yet stirring, and the two women sip their coffee standing side by side. Both like silence first thing in the morning, while Maggie shoves a tape into her tape player the moment she opens her eyes and starts the day to the loud, soulless music Lannie remembers without fondness from her student days in Saskatoon. If she could, she would wipe out every trace of her past; she would forget it all.

Lucy, on the other hand, tends to pray, audibly, endlessly, before she emerges for breakfast. They've all grown used to the murmur coming from behind her door. A plain, dark girl, she has on occasion tried to talk to Lannie about Jesus. At first, Lannie laughed out loud. *Are you insane?* she'd asked her, before she could stop herself. *Look around you!* Ever since, Lucy has watched her closely, with a touch of mournfulness in her eyes that infuriates Lannie, when she allows it to affect her at all. Some days, though, she finds herself envying Lucy, some days it's hard to keep from bursting into Lucy's room and falling on her knees beside her.

Lannie is working on registrations today because of Sarah's absence, until either she returns or somebody new arrives to take her place. The others can't understand what Lannie's doing here. She's not a nurse or a nutritionist or pharmacist, she hasn't signed a contract with any of the non-governmental relief groups the way they all have, she can't boast years of experience in other countries — Sudan, Somalia, Uganda, South Africa — as Caroline and some of the others can. It was only Sarah who didn't ask.

Caroline, as if she has divined Lannie's thoughts, says gravely, "I think it's probably better if Sarah spends her contract time doing office work in Addis." Lannie clears her throat again softly before she says, "She'd have to live with her failure if she just goes home." Caroline draws her breath in slowly, her eyes distant, as if she's seeing shy

Sarah filing papers in a dingy office in Addis. She pushes herself away from the rough plastered wall she's been leaning against.

"See you later," she says. "Eat something." This last as if she's thinking of something else — Lannie knows her mind is already on the day's work ahead of them — and, taking her coffee with her, she goes out of the kitchen toward her room on the other side of the house from Lannie's. Caroline's departure always leaves her feeling the same way — faintly bereft, faintly lonely.

She knows it's her own fault she doesn't fit in with the women nearer her own age. She's not interested in the things young women are supposed to like: men, dating, dancing all night in clubs, gossip, and long, intimate talks lasting half the night. If she were like some of them, here for religious reasons, the others would forgive her her difference, or at least tolerate her better, but she isn't religious, nor is she drawn to them any more than to the ones who are here out of curiosity, out of a desire for adventure, or even because they can't find a job at home. Then she chides herself for this thought too, all-encompassing as it is, and unfair. Some, maybe even most of them, are here because they want to help the suffering. Period.

She glances at the slice of bread Caroline has told her to eat, but instead, puts it back inside the tin box on the table. Another of those baffling contradictions they're all surrounded by here, that they don't lack for food when a hundred yards away people are dying of starvation. She picks up the slightly grubby white cardigan that's draped over the back of a chair, puts it on, leaves her half-full mug for the kitchen staff to clean, and goes softly out of the kitchen, into the small, square room that they use for a living room, with its broken-legged couch propped up on bricks, the two shabby chairs, the brown, black, and cream Ethiopian rug covering most of the splintery board floor, the long wooden table with its ancient, chipped white paint.

She pauses for a moment outside the door. The sun is up now and for one instance she catches herself yearning — easily squelched — for the soaring clarity of the prairie light at home, instead of the haze this sun produces. The day is windless, promises to be hot later, although right now, in the shade of the roof's overhang that is propped up with poles at regular intervals to make a veranda of sorts, it's still chilly.

The house, once a school, is long and narrow, with six brown-stained doors across the front, each one opening from the outside into a bedroom, and each room having interior doors leading from room to room. It's actually a mud house — when she first came it struck her more than once how horrified Aunt Iris would be if she knew she was living in a mud house — but the exterior has fairly recently been freshened with a whitewash, and as the house is situated on a slope, the veranda is supported by a rough stone foundation, which gives it a smarter air than most one-room, mud, tin-roofed shacks housing eight or more people each, in the nearby town. I am living in the lap of luxury, she thinks, and would laugh did she not find it so appalling.

She descends one of the three sets of crumbling cement steps that lead to the dirt road, crosses it, follows a row of eucalyptus trees down the lane, and then strikes off down a well-trodden, narrow path across a farmer's unploughed, unseeded field toward the camp. Without rain, why plough, why seed. He probably ate all his seed anyway, to stave off starvation, Lannie thinks, or sold it, and now has none to plant. Perhaps, if it rains, some agency will give him seed. If he's still alive. The low mountains with their scruffy, sparse vegetation rise up beyond the camp, dusty in the morning's dull-lemon light. She looks off across the field and across the roofs of the city of tents and low pole-and-plastic-sheeting shelters to the gap-toothed row of trees on the far side that protrude above them. Almost a mile away, in this light they too look pale and unhealthy.

In the far distance she sees the moving black dots she knows to be the gravediggers carrying their shovels and picks, trudging up the road to the high field, to carry on with their never-ending work. She knows too, without looking, that the road from town, hardly differentiated any longer from the dusty fields it bisects, and that comes down from the mountains beyond it, is thick with people moving mutely, slowly toward the camp. The knowledge of their approach hurries her. When she puts each foot down a puff of reddish dust rises up to settle on the toes of her runners.

She wonders if she has time for a quick visit with Mariam, feels a small glow start in her chest, then squelches it; she can't take the

time, she's needed at work at once. Lannie has fed Mariam every day
for two weeks now, helping to bring her back from the brink, and she
has become attached to her, waits each day for the moment when she
enters the feeding tent and Mariam's eyes grow big at the sight of her
and she smiles and raises her arms to Lannie. Although Lannie
knows she should, she can't find it in herself to regret her attachment.

Ahead of her is the new administration building. Until two weeks
earlier it had been a tent. Glad as she and all the other workers are
for its concrete floor and corrugated iron roof, she can't look at it
without an uneasy feeling that something isn't right here. Shouldn't
they be scaling down their presence with the intention of leaving
soon, instead of consolidating it? This is somebody else's country
after all, and they can't stay here forever feeding the hungry. Sooner
or later, surely, the hungry have to find a way to feed themselves.

But whenever she thinks this she has only to do as she is now: look
out across the field to the hundreds of starving coming down out of
the mountains and across the plain toward the camp, or pause to
listen to the pained coughing of the pneumonia cases who will die
without the NGO's drugs, to the whimpering children with their
swollen, empty stomachs, the dazed adults with their cupped hands
held out imploringly to the workers, or go to the feeding tent or
hospital where the severest cases of kwashiorkor are, and marasmus
— the skeleton-people. Her misgivings don't exactly go away.
Instead, they're dissolved in the desperate need of the moment, and
she and all the others, dampening their anger, muttering occasionally
to one another about the failures of government, or the utter stupidity of war, have to leave — what choice do they have — long-term
solutions to Others, whoever they may be.

Off to her right is the tent city where those already registered and
healthy enough to look after themselves have settled in to stay until
— when? she wonders, watching the thin plumes of smoke from
cooking fires beginning to curl into the pale sky. Until the crops
grow again, she supposes. People have begun calling back and forth
to each other, babies are crying, and somewhere in the rows of
makeshift shelters, a woman's voice rises abruptly, breaking the early
morning's drowsiness with a wild, keening cry. The sound, sudden as

it is, makes the small hairs on the back of Lannie's neck prickle. A child? she wonders, a husband? One cry, then silence. Soon that body, together with all the night's dead, will be carried across the camp to be laid out and prepared for burial in the field where the gravediggers will by now have begun work. And every day the number of mounds, the pits beneath which each hold as many as twenty carefully arranged bodies, grows. Yesterday alone nearly a hundred died.

She's the first of the staff to arrive, she usually is, but already people are milling about or squatting quietly on the ground outside the door, waiting for the centre to open so they can register, be sorted out: the sick to the hospital, the hungriest to the feeding tents, the others to the segregation area where they'll stay until the staff determines their needs. She glances to her left, to the hospital building behind administration, and sees the doctor, Habte Mika'el, mounting the steps. He waves peremptorily to her, then goes inside. The hours he puts in humble her. She's only a few feet from her destination now, and tenses herself for the onslaught she has learned to expect.

"*Selam*," she says, without actually looking at the people rushing to surround her, and then, "*Tena yistillin.*" Most of them are women and children. They are wrapped in ragged cloths and garments, torn now, and dirty from their days of walking through the dusty countryside. They press toward her, hands held out, would crush her against the building but Dawit comes hurrying up, towering over them.

"*Tena yistillin*," he says to Lannie, giving her a quick bow.

"Good morning," she replies, smiling, too shy to reply in Amharic. Every time she sees him she can't help marvelling at his dark-eyed, fine-boned beauty, at how beautiful Ethiopians often are. In Amharic, loud and firm, he commands the people back, and humbly, not taking their eyes off him, they make room so that he can unlock the door. He and Lannie enter, Lannie shivering at the night's accumulated chill inside. They arrange the table and chairs, unlock the cupboard and take out the registration forms, papers, and pens, and set them out in preparation for the arrival of the rest of the admissions team. When she looks up out the open door Lannie sees Caroline, Lucy, and Maggie, the image washed in sunlight, coming quickly across the field, hurrying so as not to be late for the meeting with which the nurses' day always begins.

Beyond the eerie silence of the crowd outside the door she hears the cheerful voices of the women from the nearby town who work in the camp, as they pass by on their way to the feeding shelters. One of them, Almaz, wearing a dusty blue cotton skirt, a light wool sweater with a white cotton *shamma* over her head and shoulders, stops in the doorway to greet them. She blots out the light and her features disappear in shadow. To Lannie she says a careful "good mor-ning," and bows gravely, her head a flash of white, before she goes on her way.

The camp is fully awake now. Back at the feeding tent Almaz and the others will soon be bustling around, preparing the first batch of high-energy milk — proportions of dried skim milk, sugar, oil, mixed with water. And the *faffa* too, a hot porridge. Lannie could do it in her sleep. The day will be over before she knows it, and she's grateful, almost cheerful, for the fact of its busyness. Unexpectedly, Caroline comes hurrying in, smoothing her pale brown hair back from her face and extracting keys from her pocket with the other hand.

"Have you looked out there?" she asks. "I couldn't waste time in a meeting when I saw that crowd. And there's hundreds more coming." She unlocks her medicine cabinet and begins quickly laying out her measles vaccines and syringes. They've had one outbreak here, they don't want another. Other camps have had cholera; it is their greatest fear here — that and the government with their ready supply of functioning trucks refusing to use them to transport tents, blankets, medicines, and grain, or the army, arrogant as always and in the midst of their civil war against the Tigrayans, running rampant over them for no particular reason.

"Ready?" she asks Dawit, who nods, and then Lannie, who nods too, checking over her shoulder at the two Ethiopian women, strangers to her, and the man, Teodoris, who stand in readiness at the scale.

"Ready," she says, and allows herself now, when it's necessary, to look at the crowd in front of them. It has doubled in size in the fifteen minutes since she arrived and she sees that today will be at least another five-hundred-person admission day. Already the camp facilities are stretched to the limit. If another load of tents doesn't arrive soon, the newcomers will have to live in the open. Which means more pneumonia, more deaths from the nights which at this altitude are very cold.

She and Dawit move out into the crowd, urging and pushing them into a semblance of a line instead of a pressing, undisciplined gang. Too weak to stand for long, many of them sit down and wait quietly, the expressions on their faces unreadable. Her job now is to assist Dawit who will search the seated crowd for the sickest and take them out to be looked after immediately. Off to the edge of the crowd a young man squats beside an old man — at least he looks old — who lies on a rag in the dirt. She watches him for a moment and her heart sinks. This is triage. Behind her, as if to confirm her judgement, Dawit says, "No. It is too late. No food." She turns to him, touches his arm lightly with her fingertips. He does not look at her, walks quickly away.

Dawit is speaking Amharic to the first family in the line, a woman and her two, shivering, half-naked children, one of whom lies on a bundle of rags on the ground, her head on her mother's lap. She's in an advanced stage of starvation, barely conscious. As Dawit translates the mother's answers to Caroline's questions, Lannie is there, ready to carry the weakest child to the scale, or to take the other by his hand to lead him wherever Caroline decrees he should go.

As she moves toward them, the woman opens her *shamma* and reveals a tiny infant nestled against her withered chest. Her expression doesn't change as she looks down at her skeletal baby. Dawit, alarmed, snaps a question in Amharic to the mother as Lannie automatically reaches out to take the infant. The woman ignores Dawit, resists Lannie's gesture for a moment, then lets Lannie take the child. As soon as she touches it, Lannie realizes it is dead.

At such moments, she relies on Caroline. Caroline has spent her life in the Third World. Over and over again she's refused administrative jobs that would have taken her away from the front lines. Nothing surprises her, no emergency is too much for her.

"Over there!" Caroline snaps, the brusqueness of her voice is like a small jolt of electricity. Numbly, Lannie carrying the dead infant follows her pointing finger to where one of the Ethiopian women workers wraps the body gently in an admissions blanket so she'll be covered — for dignity? so others won't see? — as Lannie carries her to the laying-out tent. When the mother has been questioned and she and her living children tended to, if she wishes to see her dead baby again, someone will take her there. Lannie is sure the woman will not want to see the baby again.

The morning passes in a steady round of lifting, carrying, supporting, and sometimes leading children or their weakened mothers to the hospital or the feeding shelters. In between these trips, she carries messages from Caroline to the doctor, or to other nurses. Each time she returns the crowd of waiting people does not appear to have diminished.

At noon, instead of going back to the mud house she shares with the others, even knowing Caroline will scold her — *You have to keep up your strength, you'll get ill if you don't eat, then you're no good to anybody* — she skips lunch to sit with Mariam in the feeding tent.

Often, holding her Oxfam cup to the little girl's lips to make sure she drinks every drop, Lannie is reminded of being allowed to hold her baby sister Misty, when she was a little girl herself. The memory makes her want to cradle Mariam more firmly, rocking her, burying her nose in the child's freshly shaved, prickly scalp. Even though she's ashamed of using Mariam to fill a hole in her own life, Lannie still spends every spare second by the child's side.

Yesterday Mariam pulled the cup out of Lannie's hand to hold it herself. Seeing this, Belainesh, the social worker, said to Lannie, "I am trying to find her family, if she has any left." If Belainesh can find an adult from Mariam's village, she will send her home with that person. If not, Mariam will have to go to stay with the nuns who will try to find her a home. It is inconceivable to Lannie that no one would want her. She has toyed with the idea of raising her herself, but knows no one would allow it. She would have to kidnap her.

When she arrives at the feeding tent, Lannie scans the crowd of women and children squeezed into the small shelter for Mariam's bright little face, but can't see her anywhere. Almaz, who is helping dish out the *faffa,* says to Lannie in a sympathetic voice, "Some people from her village took her."

"Home?" Lannie asks, hearing the faint quaver in her own voice. She notices, in the instant she waits for Almaz's reply, that the woman who had the dead baby at her breast early this morning is sitting on the ground in the corner of the enclosure, not bothering to bat away the flies resting on her cheeks and forehead, the food on her dish untouched, the skinny woman next to her reaching furtively for it. Her other children aren't with her. Almaz, following her eyes, says in an undertone, "The second one died an hour ago. She brought her too late to save her. The other is in the hospital. Dr. Habte says he will die too. She refuses to sit with him."

"Who will look after her when she gets there?" Lannie asks, meaning Mariam, as if Almaz hasn't just told her about the woman sitting in listless silence in the midst of the hum of voices from all the people packed into the shelter.

"They say she has an aunt there. Belainesh says we must get her back to her home." Moving away, she has to raise her voice over the buzz of voices, of children crying out.

Blinking, Lannie turns away, stepping over people and squeezing between them. At the entrance, she bumps hard into a male body. Each of them steps to the right and then to the left and then laughing, at least he is, he puts both of his hands on Lannie's shoulders and says, "Hey, maybe I should put up some traffic lights here." She recognizes him as the engineer who built the admissions building. He's a true redhead, she can't help but notice again. How strange we must look to everyone here; maybe they think we're brother and sister. This whips through her mind as the heat from his hands penetrates her shoulders and spreads, causing an unexpected, answering flush in her abdomen. It's a long time since a man has touched her. She's about to pull away when he drops his hands.

"Rob Sargent," he tells her. "I'm a Canadian."

"Lannie Stone. Me too," she responds automatically, smiling, not meeting his eyes. She shakes his hand, still smiling as if she's glad to meet him.

"Actually we already met," he tells her.

"What?" she says. Lucy pushes past them carrying a child wrapped in one of their admission blankets. Lannie hadn't even noticed she was in the feeding shelter. As she passes Lucy mutters, "The hospital is overflowing." Lannie makes a move as if to take the child from her, nurses are needed everywhere, this is something Lannie can do, but Lucy says, "No, I'm going there anyway. Caroline is going to see if we can send a few patients out so there's more room."

"We'd better move," Lannie says to Rob. Dodging people, they step outside to one side of the entrance, searching for a little shade. Although it's not terribly hot, the sun is directly overhead and has more power here so close to the equator than it has at home.

"I see I made an impression," Rob says. He doesn't seem embarrassed, more curious, almost tender over the fact that she doesn't remember him.

"I — uh, meet a lot of people," she says, drawing a line in the hard-packed, red-brown dirt with her toe.

"I'm not supposed to step over that?" he asks, looking down at the line, grinning and looking back up at her. In spite of herself, she laughs.

"I remember you now," she says, opting for flirtatiousness, then thinking better of it, too late. It had been at one of the many evenings they'd all spent on the terrace of the one bearable café in town. "Much beer." She tosses her head and looks away to where the column of people are still descending the far slope, all sizes, all ages, the men walking with staffs, the women carrying babies, tramping through the dust toward the camp. She thinks, I've got to get back to work, they'll be swamped at registration. "What are you doing here?" she asks him, then adds hastily, "I know you built the administration building, but I mean, now."

"Water," he says. "You've probably noticed there isn't enough?" There's a touch of sarcasm in his voice or maybe it's irony at the whole situation, or that rage they all feel they have to keep tamped, so that she looks back at him, into his eyes which, unlike her yellow-brown ones, are a pale blue and clear, almost as clear as the cruelly cloudless sky. "We've found a bore, now we're trenching and laying the pipes. Should soon have a good supply." He looks over in the direction she has just been looking and says, "Well, it won't be enough, but it's better."

"The formulas take a lot of water," Lannie mutters, for want of anything better to say. She's trying hard not to think of Mariam. *At least she's well, at least she didn't die.* This thought helps to dissolve the lump that formed in her throat when Almaz gave her the news of the child's departure. "So do the showers and the hand-washing and the laundry and — everything."

"After work tonight, would you consider having a beer with me in town?" She can see a flush rising under that redhead's freckled, translucent skin of his that mirrors her own, and now he's the one to toy in the dust with the toe of his boot. She thinks, no, remembers she owes her Canadian churches a new story and should write it tonight. About Mariam? No, not Mariam. But always on the lookout for camouflage too, not wanting to be labelled as eccentric, too much a loner, after a short hesitation she says, "Okay, but it'll be late. Eight, maybe?"

"I can pick you up at your house," he offers, "We can walk together." She nods again. The girls all tease her about being a recluse. Sometimes it isn't a joke. She knows they find her strange, cold, not pleasant. This will help, make her seem more normal. Provided one of them doesn't already have her eye on Rob — he's a nice enough looking man and he isn't a Russian or an Italian or an Ethiopian — but if somebody else is interested in him, there'll be trouble. A loud cry comes from a tent off to their right, a wail of grief, and then another. "My husband is dead, my heart has pain. It is finished, my husband is dead." Such open mourning is not the usual thing these days. With so many dying, eerie silence has become the pattern of grief.

"I have to go," she says, urgent now, raising her voice to be heard over the noisy buzz of the feeding tents and the sounds of grief. Rob's face has gone blank behind his freckles. It is a stoicism she recognizes: *Don't think about it, be strong,* it says. Another infant in the feeding tent has begun to howl.

"Yeah, me too," he says, giving her a solid, assessing look. Then he walks away carefully, firmly, only a slight jerkiness in his stride giving him away.

*

"We should go and check the tents," Caroline says. They've closed registration for the day, in a half-hour it will be dark. "I'm starving," Caroline goes on, "but with so many coming in and the hospital so full, I'm afraid there might be sick unaccompanied kids in the tents nobody's noticed."

"Okay," Lannie replies. She'd just as soon work right through until eight and then go out with Rob directly from here, get something to eat in town. Caroline will drag her off to supper with the others though, she supposes. And if she isn't hungry right now, she knows she will be as soon as she smells food cooking. She can't remember for sure, but thinks that today she has eaten only a couple of cookies and some juice at the afternoon break.

Dawit has gone back to his family in the nearby town for the night, so Caroline calls Teodoris, who is still tidying the office behind them in preparation to locking up. Teodoris will interpret. They all go to Amharic lessons two or three times a week, but after a day's work most of them have trouble concentrating.

They set out to walk through the tent city, unable to go ten feet before children healthy enough to walk about and play a little have begun to hurry along with them, the bolder ones taking their hands, the others giggling and running alongside. Even though it's almost dark they want Lannie and Caroline to stop and play ball with them as the staff sometimes does. It amazes Lannie that children can still play in the midst of such devastation, and this makes her think of all the ones who can't, of the dead baby at the woman's breast. Of Mariam, gone away.

Even if Mariam's aunt comes back in a month's time for rations, she thinks, she doubts she'd bring Mariam with her. She finds herself wiping moisture from her eyes, glad of the night falling rapidly over the camp, the people retreating inside their shelters to huddle together for warmth.

Caroline, Teodoris, and Lannie split up and thrust their heads into tent after tent. Teodoris calls, "Caroline!" and comes to her where she's paused down the alley beyond him. He's carrying a tiny child in his arms. The child's limbs and his head against Teodoris's chest bob loosely with his long steps. Lannie comes up to them, the only one here with little Amharic, ready to take the child from Teodoris.

"He is seven years, they say," he explains to Caroline. The boy can't weigh more than twenty-five pounds and is the length of a three-year-old. Lannie can't contain a gasp. Caroline, peering at him, says nothing, although for an instant she stands perfectly still. "He came in last night," Teodoris goes on. "His mother died in the night. They have taken her away." Caroline feels the child's pulse gently, lifts one of his eyelids, says, "Lannie, take him to the hospital. We'll finish up here and I'll check on him before I go home." Lannie had initially looked away at the sight of the child in Teodoris's arms, then made herself look back again, feeling for a second that her face is acquiring the set of Caroline's when she studies suffering: grave, gentle, clear-eyed.

Lannie takes the child from Teodoris and holds him carefully against her chest — a bundle of worn, chilled cloth. She shifts him so that his head rests against her neck as she walks carefully so as not to jostle him, down the row of shelters in the gathering darkness toward the lighted hospital. The child does not move or make a sound.

As she walks she remembers the first camp in Sidamo province where, not trusting the government who said there was no drought, no famine there, she'd managed to get a travel pass and gone to see for herself if this was true. She remembers lying awake listening to the drums celebrating the third day after the birth of a son. Sons, always sons, she thinks distantly, securing the child more firmly to her. Didn't Iris say she'd once had a brother? One who'd died as a baby? She stumbles over a small rock, catches herself before she falls, and in that instant, her short time in Sidamo rushes back in . . .

When she'd seen blood pouring from the woman, her head lolling over the arm of the man carrying her, Lannie had instinctively run toward them, without remembering she wasn't a nurse and couldn't help. Abebe, the nurse on duty, appeared in the doorway of the examining room and shouted to her, "Here! Come!"

She moved toward him through the noise and too-bright light to the blood-soaked bundle of rags lying now on the examination table. The woman's relatives, four or five of them, crowded around the table, looking down at her, one woman keening softly. "She must not bleed so much!" Abebe said, turning his back to the woman on the table, pulling open the cupboard where instruments, bandages, and medicines were kept. "Get her clothes off!" He handed her scissors over his shoulder and she began to straighten the limbs of the bundle on the table who she saw now was a thin girl of perhaps fifteen years, her eyes rolled back in her head. But as Lannie touched her ankles she felt warmth. She started to cut away the soggy fabric and saw, or already knew, the blood was pouring from the girl's vagina, had already thought it a miscarriage, when she caught a glimpse of the flesh torn away, red and pulpy, and she would have fainted or vomited at that and the blood pouring out all over the table had not Abebe pushed her back, lifting the girl's hips and sliding a sterile pad under her, and then the Swedish nurse Inge shouldering Lannie aside, taking in the situation at a glance.

"Take them out!" she commanded Lannie. Lannie, clenching her teeth to keep from throwing up into the puddles of blood, removed the relatives from the room, going with them herself, closing the door behind them. She leaned against the wall shaking so hard she was afraid she might fall. After a moment she got a basin of water and a brush and began to scrub the puddled trail of blood from the cement floor.

It was a botched genital mutilation, Inge had told her later. The woman who did it was drunk, the relatives said, had cut clumsily and too deep, had — God, she mustn't think of it. She's glad she's not a nurse; she doesn't have the courage. She'd finally written a piece about it, but is certain the church magazines she was writing for didn't print it. Maybe they didn't believe it, not that they'd think she was lying, but out of a sheer inability, born of their utter naivete, to assimilate the story. Like Iris, she thinks. She can't imagine telling Iris such a thing either. It's one of the reasons she doesn't write.

Climbing the hospital steps now, she edges sideways through the door, letting it slap shut behind her. Rita, the nurse on duty, looks up from where she's bending over one of the pallets, soothing a skeleton who whimpers softly, too weak to form words. She hurries over, takes the child from Lannie's arms.

"Set up that camp bed," she tells Lannie. Lannie runs to the bed leaning against the wall and pushes the legs down as quickly as she can while Rita waits, holding the child. She sets the boy gently down on it and Lannie waits as Rita takes his pulse. "It's okay," she says to Lannie, glancing at her over her shoulder as she crouches by the child. "I'll take it from here." Then she hesitates, staring up at her, and says, "You should go home now." Home. For one instant Lannie sees the farm kitchen, its bright yellow walls — Iris loves colour so much. Before that they'd been turquoise and before that, hollyhock pink — Barney grinning a silent good morning at her over the paper, his eyes brightening at the sight of her, Iris turning from the toaster to say, *Did you sleep well, dear?* as if there were no horrors in the world lurking in the shadows just out of arm's reach. "You look exhausted," Rita tells her.

"But I'm not!" Lannie answers, flushing. She pushes loose strands of her hair back from her face, forces a laugh, and its falsity makes her blush more. Rita doesn't answer her, rises, goes quickly to the medicine cupboard. Lannie turns away. She catches a glimpse of her reflection in an aluminum basin hanging on the wall. She's a ghost, the freckles dusting her high cheekbones and the bridge of her narrow nose barely visible. Two dark holes for eyes, a blur of palest pink her lips. Shaken, she skims her eyes away from the image, erases it, leaves the hospital.

And yet she does not wonder what she's doing here. She knows now, in this camp, what it is: it is escape from her own too-marginal, too-pitiful, too-ugly history. There is a part of her that is grateful for this famine, this drought, this pneumonia, this tuberculosis, leprosy, the spear-wounds, the kwashiorkor and endless, desperate cases of marasmus, even the grenade wounds — no, not for the bloody, inhuman war — she is grateful for all the rest of it because it saves her from her own hopelessness, from the pointlessness of her life. But she hates herself at the same time, for her heartlessness, that she would use this devastation to escape the pain of her own wounds.

Rob is sitting in their living room being entertained by Lucy and Maggie when Lannie and Caroline get back. Lannie sees at once that Maggie is smitten — the way she laughs too much, fingering her long, blonde hair that she has to keep pinned up at work, as if she's calling his attention to it. In the background they're playing a tape of a rock group unfamiliar to Lannie, and it seems to her annoyingly loud.

"There's some supper left in the kitchen," Lucy says. "If the bugs didn't get it." They all laugh.

"Thanks, but I'm having supper in town," Lannie says. Rob doesn't say anything. She doesn't want to sit here with all of them trying to eat while Rob waits. She isn't really hungry anyway, would rather have a plate of *injera wat* in town.

"I'm ready whenever you are," Rob says. "Thanks for the conversation," he says to Maggie, smiling at her. Maggie smiles back, brightly. She wants to make an impression.

"Don't forget curfew," Caroline sticks her head out of the kitchen to warn them. Rob says, "They kept Todd and Larry in jail overnight a couple of nights ago when they didn't make it back to the camp before curfew. Our director had to get them out. He was pretty mad."

"Wars!" Caroline exclaims, a mixture of disgust and acceptance. She should know, she's seen enough of them, Lannie thinks, in northern India, in Guatemala, in Angola, and elsewhere. But just this, the famine and the war in Ethiopia, are enough — more than enough — for Lannie.

She and Rob go out, shutting the door carefully behind them; if they leave it ajar, rats and snakes get in. Rob steps away from her, then comes back quickly. She sees with gratitude that he's carrying a long, heavy stick.

"A man came into the hospital today with a hand half-eaten by a hyena," she says. "I didn't see him, but Lucy said he was trying to save his son. Some other men came along and drove the pack off."

"We found a body," Rob says in a low voice. "Or what was left of one. Not here, out of Dire Dawa. I was working on a water project there. She was collapsed from starvation, we think, that was how they got her. It was pretty awful." They walk along in silence for a minute. She shivers and Rob draws close to her, puts his arm over her shoulders. "Are you cold?"

"A little," she responds. Her impulse is to shake his arm off, it's heavy, and allowing it to stay says too much about the possibilities of the relationship, possibilities she doesn't want to contemplate. But its very heaviness is comforting. His Canadianness, the world they've both come from that they know exists solid and stable back there — that, like it or not, must surely be what gives them the courage to stay here — is implicit in the warm weight she feels across her back, stilling her. It's shaking down the day's horrors, steadying her, loosening her stride. After a while he drops his arm and takes her hand in a light, casual grasp. Again, she's glad it's dark. And she wonders, too, which of the kitchen or the camp staff is the government informant who will report that she and Rob have walked to town together.

Now, from the round thatched houses on the edge of the town, they can hear the sound of drumming. Voices, impossible to tell if male or female, rise mournfully in singing, sounding more Asian or Arabic than African. The voices fall away slowly, but the drums go on. Lannie and Rob walk, listening without wanting to.

"The army came into town today," Rob says. "They were looking for boys." Lannie doesn't say anything, although this would be what the drumming is about. "They went straight for the school. The story is that the teacher's helper held them up at the door while the teacher dropped the boys out the window so they could run away." He laughs a little at the audacity of it.

Lannie draws in her breath quickly. "Did they take the teacher away?"

"No," he says, "but they got two of the boys for cannon fodder. Twelve-year-olds. Their parents are devastated." They listen again, in spite of themselves, to the elaborate rhythms of the drums. A single voice rises eerily, discordantly to Lannie's ears, full of woe.

"What a country," she says. Surprisingly, her brother, Dillon, comes to mind. Of how she'd feel if she knew he'd been conscripted. But I hardly know him, she thinks, and anyway, by now he'd be old enough to go on his own. Still, she's glad there's no war back in Canada.

The group of workers crowded around a long table on the deck of the café is too boisterous for Lannie's taste, bringing back her years at university in Saskatoon, Tim and Armand, and all the nights she'd spent with men — she would not think about it. It was done with, it would never happen again. In the light of what she has seen here in this country, all her transgressions seem so much less horrifying, have dropped into the realm of the truly trivial, another reason why she isn't sorry she has come here, another reason to stay, to never go back again. She thinks again of Iris and Barney, but their faces are remote now, and fade quickly.

Shouts of welcome greet them and Rob, smiling, slides a beer toward her. She stops it with her hand, smiles back at him. She mouths her thanks, since he can't hear her over the laughter. Two of the workers she doesn't know, one with an Irish NGO — the short-hand they all quickly fall into for non-governmental agency, mean-ing everyone from obscure little church groups to the United Nations — and the other from the United States, have begun to sing "Michael, Row Your Boat Ashore," while a second Irish nurse accom-panies them on a guitar. They've just begun to sing, and for a moment nobody joins in.

The Ethiopian men sitting here and there at the rickety tables against the corrugated iron wall turn their heads and listen, interested. Slowly others gather, amazed by these *ferenjis*, men who allow women to sit with them in a café, treating them like equals, women who sing, too, and laugh and touch the men with their hands, rub shoulders, even kiss them briefly in public. Rob opens his mouth and softly half hums, half sings. Soon all of them are singing, even Lannie.

Much later when Daniel drops them back at Lannie's door, then roars off to drop another worker at his house a mile down the road, Rob steps close to her, gathers her slowly, tentatively at first, and when she doesn't resist, more firmly in his arms, and kisses her. She kisses him back as hard as he's kissing her. She kisses him as if his mouth, his body, will blot out all the outrages and sorrows around them. She can't stop herself, even though a part of her knows all too well that she — they — will pay for this down the road. He pulls back abruptly.

"Do you think a person can fall in love with somebody the first time they go out?" His voice is husky.

"I'm not in love," Lannie states clearly. She can feel him go rigid, for just an instant, holding himself away from her.

"You're right," he says. "All right." They stand like that for a moment longer, close enough to feel the heat radiate from each other's body, but not touching. Hyenas yelp and growl at the far edge of the black shadow that is the field. He sighs, the sound is diminished by the rumble of Daniel's vehicle coming back down the road toward them, the headlights appearing and disappearing with the dips in the road.

She wants to explain to him that she can't fall in love, that she's a bad choice, that she can only damage men. But while she's still struggling to find a way to say this to him, or something like this, the Land Rover pulls up beside them. Its headlights pick out a figure making its way down the path from the hospital with the help of the wavering beam of a flashlight.

"It's Caroline," Lannie says. They wait in silence, the Land Rover rumbling beside them, until she reaches them.

"An emergency?" Rob asks Caroline as she nears. Not waiting for her answer, he climbs into the vehicle to sit beside the driver. It's as if he and Lannie hadn't been out on a date, hadn't just begun to talk about love.

"A birth," Caroline says in that even tone all of them have come to rely on. "Dr. Habte had to do a Caesarean. The baby's dead, but the mother made it." She blinks away from the headlights, but not before Lannie sees her face.

"We've got to hurry," Daniel warns. Rob says good night and they drive away, Daniel stepping on the gas so as to get back to their camp before curfew sounds.

The two women stand quietly for a moment side by side in the chilly Ethiopian night.

"She didn't want the child anyway," Caroline murmurs. "She already has eight children. I shouldn't be sad."

"I'm thinking of asking for a transfer," Lannie interjects. She's been thinking of no such thing, until now, until Rob.

"You don't work for anybody." Caroline's voice is sharp. "You can go if you want to." Lannie is silent.

"I need somewhere to go," she says finally. "Any ideas?"

"Yes," Caroline answers, still harsh. "Go home. Go home before you wind up like me, with no home to go to. Until home is a camp like this one, in some godforsaken country where it never rains, or it rains too much, where wars never end, and people never have enough to eat."

Her words frighten Lannie. Caroline is the heart of this camp, she's the one all of them turn to for advice, for help, for the courage to continue. If Caroline gives up, Lannie knows, all the camps in the whole country will collapse, because the Carolines, with their quiet hope, their bottomless courage, their gentle certainty that they are doing the right thing, the very thing required by human decency, are all that keeps the weaker of them, like Lannie herself, from bolting during the moments when they can't tell their days from their nightmares.

"Today we fed — how many hungry people?" she asks, knowing the count perfectly well, as does Caroline, and a little surprised at finding herself the one to comfort instead of to be comforted. But she puts out her hand and rests it briefly on Caroline's shoulder, then lets it slide away.

"And tomorrow they will be hungry again," Caroline says. Then she laughs, a sad, tired laugh. "I'm sorry. You're right, of course. But when this is over, I'm going to find something to do that will have a longer-lasting effect."

"Like what?" Lannie asks.

"Oh, I don't know. Help set up health-care clinics, maybe, with local staff, in the farthest out-of-the-way places I can find."

They don't say anything, each of them thinking her own thoughts of Ethiopia. Of the fight against local medicines, of prejudices and superstitions. Of Sidamo, where malnourished people live beside a lake teeming with fish and won't eat them, eat instead the false banana, a species providing only carbohydrates. Of Mengistu's government with its hidden agendas and priorities, caught up in imperatives out of a hideously long and convoluted past nobody but Ethiopians understand, and maybe not even them, but none of these agendas apparently having much to do with feeding hungry people. Of the vast, roadless countryside, *the trackless waste,* cut with perilously deep, straight-sided ravines, and too-high mountains, the unbridged rivers, the deserts. Lannie thinks of Rob, an engineer, of all the roads that need building. She thinks of Mariam in her village, watching the child recede from her forever. The drums are still muttering in the huts on the edge of the scattered, rubbish-ridden town. They've become one with the Ethiopian night.

From across the blackness of a farmer's barren, unploughed field, they cannot so much see or even hear as feel the presence of the thousands in need of help. They hover in the darkness, a vague, dark shape with a million glittering eyes and listening ears, thinking of history, of how it has always been so, and maybe always will be, coughing, whispering, sighing, moaning, waiting in the shadows for the return of the intractable, burning orb to illuminate the darkness for one more day.

Lannie shakes herself, puts a hand against the rough mud wall of their house to anchor herself.

"Have you noticed," she asks, looking up past the leaves of the eucalyptus trees to the dark night sky, "that Ethiopian stars are in all the wrong places?"

The Farm

This spring from the banks of the South Saskatchewan River all the way down to the Montana border nobody has so far put a single seed in the ground. Even if it doesn't rain another drop after today, it'll be two weeks at least before anybody can, Iris thinks, the land's so wet a tractor on it would sink out of sight. It's a circumstance so unusual in this near-desert country that it's beyond surprising, must be accepted as the end of the known world.

She's on her way to town to help at the annual strawberry tea whose purpose is to raise funds for the upkeep of the cemetery — some call it the Cemetery Tea, but Iris has always found that name distasteful when it's possible to make so unavoidable an event sound happy and a celebration of spring. As she turns off her own farm access road and begins to fight the muddy grid road, the car splashing through the water-filled ruts, slewing sideways when she gives it too much gas, a weariness overtakes her. Her usual good spirits have leaked away bit by bit over the last two months, she's tired out from the arguing, the waiting, the hoping, from the loneliness with Barney away.

But at least it isn't raining, for the moment anyway, and who knows, maybe it's finally going to stop, this interminable downpour. The vast, soaring sky that normally fills most of her windshield is blocked off by heavy, round-bottomed, steel-grey clouds and she notes how the wet and the dull light intensify the delicately coloured landscape, giving it a rare, almost tropical richness of tone. She turns her head left for a glimpse of the deep, wild coulee that joins her land to that of her neighbours, the Normans, and for the blue river cliffs beyond and above it, with their dashes of white clay shining in the light, but the view at that distance has vanished into thick grey drizzle.

So she watches the near fields stretching out on each side of the deserted road: field after field of stubble left from last year's harvest, or summerfallow beginning to acquire a greenish cover of weeds. She's passing the only small pasture of native grass left on the road that leads from the farm she has lived on nearly all her life to Chinook, the town she's driving to, and she can't help but think, even though she's a farmer's daughter and a farmer's wife, how pretty it looks, all blue-green, with tints of aqua and mauve. The pasture looks as if it's drinking up the rain. Everything else looks in need of care, everything else is waiting for the rain to stop so life can go on.

She thinks again of pointing out to Barney that they should be getting their equipment ready to do their spring seeding; she hasn't so far because she's afraid he'll say he isn't coming home to seed, that he'll hire Vance Norman to do it. If he says that, she'll know their life together really is over. And the new air seeder is beyond her, all computerized, with depth gauges and a bank of mysterious lights and numbers. And Barney fertilizes at the same time, which makes the whole thing even harder to learn. This new farming is too complicated.

She remembers her father filling the drill box with bucket after bucket of pale gold seeds, she hears the rich *shshshsh* of the seeds as they pile up and spread out, smells its welcome, dusty scent. She would put her arms into the yellow seed and push it sideways, spreading it out evenly through the long box. They were cool against her palms, they flowed willingly at her touch, the precious cargo inside them protected, waiting for the right moment to spring to life. Nowadays, when Barney augers seed into the hopper of his air seeder, you can't see it, and all you hear is that heartless, high-tech whine that she hates. She thinks how farm machinery used to clank and roar and growl in a satisfying way that sounded almost like a hard-working human.

She has reached the lip of the valley where the straight-as-an-arrow road winds down its wall to the small town clustered around a bend in the narrow river, its grain elevators — dark wine, drab grey, bright orange and gold — thrusting themselves boldly above the trees,

higher even than the slim white spire of her church on the other side
of town. She has been seeing Chinook all her life and barely notices
it now: its few, tree-lined blocks of small, square frame houses
painted white or the palest, most unassertive pink, green, or grey; its
excessively wide main street, attesting to the failed dreams of its
founders, and lined with the typical western false-fronted buildings,
newly re-sided in up-to-date building materials. She can remember
every one of their transformations over the years. Bank, grocery
store, café, credit union, gas station, hotel — it feels as if the car
drives itself over to the community hall and parks itself in the lot
between Ardath Richards's shiny new white half-ton and Marie
Chapuis's dark red sedan. She picks up her purse and her shoe bag,
takes the angel food cake she got up early this morning to bake from
the seat beside her, gets out and goes inside.

The big wooden door slams shut behind her, the sound echoing
through the shadowed emptiness of the hall. It's only noon, the tea
isn't supposed to start till two, but she can hear by the distant sound
of female voices that the owners of the other two vehicles are already
at work in the kitchen. She notes that no tables and chairs have been
set up yet, but the rush of energy she usually feels at a job to be done
doesn't come.

The wide entrance area is also the cloakroom and Iris sets the
wrapped cake, her purse, and her shoe bag containing her beige
pumps — her homage to the season, this is the first time she has
worn them since the previous summer — on the floor and leans
against the imitation-wood wallboard, its ghastly brown surely the
colour of no wood on earth, pulls off her muddy boots, shakes the
shoes out of the bag and slips her feet into them. How many times
has she done just this?

She waits, arrested by the pictures she has unexpectedly conjured as
they flip backwards in time like pages on a calendar in an old movie:
standing here next to the coat racks with a frozen lemon dessert to
serve at a wedding or two pumpkin pies for the Fowl Supper or Santa
Claus-shaped sugar cookies for the children's Christmas party or sandwiches or a pan of iced squares or two dozen buns for a wedding
shower, an anniversary tea, a funeral reception, a fund-raising tea like

this one. She wonders if in an eternity of other lives she was just as she is now: a wife, a middle-aged member of a big, prosperous family, a leading member of a rural community as her mother was before her, and her grandmother before that. Her head feels thick, the beginning of a headache hovering behind her brow.

Then, still leaning against the wall of the dimly lit cloakroom, her raincoat partly unbuttoned, she lets her arms fall to her sides, her head drift back to rest against the fake wood, and closes her eyes. She hears the voices from the kitchen rise to bright laughter, but she feels no answering desire to join the other women, although she knows in a moment she'll have to give up this interlude of solitude. An ambience overtakes her, for the barest instant she's plunged back into last night's dream: a foreign country, hot, there are palm trees, and low, flat-roofed, rectangular houses. She is seated at a round table on a hill. A woman is seated there too. She is perhaps middle-aged, with a smooth olive-skinned face, not a line or a wrinkle, and very dark eyes. Her flowing white robes and headdress with its black band are a cross between an Arab woman's and a nun's. The woman gazes hard at Iris with eyes that show no fear, nor any favour. Eyes that see right through into her heart and her soul, that know everything there is to know about her. Eyes before which she feels reduced to a child again.

She is still troubled by that piercing gaze, as if the woman were real and not merely a figment in a dream. More, she is troubled by her dreams themselves; in the last months they've become too vivid and powerful to merely dismiss, but she doesn't have a clue what they mean, although she suspects they do mean something. She supposes they'll eventually go away as mysteriously as they've come.

She rouses, is about to pull away from the wall, but there's another burst of laughter from the kitchen. No, she doesn't want to go there, she wants to — what? Follow that dream woman to some place where — where there are no strawberry teas, no farms needing seeding, no baffling husbands. Resolve deserts her. She slumps back against the wall, again lets her eyes close.

*

She'd been wakened by a crow. Barely dawn and it had come, calling faintly from a distance, its voice confused in her mind with the early morning twitter of songbirds and the elusive sounds of her fading night's dreaming, growing louder as it drew closer to where she lay motionless on her side of the bed in the upstairs bedroom she now rarely shared with Barney, her husband of nearly thirty years, his half of the quilt depressingly smooth and untouched. She'd listened, her countrywoman's senses aroused. It couldn't be a crow, surely it was too early for crows to be back? But it drew closer and closer, cawing as it came, and then it was against her window, must have lighted on the poplar branch that in the wind would rasp the window frame. From there it cawed peremptorily into her very ear, stentorian, three times: *Caw! Caw! Caw!*

She couldn't fail to note — a slightly accelerated heart rate, a still-ness that was all listening seizing her — it was as if the bird had been sent to speak directly to her, a messenger from regions she'd not yet been to, and she waited, bewildered, but feeling sure from the sudden uneasy stirring in her gut that there had to be more. But all she could read in the strident finality of its voice was that she should rise and go about the business of the living.

She stretched one leg toward the edge of the bed. The crow had now retreated some distance, its voice growing fainter, its crowing no longer having rhythm or pattern — or maybe it was a different bird? Or maybe she'd dreamt the whole thing? She pushed the lilac quilt back, and the flowered sheet, kicking to free her legs, and sat on the side of the bed.

The clock, sitting beside the crystal-based lamp and the mauve phone with the imitation gold trim on her bedside table, read six in the morning and by the clarity of the light filtering under the blind Iris was able to tell that it had stopped raining. She groaned softly in response to another morning, another Barneyless day, and straight-ening, placed one hand under each breast, as if to weigh them, not in pounds, but in womanliness, to reassure herself of her existence. She listened, heard the familiar chatter of small songbirds beginning in the trees, a tiny embroidery of sound on the vast silence of her house. How she hated waking each morning now into its emptiness, the wide oak dresser, the white-painted door, the mauve satin-covered chair that Barney complained of as useless, that he was always stumbling over, looking stranded, homeless, even though they'd always been there.

And the crow's toll had disturbed her, its harsh cry had torn an opening in the blurred shadow of her most private self which she kept hidden because she who had everything, who had always had everything, had no right to unhappiness, to these puzzling, seemingly objectless yearnings, these unattached dissatisfactions. She kept them all shoved down well out of sight, telling herself, surely everyone has this bundle of wide, nameless desire, surely everyone has to live with this mysterious, powerful undertow?

Realizing she still held each heavy breast cupped in a palm, she dropped her hands, embarrassed. She stood slowly, reaching for her dressing gown. As her fingers touched the cool, bright silk it came flooding through her that Barney had failed once again to come rushing up the stairs to take her in his arms, to bury his face against the white hollow of her neck and then against her warm breasts, his mouth open, breathing to her how mistaken he's been, how he can't live without her, Iris, his darling, his woman, his one true love.

The door beside her bangs. Iris is so startled her heart leaps into her throat. She straightens and turns her back to the door, rapidly unbuttoning the rest of her raincoat with fingers that tremble over the stiff, shiny fabric and the plastic buttons.

"Iris! You scared the wits out of me!" It's Audrey McCormack, her bleached blonde hair elaborately curled and sprayed into precise place, the collar turned up on her neat black raincoat. The sound the door makes divides itself into the rattling clang of the bar handle, the thud of the door against its wooden frame, the dull echo as the noise pushes out through the hundred feet of empty hall to bounce slowly off the walls and stage, dying away to a muffled sigh against its dusty wine velvet curtains. Audrey stamps her feet on the mat to get the mud off her boots, reaches out over Iris's head — Audrey is quite a bit taller than Iris, but who isn't, Iris thinks — and flicks on the rest of the lights. "What are you standing in the dark for?" she demands.

"Hi, Audrey," Iris says weakly, but Audrey is already whipping off her boots, unbuttoning her raincoat to reveal a flowered pink-and-green dress, turning to say hello to Donna and Irene Meadows, thirtyish sisters-in-law, who've entered together, each carrying the obligatory fresh-baked angel food cake. Iris has her coat off now, she's straightening the skirt of her favourite cherry red suit, chosen because the colour sets off her fair skin and dark hair so well, and fluffing with her fingers her loose-hanging, mid-neck-length hair that, despite her fifty-two years, unaccountably still refuses to show even a trace of grey.

The cloakroom is filling up with women greeting each other, complaining about the weather, fussing over their clothes, whispering to each other about some commotion in one of their families that Iris doesn't know anything about, and today finds she doesn't care to know. She rescues her cake and her purse from the floor and makes her noisy, high-heeled way across the hall's wooden floor, where she has danced away two dozen or more New Year's Eves and as many or more wedding celebrations, to the kitchen where she sets the cake on the long table with six or so others already there waiting to be cut.

Flats of red strawberries, so bright they light up the entire room, march down the length of one counter, scenting the air with their tangy sweetness. Mavis Miller stands at them, looking smart in her pale blue fake-linen dress. She's past fifty too, but she dyes her short, crisp hair a pale, elegant blonde. Her small diamond earrings flash light as she bends over the radiant berries, picking them up one by one and turning them over, dropping an occasional one that has a spot on it or isn't ripe enough into a plastic basin she's balancing with her left hand against the table edge. The ones she hasn't touched are still resting, smoothly tucked into the individual baskets that make up the flat, but those she has picked over are heaped up in the flat, spilling over the sides and across the table, a few have even fallen off to lie as gay crimson splotches on the floor.

"Really," Mavis remarks officiously, without glancing up from her work, her fingers stained ruby red from them. "Half of them aren't ripe."

"What's the flavour like?" Iris, approaching, asks.

"The usual." It's Audrey who has come up behind Iris again and speaks into her ear. "Like strawberry-flavoured cardboard. They pick them too soon. California's too far away," she scolds, taking an apron out of her purse, shaking it, tying it on over her dress, and joining Mavis at the berries. Nobody pays any attention to her; she has always been this way.

The scent of the fruit increases in a wave, like heat from an opened oven door, filling Iris's head with its fragrance. The hint of headache retreats and disappears. She opens the door of the commercial-size fridge that sits along the back wall. Quarts of farm cream the colour and density of mayonnaise fill an entire shelf.

"I hope there's enough here," she says dubiously.

"If there isn't, somebody will have to run over to the co-op and buy a few more pints of that thin stuff they call cream," Audrey tells her.

More women have arrived — Shirley Austin, Margaret Wolf, Janet McPherson — and before they begin to work they pause to chat with each other, laugh a bit, ask a quick question about family members, how an afghan somebody is crocheting is coming along, did John find his stolen truck? The long table in the centre of the room is covered with cakes now, and their sweet scent rises to mingle with the piquant aroma of the berries. Ardath Richards, with whom Iris went to public school, begins to set the cakes on aluminum carts to take them into the hall where later they'll be sliced and set on plates to be served. And the cream still has to be whipped, Iris thinks. It's tricky though, such thick cream will turn to butter in an instant's inattention.

"Guess what?" Her young second cousin — or is it third? — Joanne, is speaking from the sink where she's washing berries. "Jerry and I are building a new house as soon as the ground dries enough to dig a basement." She turns back to her work, her long brown ponytail bouncing against her back, but not before Iris sees the delight in her eyes.

"That's wonderful!" Iris says, remembering how young couples yearn for a new house of their own, even though she never did. She lives in a house built by her parents when she was six or seven years old. "Are you building out on the farm or in town?"

"In town," Joanne tells her.

At the next sink two of the women have opened a tap to fill one of the massive coffee urns and the water gushes noisily out; farther over somebody is emptying the cutlery drawers and clattering forks and spoons onto metal trays to carry out to the hall. Iris has to raise her voice to be heard.

"When Barney and I got married Mom wanted Dad to build us a new house in their houseyard, but he wouldn't hear of it either." She doesn't explain that Jack hadn't wanted to use up good farmland. He liked to seed every acre: road allowances, deserted homesteads, slough — waste not, want not, and all that. Her mother Lily who, as she often said, liked grass, was perpetually annoyed with him over that obsession of his. Leave a little for the animals, she'd scold, and he'd smile at her sardonically.

As Iris cuts neatly, rapidly at each berry with Joanne chattering on beside her about rug colours and whether they should have a bay window or not, she thinks of the first home she and Barney shared: a shabby farmhouse on a small farm her father bought when its owner went under. She remembers how for the first year she hadn't really noticed its many shortcomings, knowing the big, two-storey, brown-frame farmhouse with its smart cream trim was waiting for her, dreaming of the day when she would be its mistress as her mother was, its chatelaine, and Barney would take over her parents' and her grandparents' farm, as soon as — her father said — he knew the place: the names and soil characteristics of each field, the weather patterns over each one, the places first and last to dry in the spring, and the business side of things. *Ranch-raised*, her father said sceptically, when Iris declared her intention to marry him. *Doesn't know much about farming* . . . And her mother, shocked and frankly disdainful, *A cowboy from up in the hills!*

A year and a half they'd lived in the old Daniels farmhouse, until Iris began to chafe at facing another winter in it with its freezing floors despite the thick new rugs her father had installed, all the hot air from the ugly propane heaters rising straight to the ceiling or out the apparently unfixable, rattling window frames. She'd grown tired of its uncertain water supply, its inadequate electrical wiring, its crampedness. She'd balked then, demanded a better place to live, but although she was waiting with less and less patience for her parents to retire so she and Barney could have the big house, she knew better than to say so directly. Hadn't been above planting a few hints, though, she remembers, which her parents studiously ignored.

And yet, as she stands here in the bustling hall knifing the stems out of the berries, discarding the occasional one Mavis missed that's bruised or not ripe enough, she finds that shabby old house appears now in her memory suffused in a soft golden light; how in love she and Barney had been, their tender and joyful nights together in the tiny bedroom with its rough plaster walls and the ice forming on the windowsill, lying under the warm feather quilt her grandmother had made when she was a bride.

"I'd like to stay on the farm," Joanne says, wistfully, "but Jerry says Daddy's right. If things on the farm don't work out — " she pauses, but Iris knows what she's thinking: *If we lose the farm . . .* "We couldn't even sell the house, but a house in town will sell eventually . . ." The coffee urn is full now, the tap turned off, and the women have finished filling the trays with cutlery. Now the kitchen is peaceful, the voices of the women as they go about their work harmonious, even musical.

"First we moved into an old farmhouse when we got married," Iris says. "Then we lived in my parents' basement for two years."

"What a drag that must have been," Joanne exclaims.

Then, without any warning to Iris and Barney, the day of his fifty-second birthday, the same age Iris is now, Iris's father announced that he and Lily were moving to town.

"Not to retire," he'd said, a touch of grimness breaking through the joviality he'd found for the occasion, "but to leave you two on your own here." Delight flooding over her — *at last* — Iris had glanced at her mother. Lily didn't speak, but Iris can't forget how at that moment she wouldn't meet her eyes, or even look at her. Her mother never did reproach her or even express any regret. Iris no longer tries to squelch the pang of guilt she feels at the memory. Youth! she thinks wryly, you'd think there could have been a less painful solution, although she doesn't know what that might have been. And anyway, isn't it a given that the younger generation will always try to push out the older?

"Iris! Can you come here?" Mavis's imperious voice breaks her reverie. She swishes her hands quickly through the chilly water, wipes her fingers on a soggy tea towel, hands her paring knife to Joanne, and hurries away into the hall.

"We thought you and Irma could pour over here. We'll put the coffee urns over there." Iris nods comfortably, as if being asked to pour isn't an honour going only to the women of the community's first families. She's used to such tributes; nonetheless, she feels a twinge of pride. The tables are arranged throughout the hall now, the chairs set in place around them, the white tablecloths have been laid, and two of the women are setting small yellow baskets of pink cloth flowers and stacks of pink paper napkins on each table. An elaborate silver tea service has been placed on each of the two tables Mavis is indicating.

"I could have brought my grandmother's set," Iris says. "It's just sitting there in the dining room getting tarnished. I never use it." She remembers how, when Lannie was a little girl and home from school with a cold or flu, Iris would carry it upstairs to her bedroom, and Lannie would spend the morning carefully cleaning and polishing it, her pale little face solemn as she worked, until the whole set, tray and all, shone so brightly it hurt your eyes to look at it. Mavis says, "We asked a couple of the old ladies to use theirs. They were thrilled."

The main door at the far end of the hall opens, and a plump, young blonde woman in a faded blue winter coat, carrying one child on her hip and herding two little girls ahead of her, pushes her way in. In the second before she moves toward the coat racks and is hidden from Iris's view, Iris recognizes her: Angela, Lannie's best friend from school. She excuses herself and, skirting tables, walks the length of the hall to the cloakroom. Angela has set the little boy down and is straightening his bow tie with one hand, her children's coats over her arm.

"Angela!" Iris says. "It's been ages!" Angela straightens awkwardly from her task, smiles when she sees it's Iris and says, "Emma, take Cory to the bathroom. Make sure he washes his hands." The girl grabs the boy's hand and leads him away. The second little girl peers at Iris from behind her mother's skirt.

"Hasn't it," Angela replies. "I'm so busy these days I hardly know if I'm coming or going. I've got two pre-schoolers now, you know. Orland stayed home to look after the baby." And Lannie, godmother to Emma who must be ten years old by now, an infant when Lannie left home.

"Are you well?" Iris asks, confused, not sure any more what to say or not say, pushing away the memory of hanging up the phone on Angela to rush upstairs to Lannie's room, finding her there unconscious on her bed, God knew for how long —

"Oh, sure, although I'm fat as a pig. You'd think with all this running around I'd weigh about four pounds, but no such luck." She sets the children's jackets in a pile in the corner, struggles out of her own coat and hangs it up.

In that moment's pause Iris tries not to, but sees the letters. Not letters, really, just scraps of paper torn from notebooks or stick-it pads she'd found in Lannie's macramé book bag when, long after Lannie had left and it looked as if it would be a long time before she'd return, Iris decided to do something about her bedroom. From men, they were, boyfriends: "*Hi, Lan — meet me at the Sub at eight. Tim.*" Iris knows from her year at university that the Sub is the Student Union Building, and she's met Tim, a nice boy, she'd thought, and clearly in love with Lannie. The others —

"I knew you'd be here today," Angela says. "I wanted to ask . . . I was wondering, have you heard from Lannie lately?" Then, not waiting for Iris's answer, she rushes on. "I'm really sorry to upset you. I mean, if you haven't heard from her, but, it came into my head this morning when I was vacuuming and it wouldn't go away — you know how that is?" She means, of course, when an intuition hits you, but Iris hasn't Angela's gift.

"I haven't, no," she says, trying to sound cheerful. "And you haven't upset me. Do you know something? Have you had any letters? Any cards?" She laughs, pretending to be amused. "No telegrams? Smoke signals maybe?"

"Not since that postcard maybe three years ago. You know the one, from Iraklion, was it? In Greece — some island. Oh, Crete, I think. She must have been travelling."

"What I'm thinking," Iris says, "is that maybe she travelled herself right off the globe. Right into oblivion." She's appalled at her flash of anger. *I'm going back*," the card had ended. But back where?

"Don't think that," Angela says. "She's all right. If I felt there was something wrong with her, I'd have told you." Her voice is steady, clear.

"I really hope we'll hear something soon," Iris replies, retreating. Angela's little girl, who looks to be about eight, is walking the length of a rack of coats, humming and running an arm down them, making the coats sway.

"Don't Sarah," Angela cries. "Stop that."

Iris wants to point out — in a confusion of self-justification and defence of Lannie — that after all Lannie is only her niece, it's not as if she's her daughter. In the end, she doesn't; Angela must understand how much they once meant to each other. Still, she feels a pang of guilt at precisely what she isn't sure — that Lannie's failure to write is somehow Iris's fault? That Iris hasn't tried very hard to locate her?

Angela has had to ask her twice, "How's Barney?"

"Oh," she says, too quickly. "He's fine. He's gaining weight, too. I'm going to persuade him to see the doctor as soon as he finishes calving. He looks tired out." Beside them the door is opening and closing steadily as people enter, stomp their feet to shake off clods of mud, and crowd toward the coat racks.

"I heard about that! What a funny thing for him to do. But there's no accounting for . . . whatever," she finishes, looking away.

"No, there isn't indeed," Iris says briskly. She hesitates, then moves close to Angela and plants a kiss on her warm cheek. "Thanks for still caring about Lannie," she murmurs, although she means to say — she feels — much more than this. How can it be that Angela who's so much younger, seems to know more than she does about the world? Is it because of her children? "I'll call you the minute I hear anything."

Time passes, more people arrive, pay their money at the door, leave their coats and rubbers in the cloakroom, and slowly fill the tables. There are, as always, mostly old people here, Iris notes from her position in the centre where she's filling cups of tea from the silver teapot that Audrey has to scurry to keep full. Catholics, Protestants, Jews, and infidels alike are buried in the town's one cemetery; every family that has been in Chinook more than twenty years has somebody buried there; thus, most families come to the tea. Iris sits demurely, filling cup after cup to be passed to the members of her community, people she has known her whole life. In an unguarded instant, they feel to her like a huge, extended family. Small plates heaped with cake, strawberries spilling over its sides, and a mound of whipped cream on top of the berries sit in front of each person, and servers place cups of tea and coffee on trays and distribute them efficiently among the tables.

"Come and sit with us, Iris," a quiet voice says. She glances up to see her mother-in-law standing beside her. She's short and thickset, wearing that same dark red polyester dress with the rhinestone buttons marching down the front that she has been wearing for years. She's put on weight, Iris notices, the dress pulls slightly across her bosom and stomach.

"Mary Ann! I didn't see you come in. I bet the roads out your way were a nightmare. I'm supposed to be pouring — "

"Somebody will take over for you," Mary Ann insists, with authority born of years of experience at women's work. Iris catches Mavis's eye, who comes over at once, eager to take her place. Iris follows Mary Ann to a table near the cloakroom where she sits down kitty-corner to tall, spare Luke Christie, her father-in-law.

"Hi, Luke," Iris says. He's eating cake grimly and doesn't look up. "Barney showed up yet?"

"Oh, I don't expect him," Iris says cheerfully. "He'll never leave his heifers to come to a tea," she adds, making her voice sound humorously disparaging. Luke doesn't answer.

"I'm just waiting for the mud to dry up so I can put some new artificial flowers on Wesley's grave," Mary Ann explains. Wesley was Barney's older brother, born mentally handicapped, dead a couple of years earlier of a heart attack. Iris had forgotten that of course it would be Wesley's grave that would bring the two of them, fighting mud all the way, from their ranch where Barney was raised, far off the beaten track to the north.

"Deer ate the last ones," Mary Ann says. "Thought they were real. They got a surprise!" She and Iris laugh. Luke grunts as if he disapproves, but doesn't look up from his rapidly diminishing mound of dessert. Iris casts about for something to say, thinking glumly how it's always this way, she and her in-laws never have much to say to each other. And Luke and Barney always at each other's throats.

"Barney's been calving a while already, eh," Luke says gruffly. His plate is now empty and he's gazing across the room instead of looking at her. Iris nods without speaking, a little game she's started, to see if she can make him look at her. But he doesn't bother, just pushes his plate away and slowly stands to his full six feet, looking around at all the people chatting away to each other. Without speaking, he walks away. Mary Ann appears not to notice his going. Iris knows he has spotted cronies somewhere in the crowd and won't be back until he's ready to go home. It isn't simple rudeness, she knows, it's just how tough old ranchers, weaned on blizzards and raging thunderstorms and rangy mustangs and hard, hard times behave; it doesn't mean anything. Farmers, on the other hand, she thinks, aren't tough any more now that they farm with machinery instead of horses.

"You going to try to go back there yourself tonight?" Mary Ann asks. Startled, Iris can't think what she means — Oh, Barney's ranch. She's never told her in-laws she doesn't go there with Barney, in fact, she's only been there once, when he was trying to decide whether to buy it or not. *Over my dead body,* she'd said, pretending she was joking, but Barney ignored her, as if he'd suddenly gone deaf, couldn't hear a word she was saying. Fortunately, she doesn't see that much of her in-laws, it's easy to keep secrets from them.

"Oh, I can't handle the roads in there right now," she says. "And Barney's got the four-wheel drive. I'm staying at the farm for now." When she'd made it clear to him that she would never, never move there of her own free will, all Barney said was, "I have to do this, Iris. I never asked nothing of you, but I'm asking this." When she asked him, over and over again, "But, why?" he would only turn away, and she couldn't tell if it was because he knew she wouldn't understand his reasons, or if it was because he didn't understand them himself. Mary Ann is giving her a sidelong, speculative glance, but she decides it's safer not to add anything to what she's already said. Mary Ann would say, A wife belongs with her husband. And what would her own mother say? She finds she can't guess.

A plate of cake heaped with strawberries, the whipped cream spilling over the edge, appears with a thump on the tablecloth in front of her and she looks up in surprise to see Ramona Norman grinning down at her. Ramona is her lifelong neighbour, they played together as children, in high school they'd been best friends.

"Gotta keep your strength up," Ramona says, licking whipped cream from her fingers and pushing her glasses back up her nose with the other hand.

"Sit, Ramona," Mary Ann says, indicating Luke's chair.

"Can't. I'm with Mom and Dad and we have to get Dad home. He's played out already. Only been here fifteen minutes. And we're calving, gotta get back. See ya." She's gone as abruptly as she arrived, turning sideways to make her way between the crowded tables.

"Thanks for the cake," Iris calls to her retreating back.

"We should be going soon, too," Mary Ann says. She looks around the hall as if she's going to find Luke and tell him it's time to go, but of course she doesn't move. "Your mother okay?" Iris's mother is in a nursing home.

"I'm going on to see her as soon as I can get away from here. It was raining so hard on Sunday, and Barney was ho . . ." — she corrects her remark quickly — "was too tired to drive all that way to Swift Current and back. So I'm going by myself right away."

"Luke and me are going up on Thursday," Mary Ann says. "We'll have supper at Fay's, haven't seen the grandkids in quite a while." Fay is Barney's younger sister. Iris doesn't think she can endure much more of this halting, boring conversation. "Funny thing," Mary Ann continues, resting one elbow on the table, rubbing the tablecloth with swollen, arthritic fingers, "but all I can think about with all this rain is them drought years." Iris's mouth is full of the cake Ramona has brought her. "The dust years," Mary Ann goes on. "There was a book in them days — no, maybe when the worst was over. About the Okies?" She looks up at Iris. Iris nods. "In the States. How they lost everything in the dust bowl and went away, left everything behind, tried to get to California, I think it was. Funny," she says. "That book got passed around from house to house all through the countryside till most everybody read it, even them that didn't read books much." She sighs and straightens her back as if it's aching.

Iris thinks, oh brother, am I going to have to listen again to how people were happier when they were poor in the Depression? How people stuck together then like they don't now? This makes no sense to her, never has, even though all the old people swear it's true. She would like to ask Mary Ann, were they happy when they had only potatoes to eat? When their kids couldn't go to school because they didn't have shoes? When their cows got too thin to give milk and their horses weakened and died of starvation?

But Mary Ann is staring around the room as if she's not seeing a thing there. "Too much of a good life — too much *things* — it kills something in people."

Her words arrest Iris's movement as she brings the cake and strawberry-laden fork to her lips. She sets it down, then, keeping her voice mild, trying to erase any hint of complacency, says, "They say the drought in the eighties was worse than the one during the Depression, but our improved farming methods and our new genetically engineered seeds and our technology all made it so we still got crops."

"Lotta people lost their places during the eighties," Mary Ann points out. Iris shrugs.

"Bad management, places too small, you know." She lifts her fork again and takes another mouthful — delicious.

Mary Ann says sharply, "You wouldn't shrug if it was your place." Iris stops chewing, surprised. Her place? It's the biggest, most prosperous farm in the district. She and Barney, and her parents before them, are rich from that farm. Lose it? Never! She glances at Mary Ann, sees the set to her jaw. Remembers the poverty Barney grew up in.

"Yes, you're right," she says meekly. "Of course, you're right." She mustn't quarrel with Mary Ann too, she's Barney's mother, she has to get along with her. Besides, she likes Mary Ann, her stubborn, down-to-earth good sense, her courage at living what has been a hard life, driven almost wholly by men's desires and needs.

She pushes her half-eaten plate of cake away and takes her leave of her mother-in-law quickly, promising to drop in whenever Barney can make the time to drive up, knowing that it'll surely be summer before that happens, and with Barney as good as gone — but she won't think that; it isn't as if he's declared their marriage to be over, or that he's died on her. Still, what she wouldn't give to have him forget his ranch and come back and be her husband again.

Without saying goodbye to anybody — if she did, it would be another hour before she gets away — she leaves the tea, pushing back coats jammed into the overfull coat rack to locate her own and then scrabbling among the rows of muddy boots for hers, putting them on, then sliding out the door between a family of newcomers entering the hall. She has told the others she can't stay to clean up. Knowing there's always plenty of help, no one will mind.

As she's driving out of the parking lot an unaccustomed relief floods over her. She has never minded these events before, even enjoyed them, nor has she ever questioned their necessity knowing, as she does, that they are what make the community. Still caught up in surprise at her reaction to leaving the hall full of her relatives, friends, and neighbours, she momentarily catches a glimpse of Barney moving slowly on horseback through the lodgepole pines that surround his cabin in the wilderness and she understands a little about why he's gone. Abruptly, she's gripped by the desire to reverse herself, to throw everything up too, run to him, and throw her arms around him: *I give up, you're right*, she'd say.

Somehow she's turned the wheel left when she meant to go right, and there it is on the corner: the house where James or Jake Springer used to live, newly painted a pale blue with white trim, its big yard still framed by the ancient sixty-foot poplars the pioneers planted. The memory of their lovemaking, so long ago now, hits her low in her abdomen with an immediacy that stuns her — his mouth on her breasts, his gentle, insistent hands on her body, his . . . She catches her breath. The one person who loved her wholly, without equivocation, dead now, gone forever. And she can hardly believe she could ever have done such a thing — her, a respectable married woman, a woman in love with her husband, and him a good man who didn't drink or abuse her or even look at other women. Even more puzzling is her lack of shame at her adultery, as if the pure, desperate love she and James shared is its own justification.

And what about the pain? she asks herself. The need to sneak around, lying to Barney that she was cleaning his house and seeing to it that he ate the occasional decent meal, when in fact her cleaning was perfunctory and she rarely did more than make a pot of tea. What about the constant terror of being caught, her life ruined by her own unaccountable, driven need for an old man? Not for the first time, and not without perplexity, and something else less easily nameable, she thinks there was something in their relationship that felt like father and daughter. Maybe that was part of why it was so good. Her own father so distant. She pulls back in distaste from this line of thinking. It was love, she tells herself, that was all, and we were a perfect match sexually.

Sex with Barney has become a disaster. When he comes home for a night every week or so she is so ardent, so tender, eager to woo him back, trying to please him with all the things she knows he likes best: touching him just so, her kisses studied, expert, filled with desire, and him apologizing afterward — "I dunno what's — the thing is — " She can feel the effort it takes him to respond at all. Then lying silently beside her, awake but pretending not to be, while she does the same, hurt and angry, desperate to speak to him about this nameless thing that's spoiling their love, but afraid to say a word for fear of hurting him, or of having him say something she couldn't bear to hear — or even worse — of scaring him away so he stops coming home at all. She holds back tears and grips the steering wheel more securely. She has decided he's having an affair with his ranch, and until he tires of it, or begins to remember all the bad things about ranching that he once couldn't wait to get away from, she'll have to settle for being second best, even if she hates it with every fibre of her being. Patience, her father would say. Wait it out. You got time. That's how he did business, she remembers grimly, it always worked for him.

The small, muddy town recedes behind her now, as she climbs out of the valley and begins to gather speed on the highway. Sun has broken through the clouds; the haze that has for days obscured the distance has dissolved and she can see the prairie, varying from flat

to slightly rolling, and nearly all of it cultivated, unfolding for miles
out on each side of the road, tilting upward to a faint line of purple
hills at the bottom of the sky. She sets the car on cruise and loosens
her grip on the steering wheel. Driving through this vast, open landscape always has this relaxing effect on her, and makes the town seem
claustrophobic.

Why won't Barney come home? When he does, he gets out of the
truck and stands for a moment with his back to the house and to her
and stares out over the farm: field after field, a rolling green carpet in
the late spring, a sea of pale gold by August, shadows dappling its
stately, slow-moving waves, in winter a blue-shadowed, gleaming
white ocean. Or he looks out to the sky-filled space that is the river
valley with its white-flecked cliffs and its steep dun-coloured sides.
It's as if he's searching for something there that, judging by the
puzzled expression he wears when he at last turns to her, he never
seems to find. How could he have chosen thick coniferous forest and
precipitous hills, a landscape where he can see neither the sunset nor
the sunrise, over the heart-stopping vistas of the farm?

That moment of clear sunlight has gone, it has begun to rain
again, and, with an exasperated "Damn," she turns on the wipers.
She hasn't told Barney where she's going, and for an instant she
tenses again — what if she misses his call? She'd have phoned him,
but knows it's hopeless to try to catch him inside. I'll be home by ten,
she tells herself, and he never phones before dark; if I don't answer,
surely he'll keep trying. She reminds herself, too, that as soon as calving is over in another month at the most, he'll spend more time at
the farm with her, but this thought doesn't comfort her the way it
used to. She no longer holds the key to his heart. He's retreating from
her, growing smaller and smaller, and she doesn't know how to bring
him back.

By the time she reaches the outskirts of the small city spread down
the wide, shallow valley and partway up its sides, it has again stopped
raining. She drives to the nursing home where it sits high on the
sloping valley wall. As she parks, everyone Iris sees around her is a

stranger. This too is something she can't seem to get used to. What with the rapid, bewildering changes in the farm economy, bankruptcies and land losses, consolidation of small farms into big ones like her own have emptied out the countryside. Half the people she knows have gone to British Columbia or Alberta, to the cities, to find work, her own once huge extended family reduced to a fraction of what it was when she was a child.

As she approaches the nursing desk to make the obligatory inquiry about her mother — not that they ever have anything to tell her that she can't see for herself — she meets a handsome woman walking out. The woman glances at her, a glint of something, recognition maybe, passes over her features, but she doesn't speak or nod. Iris thinks maybe she ought to know her, although she can't place that assured stride, that smooth cap of fine fair hair, that delicately boned face with its haughty expression.

"Who was that?" she asks the nurse on duty, Rosalie, who'd been a couple of years ahead of her in high school in Chinook. The woman is moving quickly down the steps on the other side of the glass doors.

"Daisy Castle," Rosalie says. "Don't you know her? She lives over west on the border. Her dad's Irv Castle?" Iris remembers now. Wild as a coyote, people said, when she was a girl. "Her mother's here too," Rosalie goes on. "Alzheimer's." She reaches for Iris's mother's chart. "Nothing new here," she says of Lily. Old people totter past, or roll by in wheelchairs. A TV set in the corner is on too loud, a soap that nobody's watching. Iris, staring down at Rosalie's tight bun of grey hair, is thinking vaguely, she ought to colour it, it makes her look so old that way. Rosalie is religious though, nursed for her church for a few years in Bangladesh or Thailand or somewhere.

"You know, Iris," Rosalie says, still not looking up, "your mother could be at home. There's nothing much the matter with her." Iris can't think what to say. What about her mother's heart? What about her forgetfulness? She's about to respond with a polite "Oh?" but Rosalie goes on. "She's stable enough. And that disorientation she has sometimes — who wouldn't get disoriented with nobody to talk to day after day after day?" She looks up now, something glimmering in her dark eyes that are so striking in that plain, aging face that Iris is taken aback.

"That's one reason we brought her here after Dad died," she replies stiffly. "So she'd have people her own age to socialize with. We couldn't leave her on her own in town and she'd have been lonely with us out on the farm." Rosalie doesn't say anything, just looks down to her papers. After a second's silence, feeling as if she's somehow been humiliated, Iris walks away.

Her mother is sitting across the room in a leather armchair, her legs covered with an afghan composed of white daisies with yellow centres that Iris remembers her, in better days, crocheting herself. She lifts her head slowly when Iris enters, as though she has been napping. Beside her the television set flashes soundless pictures and Iris reaches over and snaps it off.

"How are you, Mom?" she asks, crossing to her mother, bending and kissing her forehead. Her mother looks down with quavering head at her body, so wasted now that it barely disturbs the afghan.

"I'm not well at all," she says, smiling — she's making a joke. She turns her head to the window, sighing, and for an instant Iris sees the woman her mother used to be, the fine nose, the high cheek-bones, the patrician mouth. How haughty she could be, Iris remembers with a trace of irritation. "I'm going to die soon," her mother says.

"I'm sorry I didn't come last week," Iris explains. Confronted by her mother's frailty, she's overcome with her failures as a daughter. "I'm really sorry," she says again, meaning it this time. Her mother observes her, and Iris is surprised to see how blue her eyes are today. It seems to Iris that the colour has been progressively leached from them over the years she has been here, as all excess flesh has slowly melted from her bones.

"I've never been so tired in all my days."

Iris recognizes this as something she has heard before, as far back as she can remember, whenever her mother had finished the canning, or the spring cleaning, or given a family dinner. "Where's Barney?"

"At the ranch."

"What ranch? His father's?"

"No, ours." She pulls the visitor's chair closer to her mother's, seats herself, and leans forward to take her mother's hand in hers.

"What's this?" her mother asks, her eyes widening. Iris has told her about the ranch, more than once, as a matter of fact, but she explains again.

"Barney bought a ranch late last fall, and now he's calving so he's there all the time — " She wants to go on, she wants to tell her mother everything, suddenly tears prickle behind her eyelids. She wants to say, *He's left me, Mom*, even though she knows Barney would deny this, and her mother would not say, *I told you he's not one of us*, although this is what she'd always thought, had barely troubled to hide behind the cool formality with which she'd treated Barney. Her mother's hand is cold and Iris rubs gently to warm it. She lifts her eyes and finds her mother staring at her in that piercing way she always had whenever she suspected there was something going on that Iris didn't want her to know about. But now Iris sees a remoteness, a distance, as if Iris is some woman her mother hardly knows and is only moderately interested in. In an unexpected flash she sees too in her mother's face an echo of her grandmother's — her mother's mother — before it disappears as quickly as she found it. Confused, unable to tolerate so probing a gaze, she blinks and looks away like a guilty child.

"People grow away from each other," her mother says, no longer looking at Iris. "Your father and I did."

"No!" Iris says, shocked. This is news to her. In her memory her parents were the ideal couple, community leaders, solidly a pair in everything they said or did. She thinks of their brief antagonisms that flared up and then died away as quickly as they'd come — or so it had seemed to her. Now her heart begins to beat faster. It trips in her wrists and throat, tiny thuds that propel too much blood up into her cheeks.

"When Laurence died, Jack changed forever." Her mother pauses. Lily — what a lovely, melancholy name, Iris thinks, and wonders if it's true that your name helps set your destiny, remembering Lannie telling her from her hospital bed that Iris is the goddess of the rainbow. Lily pushes Iris's hand away, but gently, slowly. Laurence was Iris's brother, stillborn when Iris was a year old, nothing more than a story, no, a myth, to Iris. "Men want sons," her mother says. "God knows why," and she smiles, so that Iris knows she's making a joke again.

"How did he change?"

Her mother stares down at the afghan, then she says, poignantly, "He wasn't any good at loving any more." She swallows perceptibly, as if her throat hurts her. "He grew to love land more than anything — more than me or you."

Iris sits back startled and puzzled. Her father had stopped loving them? Is that what her mother means? She'd never doubted her father loved her; hadn't he given her anything she asked for? She knows her mother thought that they had spoiled her. Except that time when she'd asked for a horse. It can't be. They'd gone everywhere as a family; there'd been no quarrels, no shouting, no cold silences, and when her mother was busy with her church work her father took her with him, even to auction sales where mostly men went. *Thomases don't sell land*, he often used to say, *Thomases buy it*. When Barney married her, he married that dictum, too. Now it jolts her a little, as if she's hearing it for the first time, she who'd always taken its senti-ment for granted as wise and right, the way the world needed to be. She waits uneasily for her mother to go on.

"He got land fever," her mother says, and laughs gently at the old phrase, or maybe it's that she finds the condition amusing, although the tears still sit, pooled in the wrinkles at the bottom of each eye.

Land fever? Was that what happened to Barney? But no, she answers herself. Barney's buying the ranch had to do with — turning away from everything he'd become since he'd left his father's dirt-poor ranch up in the hills to marry her and become a farmer, for some incomprehensible reason needing to go back to his beginnings. Articulating this for the first time, she feels a cold relief.

"That's how you wound up with the biggest farm in the district, Iris," her mother says. "I guess you should thank him for it. I'm sure Barney does" — that wry, faintly contemptuous note still there after all these years. But Barney doesn't, not any more, Iris knows.

"I don't know how you can say that Dad didn't love . . . you," she

says in wonderment. "You never fought. You always seemed so —
comfortable — together."

"About this ranch," her mother says abruptly, as if Iris hasn't
spoken. She drops her eyes from Iris's and picks at a daisy's yellow
centre. "You haven't gone with him to live there?"

"No." Iris shakes her head, watching her mother's fingers as they
pluck, pluck at the daisy.

"Why not?" The question is firm, and in its surprising lack of
rebuke Iris remembers the gaze of the woman in her dream.

"It is a beautiful place," she says. "It's over west in Fort Walsh
country, you know? It has lots of trees and deep coulees and valleys
and streams . . ." Her mother doesn't appear to be listening.

"You better go there, Iris," her mother says, startling Iris with her
firmness as if she knows something Iris doesn't. She closes her eyes.
Her fingers stop their restless picking.

"I don't want to," Iris says bleakly. She hears the hint of anger in
her own voice and tries, too late, to soften it. But there it is, out at
last. She just doesn't want to.

"Why not?" her mother asks in a whisper, her eyes still closed.

"There's no running water, no electricity, no decent roads. It's fifty
miles to the nearest town. I'm past fifty, Mom. It's too late for me to
start living like my grandmother did. And I don't know a thing about
cattle, you know I don't." She's trying to find good reasons to tell her
mother, explanations nobody could find fault with, but instead she
finds herself recalling the dehorning so long ago on the Christie
ranch, before she and Barney were married, the blood drenching
Luke's shirt, Barney's half-brother Howard's barely concealed rage,
the screams of the animals, and Barney trying to hide it all from her,
afraid if she really saw it, she'd go away and never come back. And
never telling her mother about this, not wanting her to be right. "I
still love him, Mom," she whispers.

Her mother is asleep. Iris leans toward her and whispers, "Mom?
Mother?" There is no response. She peers at her mother's delicately
lined face, the fine skin, the palest flush in her cheeks showing she's
still alive behind her stillness. "Help me, Mother." Her mother's
eyes are still closed; she moves her head irritably, a tiny, almost

imperceptible jerk, and a frown passes across her features and disappears.

The door opens and a nursing assistant enters the room quietly. She's carrying the supper tray which she sets down on the table by Iris, snapping on the lamp beside it.

"Will you feed her or do you want me to?" she asks.

"I'll feed her," Iris says. The nurse bends over her mother.

"Wake up, Mrs. Thomas, suppertime," she calls. "When she finishes eating, call me and I'll help you put her to bed." Lily says, "Don't worry, I have the garden planted." The nurse turns to Iris with a smile and says, "She's alone too much; all our old people are." She gives the afghan a little pat, then leaves the room quickly.

Lily doesn't want to eat, and when she lifts one thin hand in a gesture of refusal and turns her head away to stare into the shadows at the end of the room, Iris makes no effort to persuade her. After a while she pushes the buzzer at the head of her bed, and together she and a different nursing assistant, this one a dark-skinned, slight woman whose accent Iris can't penetrate, help her mother into the bed. Lily soon falls back into sleep or wherever it is the very old go when they close their eyes. Perhaps she will die tonight, perhaps this is the last night they, mother and daughter, will spend together. And when she goes, Iris thinks, watching that scarcely discernible quiver in her mother's chest, who will take her place? For in this instant she understands what she has not known before, that there will never be any kind of loss as whole and irrevocable as the loss of her mother.

Evening has come and the room is filling with shadows, dissolving the walls and ceiling. Iris sits on, lost in reverie, this place, this room, this woman who bore her, introduced her to life, nursed her and cared for her and taught her, filling the space left by Barney's defection. She thinks, I could take her home with me, right now, tonight. She tries hard to think what it would be like with her mother at home, but her mind won't deal with it. Not in the new uncertainty in which she lives with Barney neither fully gone nor fully present.

She remembers her answer to her mother's *Why not?* A sulky *I don't want to.*

Suddenly it's as if an axe has cleaved her bloodlessly in two, from the crown of her head right down through her womb, and in that remorseless opening into her own soul, she sees what she's been: selfish through and through, a stubborn child blindly wanting her own way. And more: terrified by Barney's attempt to drag her out of her complacent, comfortable rut of a life. Utterly terrified. And that — that is the real reason she has refused to go.

The Wild

It's noon by the time she and Luke set out for Barney's ranch. Driving home from Swift Current in the darkness last night she had felt her loneliness as close to unbearable. If she could not thank Barney for forcing her into so radical a change in her lifestyle at this late stage in her life, faced with her own childish stubbornness, she knew she had at least to try to meet him halfway. As she drove the wide, curving highway toward Chinook, the damp blacktop eating up her headlights, she thought ruefully and with a touch of something close to shame at her own newly glimpsed wilfulness: if I don't go to him, our marriage will never be the same again.

Having made her decision, she has been forced to ask Luke to drive her to Barney's ranch, since most of the road there is impassable this rainy spring without a four-wheel drive, and Barney has theirs with him. Sitting beside Luke on the hard seat of his scarred and dented old truck, her side of the seat covered with a faded quilt which she knew Mary Ann would have insisted on spreading where Iris would sit — this out of some indissoluble embarrassment at her family's life even after all the years Iris has been her daughter-in-law — Iris glances quickly at him. The same clean, sharp profile, impossible to tell by it he's seventy-five, and he's as handsome as ever, although his handsomeness is forever spoiled for Iris by the implacable set of his face. She'll never get used to these hardbitten old ranchers with their grim ethic, never smiling for fear somebody might take them for soft, still testing and finding wanting their fifty-year-old sons. It had taken years, no matter what Barney said, before she stopped feeling a bit scared around him.

At the moment they're driving down a narrow paved road, for which Iris is grateful, as she needs a respite from being thrown around in the cab by the muddy, deeply rutted roads they've had to travel before they reached this twenty-mile stretch of pavement. She rearranges her shiny blue raincoat, pulls her damp silk scarf off her head and spreads it out on her knees to dry. Luke turns on the windshield wipers, spraying the windows with cleaning fluid at the same time. Neither of them can see anything as the lumps of pale brown mud dissolve and smear the view of the narrow black road and the drenched yellow fields stretching away on both sides of it. Bit by messy bit the wipers clear two fan-shaped openings.

"The sun is shining!" Iris says in amazement. Luke grunts. The sight of the clear blue sky and the sunshine glinting off the puddles on the asphalt ahead of them so encourages her that she makes an effort to talk to Luke.

"Are you calving?" She can never remember whether Luke calves early or late, the choice being a source of disagreement among certain cattlemen. Of course, Luke calves late. He has nothing but contempt for those who breed their cows so they calve in the middle of blizzards or in forty-below weather in order to have extra-big calves at the fall sales, or because they're really farmers and don't want to be calving and seeding at the same time.

"Couple more weeks," Luke says. She looks at his knobby hand on the gearshift. In it she sees his life written, his fingers thick with muscle, his skin roughened and tanned even in winter, his knuckles arthritic. If he weren't so tough, he'd be dead, she thinks and is a little ashamed she has never tried to get closer than hailing distance to him. And Mary Ann's hands are big and thick too. The only time Iris's hands show any signs of having done work is during gardening season when her nails break off and the skin grows rough from the constant scrubbing to keep them clean. Her diamond wedding ring and the sapphire, a gift from her parents on her high school graduation, glimmer gently at her and she thrusts her hands into her coat pockets.

Looking at them, though, reminds her that soon she'll be able to start planting her garden. She sees herself dropping the seeds from a mound in her palm, the dark furrows accepting them as she kneels

in the slowly warming earth, losing herself in the rhythm of planting. The bumping of the truck reminds her that she won't be planting at the farm this year. No use if she isn't going to be there, nobody
to weed or water it, and the deer eating whatever grows. She wonders
if you can plant in forest soil, and doubts it. This is the first thing —
other than all her comforts, she thinks wryly — that she really cares
about she'll have to give up, and she wonders briefly if it's not too late
to ask Luke to turn back.

"I can't thank you enough for doing this," she says instead. Her
resistance has crumbled, her anger at Barney has been replaced by her
need to touch him, to lie full length against him, skin to skin, breathing in his breath, her mouth on his.

"I don't mind," Luke says. Startled, she glances at him, having
forgotten her own remark. "Mary Ann wouldn't let me do nothing
else," and he makes a noise that might be laughter. She recognizes his
words for the usual sentiment: If you do something that might be
seen as nice or good, it's only because the women made you. And yet,
it's true. Even Luke in such matters yields to the wife he otherwise,
apparently, pays no attention to. She considers that power women
seem to have, what it is, where it comes from, in a world otherwise
run by men.

Or maybe he really doesn't mind. Maybe he's looking forward to
seeing his son, especially now that Barney has returned to the
cowboy life he was raised in. Her face heats up at this thought. The
truth is, she has always felt a sort of perplexed guilt at stealing him
from his family. Now she realizes Luke and Mary Ann had expected
that from his bride; what they hadn't expected was that their own son
would turn his back wholly on their way of life and everything they
stood for, trading in the ranching way of life so casually for what
seemed to them — to all of them — its opposite, farming. But surely
she's not responsible for that? Surely that was his choice?

"I tell ya," Luke says. "Don't know what he's thinking about. Past
fifty and still can't make up his mind what he wants." He shifts gears,
usually an effortless push and click but this time it's a rapid and hard
movement, and when she glances at him, his lips have tightened.
Change the subject, quick.

"How is Mary Ann these days?" she asks brightly. "Her arthritis not too bad?"

"Pretty sore mornings," Luke says.

"The doctor's no help?" He shrugs, she struggles on. "And Fay and the kids?" Has she gone too far, asked too many questions, begun to seem nosy to touchy Luke?

"Don't see too much of 'em. Fay lost her job in the drugstore when it closed. She's looking around. Barry's at home."

"Oh?" Iris is startled, and bites her tongue to keep from saying more. Fay's husband hasn't been home regularly for years.

"Getting too old to rodeo," Luke points out, as if he knows what she's thinking and isn't going to pretend to her everything is fine between his daughter and son-in-law. Recognizing this for what it is, that she's finally family, she feels only exasperation. "Guess now he figures he needs his wife and kids. Got a job at that feedlot outside Swift Current."

"Quinn will be glad to have him home," Iris remarks, thinking of him at twelve when he used to come and stay with her and Barney — and then run away — every single time, back to the city, or to whatever town his father was rodeoing in. Luke shrugs again. She'd like to ask if Fay is still drinking, but of course can't since it isn't supposed to be happening. She's running out of things to say.

When she'd tried to phone Barney to let him know she and Luke were coming, the phone rang and rang into a muffled silence. Out in the corrals, she supposes, or riding the steep, wooded hills looking for cows. Thank God it's stopped raining, really seems to mean it this time.

"How many cows Barney got to calve out?" Luke asks.

"I think about eighty. He said he'd start small till he got back in the swing of things." Luke grunts, whether in amusement, exasperation, or agreement, Iris can't tell.

"Wolves, grizzlies, all gone from them hills now," he remarks. "Used to be stories, you wouldn't believe . . ." Iris remembers now the importance of waiting. Luke speaks when he's good and ready and if you interrupt his thoughts, he quits talking, period. "Used to take Howard and Barney when they were kids up to the old Sullivan place for roundups. A long time ago. Old Man Robinson would be there. Jerretts, Castles would come with all the kids. We'd camp there, three, four days, while we brought in all them cows, sorted them out." The hint of sadness in his voice makes her risk a glance at him. As far as she can tell, his expression hasn't changed. "Yeah, Castles'd be Barney's nearest neighbours. Irv is running the place now. His boy Dennis helps. That Daisy comes and goes."

She's resting her left arm on a sports bag full of clean jeans, shirts, socks, and underwear for Barney that, because of the mud and the other things they're carrying in the back of the truck, they've had to put on the seat between them. In the steel toolbox, besides the bag of Iris's own clothing, there's a carton of groceries, fresh baking, fruit, even lettuce and tomatoes for salad, something Barney won't have seen since he was last home. There isn't even running water to wash the lettuce in, she'll have to pump it at the well. Grandma pumped water at the well her whole married life, she tells herself. It didn't kill her. But there isn't much comfort in the thought. All those women worked too hard, never had a second to themselves, never got to do anything that was fun or just for themselves and nobody else.

The truck slows, and Luke turns the wheel west off the highway. He reaches down and jerks the knob that puts the truck back into four-wheel drive. The truck bucks and growls, but it pulls on through the mud. Iris hangs on to the armrest when they slew sideways and appear to be going straight for the ditch. Mud and water spray up and hit the windshield and the side windows, it's hard to believe anything could get through this mess. She peers through a splattered window and sees a broken landscape of pines and steep, sloping hillsides and knows they're well into the Cypress Hills. Soon — if they don't get stuck or slide off the road — they'll reach Barney.

"Not far now. Wind's up. Could be a good drying day," Luke says. Unexpectedly, he goes on, "I told Howard I'm ready to retire, told him to come home. I think he's got a woman where he is. 'Bring her, if she's a good woman,' I told him." His words are broken by the roaring and bumping of the truck. Iris opens her mouth to speak, but abandons the attempt, the truck is making so much noise she'd have to yell. And anyway, she doesn't know what to say about

Howard, Barney's half-brother who is also Lannie's father. It's nothing to me, one way or the other, she tells herself, but I'll never be able to like him, not after the way he dumped poor Lannie on us and walked away and never even looked back.

She finds herself smiling, remembering Lannie as a little girl, kissing her good night as she lay in bed, tucking her in, leaving the door open so a shaft of light brightened the darkness. How she missed her when she went off to university, how — those letters again, the ones she found in Lannie's book bag. Surely they must have been someone else's? But no, her name was on most of them. Why would anyone write obscene notes to her? Why would she keep them? Iris shakes her head quickly, she's been down this frightening path a thousand times before and is never any the wiser.

They're climbing a high, narrow, winding road that she recognizes as the one that will lead them over the last barrier on this long trek to Barney's godforsaken ranch. At the top they'll see through the filthy windshield far below them and across the narrow, grassy valley, nestled in the dark pines near the bottom of the far slope, the small log house that's become Barney's home. A wave passes through Iris — nausea, heat, excitement — she can't name it, just wishes it would pass, it scares her. Maybe she's making a mistake. Maybe she has been right all along, and Barney wrong. And yet — she sees Barney as he was when she first knew him: tall, lean, slow to smile, staring at her as if by the sheer intensity of his gaze he might make her his. She smiles to herself, suddenly sure that he'll be glad to see her, and her old contentment in her marriage returns to move slowly through her.

The truck gives one last lurch, Luke says "Whoooaa" to it, it straightens itself, and they've reached the top of the ridge. He stops the truck, pushes the knob that sends out a steady stream of cleaning fluid, the wipers thump on high for a minute and as the windshield gradually clears, Iris leans forward to peer ahead and below. There's one more barrier she's forgotten about. Below them, partway across the valley, where normally there's a narrow, shallow but fast-running, clearwater stream whose gravel bottom a truck rolls easily over, lies a wide expanse of rushing black water. They sit silently, staring down at it.

"Hell," Luke curses, mildly enough, then, "must be some way through it." He puts the truck back in gear and they inch their way down the narrow trail that winds down the hillside. Frowning, Iris says, "There's no smoke coming out of the chimney."

"He must've been out too long. Fire went out. It ain't that cold." They reach the bottom of the valley and make their way a few yards along the trail to the very edge of the water. For a minute Iris thinks Luke is going to drive right on through it. But he stops the truck again, leaves it idling, gets out, and walks to the place where the creeping edge of the water forms a small pool on the road before it eddies rapidly away downstream. He stands so long Iris considers whether she should get out of the truck and stand with him.

She peers across the water to the cabin. There's no sign of movement, but over the hiss and burble of the water she hears cows bellowing. The sound makes her uneasy. She stares harder across the water's silver expanse, and sees two saddlehorses standing motionless against the fence in the pen closest to the house and, in the next pen, cows milling about, calling or stopping to watch her and Luke.

Luke opens the truck door and climbs in. Iris's palms have begun to sweat, and the back of her neck is damp against the stiff edge of her plastic raincoat.

"What?" she asks uneasily, breathlessly.

"He's only got two saddlehorses here." Iris waits for him to go on, but of course, he doesn't, and it dawns on her that he means Barney must be around, inside the house maybe, since both horses are in plain sight. Luke leans on the horn, then beeps it rhythmically. Nothing stirs, then Iris notices what Luke probably took in at a glance: Barney's half-ton parked by the side of the cabin under a couple of tall lodgepole pines. He has to be inside. Now her heart is thumping in her chest; the strength of its beating tells her she's anxious before she recognizes the nausea again in the pit of her stomach. She turns her head to Luke quickly, out of control, is about to say "Luke!" but he's speaking.

"I'm going across on foot."

"Can't we drive?"

"Nope," Luke says. She waits. "Road's washed out right in front of us. Must be a two-foot drop."

Iris feels she should protest, however futile. Luke is an old man, and they don't know how deep the water is. But he's getting out, reaching into the carry-all box in the back of the truck. He pulls out his long yellow riding slicker. When he has it on, he reaches inside the cab and shuts off the motor. "This is as far as we go," he says, and Iris smiles. She sees it's grim cowboy humour.

"I'm coming too," she says. In the abrupt silence her voice is too loud.

"You wait here," Luke says amiably, as if she hasn't spoken. "I'll come back for you. Or Barney will." This last is so clearly an after-thought that Iris realizes Luke thinks something's happened to Barney. The heat envelops her again, she feels as if she'll stifle in her raincoat and jacket and in the cab. She pushes herself quickly across the seat and clambers out on the driver's side, her scarf clutched in her hand. Luke is standing meditatively at the water's edge.

She cries, "A rope, is there a rope?" Luke turns back to her, not looking at her, and goes to the truck box again. He rummages around inside while she stands, worried, behind him, her hands in tight fists at her side. She's holding her breath and lets it out in a sudden rush as Luke pulls out a coiled yellow nylon rope.

"Never go anywhere without it," he says, and she realizes this is more humour and it frightens her even more. That's what she is, she's scared to death. She pulls open the truck door and leans hard on the horn again, then waits. Nothing. Silence. Even the cows have stopped bellowing, and she thinks now that cows only bellow when there's something wrong — they're hungry or thirsty or have lost their calves — a fact Luke would have noted instantly.

"I'm coming too," she repeats. He doesn't answer or even look at her, but walks around her to the front of the truck where he fastens one end of the rope with one of those fancy cowboy knots Barney is so good at to the big truck's grillguard. The noise the water makes hurrying by seems to grow louder, and behind it Iris hears some other higher-pitched hissing or whoop she can't identify that mingles with the cows' renewed calls. Luke goes past her back to the cab where he reaches in and does something to both gears and pulls on the emergency brake. Iris looks again toward the cabin. Still no movement from it but the tops of the pines all the way up the ridge behind it are in motion, and she understands the other noise she hears is wind, thinks automatically, good, Luke was right, it'll dry up this mud.

Luke looks at her now, he's got a funny sort of smile on his face. She recognizes it as an attempt at reassurance. A peculiar lightness has entered his voice. He's good at trouble, comfortable with it. Sensing this about him, a flash of anger briefly knifes through her. Irrationally, she would like to blame him for this.

"This here's a forty-foot rope," he says. "I'd say that stream's maybe fifty feet across. Can't be deep all the way — maybe only twenty feet or so down the main channel. Should be long enough." Iris looks wildly around. Seeing what she wants — she can be good at trouble too — she pulls a rain-swollen tree limb about two inches in diameter out of the roadside water and struggles to strip off the small branches. Luke is busy tying a loop in the other end of the rope. She expects him to tie it around his waist, but instead he loops it over his head, across his shoulder and chest and under his arm. She hands him the stick. He takes it as if it's all he's been waiting for and turns his back on her, then turns back again.

"Here." He hands her the thick coil of rope between the end tied to the grillguard and the end he's formed into a loop around his body. He moves the knot until it's resting against his shoulder blade. "Let it out slow." He steps into the water and for the first time Iris sees the washout. The water's mid-thigh on Luke already. He wavers a bit, then regains his balance.

"There's probably a boat on the place. This must happen all the time. I'll come back for you." She doesn't want to wait but something holds her back from insisting, some last-minute fear. It isn't this violent flow she's afraid of. It's whatever is on the other side.

The rope is stiff and hard in her hands and each loop stays formed until Luke moves ahead and pulls it taut. Then she lets another loop go. He moves slowly, prodding ahead with the stick before each step. Every few steps he wavers a bit, as if he's lost his footing. He's an old man, she reminds herself, his balance probably isn't that good any more. I should have gone myself, but the very image of striking out through the water while Luke waits in the truck makes her laugh out loud. She's glad Luke can't hear her over the stream's racket.

It's getting deeper and deeper. There isn't much rope left. Luke's a tall man, as tall as Barney, but the water must be waist-deep by now, she half expects him to strike out swimming. His long coat billows up around him like a sail filling with air, she's holding her breath when she sees him begin to rise up out of the water and realizes he must be through the deepest part and climbing what would be, in normal times, the far bank. She has no more rope to play out. Luke seems to realize this at the same time as she lets the last loop go, because without stopping or turning back to signal to her, he lifts the rope over his head, slides his arm out, and drops it. Instantly it swings out into the current behind him and begins to move, undulating like a sea serpent, toward her side of the torrent. The water strains and pulls to drag the rope free of the truck.

Now Luke's out of the river, pausing to empty his boots which must be too heavy with water to walk in. He nears the cabin, hesitating again to look up as if whatever he's looking for might be on the roof or in the tops of the forty-foot pines beside or behind it. Go in, she wills him, for pity's sake, go in, Luke. Hurry.

Still moving slowly he disappears inside and she stands, her hands pressed flat against her chest, above her breasts, waiting. He doesn't come out and she waits some more and then, caught in the roar of the water and the wind, she knows something really bad has happened and she finds she can't stay there any longer. She grabs the rope and reels it in, fishes the soaking loop out of the water and drapes it over her chest and shoulder the same way Luke did and steps down into the water.

Instantly the water is at the tops of her thighs, and freezing cold. It plasters her pants against her legs and lifts her raincoat to float out around her; the stream tugs on it, trying to sweep it away with her inside it. The stream has taken on a fierce, cold soul that insists she go away downstream with it. She makes a misstep, reaching out with her foot to a place where the ground has dissolved in the rush and sweep of water and she's over and down, being swept away, the water washing over her head, and rushing up her nose and into her eyes.

Flailing wildly, she grabs the rope before the water pulls it off her shoulder, and with its resistance finds her footing and stands, coughing and gasping. She's scared, really scared, but then she tells herself, *Smarten up, you've got a rope, you won't drown.*

The water has reached her chest and its untamed tugging and pushing is almost more than she can resist. She pushes doggedly on, fighting her way back upstream to get as much length out of the rope as she can, at the same time as she crosses. She tries to keep her eyes on the open cabin door hoping Luke will reappear. Her foot hits a rock and she falls again, but it's shallow enough here so she pushes herself upright on the stream bottom and realizes it has begun to slope upward, not downward, and that she has reached the far edge of the main channel and she can make it from here all right.

She tries to run, but the current makes her stumble forward, splashing. Suddenly her body gets very light as she rises out of deep water. This surprising lightness makes her stumble again and then she's jerked back by the rope. She flings it off without looking, the way Luke did, and tries to run up out of the water, off-balance, jerky, her feet are numb with cold, water pours out of her boots with every step, until one simply pulls itself off. She doesn't stop to retrieve it.

At the cabin door she stops and kicks off her remaining boot. It falls off the railway tie that forms the step into the dripping grass beside it. She hesitates for a second, the wind howls at her back, and behind it the river surges by with a malevolent roar. She puts out stiff fingers to push the partly open door to widen the gap, then steps into blackness.

She can't discern much, but she doesn't wait for her eyes to adjust. She knows she's in the kitchen, knows the way is straight through in the direction of that square of light that is the window on the end wall of the only other room that serves as living room and bedroom. She bumps against the corner of a table, keeps moving, stumbles against a chair, pushes it aside and hears it fall over as she crosses the threshold of the second room.

Slowly she makes Barney out. He's lying there on the couch, and she's dimly aware of Luke standing with his back to her, blotting out the light from the other window, his head down, his back bent. Barney is so still. Why doesn't he get up when he sees her standing there in the doorway, water pouring off her? Why doesn't he say something?

Luke doesn't move at all, but there's a soft sound coming from him, as if he's caught cold, a kind of snuffling or wheezing. She goes forward, her wet clothes heavy and bending like cardboard, impeding her movement as she goes toward the couch. Get up, Barney, she almost says. Get up! But he just lies there, one arm up above his head, the palm opened to the ceiling. When she reaches him, Luke still hasn't moved.

"Don't do this, Barney," she whispers, as she bends over him. "Please." She touches him with her fingertips, gently, his cold denim shirt, his dear, familiar face. "Please, I love you," she whispers. But when she feels how cold his face is, like ice and stiff, not the real Barney at all, when she sees how dead he is, how he has gone away somewhere, he isn't there, not there — her legs give way and she finds herself kneeling on the cabin floor, leaning against Barney, her arms reaching out across him, her fingers clutching his shirtsleeve where it's pressed against the back of the couch, as if to pull him back to her.

"Luke," she says. "Luke — " She means to ask him to explain this thing that has happened, she wants him to make it stop. "Luke!" She knows by the feel of her throat that she has screamed his name and this, too, seems absurd, as absurd as Barney's deadness, so she calls instead the name she surely meant to call: "Barney!" Behind her Luke's feet are making the old plank floor creak as he rushes toward her.

"Get up, Iris," he growls in her ear and the sound is so fraught with rage or anguish, or the two mixed and only half released, that when she feels his arms sliding under hers, his whole strength roughly pulling her to her feet, she's afraid to resist.

Standing now, she leans into Luke, feeling his body's rigidity with revulsion. She wants to hit him, she wants to pound his face with her fists. Her anger with Luke and his rage with her is out in the open at last.

With legs that feel heavy and numb as posts, she staggers rapidly away from his reach, letting her breath out carefully, her chest shuddering with it, the sound audible. In her ears the tension in the room is discernible, the sound as high-pitched as the wind's wild scream through the tall black pines that surround the cabin. Her head filled with its whine and keen, her heart swelling to fill her chest and throat and mouth, she stares down, voiceless, in slowly growing belief, at her husband's body.

The Promise of Heaven

Iris's eyes snap open into the half-light of her bedroom, the awareness that it's morning and she has to get up as immediate as consciousness is. She feels exhausted and strained, yet no dream, no echo of the passing of the night lingers. Something is tugging at her memory though, but whatever it is refuses to dredge itself up and confront her. The room's shadows are lucid but convey no information. She waits motionless inside the cool sandwich of sheets for that phantom just out of her view to come into focus, glimpses its craggy, horrifying shape, holds back, then edges her hand out to feel the blank sheet beside her, as the spectre moves into reach and slowly encompasses her.

Barney is dead. It's the day of his funeral. She has wakened this morning a widow, she doesn't have a husband any more; she can't quite believe it and would laugh, just a quick snort of surprise, except that she knows she mustn't laugh because it isn't funny. If she laughs, she knows she won't be forgiven. Forgiven for what? For laughing, she tells herself, then, irritated with the nonsense she's babbling to herself, she wobbles her head back and forth briskly on the cold pillow to clear it out. The room rotates rapidly on an angle, and she holds still until, with scarcely perceptible swishes and thumps, it settles back into place around her.

She sees Barney clearly as she and Luke found him only three days ago, that dear body lying on the old davenport, one arm stretched above his head, his eyes closed, his expression calm. It occurs to her that Luke might have closed his eyes. Had he screamed as death descended on him? Or had the blood vessel in his brain swelled and burst while he was peacefully asleep —

I've got to stop this, she tells herself, and lies still, waiting for the full knowledge of his death to overtake her. She tries to call up his face, his straight nose like Luke's, his thick, golden-brown hair, but even that won't come and her inability to mourn, even to feel her love for him, makes her uneasy and faintly shocked at herself. All she has that might be called sorrow is an emptiness in her chest that takes up all the space and makes it hard to breathe.

She thinks of other widows she's known: Poor Marie Chapuis who couldn't manage a coherent word all through the funeral and the reception for sobbing and had to be led away by relatives, Gladys Warkentin who sat frozen-faced and silent, young Melody Friesen who talked and laughed and then stared into space with eyes so deep nobody could look at them. The thought that today she will have to find a way to be a widow makes her automatically push back the covers and get out of bed.

The room's too cold. She goes to the closet and takes out Barney's dressing gown, a thick, deep wine velour that he refused to wear because, he said, it made him feel silly. Said it in such a helpless, baffled, and yet pained way that Iris who had given it to him had to laugh at this display of his untempered maleness, and stopped nagging him to put it on, even if she couldn't understand what it was that bothered him about it.

She slides her arms into it, wraps it around herself as tightly as it will go, and ties the belt in a knot, then pulls the wide collar snugly up around her neck. It feels warm against her skin, its heaviness comforts her, and the assertive way it flaps against her ankles. On Barney it was knee-length. She looks for her slippers, finds them under the bed and slides her feet into them. She isn't sure what to do next, caught in the desire to crawl back into bed and refuse ever to get up again, not even for Barney's funeral. Instead, she goes to the door, puts her hand on the doorknob that's so cold it feels like fire on her palm, and opens the door silently.

The house is without sound, yet there's something in the air that reminds her it's full of people; she can feel them, their sticky bodies, their mingled breaths, their sighs and coughs and their tumbling dreams. Barney's sister Fay and her teenagers, Iris's nieces and nephews, are asleep in the guest rooms and in the basement. This house full of people feels strange, oppressive, when for so long now there's been nobody in it but Barney and herself and then not even Barney.

Now that she's out in the hall she realizes she needs to use the bathroom and would go back, but hesitates because she's afraid flushing the toilet would wake everyone, and the thought of them rising, moving up or down the stairs into the kitchen, making toast, pouring cups of coffee, staring at her with measuring eyes is unbearable. She feels dizzy and has to put a hand out to support herself against the wall. It's probably all the pills they've been feeding her. Tranquillizers, she supposes. She's vague about this, as she is about everything, including where she's going at this time of the morning on the day of Barney's funeral.

Somebody is snoring. The door to Lannie's room is open and she peeks carefully in to see who it is. It's Fay lying sprawled across the single bed, her blonde hair tangled across the pillow, her long nightgown hitched up to reveal her wide, pale, vein-etched legs. The smell of cigarette smoke and some other unpleasant odour reaches Iris now that she's closer. It's that spent alcohol smell; Iris supposes Fay went to bed drunk. She sighs for Mary Ann's sake, for Fay's children's sake, for Barney's sake, but her ruefulness is mixed with pity. She hasn't forgotten Fay's wedding all those years ago, Fay beginning to show with Quinn, Barry sneaking out during the wedding dance for a couple of drinks with his buddies in somebody's half-ton. Iris backs away softly.

She can't recall much of the evening before, although there'd been visitors. The women had made her go to bed early, she remembers that. She must have been acting funny. Placing her feet carefully on the stairs, one by one, till she reached the top, Fay on one side of her who kept stumbling slightly, then catching herself, and Ramona on the other. As if I couldn't walk upstairs myself, she thinks, and decides that she's not going to swallow any more pills. She hates this fuzziness, this sense of drifting.

She wishes Ramona were here right now; Ramona would know what to say to her. She doesn't know herself what it is she needs to hear that might fill this hollow in her chest, that might bring the unreality of this day out of the realm of madness and error and back to some kind of normalcy.

She moves quietly down the hall to the top of the stairs and starts carefully down, intending to use the bathroom by the kitchen door. At the halfway point the sickening scent of flowers flows up the stairs to meet her: lilies, roses, irises because it's spring, God knows what all else. Now, as she reaches the kitchen, the fragrance of squares and cakes brought by neighbours and left on the counter because the deep freeze and fridge are stuffed overwhelms her.

An intense heat has begun to spread itself through her, it has started deep in her centre and radiates outward inexorably, rapidly, building till it reaches her skin and a thin film of sweat breaks out on her forehead, the back of her neck, between her breasts, down her back, even the backs of her knees are slick with it. How can she be so hot when this morning the house is so cold? She crosses the kitchen with quick tapping steps as her slippers slap against her bare heels and bounce off the vinyl floor, tugging at the belt of the heavy dressing gown to loosen it. Flinging open the back door, she steps out onto the deck, the robe wide open, and feels the relief of the pristine early morning air.

The sun hasn't yet climbed above the horizon and the glow of night still rests in the hollows of the land as it spreads out around her. The caragana hedge, the trees of the yard, block most of the view, but she knows the land is there. It's imprinted on her psyche; her mind's eye sees over the deck and the driveway, through the hedge, past the trees, to the peaceful, wide fields that lie beyond her farmyard. It would be utterly silent except for the waking twitter of small birds in the unleafed caragana hedge and the lilacs by the steps. She walks farther out onto the deck, retying the dressing gown tightly around her, as now that she's outside in the clean, cool air the overwhelming heat is dissipating and she feels the chill.

She kicks off her slippers and steps into her muddy rubber boots that stand by the door. She can't remember putting them there and doubts she was the one to do it, but it crosses her mind that her boots are witnesses to her plight, they are companions, so she doesn't mind their cold interior and dampness on her bare feet. In her urgency to be away from the house, she hardly notices.

She crosses the deck, goes down the steps, across the gravelled drive, and hurrying now, she has to do this before the others wake, she squeezes through a gap in the caragana hedge, a shelter belt from the wind, that makes a square around the houseyard except for part of the way across the front where the driveway enters. The house, with its weight of expectations, its sleepers, recedes from her.

Barney has left a strip of grass maybe five feet wide between the hedge and the summerfallow field beside it. She sets out south, following the hedge's rectangular boundary. The grass, genuine prairie grass, is a dull gold, about a foot high and so fine it has fallen over on itself, so that she walks more on top of it than actually in it. Her boots have a wet sheen now and the hem of her nightgown will be soggy, not that she cares. But the air is so delicious in her head, her lungs, she can feel it filling some of that emptiness in her chest. She forgets about the damp and keeps going, now turning west when the hedge does along the back of the house, past the row of shiny steel grain bins.

As she walks she turns her head left to study the southern horizon. Spread out before her in a long undulating wave is her farm, the biggest farm in the district. It washes slowly away from her, descending as it goes, across faded stubble till it begins to rise again, now a blackened rectangle that reaches out to touch the bottom of the sky. Ahead of her and to her right, less than a half mile away, is the fence-line that marks the border of Ramona and Vance Norman's ranch. Her eyes follow the barbed wire to the deep coulee that the fence fails to contain, that reaches into Iris and Barney's land. That quarter had once been pasture, but Barney had broken most of it. She had resisted his plans only when he'd wanted to burn the homestead buildings. An eyesore, he'd said, and she'd closed her mouth tightly in disagreement, mutely refusing consent to his burning them — it was bad enough her father had sold the house to be moved to town. This morning her mother's parents' falling-down barn and two decayed sheds are tugging her toward them, as if there's some comfort to be had on the ground where her grandparents first made a home, where her mother was born and grew up, an explanation maybe, an answer to the question that has emptied her chest: *Why?*

A noise, not too loud, intrudes and she stops to listen. It's a distant sound, higher pitched than farm dogs or coyotes, more musical, growing louder by the second. She lifts her head to search the sky, and finds to the east of where she stands, flying not very high, as if they've just taken off or are searching for a place to land, a chevron of geese heading in a northwesterly direction. If they keep to their heading, they'll fly right over her. One arm of their formation is very long, while the other has only about five birds in it. It's not that this is so unusual, but she wonders why it would be so on this windless morning when it's nowhere near hunting season.

As they come closer to where she stands a few feet from the hedge, she sees that it's only the lead goose and the birds in the short wing who are honking. She suspects that soon geese will reply from the far end of the long arm, and in a moment a couple of them near its back do, which satisfies her. Soon they're just above her, like the skeletal shadow of a phantom airship, breaking into individual birds as she watches. They hold their speed steady, their wing-beats constant and regular so that she feels sure in their view she's only part of the hedge or tree or rock. Over her they go, one after another. The light is such that she can make out no details of their bodies, just the black shape of bird after bird as they pass overhead in a line that wobbles faintly with their uncoordinated wing-beats.

Then they're gone and she stands transfixed, still staring up to the section of sky where their bodies were, even though she can hear them receding behind her. When she finally turns to follow their flight, they're almost out of sight, soon to pass over the river valley to the northwest where the rising blue-shadowed cliffs sweep against the horizon.

In the few minutes she has been outside the light has changed dramatically with the higher position of the sun. Now it's just above the horizon — it's past seven she thinks, soon everyone will be up and I'll be caught — but she forges on, hurrying now, trying to beat the rush of the sun behind her, in the direction of the coulee.

In the rising light the decaying, grey buildings ahead of her are precise again. And Barney wanted to burn them, she thinks, still indignant. *I don't care if you are dead*, she says to his shadow, realizing its presence has been with her since she squeezed through that gap in the hedge. *You were wrong about that. I know it*, he says, and she feels his arm across her shoulders hurrying her, as she slips a little in the mud, down the rutted track that was once a road, in the middle of the stubblefield.

At the coulee's lip every little knob and rock, every dip and badger bush stands out sharply. It's the light the Great Plains is famous for and she's grateful for it, too, on this brisk morning of her husband's funeral. Even the drugged sluggishness is leaving her in the morning light and the cool spring air. In another fifteen minutes that precious light will have spread itself out more evenly and with less extreme attention; the high spots will flatten a little, the low spots will rise to meet them, and the promise of heaven will be gone until, as the sun lowers itself gently down the sky, its rays will once again make every stone and blade of grass ring with golden light.

When she reaches the dull, matted grass, she pauses, not out of choice, but by the gentle force of the place itself. Barney is still with her; she's begun to suspect he's the one who has called her out here on this errand so early on this chilly morning of the day she has to bury him. She crosses the narrow patch of grass, going slowly. First her father and then Barney had ploughed as close to her grandparents' buildings and to the edge of the coulee as they dared, fearing Iris's mother's wrath and then her own if they edged over too far and brought down one of the shacks or lifted and tumbled a rock that Iris knew must be left as it had been since the last ice age.

She finds herself standing at the edge of one of the two tepee rings that are the only ones left of what was probably an encampment, but the rest of which her grandfather had destroyed with his first ploughing, seventy years earlier. Probably didn't even notice they were rings. *He knew*, Barney says, in her head, and Iris gives him credit for having a grasp on the truth now. Besides, it's an old grief, as old as the hills and the valley bottoms. They were always doomed, Iris thinks. *As are we*, she hears, and Iris is surprised that he would think such a thing.

But the stones still lie there, half-hidden in the damp yellow-grey grass, so lichen-covered and crumbling with age that if she looks too long, instead of seeing them more clearly they disappear into the texture of the grass-covered earth. Some days when she comes here she is able to see most of the individual stones, but not the order or design she knows to be there. It's the strangest thing, as if the stones were alive and could hide themselves from her if they chose to. This morning, arrested by the light, the circles rise clearly in the grass, and she stoops and rests a hand on the curve of one that's covered with a thick coat of pale green lichen. It's satisfyingly scratchy against her palm, and the contrast — her fingertips touching a bare spot of hard, cold rock — makes her fingers tingle.

She rises and walks to the entrance of the decaying barn. Its big door lies broken and decomposing in the grass where a typically savage wind put it years ago — and standing in the opening where it used to be, she gazes upward to the patch of sky she can see through a wide hole where there was once roof. A beam of light pierces it and spotlights the opposite wall, up high, so she can make out the soaked brown wood, still tightly joined horizontally, and an old bird's nest of mud and twigs — swallows, she thinks — nestled under a cracked rafter. Here her grandfather harnessed Clydesdales — he was famous for his beautiful, matched teams — and sat on hay bales with his hired man, both puffing solemnly on pipes, while across the way in the house where now there's only a grass-lined, indistinct depression, her grandmother was baking the breakfast buns she'd set the night before, or checking the Sunday roast. She cannot think what all this means, both of them dead now since Iris was a teenager, and their children too, dead or dying. The barn not likely to stand more than another year. Her grandmother's face is suddenly before her, her image as clear as if she were there in flesh and blood: the halo of fine white hair, the habitual half-smile she wore as if she knew something the rest of them hadn't figured out yet, her startling blue eyes that in old age instead of fading, grew darker.

The memory ebbs and Iris turns away, her chest suddenly hollow again, when she thinks she hears Ramona's voice on the wind. She looks around quickly, but no, the sound has faded, she's alone in this precious space of clear air, of walking spirits. Over by that small pile of rocks, so old they've grown together, Ramona had knelt before her, her cheeks flushed with joy, her eyes lit up with a new, deep light. *I'm going to have a baby.* Iris remembers herself as outraged at this betrayal. Wailing at Ramona's news, *But we were going to go away to school together!* Ramona so caught up in her own adventure she never saw Iris's selfish anger, or if she did, she thought it childish, something that would pass.

Iris had been gathering the first crocuses to take to her mother. She'd dropped them, left them there to die in the damp grass. *This is what I want,* Ramona said, grasping Iris's hands in hers, trying to see into Iris's eyes, into her very soul. And Iris pulling away, her anger turning slowly into sorrow because Ramona was leaving her, going off into some foreign, grown-up world where Iris wasn't ready to follow. The coulee was filling with purple shadows, a chasm opening to swallow them, dropping down to its bottom more than a hundred feet below, passing through time incarnated as layers of earth, to those millions of years earlier. And hidden in the grip of the soil and rocks, the fossilized bones of monsters.

Now Iris moves to the coulee's edge and stands looking down into it, following its geography with her eyes to where it widens and deepens on the other side of the fence. With the melted snow and the long spring rains the slough at the bottom is twice its usual size; it has drowned out rosebushes up the coulee side. In the shallows the bullrushes and pale, rustling grasses stand motionless, and farther along, out of her sight, she knows the coulee drops off more and widens into clay-bottomed, rock-strewn badlands, with a view of the wide river valley into which its waters — when there are some — drain.

She and her mother used to walk here carrying a mesh bag with a picnic lunch in it when she was a child. The patch of grass had been bigger then. Her mother would name the plants, the ones that her mother had taught her; once she'd picked up a stone scraper and told Iris that a long time ago, in the very place they were standing, a Native woman had knelt and scraped a buffalo hide clean of flesh. They'd startled swans in the slough, and often deer bending to drink. Far, far down the coulee, high above the river, golden eagles sometimes circled. You could tell them from hawks by their size and by the mastery of their soaring, as if moving their wings was too much trouble, and then, sailing off with an unconquerable, lazy power that made Iris's heart do funny things in her chest.

I loved you, old man, Iris thinks, I know you're gone, I know it, and it's been too long to cry, and is bewildered, realizing it's James Springer she's grieving now, and not her husband. James doesn't reply. She wants to believe she was wrong, she wants to beg God for forgiveness, and Barney's ghost too, but no matter how she tries, there's a core that won't accept that she sinned. Now that both James and Barney are dead, what can any of it matter anyway?

But it's Barney's warmth that envelops her; his presence is so intense he has crept into every pore of her being, and even the wind that has risen, as it always does on the prairie when the sun is well above the horizon, can't shake him off. He has come to get her through his funeral, he will help her find a way to be a widow.

I loved you too, Barney, she tells him. You were my life.

The wind flaps his dressing gown around her shins; she pulls it tighter, holding the collar in both hands, and hurries down the strip of grass between the two wheel ruts, back to the house in the full morning light. Now her fingers are icicles, and her toes inside the boots she crossed the river in are numb. At the back door she steps out of them and into her slippers, enters the kitchen, and almost bumps into Fay who's just emerging from the half-bath by the door.

"God, I need a cigarette," Fay says. "I'm out."

"Somebody'll be here soon and give you one," Iris replies. She's certain Ramona will drive up in her battered old half-ton any second now asking, "What can I do to help?" Fay coughs raggedly into her hand. "Where were you?"

"I stepped out to get a breath of air," Iris says, with such firmness she knows the subject won't come up again.

"Are you okay?" Fay asks, studying her now, just as Iris feared.

"I need some coffee." She goes to the counter where the coffeemaker sits, but Fay has already made some. Now Iris feels her full bladder and crosses back again to the half-bath, stepping around Fay who has gone silent to stand with a lost air, looking out the window in the back door. She's still in her dressing gown, a faded pale green terry-cloth robe with long pulls of thread hanging down here and there and the cuffs bleached to white with washing. Her blonde hair hangs messily to her shoulders and her skin is grainy with a yellowish tint, her eyes puffy and red from crying. She looks ill, but then she usually does, especially in the morning.

"Why don't you go bathe," Iris suggests gently. "I want a cup of coffee before I dress, and the kids'll be up soon and neither one of us will see a bathroom again for hours."

"I'll have some coffee first too," Fay says, rousing herself from the window. "God, I wish I had a cigarette." Iris goes into the bathroom and relieves herself. When she has rearranged her robe and comes back out, Fay has poured two mugs of coffee and set them on the table along with sugar and cream in blue pottery containers.

"Lannie gave me those, a long time ago," Iris says, noticing them for the first time in ages. "They look pretty with the yellow walls, don't they? She should be here, you know."

"Nobody knows where she is," Fay replies in her blunt way, meaning, Iris sees, that the family has tried and failed to find her in the days since Barney's death. "Even Howard doesn't know. Ten years is a long time." Iris wants to argue — it hasn't been ten years — but a voice inside her that she usually keeps muffled tells her that Fay is probably right.

"Are the other kids coming?" she asks. Misty and Dillon, Lannie's brother and sister.

"He didn't say, probably doesn't know where they are either." There's a hint of contempt in Fay's voice. "Barry'll be here in an hour or so." There's no rush, the funeral's not till two. Soon Iris will have to bathe and dress, put on makeup, compose herself for the biggest ordeal of her life.

She's no longer worried about it. Instead, she's remembering the morning of her father's funeral, sitting here in silent misery at this same kitchen table with her mother, before the onslaught of family and neighbours began. How still her mother had been, her straight posture more rigid than usual, but her eyes pale and misted over, as if her husband's death had blinded her to the palpable world around her.

Tears drip silently down Fay's roughened cheeks and she wipes them away absently. Iris sits peacefully, her mind wandering to the coulee, the shacks, the barn, to the ancient circles of stone.

"I think I hear a vehicle," Fay says, in her rough smoker's voice, and stifles a cough to listen. Iris listens too, but hears instead the soft fall of bare feet coming up the basement stairs.

She rises and walks rapidly toward the door, anxious to escape without facing whoever it is about to enter from the basement.

"We'll take care of any company till you're ready," Fay calls to her. Iris doesn't answer or look back, just moves on steadily, quickly, down the hall and up the stairs.

Now, staring at the dress she's picked to wear to the funeral as it hangs, freshly sponged and pressed by Ramona, on the closet door, it crosses Iris's mind that her mother might not approve of her not buying a new dress, then remembers that they've agreed not to tell her mother about Barney's death. She's so frail, Iris protested to Mary Ann over the phone, and then to Cousin Eunice, and Aunt Mina, and to her minister, Henry Swan, she's so frail now, I have to be with her when she's told. She takes the black crêpe dress from the door and throws it on the bed, thinking her mother might not be very upset, she never liked Barney much anyway.

Suddenly tiredness sweeps over her in a wave, irresistible, and she crawls onto her bed, clasps her hands together under her chin, brings her knees up tight against her abdomen, and closes her eyes. She's sorry now that she didn't let her mother know. She needs her mother here, with her; without her mother she can't face another second of this horrible day.

Someone is knocking on her door. Startled, embarrassed to be caught like this, she uncurls herself and pulls herself to her feet so rapidly that for a second she's dizzy. She tightens the robe's belt and, turning her back to the door in the pretence of doing something to the dress, calls, "Yes?"

"Are you all right?" The door opens a crack — it's Fay — and Iris says over her shoulder, as cheerfully as she can manage, "I'm fine, I'll be down soon." Silence. The door clicks shut. Now the doorbell is ringing, and through the open window Iris hears the muffled crunch of tires on the gravel driveway around the corner of the house. She goes into the bathroom and turns on the taps to run her bath. The noise of the rushing water blots out all sound from below, the door between her and all of them, between her and the rest of this night-marish day, is closed, locked. Barney's been dead three days, she thinks, and already the world has lost its customary face, begun to reveal parts of itself she has known nothing about, parts that, even though so far benign, scare her.

She lifts a soapy hand to her eyes. It's the first time she has cried, comforted by the release of tears as they slide soundlessly down her face to flow off her chin and cheeks into the bath.

As she's coming out of the bathroom there's a sharp, fast rap on the bedroom door and Ramona enters. She's wearing jeans and a creased white sweatshirt, her eyes are reddened and puffy behind her glasses, her straight brown hair pulled back in its inevitable ponytail.

"Want me to help you get dressed before I go home to get ready?"

"Please," Iris says. She needs Ramona's brusque matter-of-factness, her lack of sentimentality. With Ramona she can just be herself. "Everybody is going to be staring at me," she says, not liking the hint of a whine she hears in her voice. Ramona's all business as she picks up Iris's hairbrush from her vanity.

"We better do something with your hair first. You want to be neat, but not showy, I think. No eyeshadow or blush," she tells her. "Remember, it doesn't matter how you act. This is one time no matter what you do, people will forgive you. Anyway, I've never seen you be anything else but a lady." Iris smiles faintly at this, and gives herself over gratefully to Ramona's ministrations.

Finally, she's ready. Her thick, wavy hair is pulled smoothly back from her pale face and fastened with a black velvet bow, she's wearing the smoothly fitting black dress, her feet are clad in neat black pumps.

Just as Ramona clasps on the strand of pearls Barney had given Iris as a wedding present, Eunice, Iris's cousin on her father's side, bursts into the room, holds out her arms, and says, "I-ris!" in the very tone Iris dreads most: heavy with false sympathy and false affection. Eunice is married to a man who was once an accountant but now does something with stocks and bonds. He's rich, nobody from the family ever sees him. She's still wearing her dark mink coat, she must have just arrived from Regina and come straight upstairs. Iris allows herself to be enfolded in the scented silkiness of the fur, then extracts herself quickly. Before she can speak, Eunice has turned to Ramona. "I'll take over now, Ramona." Her voice is brisk, her tone patronizing. "It was good of you to help." For a second, Iris thinks by the abrupt flush in Ramona's cheeks that Ramona is going to tell Eunice to bugger off, but after an instant's hesitation, Ramona gives Iris a rough, quick hug, then leaves, closing the door a little too hard behind her. Eunice sweeps off her coat, drapes it over the satin chair, and smooths her smart navy dress over her gaunt hips with bony fingers that end in long red nails. She turns to Iris with a glance devoid of sympathy or tenderness or pity.

"A little lipstick would help," she declares.

The rituals of bereavement begin. One by one the female relatives from more distant farms and ranches or the city come up, knocking softly, and are ushered in by Eunice in her queenly manner. They kiss Iris, tears in their eyes, mumble a few words, then, glancing apprehensively at Eunice, exit as quickly as they decently can. Iris replies stiffly the same rote phrases: "Thank you for coming; It was good of you to come; I'm fine; Thank you for coming."

At last Fay pounds up the stairs and knocks sharply on the door. The funeral parlour's limousine is waiting. Iris's stomach goes queasy. Eunice says sharply, "I wish you'd put some earrings on." Iris shakes her head mutely, no, at the pearl and diamond pair Eunice holds out that she has found in Iris's jewellery box. A gift from Barney on their tenth anniversary. "Here!" Eunice says, she'll not take no for an answer, and seeing this, Iris capitulates and puts them on. She takes a quick glance in the full-length mirror and is taken aback at what she sees. It is her face, the fine-grained, pale skin, the prettily bowed lips, the small, straight nose, the black eyebrows and lashes framing the brown eyes that she'd always wished were blue. But all colour has fled from her cheeks and mouth, emotion has drained from her features, leaving behind a heart-shaped, ghostlike mask. And how can she appear so composed and elegant when on the inside she's all tremulous chaos? And the earrings — Eunice was right: they've taken her from grieving penitence into regal sorrow.

Eunice gives a quick brush to the bosom of her own silk dress, her diamond rings flashing, pats her rigidly coiffed, silver-blonde hair, picks up her coat, and leads the way into the deserted hall and down the stairs. Iris follows, her body feeling heavy, weighted down, moving carefully so as not to fall.

Downstairs Eunice opens the closet by the front door and takes out Iris's spring coat. They stand staring at it — bright red, it's out of the question — while a few feet away in the doorway to the living room Fay brushes lint off Barry's shoulders and assembles their family: two young adults, two bickering teenagers, and in the kitchen the phone rings mutedly, insistently, nobody answering it, cars start up in the driveway, and the back door slams: the noises swell, a cacophonous din.

"Your fur coat," Eunice decides.

"No, wait — I — " Iris puts out her arm to support herself against the open closet door.

The house levels, her heart slides back down into her chest, the humming dissolves into the spaces between the too-bright molecules of air. Slowly, she feels something she imagines as a fragile, translucent shell descend around her, seizing her in its softly gleaming tranquillity. The noises in the house dim and retreat. In the carapace's shelter she is light, weightless, and her dread, her terror, like baying dogs that have been quelled, move back to settle watchfully in the distance.

"Mother's good black coat is in the closet in the guest room." Eunice rushes back upstairs, leaving Iris standing alone in the hall, virtually unnoticed, while Fay and Barry and their children file past her out the door. Quinn is last. At twenty-two, he's a smaller version of his uncle Howard, as heavyset but much darker. He shoots a black-eyed glance at her as he passes, some message in it she can't begin to read. He looks Indian, she thinks, and an unresolved suspicion she's held back for years takes firm shape. Is Barry not his father? That would explain — But here is Eunice holding up Iris's mother's coat for Iris to slip into. It's too long, but fits well enough otherwise.

"Perfect," Eunice pronounces. She holds open the front door and stands back while Iris goes slowly out onto the deck. At the bottom of the steps the gleaming black limousine sits, its young driver in his black overcoat waiting by the open door, faint anxiety in his glance up at her. She shivers, and raises a hand to lift the coat's collar up around her chin. Wafting from it is a delicate trace of scent; she recognizes it, lilies of the valley, her mother's cologne. Her mother has come to comfort her after all.

Now she can't stop herself from a quick glimpse around the driveway. Fay, Barry, and their children are in a second black car behind the limousine that waits for Iris, and behind them, all the rest of the aunts, uncles, cousins, nieces, and nephews from both sides of the two families follow in trucks and cars. Ramona and Vance, their five children and their children's spouses and children are back there too, she knows, since she has asked them to sit with the family in the church. Only Lannie is missing.

She will not think at all. She will not cry. She bends and lowers herself carefully into the limousine.

Eunice, Luke, Mary Ann, Howard, and her own family's senior representatives, doddering Uncle Raymond and Aunt Mina who no longer go out except to funerals, arrange themselves circumspectly in the seats around her, Aunt Mina on one side of her and Uncle Raymond on the other. Eunice sits across from Iris, her beringed, clawlike hands with their too-red nails resting on her lap.

Mina takes Iris's bare hand in her small, minutely trembling, white-gloved one and holds it gently. Iris stares straight ahead.

Tears would be appropriate, but since her quiet cry in the bath, no sensation of them remains, and none returns now to her chest or throat or eyes. Through the windshield she catches a glimpse of the river cliffs hovering in the cloudy sky on the far side of the valley, and she remembers her early morning walk, the clean air, the pale, damp grass folded over on itself, the stone circles. No one speaks or moves, the only sound is the whisper of the car's motor, Mary Ann's suppressed sniffles, and the rustle of her tissue. Perhaps Iris should say something? Nothing comes to mind though, and anyway, she doesn't want to talk; her head is full of the rough, blue-shadowed coulee, the scarred white dolomite rocks, the lichen-covered granite stones, the way the coulee serpentines, dropping, out toward the wide, glacier-torn channel that was once a rushing sea.

Loaves and Fishes

"I don't know how you women do it," the minister, Henry Swan, says to Iris. He's a stocky man only a couple of inches taller than she is, and as he peers at her, his face close to hers, the light glints off his thick glasses with their narrow gold frames, so that she can't see his eyes. "Everybody swears nobody coordinates them and yet at these potluck suppers there's always enough food, and in all the years I've been here we've never wound up with twenty-five jellied salads and nothing else."

Something in the neatness with which he delivers this long sentence tells Iris that either he has just rehearsed it as a conversation-opener, or that it's one of his stock lines. She says, "It must have something to do with the law of averages." He throws back his balding head and laughs as if she has made a great joke, and she stands there, wishing he'd stop. It occurs to her then that he's not the person he's supposed to be. All these years she's never noticed before how falsely he behaves, and it seems to her sad that out of his desire to get along with every member of his congregation and to be seen to be a good man, he has so twisted himself that she doubts he knows any more who he is.

She has hit on a truth, she knows it by a certain solidity she feels that surrounds the thought. Such an insight is unlike her, she feels. She has never been a perceptive person, and it so clearly puts a barrier between herself and this man she has known a dozen years and unquestioningly respected, that not for the first time she wonders if Barney's death has done something to her, stripped her of a layer of protection, maybe, that in the past saved her from such unwelcome insights.

"Supper's ready," a woman calls over the voices of the small crowd gathered in the basement of the church and, grateful, Iris turns away from him toward the buffet table that's laden with steaming pots of meatballs and gravy, lasagna, cabbage rolls, rice and noodle casseroles, platters of cold meat, green salads, jellied salads, potato salads, freshly baked buns, pickles, cheeses — there's no end to it, and there's a second table at right angles to it covered with desserts smothered in whipped cream and decorated with dark chocolate or glowing, colourful glazed fruits. A regular cornucopia, she thinks.

As she moves toward the feast, Iris notes the satisfying way the blue carpet perks up the otherwise shabby basement. The church, a large white frame structure, had been built after the Second World War, a time when the community was filled with hope, and it seemed the town would keep on growing, maybe even be a city one day. It has a bell tower, complete with a huge cast-iron bell from a foundry in, of all places, Quebec. Iris listens, as she has since she was a child, for its deep-throated pealing as she enters the town every Sunday morning. Imported from England, behind the altar, there's a large stained-glass window of Jesus and the miracle of the loaves and fishes; a brilliant blue sea roils up behind Him, and white fishing boats gleam in the lower corner. As a child, she'd thought it the most beautiful thing she'd ever seen, but when she'd said so, her father grunted, "You'd think there weren't any wheat fields in the Bible." Now he, along with her grandparents, are buried in the cemetery on the hillside above the town.

It was a short-lived boom; the town's population steadied at eight hundred, then began a slow drop to its present six hundred souls. Now the church is almost too big for its diminished congregation to keep running: the huge fuel bills because of the long, bitter winters, the repeated roof repairs from winds that regularly gust to near-hurricane force, the cost of the expert hired to repair the window when the soldering holding the lead in place crumbled away. These came first, ahead of the refurbishing of the basement. In the end, she and Barney had donated the money to buy the new carpet.

"Did you bring this?" Angela asks, dropping a slice of cold roast beef on her plate, and shepherding her son ahead of her. Iris nods.

She's surprised to see Angela here, she doesn't always make it to church events, but tonight not only are her four kids in tow, but so is Orland who is holding the baby and arranging the other two at a table across the room. Iris tries to imagine Lannie at a table with a husband and children, but it shades off too quickly into the dreams she has been having about her. Silly, pointless dreams, eventless dreams: Lannie playing with her cat, Fuzzy; Lannie in her pale green silk graduation dress they'd gone all the way to Calgary to buy; Lannie in the kitchen learning to bake bread with Iris. In the dreams she and Iris chat cheerfully together as they never did in real life. The dreams disturb Iris and she wishes they'd stop.

"Not everybody can eat those spicy casseroles," Iris explains. "Barney — " she's about to say, "hated them," but Angela is bending over her small son, not hearing her.

"Some of us can't live without them," a voice says in her ear. Its masculine timbre so unexpected and unfamiliar sends an abrupt shiver down her back. She looks to her left and sees a stranger, a rare thing at one of these occasions where mostly it's the same people week after week, year after year. His sleeve brushes her arm as he reaches for the lasagna and the skin of her forearm prickles. She steals a quick look at him: dark eyes, wavy, chestnut, too-long hair — too long for Chinook, anyway — a threadbare black sportscoat over a crisp white T-shirt, faded blue jeans. Not exactly the standard costume around here. Somebody's relative from the city, she supposes, piling lettuce salad onto her plate.

She takes her full plate and follows Angela and her son, planning to sit with them, realizing too late that Angela, Orland, and their children, plus Orland's parents, fill the entire table themselves. Feeling marooned, alone among all these families, she glances quickly around. People are milling about, two tables are already full, people are standing by others waiting to be joined by their spouses and relatives or friends, and dreading that second when, seeing her standing alone, all of them at once will call to her with forced joviality, she plunks herself down on the nearest available chair and pulls it up to its empty table. Immediately it begins to fill with, not couples, she notices, but other single — that is, widowed — women: Isobel

Gallant, Marie Chapuis, Ardath Richards, spinsters being almost non-existent in Chinook. The perception that now she's a member of their unenvied ranks fills her with a dismay that makes her lower her head. Only a month ago people would have been flattered to have her sit at their table.

Henry Swan's voice rises above the confusion of sounds. He wants to say grace, there's much scraping of chairs and then a moment's silence during which he says a quick blessing, ending with, to Iris's ears, a too-hearty "Dig in, everybody!" Everyone sits and immediately voices rise around the room.

"Jay Anselm," that same voice says, and she looks up quickly to see the man from the buffet pulling out the chair on her right, the only one left at the table. His plate is piled high with food, and at the sight of it she has to hide a smile.

"I'm Iris Christie," she says. The others seated around the table give their names and then go back to eating and chatting with their neighbours. He can't mind being the only man at the table, apparently doesn't realize how rare it is.

"Have you just moved to town?" she asks, after a long silence.

"I'm just trying to decide whether to move into town or not," he tells her. Puzzled, Iris says a non-committal "Oh."

"I'm working on a novel," he explains, although she hasn't asked. "It's set in Western Canada, in a small town, and I'm looking for one that *feels* right. You know?" In that last phrase his tone becomes so urgent that, a little startled, she glances involuntarily at him. He's not as young as she'd thought, must be in his mid-to-late thirties. In that quick, surreptitious glance she sees too that if he let his beard grow, it would be very dark, and that his nose is straight, his lips sensuous and full. She wants to ask, What do you mean, a novel? or, Feels right for what? — she has never met a writer before — but, out of her depth, she falls back on formula.

"Have you been in Chinook long?" She can tell by the falling away of all the voices that everyone at the table is listening for his answer.

"Got here a couple of days ago. What is this stuff?" This is so abrupt and loud that everybody stares at him. He grins sheepishly. "Sorry," he says, to the table at large. "It's really good, I've just never tasted anything like it before." The woman on his right says, "That's Shirley Manning's recipe. She brings it to all the suppers. It has Chinese noodles in it, and . . ." She and the other women begin to discuss with what Iris regards as excessive seriousness the ingredients of the casserole and how to make it. Jay leans close to Iris and whispers, "It's awful," and startled — the comment is so like Barney — she chokes back a laugh, remembering that people are watching her, that it's too soon for laughter, that she's talking to a stranger.

After the meal the men sit in groups talking, the children run around screaming until the adults hush them, and the women begin cleaning. As Iris is washing dishes, Jay comes and dries them along with Ardath Richards and Marie Chapuis. Ardath and Marie come and go, putting away the clean dishes and wiping the tables, but Jay stays beside Iris while eagerly looking around the room as if it and everything in it is of special interest to him, halting occasionally to study a dish he's drying, but in a way that tells Iris he really isn't seeing it. Iris is missing Barney; his absence has settled into her bones, a steady, intimate ache that never leaves her. She supposes she'll grow used to it, but still, she can't stop herself from glancing quickly over her shoulder to the big room full of people she has known all her life, as if she might find him there.

"Are you a farmer?" Jay asks her. "Henry said you've just been widowed." She ducks her head, tears have risen at the suddenness of his comment. "I beg your pardon," he says. "I'm not very good at this." She wonders, then realizes he means at making small talk.

"You better get the hang of it soon if you're going to stay here," she says angrily. He's maybe five foot ten to her five foot three, she notices, but very slender. Skinny, would be a better word, she thinks disapprovingly. Relenting a little she explains, "In small-town life . . . " then hesitates.

"Yes?" he says, in the same urgent tone he'd used earlier, giving her his full attention as if she's about to make some world-shattering pronouncement. It makes her face feel hot and she says quickly, "Nothing, it's just that everybody knows everybody else, and a person's sorrow . . ." She hesitates again, wishing she hadn't begun this.

"Yes?" he repeats, leaning closer to her, trying to see her face.

"It's — it belongs to everybody. I mean, we all know each other's lives pretty well, and we try to be — kind to each other. All the time — " She wants to say more, but the hopelessness of explaining to a stranger — a city person — what it is like to live your whole life in a small rural community forces her to a halt.

"I'm sure *you'd* be kind all the time," he says, "but you'll have a hard time convincing me that everybody out there always is." He's gazing out through the wide archway into the big room where people are sitting in groups chatting with each other. She follows his gaze, tries to see what he sees. She can't. She doesn't know what they all look like to him, and she glances up at him, searching for clues in his face. How beautiful he is, she bets all the young women are mad for him — but the glitter in his eyes as he stares out at her friends, her own *people*, disconcerts her. It's too intense, it's almost *avaricious*, she thinks — as if he were a hungry wild animal sighting his prey. She turns back to the sink quickly.

When the dishes are done, Jay pulls a chair up by Henry Swan and the men he's talking with, while Iris goes to sit for a moment with a group of women, but now that the evening is almost over, she can't wait to get away. She thinks she has done pretty well for her first time out, hasn't cried once — well, almost — has managed to find suitable replies to all the commiserations and exited gracefully whenever the conversation showed signs of getting maudlin. She plans to sneak out quietly so she doesn't have to go through the interminable good-byes and stop-in-for-coffees, and when she moves slowly to the cloakroom, nobody appears to notice. She has become invisible.

She picks up the clean platter she brought her roast on and hurries up the stairs. At the top, she turns, goes through a small, carpeted vestibule, and steps into the church itself. It isn't until her high heels clack on the hard vinyl tiles that she realizes she has gone too far, having meant to go straight outside through the door at the top of the stairs. She attributes her error to déjà vu, a moment's involuntary return to her high school days when she sang in the choir and, instead of going outside, made the turn this way into the church every Sunday morning.

She's at the end of the church next to the altar. No light leaks through the tall windows spaced down the walls, but a glow at the opposite end of the church where the main entrance is she knows is from the streetlight on the corner. It has gifted the long, narrow space with bluish light, bringing into relief the rows of dark pews, and the shadowed altar on her left. She pauses, listening. The air is still, all sound from the basement muffled into silence. It is as if she is alone in the world. She peers into the shadows on the altar as if, caught unaware like this, she might catch a flicker of movement of something holy, a feather floating from an angel's bright wing; or hear a celestial voice whispering a syllable of comfort, or of wisdom.

A chill runs down her spine; she makes a subdued exclamation at her own foolishness, turns, hurries the few steps through the vestibule back to the outside door, pushes it open, and rushes out onto the lawn in front of the church.

The tension she has been labouring under and not fully realized flows off her shoulders, neck, and back once she's outside in the welcome darkness. The cool night air is such a pleasure after the vacant hollow of the church proper and the stuffiness of the room below it that she lifts her face to look up at the clusters of stars in the indigo sky, thinking, how long it's been since she noticed the moon. It seems to her a grave dereliction of duty to have forgotten the moon.

Ah, but there it is, just rising, half-hidden behind the small ragged shadows that are the young leaves, the thinnest crescent of silver light that makes the night sky around it all the more darkly mysterious. Suddenly the basement door opens, light rushes across the dark grass, a figure steps out, and the door shuts quickly.

"Amazing, isn't it," Jay says. "You know, I've lived without this nearly all my life?" Her skin prickles. She tries to see him, but he's a black patch in front of the hazy bulk of the weeping birch, the church a looming shadow behind it. "Today I was thinking I'd like to see the land — I mean, walk on it. You know?" Ideas, notions, words are tumbling about inside Iris like clothes in a dryer, and she struggles to sort them. What is it he has said?

"It's not good for a person not to know the night sky," she says, "especially a writer," and is a little surprised at what's come out of her mouth.

"What?" he says, then, "Oh, yeah." A pause. "You're right, probably more than you know." She wonders if this is a slight, meaning she's only a stupid countrywoman, or she's only a woman. "I can see it can change your understanding of life, or deepen it, or something," he goes on. "You're right. I do need to see this." He moves toward her slowly, still looking upward, and some distant light, a coating of silver from a star, is shining on his face, and she forgives him, thinking now that perhaps it wasn't a slight. "I think this craving I have to walk on some land is something I should pursue," he says, with such seriousness that she would laugh, did she not recognize that note in his voice — longing, sorrow, or something deeper even than that, nameless, maybe unresolvable — Before she can stop herself, she says, "I could show you my farm."

"I've seen about five farms already," he answers sharply. "They're not very interesting. I mean — *the land*," emphasizing the last two words, as if she isn't very bright. "But nobody seems to have any," he goes on, rueful now. "I can't figure it out."

"No, no," she says. "There's lots of unbroken land around." An inner voice unexpectedly quibbles with this, but she ignores it.

"Not a park," he warns her. "Parks aren't the real thing." She's irritated again, as if she needs this city dweller who has never even seen the night sky to tell her about land. And yet, she's curious about him, she suspects him of having fastened himself to her, as if he has decided she's the one who can give him what he needs. In the stillness and the pure night air she can feel emotion wafting from him, how he's worn out with wanting. It makes her gentle with him.

"Tell you what," she says, and at her new tone, his feet make whispering noises as he moves closer to her across the lawn. "We — I have some unbroken land and my neighbours have more. I'll take you walking there if you like."

"I'd like that very much." There it is, that rich, masculine sound again.

"I have to go, it's late," she says, and begins to walk quickly away.

"Good night," he calls to her. She glances over her shoulder, but he's blended into the shadows; she can't make him out.

Driving home, she wonders if she has lost her mind, with her community and church work, the visitors and the housecleaning and baking that goes with them, with the decisions about the farm she still has to make, and what she's half afraid might turn out to be in him only simple neediness, the everyday kind that ends by sucking up the life of others, then moves elsewhere to do it all over again.

When she goes to bed though, her solitariness is so all-encompassing it's almost more than she can endure. That amorphous, steady ache that is Barney's absence has coalesced into a ball in her chest and she lies with one hand pressed flat between her breasts, as if to keep the pain from spreading.

She falls asleep and dreams she's making love to someone, she doesn't know who. But his mouth is open on hers and he's deep inside her, ecstasy is rippling up her body in waves that grow stronger and stronger. He begins to pull away, she's lifting her head, open-mouthed, to get closer to him. But the more she strains to reach him, the more he retreats from her until she wakes alone in her empty bedroom, sweating, gasping, and appalled.

Asleep once more, she dreams she's in water, swimming. It's night, she's all alone out in the open ocean. The water is black and cold, chunks of ice float past her now and then, and waves roil up and slap at her, and although she's afraid when the water threatens to wash over her, by kicking hard and flailing her arms she manages to stay afloat. The waves build up higher and collapse, foaming, over her head or inches from her face, but when she rises with a swell she catches a glimpse of a thin line of lights along a shore in the far distance. There's a city there, she sees, she's trying to swim toward it through waves that threaten to drag her down into their freezing, black and bottomless depths.

She's talking to Ramona on the kitchen phone when she hears somebody knocking on the front door. Ramona has taken to calling her every morning as soon as she has Vance out the door to his fieldwork and Ryan and Cody, the only two left at home, off to school. It's just for a quick chat to see how Iris is doing: Did she sleep? Should she drop over right away, or is Iris okay this morning? What are her plans for the day? Iris is faintly chagrined at how much that early morning call has come to mean to her. Today Ramona has invited her for supper — what a spate of invitations she has been getting, they're almost more than she can cope with — and now they're trying to find an evening when they're both free. She tells Ramona she'll call her later.

As soon as she enters the hall she can see a man's head through the small window in the upper part of the door. She sighs inwardly, her eyelids feel gritty with lack of sleep; she'd hoped to find a few minutes for a nap, although her dreams are so relentless these days she's become apprehensive about closing her eyes.

Years earlier Barney had torn off the wide, old-fashioned veranda that had originally fronted her parents' big frame house and replaced it with a more stylish plank deck that runs continuously across the front of the house and down the side to just past the kitchen door. The man standing there is small and middle-aged, his greying hair slicked back neatly, his light tweed jacket worn-looking, his grey trousers in need of a press. She notes his briefcase and thinks at once, salesman, not a Jehovah's Witness or a Mormon.

"Mrs. Christie? I'm Jim Schiff. I'm with Harris and Block Holdings." He offers her his card which, after a second's hesitation, she takes. "I'd like to talk with you about your farm."

"It isn't for sale," she says, but her voice is dubious, not because it is for sale, but because only yesterday the Hutterites had sent a contingent of men to her. There were two of them, one young man, one old, both dressed in their home-made heavy black cotton suits, their plaid shirts buttoned securely to their tieless throats. She'd invited them in and they'd taken off their straw hats and held them against their chests, staring around them at her elegant living room, then seating themselves gingerly on the grey velvet sofa.

"Listen," the old man had said. "Us Hutterite seed for you, if you need. Move on three, four air seeder, be done in couple day. If you want — " Then he'd lifted a finger to silence her in case she was about to reply before he was finished. "But, we want to buy your land."

Joe Morris, her lawyer, had said, "I must especially caution you, Iris, not to make a deal or even sound like you're making a deal with anyone before you consult Luke or me. You cannot believe how many sharks there are out there, just waiting to get rich on a widow's misfortune." He'd smiled at her and she'd smiled back, not really believing him. "I mean it, Iris," he'd said, frowning at her, as if she were a recalcitrant child. The two of them had gone through high school in the same class, then off to university together such a long time ago, only he'd stayed, years later coming home to practise law, while she'd come home at the beginning of her second year and married Barney. "You always want to think the best of people. But listen, some of them search the papers for estate sales, hoping to catch you when you're weak. And then when you do sell, it'll be the same thing over again, only this time it'll be financial managers, investment people, bankers, after your money." He'd shaken his head, giving her the impression he was sparing her stories he knew that would curl her hair — widows and children thrown out on the street without a crust of bread — but what Iris was thinking was that he was taking it for granted that eventually she'd sell. But not to the Hutterites. She'd thanked them politely, vaguely, served them tea, and they'd gone away.

The man standing on her deck — Jim Schiff, he has said his name is — is shifting his briefcase to his other hand.

"I think you'll want to know about our plan," he says, and she recognizes his remark as his first ploy. Suddenly, beginning to see his visit as the inevitable, she capitulates, "Come in," and steps aside to let him through the door.

In the living room she sits in the grey velvet wingback chair and offers him the sofa where the two Hutterite men had perched so gingerly. He sits quickly, relaxing for a second, as if it's a relief to have a soft chair under him. He sets his briefcase on her polished teak coffee table and snaps it opens. A stack of colourful, shiny brochures spill sideways and he takes one out and closes the case with a small thud. Now she notices what might be broken veins in his cheeks and she suspects him of being a drinker.

"You have a plan for my place?" she says, pleased at having said "my place" instead of "ours" first try. She remembers her father's advice that in making deals you never show your weakness.

"I see nobody's out there working your land," he says. "I — forgive me — but I made inquiries in town and was told you're newly widowed. I'm sorry to hear it."

"Thank you," she says, and clears her throat softly, letting her eyelids rest shut for an instant.

"I imagine what to do with your land is rapidly becoming a problem for you."

"The Hutterites offered to come and seed for me in a week or so when it's dry enough." She offers this casually to see what his response is.

"I imagine they offered to buy too," he laughs, as if he finds Hutterites amusing.

"Your plan?" she reminds him, barely keeping the annoyance out of her voice. She turns her head away to look out the big front window where she sees the rail of the wide deck, and beyond it the roof of his white car glinting in the sun. Behind it the leaves of the young poplars shine like silver coins, and above it all is the sky, a cloudless, rich blue. Sleepless or not, she would like to be outside, walking.

"I must first ask you not to discuss any details about our conversation. We find it considerably easier to do business if its nature stays among the people directly involved. Innuendo and rumour just confuse matters."

"I see," she says vaguely, thinking, surely not telling people what's going on is what causes rumours.

"We're in the process of assembling a parcel of land." His voice is easy now, casually confident. He picks up the single brochure he has taken from his briefcase and hands it to her. She glances at it, seeing a checkerboard of photos of couples standing with a third person, presumably a real estate agent, in front of a Cape Cod farmhouse, a row of attractive condominiums, a California-style split level. She sets it on the side table beside her chair. "It involves most of your neighbours. If you don't know that now, I expect you soon will." She's startled by this, now wholly attentive.

"How big a parcel?"

"Oh, roughly, a hundred sections," he says, watching her face. She does a rapid mental calculation: a section is a mile by a mile — that's ten miles by ten miles.

"That's a lot of land." She'd give anything for Barney to be here; she can't think how he'd react. Once he would have tried to figure out how to outwit this company, as her father would have done, but lately — He'd throw him out? He'd sell?

"You have a good part of it," he says. "I believe you own or control — "

"Own," she says stiffly.

" — something like eight thousand five hundred acres?" Schiff snorts. "Forgive me, I'm from Iowa, actually, but even now the size of some of the farms up here astonish me."

"It isn't all arable," she demurs.

"Nearly all. I'd say just about all."

Iris realizes then that this isn't just a feeler on his company's part. Maybe even, during the last couple of weeks when she's been staggering around in her widow's daze, somebody's been out driving around on her land. It shakes her a little.

He takes a folded map out of his briefcase and spreads it on the table. Iris is shocked. It's her rural municipality with a large area shaded in a variety of pale colours and the resulting coloured block, a huge rectangle that encompasses most of the township, outlined in black felt pen. Her farm is pink, she sees. Next to it Vance and Ramona's place is yellow. The farms Schiff's company wants to acquire extend from the far side of Iris's all the way to the edge of Chinook on two sides of the town. There must be twenty or more families involved.

"Why do you want so much land?" she asks suspiciously.

"I work for a big company. We want to get into grain marketing and it isn't worth our while to farm anything smaller." She takes another quick look at the map, wondering if they actually own any of this or if it's merely speculation. She would ask, but thinks he wouldn't tell her anyway, it would be tipping his hand.

"That will take a lot of money," she says instead, dubiously.

"Yes," he answers her, nodding and tapping the coloured block with his finger. "But, we have it."

"American? You must know we have foreign-ownership laws here in Saskatchewan. Foreigners can't own more than ten acres, I think it is."

"There's no law about foreign money backing a resident owner. Anyway, I'm not the buyer." He looks up and smiles at her. "We're offering, say, fifteen times the assessment." She no longer has any idea what her land is assessed at for taxation purposes, which for years has been less than its market value, although times are so uncertain this could always change. "That's better than fair," he says, as if she's objected. "Now, wait" — lifting his hand, palm toward her, like a traffic cop — "you haven't heard the whole proposal. We'll buy it lock, stock, and barrel. You just take the money and walk away." Her face is suddenly hot, her pulse has begun to thud in her throat. "We're talking about two million dollars, depending on what you have for machinery. If your machinery's new, probably more," he points out. "That's only a fraction of the total investment in this project. My employers — "

"Where's this money coming from, if it isn't yours?"

"I'm not at liberty to say."

"I don't understand," she says. "Markets are so — the competition's so stiff and it's getting tougher every year and you want to go into growing grain in a big way? It sounds crazy."

"You have to see the big picture," he explains, leaning toward her. His pale eyes have grown dark with some vision he sees that he's determined to impart to her. "Do you realize how many bushels of grain you can grow in an average year on sixty-four thousand acres? One point six million bushels. We own oil-seed crushing plants, we've got flour mills, we make pasta for a flourishing — I mean *burgeoning* — near and far East market. Our people are at this moment drawing up the plans for a doughnut franchise with who knows how many outlets around North America." He lifts his head, not looking at her now, and goes on. "We'll almost certainly build a feedlot to use the by-products. We'll make ethanol. The ethanol by-products feed cattle too . . . " He's still talking, but she has stopped listening. A feedlot means a slaughterhouse and a packing plant and that means jobs.

"Our little river would never provide enough water for all that," she points out.

"There are ways to enhance what's here," he says, calm again. "And solar power and wind power will work here."

"If they will, why haven't they already been established?"

"Capital," he says simply, and she's silenced because she's pretty sure he's right. She asks again, "And this capital? It's what — Hong Kong money, I bet." He doesn't answer her. Suddenly it's all too much for her, everything changing so drastically and so fast, she can't get a grip on it. Did Barney have some inkling of how things were going when he bought his ranch? Is that why he did it? She feels abruptly that she might burst into tears. And she's tired, God, she's tired. If only Barney were here — but he's not, she reminds herself wearily.

"No," she says. "No, no, no." She means, no, stop bothering me, go away. She sees the rising waters of her dream, and makes a pushing motion with her hand, as if to shove it away.

"Don't be too hasty, Mrs. Christie. We're not in a rush. I'd like to talk to you again in a few days, after you've had a chance to reconsider — " But she's standing, conscious that her face must be flushed it feels so warm, that her knees may give way.

"Please go," she says. Sell this place? What would her father say? What would Barney say? She looks around the living room of the house where she has spent most of her life and she's suddenly wondering if maybe this stranger is crazy? No, no, she's the one who's crazy without Barney. He's standing now.

"I'm sorry if I've distressed you," he says, looking genuinely penitent. "I'll drop out again in a few days," he adds as he goes into the hall. "I'll let myself out." And he's gone, the front door clicking shut quietly behind him, before she can move or speak.

For a long moment she stands motionless in the centre of the room, one hand resting against her throat. Then she hears a car door slam. This mobilizes her and she goes to the big window and sees him drive away in his plain white Buick.

*

She's still staring out the window when a small red car comes slowly up the driveway. It stops where the Buick did, and Iris is thinking, go away, when the driver's door opens and Henry Swan gets out. Sylvia, his wife, is sitting in the passenger seat. They've paid her a couple of duty calls already, Iris doesn't think she can face another one. But now Henry is pulling his seat forward and waiting while somebody climbs out of the back seat to stand on the gravel as Henry gets back in. It's Jay Anselm.

She steps back from the window hurriedly, pushing her hair back from her face, then fluffing it with her fingers as the front doorbell rings. When she opens the door, he seems bigger than he did a couple of days earlier. She thinks again that his hair is too long and notices he has changed his black jacket for a warmer-looking brown leather windbreaker.

"Remember me?" he asks. "Is this a good time?" Behind him Sylvia rolls down her window and calls, "Sorry we can't stop. Henry has calls to make."

"That's okay," Iris calls back. "I'll see you at church." Jay is examining the long, wide deck that's painted a dark brown, the big front window, craning his neck to look up at the second floor as if he's a workman come to estimate a job. She can hear the gravel crunching under the car's tires as the Swans drive away.

"Of course it's a good time," she says.

"It was such a great day," he remarks, following her down the hall to the kitchen, "that I just couldn't stand to stay in town. Anyway, I'm not sure what I'm looking for is there." Uncertainly he adds, "I suppose I should have phoned." They're in the kitchen now and Iris stops and faces him.

"No need," she says brightly, not wanting him to know how peculiar she's suddenly feeling. "I'm pleased to see you. Coffee?" She sees his eyes which she remembers as black are really a rich brown, and today she detects a puffiness under them that she wonders about. Maybe he can't sleep either; maybe he too has dreams that make him thrash in bed and lie awake.

"I'd like to go for that walk you promised me." Promised? she thinks, and is for a second irritated. "I mean, if it's okay . . ." His voice trails off and he looks down at his feet. She sees he's wearing stiff new tan cowboy boots.

"Those boots won't be easy to walk in," she says, and hears a girlish note in her voice. He grins and she feels her heart speed up, gives a quick, embarrassed laugh and goes to pull on the jacket she keeps at the back door. He's there instantly, opening the door onto the deck.

The unfettered light and the feel and scent of the spring air take her breath away. How could she have stayed inside and missed this brilliance, this exquisitely scented air? Impulsively she puts her hand on Jay's arm.

"I'm glad you came," she says, but what she's really saying is, I'm glad it's spring. I'm glad I'm out of the house. Maybe life is possible after all. He doesn't say anything, doesn't even smile, and she drops her hand quickly, embarrassed again, and leads the way down the steps and across the lawn, through the hedge, and out onto the prairie grass. They don't speak as they walk, and Iris, glancing at him, sees that his expression is clouded, it's that look of unease again. Catching her studying him, he smiles.

"You okay?" he asks. She nods. They walk on in silence and by the way he's holding his head she knows he's listening to the birdsong, trying to find the birds singing in the long grass or on the wing. She thinks briefly of Jim Schiff and his money and feels a quick rush of excitement in the pit of her stomach, then realizes: it wouldn't bring Barney back. And I'd have to give up this place. But I may have to give it up anyway, and her joy deserts her.

The grass lies ahead of them, a smooth, creamy yellow patch beside the neat rows of stubble that stretch off to the left and far beyond. The old barn and the sheds are like three old men, all warped and twisted, leaning patiently into the weather, their window-glass long since gone, shingles split and torn and blown to the four winds. She likes their greyness, their emptiness, their air of history; they speak of things she has always known. In their presence even her bad dreams pale.

"Here we are," she says, and draws a deep breath because it has always seemed to her — perhaps her mother said so? — that the air over native grass is fresher, more highly scented than elsewhere. Jay has stopped and is staring down at the stone circles.

"What are these?"

"Stone circles left by the Indians a long time ago, to hold down their tepees in the wind, they say."

"And these?" He's pointing one after the other, to four half-buried piles of lichen-coated rocks embedded at opposing points in one of the circles. "There's a pile in each direction."

"The Plains Indians prayed to the four directions, I've heard, and so I suppose . . ." She trails off, shrugging.

"They're ceremonial then," he says.

"There used to be a whole lot more circles, my mother said. Grandpa ploughed them up and used the stones to make a dam west of here." She points. "My dad tore the dam out and levelled that hollow. Got a little more land that way." Her parents had quarrelled, not raising their voices, but the air so cold around them, and her mother furious in that rigid, disdainful way of hers that Iris came to know as she grew up, her father red-faced with exasperation, stomping out, her mother saying to her brusquely when she noticed Iris standing in the doorway, *You go and play.* The abrupt recollection shocks her; she doesn't know where it's been hiding all these years. She goes on quickly, "Of course, that drove away the birds. Swans, pelicans, ducks, geese."

"And over here, what's this?" He's walking toward the lip of the coulee where there's another pile of rocks.

"Grandpa could have piled them," she says, not sure.

"They look pretty old to me," he says, and she has to agree.

"So it's Indian, for some other kind of ceremony." She doesn't say anything, suddenly irritated at his trying to teach her about her own land. "Look!" he says suddenly. "It's not a pile, it's a circle. But it's way too small for a tepee." He squats, puts his hands on the rock, touching the vivid lichen grown over their surface with his palms. Patches are cream, russet, black, gold, green. But he's looking out over the coulee to the high beige cliffs across the valley with their dashes of white brilliant against the blue of the sky.

"Those things are everywhere," she says, not trying to hide her annoyance. "If the land's not ploughed up, it's got Indian circles and Lord knows what all on it." She starts down the sloping side of the coulee, ignoring him. In a minute she can hear his boots slipping on the crumbling clay side, and little stones and small lumps of yellow soil roll down to where she's descending more carefully.

"Don't you care," he calls down to her, "that all that history got lost when people turned up the land?" She has reached the coulee bottom now and is standing beside the slough. She looks up at him where he's squatting a few feet down the hillside, squinting against the light, and speaking over her head, as if he's quizzing all those old farmers who are dead and gone, and not her.

"I made sure the ones that are left didn't get ploughed up, didn't I?" Yet, forced to think about it, she's not sure why she has been so adamant about the stone circles. A wind comes lapping down on her from nowhere; it brushes her face, rushes around her, tugging at her jacket, whipping her hair, then leaves her as suddenly as it has arrived. "We drove them off their own land. They deserve at least a memorial," she says, but this last is said wonderingly, softly, as if she's only speaking to herself.

He comes down the hillside fast, sideways, his boots making the dirt spurt out behind him, then follows her as she turns and climbs through the barbed-wire fence onto the Normans' side of the coulee. But when he's through the fence he stops her by putting his hands on her upper arms. It's a light touch, but it shocks her.

"I love this place," he says clearly. "It's the most beautiful place I've ever seen in my life." He says it with such intensity, direct to her face; her mouth and throat have gone tremulous from his touch.

She stamps her feet in last year's faded grass to get the clay off her shoes, and he smiles, staring down at his dirty new boots, making no attempt to clean them, then looks around at the pale hillsides, the hawk circling above them. "I've been working on this novel — it must be six years now. It fills a suitcase, I've done so many drafts. Nobody will publish it. Everybody says it's good, that I'm incredibly talented, that —" He's growing visibly angrier. "They just want me to change this, or change that, or drop out this character or that one, or write a new one, or — " Now he stops and breathes loudly through his nose. "But *I* think" — he looks down at her — "I think that maybe what they all dislike, or feel as an *absence* of something, is really caused by a kind of inauthenticity in it, that God knows I've felt myself — You know what I mean?" She shakes her head, no, slowly, meeting his gaze which is once again so intense she's taken aback.

"I've got the characters and the story and the ideas and the narrative drive, but I don't have . . ."

"Stop," she cries out, laughing. "I don't know what you're talking about."

"I'm talking about *writing*," he says, leaning close to her so that she sees the thickness of his eyelashes and the whiteness of his teeth. "I'm talking about authenticity, about being who you are — about *knowing* who you are," he corrects himself, looking away, "and writing out of that." She wonders whether she knows who she is? And answers, Of course I do: Barney's wife. But that thought confuses her, stops her from going any further. Besides, she doesn't think that's quite what he means.

He has gone on ahead, runs a few steps, stops, then stands gazing out across the wide expanse of sky and land, as if he can't get enough of it. She catches up to him and they stand together looking up the sloping coulee walls here at the narrow end, and down to the first bend where the coulee widens and levels out for a long stretch before it continues its descent. A meadowlark calls its liquid, melodic line and it fills her with happiness.

"What has all that got to do with your coming here to live?" she asks him.

"I didn't say I was coming *here* to live." His voice is sharp.

"Excuse me," she says. "Why are you considering moving to a small town?"

"It's cheaper to live," he says, looking away now. "It's — " he shrugs. "It's maybe a better place to . . . find yourself. Solitude, and all that."

"Oh, you mean like Christ's forty days and forty nights in the desert, or wherever it was." She's teasing him.

"And my main character is a small-town boy," he goes on as if she hasn't spoken. "The first third of the novel is set in a little town a long way from the city, and I guess maybe I don't know enough about small-town life. I thought I did, but I realize I don't. So I've come here to start over again. A year or so, that ought to do it."

"How will you — I mean — "

"How will I live? I got a grant. It's not very much, but I told the Council I was going to write some non-fiction pieces on country life and they bought it."

"You mean — " she hesitates, puzzled, and he glances at her, then looks away.

"I'm an artist! They already gave me three grants to finish my novel and I haven't been able to in that time. Who the hell are they to tell me how long it's going to take? Art is art! You can't fake it! You can't write to somebody's timetable — " He stops abruptly, turns away, but not before she sees the way his mouth has twisted, and his unexpected vulnerability fills her with surprise.

The sharply sloped clay wall they've come down is behind them and the cow path they've been walking on has given way to a long grassy slope that rises gently in two levels to the flatland above. He turns back to the rise and runs up the slope to the first level. By the time she reaches it, he has gone on and is back at the top at a narrow point that widens farther on to the west, but on the Normans' side of the fence where it's all grass. She climbs up slowly and finds him sitting in sparse dead grass on the rock-strewn coulee edge. As she sits down beside him, he stretches out and leans on one elbow, his head on his fist, facing her.

"So you want to get to know us," she says.

"I want more than that," he tells her, but he has shifted his gaze over her to the sky.

"Which is what?"

"I thought that country people were basically the same as city people, that they were motivated by the same drives. Well, in the end I suppose they are. But the other night I saw that it's all nuanced differently, that the life I thought was so simple is really surprisingly complex and — " He pulls himself into a sitting position beside her, staring out over the coulee and the river cliffs and the sky.

"Of course we're not the same," she says. Again he ignores her remark, which is probably just as well since she isn't sure she could defend it. There's a long pause. "With their high-tech equipment and their market-talk — their belief in the individual and in business, as if it were the new God." He turns to her, looks into her eyes. "I couldn't believe it. Here they've lived on the land all their lives! They've known nature in a way I'll never know it, I couldn't see a trace of — " He turns away abruptly.

"A knowledge of nature is the bedrock of all our lives out here. Just because we don't talk about it all the time . . ." Her voice trails off. He sighs, then stretches out full length again.

Sitting with her legs curled up under her makes them ache and she stretches them out, then turns on her side, and, supporting herself on her elbow, her head propped on her palm, lies face to face with him. It crosses her mind that this is a bit like being in bed together, but a stubborn part of her denies that there's anything wrong or unseemly about it. Anyway, there's no one here to see it. They lie like that for a couple of minutes, not speaking, studying each other in an intimate way.

"You're tired," he says.

"I have trouble sleeping now," she says. But she doesn't want to think about her dreams, and in the brief instant she closes her eyes she sees Lannie in her yellow dress, the sun striking fire in her red-gold hair, waving goodbye for the last time as she drives away. Lannie would be — thirty — now, she can hardly believe it. She feels his breath on her face; it makes her forget what she was thinking about. "How old are you?" Her voice comes out husky and soft, surprising her.

"Thirty-six."

"I'm almost twenty years older."

The prairie sky soars at their backs and elbows. At their feet is only the emptiness of the wide valley that extends outward to the pale cliffsides with their darker blue shadows in the draws that are stands of firs. A light breeze lifts locks of her hair and then riffles his, leaving a strand on his forehead. She wants to reach out and brush it back into place.

"How did you wind up here?" he asks her.

"I've always lived here. Except for a year at university in Saskatoon."

"Only a year?"

"I only went to please my mother."

"What did you want to do yourself? Get a job?"

"I've never had a job." She's a bit rueful.

"No kidding? How did you manage that?"

"I didn't need money," she points out, caught between embarrassment at having to say it and reasonableness.

"There are other reasons to get a job," he says, laughing a little, as if he finds her innocence charming.

"That's what my mother said," Iris answers, aware she sounds petulant. "But she never had one either."

"Didn't you have an ambition? A dream, I mean?"

No, Iris thinks, ambition was for people who hadn't enough, or who weren't satisfied with what they had. "I did lots of volunteer work, taught Sunday school, and church camp in the summer . . ."

He's continuing to study her closely as she speaks, as if he sees something in her that interests and pleases him. How long has it been since a man really looked at her? "I was in love with Barney and I wanted to be his wife. That was what I wanted." After a long minute he lifts his head from his fist and moves his face closer to hers. She sees his intention in his eyes, can't quite believe it, so doesn't flinch or move away; he comes a little closer, puts his lips on hers.

It's a gentle kiss, with closed lips, but she feels it all the way down in her vagina, that first, most exquisite flush of sexual arousal, and as he draws slightly away, she opens her lips so she can catch some air. He comes closer again, his second kiss is just as gentle as the first, but she tastes the warm moisture of his mouth and, realizing abruptly how hungry she is for a man's touch, reaches out her hand to rest her palm against his cheek, then slides it back farther to cup the hard base of his head, his thick hair tangling in her fingers. He rests one hand on the curve of her hip below her waist. She's about to pull herself harder against him, when suddenly he rolls over to lie on his back and stare up into the sky.

Her body protests, making her breath come quickly. She sees him put one hand over his eyes, and then take it away. His gesture, its meaning unclear but surely boding no good, makes her lower her elbow, and lie motionless, her head resting on her outstretched arm. What has she done? What's the matter with her?

"I'm sorry. I don't mean to take advantage of a widow," he says, as if he's angry. "I've been celibate for quite a while. I've been trying . . ." But his voice trails away. So have I, she's thinking. She almost tells him then about the last few months of their marriage, of her ardour, and Barney's attempts to respond to her but his failure — or was it her failure that she no longer aroused her husband, after all those years? But she can't bear to have him know that her own husband stopped desiring her.

"Why?"

"I just thought it was something I needed to try for — for my writing — " She feels such tenderness at his admission. How could he think such a thing would help anything? She reminds herself she's twenty years — no, sixteen years older than he is. He's not looking at her, seems to have forgotten she's there, and suddenly she finds herself desperate to have back the intimacy they were feeling.

"What's it like kissing somebody old enough to be your mom?"

He casts her a mischievous glance. "Delicious," he says, which makes her laugh, although it hurts her, too. "I'm leaving in a few days to go back to Toronto. Get my stuff together." He moves abruptly, as if he's just relinquished something, pulls himself close to her again; this time when he takes her in his arms he presses the length of his body against hers. Such a surge of electricity goes through her, confusion and desire, comfort at his maleness, an instant's longing for Barney, and more deeply, that other unnameable yearning.

He kisses her face, her eyes, her cheeks, her mouth, and in his passionate gentleness she's reminded of James. When he moves his head to nuzzle his face in the hollow between her shoulder and her jaw and presses hard there with his open mouth and begins to tug her blouse up out of her slacks, she suddenly sees she's a hair's breadth away from unzipping her slacks and pulling them off, and then she feels deeply embarrassed, as if she's gone backwards into teenagerhood, or fallen into some space of utter confusion where she doesn't know which man is making love to her: Barney? James? This stranger? She's breathless and trembling, but she manages to pull away from him. Neither of them speaks, and she feels she doesn't have to say, he knows what she's thinking: I've only been a widow a few weeks, you're too young for me, and, my God, I'm not ready yet for this.

"Sorry," he says again. "I don't think I'm ready for this." She can't tell if he's joking or not, wasn't she the one to pull away this time? "Let's go back." He jumps up and stands over her.

"I thought you wanted to go walking," putting her hand over her eyes so she won't have to look into his face.

"I've seen enough for now," he says. Slowly, still trembling, she gets to her feet and brushes off her slacks. He lifts a blade of grass from her hair, and she has to stop herself from catching his hand and pressing it to her mouth. They walk silently back toward her farmland, holding the barbed-wire fence apart for each other to climb through, then walking on in silence, past the falling-down barn and sheds, past the stone circles which have retreated out of sight in the grass, back down the machinery trail on the edge of the field of stubble.

"I'm staying with Henry and Sylvia," he says, when they're almost back at the house. "Henry's family knew my dad's family, years ago in Toronto," he explains, although she hasn't asked. "Call me there if you feel like it."

"You can call me," she says, suspecting he thinks he shouldn't phone her. Besides, she comes from a time when women did not phone men, and she can't quite imagine doing it.

At the house he stops at the bottom of the stairs, his forehead creased, his eyes that liquid dark brown, full of some deep sadness or longing. She wants to hold him, to comfort him. After a moment she says, making her voice bright, "I'll make some lunch," and goes quickly up the steps onto the deck. He follows her, then stops and leans against the railing.

"No, thanks. The Swans are going to pick me up on their way back and it's probably going to be any minute."

She wants to ask him what his kisses mean, she wants him to say something promising or final, she wants him to kiss her again, hard, she wants — but instead they stand side by side, barely speaking, Iris so intent on picking up every nuance of emotion or intent on his part that she's barely breathing, and he, sunk so deep in thought, she doubts he remembers she's there. In a few moments the small red car comes putt-putting up the driveway.

"Here they are," he says. She wants to speak to him, tries in the minute or two before the car arrives at the house, to think of something meaningful and strong, something that will bring him back to her. But she can't think of anything that doesn't sound needy or schoolgirlish, so in the end, again, she says nothing. He smiles at her briefly, without intimacy, then goes down the steps to the waiting car. As Henry pilots it away down her access road Iris stands watching. It turns onto the grid that leads to town, and as she watches it grow smaller and smaller, she feels relief and disappointment, embarrassment and excitement in roughly equal quantities, until the car disappears from view.

Good Land

Iris, still in her pink satin dressing gown, stands with her back to the front window and surveys the living room where last night the two dozen members of the Women's League met. She muses on their new gentleness with her, and the sympathy for her she'd seen in their faces whenever they looked at her, yet as the evening passed, certain nuances, it seems to her, crept into the subtext of the conversations: assumptions that she would or wouldn't do certain things any more now that she doesn't have a husband, a certain subtle drop in her status, although she can't quite put her finger on specifics, now that she's a widow. She sees why all the widows she knows holiday together, play cards together, drive to the city together. It isn't so much because of the widowhood they have in common, as she'd thought, but because of their having been pushed aside by the society of which they'd always been a part. I used to do that to them too, she thinks now, and is saddened as much by this new perception as she is by her realization that Barney's death has caused her to lose rank.

The chairs have to be rearranged, the sofa cushions need fluffing, the bric-a-brac on the tables has to be moved back into place, the rug vacuumed to restore it to its air of never having been walked on. A half-hour's work, if that. The women had washed the cups and saucers and dessert plates before they left; there isn't even washing up to do.

She wonders what she did with her days before Barney died? They always seemed so busy, and now, no matter what she has to do, they seem empty, and everything she does increasingly pointless. She hopes this is just a stage in widowhood that will pass eventually. She remembers now that she had that frightening dream again last night, and for an instant the memory freezes her to the spot. Always the same dark water threatening her, trying to drag her under. She supposes the dream has to do with losing Barney, although she can't see what the connection is. But she's beginning to feel it's trying to tell her something, she has no idea what, and she doesn't know who might be able to help her understand.

"Iris."

His voice startles her into an involuntary jerk and she snaps her head up to see Luke standing in the dining room, having entered so quietly through the kitchen that she didn't hear him at all. He's not standing straight, his back seems bent, as if he has hurt it, and in the shadows — the dining room with only one small window high in the wall is the darkest room in the house — she can't quite make out his face, but his voice — it's the quavering voice of an old man. She stares at him, her uncertainty growing.

He comes forward slowly, as if each step is painful, past the heavy old mahogany table covered with papers she has been trying to deal with, past the sideboard making the silver-framed family pictures jingle, into the living room where he stops at the sofa that acts as a divider between the two rooms in front of him.

"Come in," she says, trying to sound welcoming. "Please, sit down." He hesitates, then comes around the sofa as she comes forward, stopping with the coffee table between them. In the better light flowing through the big window behind her Luke looks every second of his seventy-five years — no, he looks ninety. And his skin has that papery look of the very old, his face grey, as if he's ill. "Are you all right?" she asks.

He doesn't answer. Iris suddenly remembers she's dressed in her housecoat and under it is only her sheer nightie. She reaches up and pulls the lapels of the dressing gown closed across her chest, holds them there with both hands.

"I had three sons," Luke says. It's as if his chest hurts and he has to squeeze the words out around the pain. She pulls the lapels tighter, clenches them in her fists. "Three sons," he says, and puts a hand out to support himself on the back of one of the grey velvet wingback

chairs. "Howard no better than he should be. I know that. Wesley —
had a good heart, Wesley, even if there wasn't nothing upstairs. But the
two of 'em — " He breathes heavily for a minute. "They shamed me."

Iris's blood has begun to pound in her ears, and over it there's a
rushing sound, it's the noise her breath is making as it speeds up and
grows thinner. Luke goes on, relentless. "Barney. He was — the one.
He was . . . my boy." He opens his mouth, he's struggling with
himself, Iris can see his struggle. "It was you."

At this, she cries out, "Luke!" A plea to him to stop before it's too
late, to not say what she knows he's going to say, what she has always
known he has wanted to say.

"You took my boy from me. You brought him here — You turned
him into — your pet — " He casts one hand out in a violent gesture
that would annihilate the luxurious living room, the entire house,
Iris herself.

"Luke!" Now she's angry. "He loved me! *He* wanted me!" Her
words hurt her throat. She thinks, *He doesn't like women.* She lets go
of the lapels, moves closer to him. "You drove him away yourself
with your meanness."

He staggers back as if she has struck him, drops his eyes to the carpet,
half turns away, and she wishes she could take back what she has just
said, although for nearly thirty long years she has wanted to say it. Luke
and Barney always quarrelled, they were always attacking each other,
she'd stood between them lots of time, or Mary Ann did, before it came
to blows. He has no right to blame her. But he isn't finished yet.

"Not even any grandkids. At least Howard had a family." It's as if
she hasn't said what she has said. "Where are my grandkids?" Then,
his face crumbling, "I got nothing left."

She's stunned by his accusation, there'd never been a word
between them about grandchildren — unless he'd said something to
Barney about it and Barney hadn't told her. Faltering, she draws on
her mother's haughtiness, although even to her own ears she sounds
dismayingly childish.

"That was between Barney and me. It is none of your business."
But suddenly she thinks, Is this what this emptiness is, no matter
how hard I work, or how busy I keep myself? Is it that I haven't our

children to comfort me, now that Barney's gone? Without willing it, she moves to a chair and collapses into it.

"You think about what I said," he warns her. He lifts one hand slowly to point at her, his small blue eyes gleaming like lasers, pinning her to her chair. "Because you've got through life so far without a mark on you. But I'm telling you, Barney's gone for good. And that little-girl face of yours don't work no more. You better just do some thinking." He drops his arm, turns away. As he makes his way out of the living room and through the dining room, she can hear the heels of his boots smacking across the kitchen vinyl. The back door bangs shut. In a moment his truck starts up and rumbles away down the road, and still she sits on in the chair where he has felled her, as brutally as if he'd struck her with his fist.

"Hi, there, Iris," Ramona calls as she gets out of their battered half-ton that's pulled to a halt on Iris's driveway. She bends to retrieve a cake in a square, flat pan from the seat. Vance climbs slowly out of the driver's seat and the sight of his worn, faded Levi's, dusty riding boots, plaid, western-cut shirt, and dented, oil-stained stetson makes her heart miss a beat — Barney had returned to dressing this way after he'd gone to live on his ranch. And although Ramona's been over often since Iris's disaster, Iris hasn't seen much of Vance, and when she did he was uncharacteristically subdued, pale behind his windburn, and dressed up in his suit, not looking like himself at all. They climb the steps to her, and Ramona, stooping to kiss Iris on the cheek, goes on cheerfully, "With all the stoppers, I thought you might be running out of stuff."

Vance bends to brush Iris's forehead with his lips too, then follows her, as Iris follows Ramona around the corner and into the kitchen. Ramona wears a loose, man's shirt over her jeans to hide the stomach she has developed since the births of her children; she carries twenty extra pounds on her big-boned, strong frame. In high school she played basketball, volleyball, soccer, and now she handles horses as well as Vance. A tiny part of Iris, although she has no desire at all to have Ramona's ranch life, envies her physical strength, the way she handles her body, a sort of ease in it, an acceptance of it that Iris knows she lacks herself and which she doesn't quite understand, thinks maybe it's the result of Ramona's always doing outdoor work like the men.

"What's all that?" Ramona asks, peering into the dining room where the table has disappeared under stacks of paper.

"Mail. I haven't touched it since the funeral, and it was just piling up — "

"Big job," Vance says.

"I started by separating the magazines and newspapers from the letters," Iris tells them, meaning to make light of the heap. "Then I separated the bills from the cards and letters about Barney. Then I separated the bills I can figure out what to do about — phone, power, fuel, crop spray, fertilizer — from the ones I can't."

Vance says, "That'd be all of mine. I can't figure out what to do with any of 'em." The bills for the funeral are there too, and brochures from companies wanting to sell her a tombstone for Barney's grave.

Ramona says in a firm voice, "What are the ones you can't figure out?" Iris sees she means to help.

"Oh, Wheat Board documents, forms that have to be filled out from Sask. Agriculture and Agriculture Canada — that sort of thing."

"You better go see your lawyer about them," Vance says. "Or Luke could help you."

Iris shrugs without replying — there'll be no help from Luke and that last, vicious remark of his repeats itself in her head: *that little-girl face of yours.* She hurries to the coffee machine while they're arranging themselves in chairs, one at each end of the table, the cake in the centre.

"That cake looks good yourself," she says briskly over her shoulder. "A lot better than the leftovers I had for you."

"You're looking pretty good yourself," Ramona says bluntly, studying her. Iris looks down at herself: neat beige cotton slacks, flowered blouse in bright pinks and greens whose cheeriness belies how she really feels. "Did you sleep last night?" Iris shrugs, she's thinking about

Luke, who only a few hours ago had descended on her like an Old Testament prophet, scaring her to death. She says only, "It's worse at night."

"Don't you worry, it'll all work out. Just time," Vance says, his voice hearty and a shade too loud.

"I sure wish I could help." Ramona's voice catches, and there's a silence during which Iris is reminded that Vance and Ramona have lost an old, close friend, and she says, her voice also breaking, "I know you miss him." Blinking, Vance looks away. Ramona swallows, then says, "Isn't this weather great? Spring at long last."

"Got any calves yet?" Iris asks, busying herself with the coffee ritual, taking mugs from the cupboard, spoons from the drawer, the cream pitcher from the fridge.

"Lots of 'em," Vance says. "Cute little buggers."

"You should come over and see 'em," Ramona says, and there's that all-too-familiar hint of hurt in her voice, which Iris hears with something between irritation and resignation. She wants to be the friend she used to be long ago, it's only that — but she can't change the facts that have spoiled their friendship: that she's richer than Ramona, that Ramona has five children and now grandchildren too, and she has none.

Without answering, she carries the mugs, spoons, cream, and sugar to the table and sits down between them with her back to the counter where the coffee machine has begun to burble softly. They've left the inside kitchen door open and Iris is aware of the scented spring air flowing in through the screen in the outer door. In the trees red-winged blackbirds call to each other. Ramona and Vance lean toward her, listening with such attention that she's disconcerted. She starts again. "I'll tell you the truth," she says, although she isn't sure she knows what it is, nor does she know why, after all these years, this moment seems the right one to start revealing things — it's just that they've been so good to her over these last few weeks. "You know I've always had a busy life — "

"We know, we know." They nod vigorously. Iris hesitates, drops this tack, hasn't she just told them she'll tell the truth? If she can just find the words — "I always felt funny at your place." It comes out

flat, insulting, and she feels Ramona stiffen. She hurries on. "I felt —
It's the kids," she says, finally, and stops, her face growing warm.

"It's true the place was always noisy, and kind of messy." Ramona's
tone is careful, slightly injured, as Iris was afraid it would be. Now
she's staring at Vance who, in his turn, is gazing at the tabletop with
an expression Iris can't read.

"I mean," she manages to say, sounding lame even to herself,
"because I don't have any." She knows Ramona will interpret this as
meaning she regrets having none of her own, which isn't exactly what
she intends at all, but she doesn't know how to say so without
making matters worse, since she's pretty sure it would never occur to
them, as it hasn't to Luke, that there's any purpose in life for a
woman beyond having children. Ramona leans forward, exhaling
gently, fastening her green-flecked hazel eyes on Iris's face.

"Oh, I see!" she says, and Iris knows that Ramona believes Iris just
finds it painful to be reminded of her childlessness. It occurs to her
that they take it for granted she and Barney are childless because one
of them, she bets they think it's her, is infertile. Did this never occur
to Luke? Or did — did Barney tell Luke that she refused to have children? Surely not!

When in her thirties and early forties she had been stricken by a
sudden flurry of misgivings — that maybe she'd enjoy a baby like all
her friends seem to, that children are a moral necessity in a marriage,
that she has no right to deprive her own parents of grandchildren —
she'd stopped taking her birth control pills only to find nothing
happened. She doesn't know why, but she felt sure that if she'd really
wanted a baby, she'd have gotten pregnant. Then Barney had stopped
talking about it, as if he'd finally agreed with her that they didn't need
children. Why suddenly, now, when he's gone, and long after it had
stopped coming up between the two of them, has the question
arisen? She drops her head and smoothes her forehead with her
fingertips.

"What're you gonna do about seeding, Iris?" Vance inquires
quickly. "I wonder if you shouldn't try canola this year. Lots of moisture for it. Good price these days, too, and wheat prices are the pits.
Hardly pays you to seed." For twenty years now, every spring and

fall, Vance has let his own work go to help Barney seed and then harvest. There's nobody left who knows the Thomas-Christie land as well as Vance does. "Got any contracts yet?"

For a second, Iris can't think what he means, then she remembers. Farmers used to work on a quota system; you had so much cropland, you were entitled to market so many bushels of crop every year. Now they sign contracts to market a certain amount of crop, never mind their land base.

"Barney would only sign contracts after the crop was in the bin," she says, realizing as she speaks that he has only been searching for a way to talk about the farm, that he and Ramona have come visiting at least partly to give her a nudge about this year's crop. Ramona intervenes softly, "Vance, maybe we shouldn't worry her about the farm right now." Colour rises up from under the collar of Vance's shirt to flush his tanned face.

"What else do we talk about every spring?" Iris asks. "Anyway, I need advice. I guess," she adds morosely.

"What does Luke say?" Vance asks. Luke? *He says I'm an evil woman*, she thinks indignantly, *I, who've always tried to be a decent person.* When she doesn't answer, Vance asks, "Got your land rented yet?" not looking at her. She shakes her head no, then realizes that if she'd been thinking of them instead of always herself, she'd have realized that the money Vance earns working for Barney is important to their income. They probably need to know if it'll be there this spring or not.

"I know I should have talked to you," she says lamely. "I'm really sorry. I have to figure out what to do."

"Have people been bothering you?" Ramona asks. Glancing quickly at her Iris knows that the question of their own income has barely occurred to them. Their goodness shames her.

"I have had some offers to buy."

"I wouldn't sell yet," Vance says slowly.

Iris knows he isn't interested in buying. Vance is from an old ranching family. When everybody around, like Iris's father, was breaking all his land because for a while there, if you were lucky and had enough land, you could get pretty rich farming, Vance and a few others like him didn't say much, but they resisted the trend, and now Vance's small place is an island of native grass in a sea of farmland. Which is why he's perpetually broke — his ranch isn't big enough to start with, and instead of overstocking to pay the bills as so many of them do, he stubbornly understocks to save his grass. He has the best stand of native grass for miles in any direction, but he has had to work for Barney to make ends meet, and looks ten years older than he is from the year-round outdoor work. And Ramona too, Iris thinks. "It's too soon to take such a drastic step," he says. "Might be the wrong move right now."

"But those people — " Ramona begins. Vance snorts.

"There's some kind of deal going on around here. Somebody's making offers on land. Somebody with money. Don't know who it is or what they want this desert for."

"They made us an offer," Ramona says. Vance interrupts.

"I ain't selling to somebody I don't even know who he is and he won't tell me! My grandfather homesteaded that place, broke his back. Died broke, too. I'm not selling it to anybody as long as I'm young enough and I got sons coming up. Besides, you heard 'em. They want to farm it. Break up all that grass, as if there wasn't enough farmland around here already. As if we didn't need grass."

"They came here too," Iris said. "Yesterday. Offered me a lot of money for the place." Vance and Ramona freeze. "I asked him to leave," Iris says finally, knowing this is something of a lie because she has made it sound as if she has refused to sell, when all she has done is put off the decision.

"They show you that map?" Ramona asks. Iris nods. Vance says, "I know the Richards are ready to retire and none of their kids wants the place. They'll sell in a minute. So will the Kandinskys."

"But we won't," Ramona says. "And I'm sure the Livingstones won't. They're doing fine and he's only in his early forties. Why would he sell?"

"Alfred Sigurd says he doesn't like the smell of the deal," Vance adds. "He figures maybe it's crooked. Where's all that money coming from? Nobody knows."

"Maybe it's drug money," Ramona says. "That's what some people are saying," she says defensively, when Iris turns to her quickly. "I don't see why not, either. Where else does millions and millions like that come from these days?"

"To invest all that here," Iris says, disbelieving. "Wouldn't our grandpas die laughing?"

"If they weren't already dead," Ramona says. They grin at each other.

Vance says, "No, I'd rent for a while."

"She'll have to find somebody she can trust," Ramona says sternly. "Men always try to take advantage of a woman on her own." Vance stares at her. "You know that's true!" Iris remembers the coffee and jumps up, brings the pot back to the table and fills their mugs.

"You'd better rent it soon," he says to Ramona instead of Iris. Iris knows he has to be careful not to be seen giving another man's wife advice. Even if the husband is dead. "Barney's got himself a bad weed problem. If you don't look after it right away, you won't have no crop at all. If there's anything you can do about it," he adds somberly.

Every year there's been a lot of talk between Barney and Vance about the weeds and how to handle them. And when Barney hired a crop sprayer, he had to be very careful to make sure that either there wasn't a breath of wind, or if there was, that it was blowing away from the Normans' land. It's the one thing that over the years Iris has seen Vance really angry about — Barney's insecticide or herbicide drifting onto his grassland. It makes her head ache to think this is her problem now.

"Iris?" Ramona says gently. "Iris? You okay?" She puts her hand over Iris's where it sits limp on the table beside her untouched coffee mug. Iris sees how Ramona's good sense, the way Iris could talk to her when she couldn't always talk to her mother, has been a mainstay in her life. And she has just taken it for granted. Nobody speaks while she struggles and at last succeeds in pushing back her tears.

"I need help," she admits finally, turning first to Ramona and then to Vance. "I've never had to run this place and I'm not sure I can. And I don't understand this new machinery with its gauges and dials and lights and computers. It wasn't anything like that when I used to summerfallow for Dad. And I don't want to sell, not yet, anyway."

Vance squirms uncomfortably, crossing and uncrossing his legs and stirring his coffee vigorously. An idea is dawning in Iris's head, and it feels so right — she tests it rapidly and finds it holds up. She says slowly to Vance, "I know you don't want to farm. But I trust you. And you know our land as well as Barney does — did. Will you look after it for me for a year or so? Rent it, I mean?"

There's a moment's startled silence during which Iris recalls how Barney had offered to buy Vance out more than once and he always refused. She remembers too what seemed on the surface to be good-natured sparring at the kitchen table over ranching versus farming that Iris knew, everybody present knew, underneath was otherwise. No, Vance is going to refuse.

"I don't have the equipment," Vance says. "I don't have the money for the seed or the fuel. You can't just pick up and start farming a place this big just like that. It takes cash and it takes machinery — " He turns to Ramona. "We gonna eat that cake, or what?" Ramona casts him a wry glance, gets up, goes to the cupboards, finds and brings back three forks and three dessert plates. Iris hardly notices, she's rushing through Vance's arguments to see if she can counter them.

"You can use Barney's equipment. I'll buy the seed and the fuel. We'll work on shares — sixty–forty — that's right, isn't it? I can ask the government agrologist, he'll know what the rate is. If it's a good year, you can pay me back. If it isn't, I'll carry it — or write it off or something. Or if you'd rather, I'll co-sign a loan at the Credit Union or the bank for you for fuel and seed. Anyway, you won't be stuck, I swear."

She has never made a deal before, she didn't know she knew how, but hasn't she been a farmer's daughter and then a farmer's wife all her life? She almost slaps the flat of her hand on the table to indicate the finality of the terms, but holds back at the last second. "Luke's already arranged for Irvine Castle to take over Barney's ranch for me until fall. So I have at least six months to make a decision about it." Ramona and Vance glance at each other.

"I saw Daisy in Swift Current," Iris says, reassuring them. "So I know she's at home to help Irvine and Dennis. The three of them can handle it."

"Oh," Ramona says. "That would be why they could take it on." There's a note in her voice Iris can't place, but when she looks at her, Ramona is busy cleaning her glasses with her shirttail.

"It takes a lot of money to farm this place," Vance says. "I wonder if you know how much." Iris's heart has begun to pound as she understands this means he's considering her proposal.

"I've seen the accounts," she replies. Their operation has been too big for Iris to handle the books, an accountant does that, but Barney would tell her about the cost of this and that, more or less thinking out loud. And she was as interested as he was in the bushels per acre they were getting, and the price of spring wheat, durum, barley — whatever they were growing. "You know I've got the cash. I won't charge interest, either," she says quickly. "You're neighbours, helping me out when I'm in trouble. I could hardly charge you to do it!"

Ramona straightens suddenly. Iris sneaks a glance at her to find she and Vance are staring at each other. If some communication is going on between them, she doesn't want to disturb it, but Ramona's face is flushed and her eyes are bright. Sharp eyes, intelligent eyes. It occurs to Iris that she's always thought of Ramona as not very bright, or at least, not as bright as she is. I suppose it was because I had more money, she thinks, and is shocked to think such a thing true of herself.

"Cody wants to go to university," Ramona says. She and Vance had three daughters, then stopped. But Vance's longing for sons had caused them to start again after seven years. Cody is the second child, in Grade Twelve right now. "He's got good marks, he's the smartest one of my kids, but where'd we get the money? And student loans — "

Iris puts her hand over Ramona's as it toys jerkily with the unused spoon by her cup. Ramona says, "And we got Crystal's wedding to pay for . . ." Vance is still thinking.

"That's some deal," he says finally. "Luke'll probably think I'm robbing you blind."

"It's none of his business." They both look quickly at her. "If there's any crop at all, you should make some money. Barney always said this place runs on volume, otherwise we'd be broke, too." She wishes she hadn't said that last thing, but Ramona is staring at Vance again as if she didn't hear her.

"Iris," Vance hesitates, "you know I always helped Barney because . . . I needed the cash. You know I don't like farming." He swallows audibly.

"I know it," she says, pleading now. "I know it, Vance. I don't mean to turn you into a farmer — "

"You don't have to do it forever," Ramona puts in. "Just for a year." There's a tension behind the calm tone and Iris recognizes that Ramona is desperate for Vance to do it. Iris is suddenly aware that Vance's principles have made life difficult for his family and she sees that Ramona has a hard layer of buried anger at him, though she has never said a word of complaint to Iris about him. Her own blindness to the nuances of her friends' marriage embarrasses her. And Ramona's integrity in keeping silent about it shames her a little, since she'd never hesitated to complain to Ramona about Barney whenever she felt like it. But that, she thinks, was because there was never serious trouble between the two of them — until he bought his ranch, and she couldn't bring herself to talk to Ramona about it, not wanting to hear perhaps that she was wrong.

"The land's already broke," Ramona persists. "It's not like you're going to have to break land or anything. If you don't farm it, somebody else will."

"What if we have a crop failure?" he asks her angrily. "Don't you see what could happen? I'd be in debt to Iris, I'd have to keep farming until I paid it off. We could be starting a drought cycle! It could be ten years before we get the rains again."

"I'd never make you stay!" Iris interrupts. "I'll take the responsibility for what happens, financial or otherwise. I'll sign an agreement. You'll never be stuck. I wouldn't do that to you. Honest." Staring at Ramona, his jaw set, Vance is holding his spoon in both hands as if he might snap it in two.

"There's good moisture to start a crop right now," Ramona says, but her voice is subdued. She and Iris's eyes meet in a quick glance — from Iris, inquiry, from Ramona, a warning: Wait, don't push too hard. A sudden breeze sweeps through the kitchen from the open door and Iris feels a chill.

"I think you'd be surprised what a profit we can make on this place in a good year," she says softly. "Even when prices aren't very good, Barney and I have done pretty well."

"Never mind what it does to the land."

"Vance!" Ramona says, sharp now. He colours.

"I know you don't approve," Iris says. "I know you think we're just mining the land here — "

"Won't last another twenty years," he states. Iris knows he'll have to have his say before he can give in. She's careful to show no sign that she can feel him weakening.

Ramona says, pressing harder, "For the kids' sake." He glances at her, then tosses the spoon down and it skitters across the table until it stops with a clink against her cup. Iris jumps, but Ramona just stares back at him, her lips tightening. Whatever is going on here between the two of them, Iris would just as soon not be witness to. Should she make an excuse to leave them alone for a minute? What would Barney do? Before she can move, Vance speaks again.

"Farmers like Barney ruined this country," he says to her. She can feel colour rising into her face, knows Ramona is holding her breath. Never mind. He has to do this. "They drove away the wildlife and they poisoned the land with their chemicals. Never could get enough. Just kept breaking more land and breaking more land till there's hardly no grass left. Old farmsteads, the road allowances that don't even belong to them. You're asking me to join 'em, Iris — " He looks away, as if he suspects he's going too far, or maybe he remembers that Iris is a widow now, with nobody to protect her.

"I worked every year on this place, for twenty years now," he says, his voice softening. "And I didn't like what I saw Barney doing, but I helped him anyway because I had kids to look after." He's silent for a moment and neither Iris nor Ramona move or speak. "I'm no farmer. Everybody knows that. But, I guess . . ." His voice trails off, but the two women say nothing, waiting. "I guess I wouldn't be much of a friend to Barney, or to you, if I didn't say I'd do it." Ramona exhales slowly. Iris starts to thank him, but he interrupts her. "But one year, that's all. I got my own place to look after. At least Ryan and Cody can take up the slack while I'm farming."

"You know I will too," Ramona says unsteadily. For a second they lock eyes again. "When you were sick with pneumonia two winters ago I kept the place running." Then, unexpectedly, while Ramona looks as if she's about to cry, Vance smiles.

"Okay, it's a deal," he says.

"I'll get a lawyer to draw up a contract tomorrow."

"I'll trust you with a handshake, Iris. Barney and me never had anything else."

"Lawyers just cost money," Ramona says. "You've been my friend since I was a kid. I'd trust you with my life." Even though it feels strange to be doing it, Iris stands, moves to Ramona and hugs her briefly around the shoulders, pressing her cheek to the top of her head. What she feels for Ramona now is nothing less than love, and gratitude overwhelming her, she takes an instant, her face turned away from Vance, to get control. Then she reaches across the corner of the table and offers him her hand, seeing in her mind's eye Barney shaking hands with machinery salesmen, or investment dealers, or men he'd hired to drive grain trucks during harvest.

"It's a deal," she says. She and Vance shake hands solemnly.

"Are we finally gonna get to eat that cake?" he asks, grinning, and they laugh with relief and excitement. Then Iris hurries to the counter for a sharp knife, comes back, peels back the plastic wrap, and cuts the cake. She serves them each a big piece, and while they're eating it, Ramona asks Iris if she's heard anything at all from Lannie.

"Everybody thought sure she'd be back for Barney's funeral."

"But nobody knows where she is to tell her," Iris says, surprised, thinking this is common knowledge around the community. People had stopped asking years ago. "I haven't heard from her — " she hesitates, about to modify the truth, then tries to think what the truth is. "It's been years, I don't know how long. At least five, maybe . . . even longer. Neither's anybody else, not even Luke and Mary Ann. And it's ten since she left."

"Why? That's what I want to know. Why doesn't she write

anybody a letter — I mean, not even her grandma? Or she could phone, at least. It's so — ungrateful. You know it is, Iris."

"But don't you see?" Iris says quickly. "That's it, you know. We hurt her — all of us, from Howard just walking away from her — her own father! To the kids at school who knew all about her: her mother dead, her no-good father abandoning her. And then, when she took the pills, there isn't a person in town who doesn't know that, too. She — " Iris is about to say, I bet they even know about her abortion, but doesn't because she has never told Ramona about it either, had managed not to for Lannie's sake. She swallows. "She's so . . . proud, and so . . . she feels so much. I think she just can't bear to even think about this place. I wanted to give her time . . . But now . . ." She thinks of the wrinkled handful of notes in Lannie's book bag. Did the fact that Lannie kept them mean she wanted some kind of help? Or was it only that she meant to destroy them but forgot? How could she forget them?

"The poor kid." There's another long silence, during which they can all hear the clock, caught in a band of sunlight on the wall above the table, ticking precisely, steadily on. A hawk cries from his airy kingdom above the farm. The sound falls down the sky, sails over the lilacs and caraganas and poplars, across the driveway and into the kitchen: that high-pitched screech, a hunting cry. Ramona stirs, looks at her watch.

"Oh, Jesus, there's a heifer ready to calve in the barn. Hurry up, Vance."

But Vance wants to talk to Iris about seeding so it's agreed that Ramona will take their truck and check the heifers, and Iris will drive Vance home once they've finished their business. As the old pick-up rattles off to town, spewing oil fog into the fresh spring air, Vance and Iris get into Barney's shiny half-ton and start out to make the rounds of the farm.

This is a ritual she's used to, having done it every spring for years with Barney, sitting beside him as the half-ton bounced over gopher and badger holes on grassy road allowances or down rutted machinery tracks between two fields, while he talked the whole time about prices, the futures markets, what fields he'd seed to durum, what to spring wheat, checking on the winter wheat and the fall rye if they'd seeded any, whether it was wet enough to try some canola or to seed into stubblefields instead of letting them lie fallow for a year as you had to do in such dry country, always seeding only half your land at a time, while the other half lies gathering moisture and rebuilding its nutrients.

Now, here she is performing this ritual with Vance Norman, and she's the one driving the pick-up. The world has turned itself on its head overnight. She turns to Vance, is surprised to see he's frowning, the window rolled down and his elbow sticking out into the air gone subtle with new warmth. She sees how worn his boots are, and his jeans are loose on him, not stretched tight over his thighs the way she remembers them being the last time she looked. He's working too hard, she thinks, just trying to stay afloat; no wonder he agreed to this deal.

"Weeds and more weeds," he says. Iris knows the wild oats at least have been getting worse each year. It didn't seem to matter how much money Barney spent on herbicides. "I hear he's got some Downy Brome," Vance says. "I heard on coffee row at least three people in the municipality have it on their land. It come up from the States in cut hay, or maybe it was contaminated seed grain. The usual." Her father always used to say the West got its weed problem from the bags of seeds settlers brought from Europe.

"I think maybe there is some," Iris says slowly. "The extension agrologist was out with a scientist from the research station. I forgot all about that." She drives Vance over to the field in question so he can have a look at it, although so early in the season there isn't much to see. "It's basically good land," she says comfortably to Vance. His silence makes her falter and she turns to him. "Isn't it?"

"Nope," he says, a dogged note in his voice. "Should all be seeded back to grass, just left alone for about a hundred years. Might get back some fertility by then." Without noticing, she has lifted her foot off the gas and they go slower and slower. "See those white patches?" He points toward low hillocks in the summerfallow field beside them. It's that time in spring when the low spots are still too wet for machinery to go on, but the hilltops are dry. The crown of each is bleached almost white. "Salts are rising all over the place. Nothin'll grow where it looks like that. You know that, Iris." The truck has come to a halt in a dip and Iris shifts into neutral.

He opens the truck door, gets out, strides into the field where at one of the dry places he bends down, clenches his fist around a handful of soil, then brings it to her. "Look at the colour of this stuff," he says. She leans over to the passenger side to see. "It looks like ashes. It ain't even soil any more. It's got no fibre, it won't even stick together." He spreads his fingers and the dirt slides easily between them to drift, pale and powdery, onto the land. "Got no nutrients left. Where the soil's got no nutrients left it can't grow wheat with good protein. Hell, Iris, don't tell me you don't know that."

Iris stares dubiously at the soil as it drifts away from Vance's hand. She can't deny it's a long way from the rich black soil she has seen in fields around Saskatoon or even north of here. Still, all Iris's life this has been the refrain: this dry country, this desert country. If it was too dry for farming, why did everybody farm it? How had her father become rich on wheat sales if this was really a desert?

"For land that's no good, it's grown a lot of wheat," she says.

"We're talking about fertility, Iris, not drought. Only reason Barney still grows something on it is because he pours the fertilizer to it. How the hell long can you keep that up? That chemical fertilizer just knocks the organic stuff out of the soil, just kills it." He wipes his hand on his pants and looks away across the fields north to where the blue river cliffs are hovering in a mirage high above the horizon. Seeing them, she remembers that only yesterday she lay on the grass at the edge of the coulee and kissed Jay Anselm and fitted her body to his.

Vance gets into the truck beside her, slamming the door shut. She says, "But why does that company want it if it's no good?"

"They'll pour the chemicals on; they'll wring every last ounce of good out of it till there's nothing left but ashes, till this place looks like the moon. Then they'll walk away, richer than — " He stops, his mouth working. "It takes five hundred years to grow one inch of topsoil, Iris. In the meantime, what do the rest of us do to live?" She hesitates, bewildered, then gravitates back to her immediate concern.

"Can't you farm it?"

"Jesus, Iris," he says. "I didn't know it was this bad. I never really noticed it when I was helping Barney harvest. You just do your job, try not to think." He takes off his hat and wipes his forehead with his forearm leaving a streak of dirt across the whiteness where his constantly worn wide-brimmed hat shelters it from the sun. Iris feels as if she has been punched in the stomach. Does this mean she'll have to sell after all? "You'll have to back me for chemical fertilizer, too," he mumbles, looking away from her, "otherwise, won't nothin' grow." Relief floods over her.

"Oh, of course," she says. "Didn't I say that? I meant to. And crop spray. Actually Barney's already bought this year's supply when it was on sale. It's in the quonset."

They sit in silence while a handful of horned larks skim the grass ahead of them with their dainty, bouncy flight. It occurs to her that this is the first wildlife they've seen since they began their farmland tour more than an hour earlier. She and Jay didn't see any either, and she wonders where all the wildlife is this spring.

"I'll farm it for you, Iris, like I said. At least for a year till you figure out what you want to do. But I'm telling you, this land's nearly dead. A few more years is all it's got left if you keep up this kind of farming."

Iris is horrified, but then doubt creeps in; Vance isn't a farmer after all, what does he know? And even though he and Barney rarely argued, they tended to skirt subjects, to say nothing when a conversation might be the expected thing, Vance keeping his land in grass the way he did and raising cows, and Barney seeding from fencepost to fence-post. So she doesn't know what Barney would have said to counter Vance's arguments. She wonders suddenly if maybe Barney couldn't counter them, if maybe he just thought his money was defence enough. She hates herself for the thought, with him dead now.

She puts the truck back into gear and they're moving up a rise. At the top, she brakes. The field beside the track they're travelling on is in summerfallow. A breeze has come up, and as they sit in silence looking out over the more than three hundred unseeded, bare acres, a burst of wind rushes across its mottled grey-and-brown expanse, picking up dirt and weeds and small rocks as it goes. For an instant the horizon is blotted from view by the pale soil as it lifts on the air and corkscrews into the distance, rising as it goes.

This is her best soil blowing away, this is gold, this is the future speeding off to fall into ditches, onto roads, onto the streets of the town where it'll do nobody any good. And not a single windbreak to be seen, since Barney pulled out the few rows of straggly caraganas her grandfather had planted. This is absolutely it, she's had it; if she could drive with her eyes shut, she'd close them so she doesn't have to see and thus to think about her farm. She sees Barney, the look on his face when he studied the land, his eyes narrowed, speculative; she did not think she saw love there.

"I want you to get Luke's okay on this deal," Vance says quietly.

"Luke!" she says contemptuously before she can stop herself.

"Did you two have some words? I don't mean to pry, but I know Luke isn't the easiest — "

Iris says softly, turning her head to look out the side window away from him, "Did you know he hates me?"

"Hate? No, he don't hate you. It's just — you know — families." He gives a small, uncomfortable laugh. Vance turns to her and studies her, looking deep, behind her skin. Then he tightens his jaw and turns his face from her so cleanly and firmly it reminds her of Luke, and she knows she could torture Vance with red-hot pokers and he'd never say another word.

They're still bumping slowly down the track, have almost reached the point where the trail turns and goes south. What she'd really like is never to have to see Luke again. No, what she'd really like is to sleep soundly at night, to stop having those dreams.

"I'm thinking of going away for a while," Iris says, then stops, surprised. But as she listens to the echo of her own words she realizes this has been forming in the back of her mind since the day she buried Barney. Now it's said, it seems inevitable. "Once you and I are all set up, I mean," she adds quickly.

"That's probably a good idea," he says finally. "I'll look after your place for you. Ramona and me. You can count on it." He leans back against the seat, relaxing for the first time and Iris realizes he's relieved that she won't be around to oversee him, maybe start giving him orders. "You should maybe try to track down Lannie. Unless you got some other plans."

She starts to respond to this, just more meaningless discussion of the same old subject, but something strange is going on inside her; she can feel that hard ball of resistance dissolving, that she knows now is made of vigilant avoidance of a deeply uncomfortable subject. And then the darkness and the immense, unfathomable depth of the water in her recurrent dream rise up and she knows that all that she doesn't understand about her relationship with Lannie, and her marriage to Barney is in that deep, black water. She says in a puzzled, uneasy way into the gulf between them, "Maybe it's time I did that."

She reaches out and turns the key of the already running truck, so that the ignition makes that grinding noise that proclaims to the world an idiot is driving.

"I'll drive," Vance says in a tone that brooks no argument, and Iris feels the warm, rough weight of his tanned and calloused hand as it closes over hers and pulls it gently back from the key.

It is that unexpected contact with human flesh, or maybe it's that it's male flesh again, but the feel of his hand makes her quiver like jelly. It's her own molecules spinning out of their places and she knows if it weren't for Vance's hand holding hers she might simply disintegrate into whirling fragments, the pieces scattering the length and breadth of creation, like the soil that's lifting off her field out there and swirling away into the sky.

Snakeskin

She'd called Joe Morris, her lawyer, told him she'll be away for a while and he'd said that there was no business to be done that couldn't wait a couple of weeks, "And anyway, you'll keep in touch with the Christies about where you are, won't you?"

"Oh, yes," she'd said, nodding briskly, even though he couldn't see her, even though she hadn't any idea where she'd end up. She phones her mother-in-law. "I've decided to go away for a while," she tells her. "To tell the truth" — how often she has been saying that phrase lately, as if up till Barney's death she'd done nothing but tell lies — "I've decided to see if I can find Lannie. I want to tell her about . . ." she hesitates. Mary Ann lets her breath out in a rush.

"You do that, Iris, that's just the thing. You go to Howard. I'll give you directions to that place where he works. If anybody knows how to find her, he should. At least have some clues or something." Her pain at her son's indifference fills her voice. "If you go see him in person, he can't put you off. I'd of gone myself, but my arthritis . . ."

"I know, Mary Ann. But it isn't up to you, it's up to me. I should have gone years ago." She tells her that Vance will take care of the farm for her. "I shouldn't be gone more than a couple of weeks." When she hangs up, relief at having avoided Luke, at least for now, floods through her. But there's still one task left: she has to tell her mother.

She'd already gone once to tell her about his death, but when, after taking a deep breath to steady herself, she'd pushed open the heavy glass door into the lobby of the nursing home, she'd been told by the nurse on duty, a stout, grey-haired woman, that her mother had had a "spell" that morning.

"Why didn't someone call me?" Iris asked, visions of another funeral rushing past her, so that she had to put her hands down on the desk to support herself until the fear diminished.

"We tried," the nurse answered, fixing her with a hostile stare. "It would help if you had an answering machine."

She wanted to explain about Barney, about the chaos her life had become, but nothing came out except a breathless "How bad is she?" And in the instant before the nurse answered, she saw before her the church where James's funeral was held. A wooden structure more than seventy-five years old, the oldest church in the district, standing alone now, in the middle of wheat fields. Simple and small with a short, plain spire and three arched windows down each side. She saw the patient air it had acquired, a kind of weary knowingness, as James had, as if nothing could surprise it any more, or hurt it, or change it. His was the last funeral held there, nobody uses it any more. All of the past vanishing, as if it didn't matter.

"She's fine," the nurse told her briskly, and Iris thought of the stone circles on the prairie, still there after hundreds of years. The thought soothed her and her heart slowed to its normal pace. "Goodness knows what upset her. But she was restless and it isn't good for them to be restless when their hearts aren't too steady. Doctor Wiebe gave her a little something to quiet her."

Although Iris sat at her mother's side for two hours, the "little something" kept her mother asleep the entire time, and dreading her task, Iris couldn't bring herself even to try to wake her. In the end she'd left without telling her about Barney.

Today, tentatively pushing open the door to her mother's room, she stops in surprise. The curtains are open, the room flooded with afternoon sun, and on the windowsill the geraniums Iris started herself from seeds and brought when they were only a couple of inches tall are starting to bloom red and pink. Her mother sits in the lounge chair facing the door and the television set, her daisy afghan covering her legs. A large book of photographs is open on her lap and she looks up from it to Iris standing in the open door. She says nothing, though, and her silence disconcerts Iris. "Hi, Mom," she says. She crosses the room quickly, kisses her mother, sets the guest book from the funeral reception on the table at her mother's elbow, and seats herself on the visitor's chair. She wonders if maybe her mother is looking at her this way because she doesn't recognize her.

"I have been waiting for you to tell me about your husband's death," her mother says, mildly enough, but Iris freezes, she can feel her face flushing; for an instant she's fourteen years old again, trying to explain away some failure of hers to her mother.

"I tried," she says hastily. "I came but — "

"I overheard it," her mother interrupts in that throaty whisper that is all that's left of her voice. "Two nurses talking outside my door. Thinking I was asleep." Her gaze doesn't waver. "It was a nasty shock."

Iris is caught between surprise at her mother's clarity and protest at being accused again: she's a widow, she's bereaved, why is everyone intent on making her feel guilty?

"I did try to tell you, Mom." That long-buried anger at her mother's attitude toward her marriage surfaces again. "You never liked him," she says and looks away.

"Indeed, I did not," her mother retorts, and lets her head fall back against the headrest. "Nor did I much like what he became."

"Which is what?" Iris demands.

"He was false," she says, in a faintly surprised tone, as if she can't believe Iris didn't know this. Iris is about to defend Barney, but this remark makes her pause.

"False?" she asks, her voice coming out rough and unsure. Her mother doesn't say anything, then her expression softens and she closes her paper-thin eyelids; Iris can see the quick movements of her eyes behind them before she opens them again.

"For a moment I'd forgotten how much in love with him you were," she says. "It was what I had to keep reminding myself. That you loved him, and — love is blind, they say." She turns her pale, delicately wrinkled face to Iris's.

"He was a good man," Iris says, too surprised to be indignant. "He was a good husband."

"Indeed," her mother says again in a newly softened voice.

"He worked hard," she points out. "He wasn't lazy, and he was smart, as smart as Dad. And he took care of Lannie when Howard asked him to . . . He took her on as a daughter!"

"None of those things," her mother says.

"What, then?"

"Oh, Iris," her mother says gently. "Did you never see that he wasn't happy farming? Didn't see that it was impossible for our two families ever to blend, that by your marriage you drove a wedge into our family life? Did you never see that Barney — " Of course she knew Barney wasn't at home in her family, she could hardly miss that, it's just that it wasn't Barney's fault. "Did you not understand the quality of his affection for you?"

"He loved me!" Iris says quickly. Her face is hot again, she can feel her hands beginning to tremble.

"My dear," her mother says so softly Iris has to lean forward to hear her. Then she sighs, as if she's lost her train of thought, or maybe decided against pursuing it. "He was a confused, complicated man." Iris's anger is again mixed with surprise. How could her mother think such a thing? Barney was as straightforward as the day is long, he was — "I always thought that in the end he would make you unhappy."

Pictures tumble swiftly through Iris's head: how close she and Barney had been, their few quarrels that were over nothing really, the way in which she'd always felt she could never quite reach his core — and then it's James she thinks of. Her affair with James, and for one instant it's clear to her why she risked her good name, her marriage, everything, to be with him: because he held nothing back from her, nor she with him. Because with him she was like a seed lying in fertile earth and he was the warmth and darkness that sheltered and nurtured her and would have helped her grow, if they could have been together all the time, if he had lived longer. While she and Barney —

"I loved him, Mom," she says, and doesn't know herself if she means Barney or James. "And he loved me." She means Barney now, and says this last with all the firmness she can muster. "Loved," she repeats. "It was love, not . . . anything else." But there is no faltering in her mother's eyes, no admission of error, no regret; instead, there is that old assessing gaze that Iris learned from her childhood to dread. It meant that once again she was not measuring up.

"I am so sorry he died so soon," her mother says. "You have a hard road ahead of you." In the long silence between them, Iris feels the sting — *the quality of his affection* — decides her mother won't reply if she does ask what she means.

But then, suddenly, a scene comes into her mind: sitting at the kitchen table with her father, just before the wedding. "Barney's marrying a lot of land," her father said gruffly, then he'd looked at her steadily, from under his thick black eyebrows. "What?" then, "He's marrying me," laughing, thinking he was making a joke. "I'm trying to tell you something, girl," her father had said, still stern. And his message had slowly begun to sink in — Barney was marrying her because some day he'd own the Thomas farm. "That's absolutely ridiculous!" she'd said, and walked out of the room.

She searches rapidly backward through the years of their marriage and finds no scene, no clue that would tell her her father had been right. No, she insists to herself, he did love me; he married me because he wanted me. All those years he was faithful to me. I was the one who was unfaithful. She thinks of Luke's remark, that she'd got through life so far without a mark on her. So what if bad things didn't happen to her — is that something to be ashamed of? She would like to ask her mother, but she doesn't.

Her mother stirs, closes the heavy book on her lap and gestures to Iris to take it away. Iris uses both hands to lift it off her mother's lap and set it at the foot of her bed. When she turns back to her, her mother has let her head fall back against the chair, but her eyes are open and she's watching Iris again in that distant way, as if Iris is a stranger, not the daughter she bore with her own body, and loved, and nourished, and taught.

"I've had some time to think now, and I realize that Lannie needs to know about Barney. They loved each other, and she'd want to know. So," Iris takes a deep breath, "I've decided to find her."

"I'm glad to hear that," her mother says, as if she's merely remarking on the weather. "I should imagine by now she's ready to be found."

"What?" Again, Iris is taken aback.

"She went away; she failed; she could not bring herself to return."

Her mother lifts one small-boned, blue-shadowed, thin hand and gives a slow, brief wave. "Too much time has passed; she needs to be found."

"How do you know that?"

"You told me she left to find her father: but Howard can't be found." She laughs softly, wryly. "No, there's no father to be found in Howard. So she's out there, wandering the earth, looking for . . . herself, one supposes," her mother says, and picks at the yellow centre of a daisy. "Yes, you go find her. And when you do, bring her here to see me. Will you do that?"

"You know I will, Mom," Iris says, and she reaches out and takes one of her mother's chilly, skin-and-bone hands and, impulsively, bends and brushes it with her lips. Even if she's not ready to admit to any of what her mother's said to her, she is humbled by the acuity of her view, and by her certainty, perhaps even grateful that it is offered since she feels so lost herself these days. She wonders, too, if age will bring such clarity to her.

She has said goodbye to Ramona and Vance and promised to phone Ramona every day and Ramona has promised to visit her mother weekly for her; she has emptied the fridge of perishables, unplugged the television set and turned off the satellite system against electrical storms; her bag is packed and standing at the kitchen door.

But she finds she cannot leave. Up the stairs she goes to wander through the four bedrooms, and down to roam through the basement, past the pool table nobody has played on since last Christmas, past the liquor cabinet full of bottles of alcohol nobody has touched in months and maybe never will again. The television set, the tape player, the table where they'd sometimes had the neighbours in to play cards on winter nights. Everything has a layer of dust on it, and abruptly, like a child, she writes on the piano lid, *IRIS,* then stands back, looking down at what she has done. It's over, she thinks. My life here is over.

Then she feels a kind of reeling in her head, as if the floor has suddenly tilted sideways; for an instant everything goes black, and when colour comes back into the rug and walls and the old plaid sofa, a picture goes through her mind so fast it hardly has time to register: she is holding out her wrist and cutting at it with something — but she won't allow herself to see that. She doesn't have to go, she can stay if she wants to; nobody is making her go. But that notion has to be cast out too. The emptiness of the house now is unbearable. She's afraid she'll never be able to sleep again if she doesn't find Lannie. She walks slowly up the basement stairs, putting her feet down heavily so that they make a noise on each step, as if to reassure herself by the sound that she exists. She goes into the dining room full of heavy, old-fashioned mahogany furniture that belonged to her parents and, before that, to her grandparents, stopping at the sideboard where her collection of family pictures sits. Women in high-necked dresses with tight bodices and long, full skirts, well-fed, pompous-looking men with drooping moustaches and hard eyes. Barney in a picture that's not even a year old. He refused to go to a portrait photographer with her so she'd had to resort to framing a snapshot taken by Ramona at one of their joint barbecues. She reminds herself that she should visit his grave, she hasn't been there yet, but decides to wait till her return. She picks the picture up and slides it into her coat pocket. Lannie's high school graduation picture is there, but it's too big to carry, so she leaves it.

She stands a moment longer, but these photos of the dead fill her with a kind of prickly annoyance. All of them, she thinks, and still I've come to this: alone, a widow, all the past in the end meaningless. Maybe *they* are what is causing her bad dreams, her sleeplessness, it's the weight of their deaths dragging her down into their darkness. She turns away abruptly, picks up her suitcase and goes out, pulling the door firmly shut behind her.

Yet, as she turns her car onto the main grid that leads away into the world, she cannot stop herself from a quick glance back. There it is: the house she has lived in most of her life, its dark brown a rich hue in the spring light, the conical peaks of the steel grain bins behind the house rising above the poplars and the caragana hedge to glint in the morning sun. She slows and stares at all of it, tries to fix it in memory, as if by doing so she will secure it forever to the spot where it stands. So it will be there when she gets back.

She turns back to the road ahead of her where above the town, the cliffs of the river valley hover mistily blue and white, and above them is the vast expanse of sky, far too big for her to see all of it in the limits of her windshield. It takes her breath away, and she experiences a moment's fleeting joy — she's free — quickly followed by: I'm alone, I have no destination. But though her hands on the steering wheel are damp with her sudden, powerful foreboding, she does not turn the car around and go back.

Once she's out racing down the highway, it gets easier, and when she remembers that her ultimate destination is shrouded in mystery, she decides instead to think only of the first step: the ranch in the foothills near Calgary. It's like learning to walk, this trying to find her new way in the world on her own.

It's cool and windy — it's always windy in the spring — but the sky is cloudless and an intense blue, and the early May light so lucid that, like a tourist, she can't stop looking at the fields and hills as she approaches and passes them. The light is merciless; it brings out every colour, every shade, every landform and slough and straggly, neglected, gap-toothed caragana hedge where there was once a settler's home. In the few places where the old houses still stand, their windows and doors boarded, shingles missing, she feels again her community's respect, maybe it's even wonder, that families of six and eight children lived in their tiny confines, without running water or electricity, and braving the horrendous winters with nothing but coal and wood fires. The light gives the shabby, greyed structures beauty, lends them a certain dignity.

To the south it's either high, grassy hills or land that falls away for miles, all the way to the U.S. border, and beyond it, to the low purple mountains of Montana. Before she notices it, she's turned north and climbed even higher — her father never failed to point out that this is the highest place in Canada between the Rocky Mountains and a point in Ontario — to the entrance of Cypress Hills Park. Then he would add proudly, as if he'd had a hand in it, that the glaciers had gone around the hills, instead of covering them as they had all the rest of the landscape.

But the sign jolts her for another reason. She remembers that this is the turn west to go to Fort Walsh, or if you're feeling adventurous, even beyond Fort Walsh, through the wilderness of coniferous forest and coulees and rushing streams — she's maybe twenty-five miles from Barney's ranch. One day, perhaps, she'll go there again, but it won't be for a long, long time.

Instead, she wills herself to remember picnics at Fort Walsh. Whenever relatives visited from other parts of the country, her parents would pack everybody into the car and off they'd go to the fort to give their guests a taste of western Canadian history. Not that Iris recalls much about it herself: the Cypress Hills massacre when drunken American wolfers killed a camp of Indians in the mistaken belief they were the ones who'd stolen the wolfers' horses; the Mounties' badly mismanaged but nonetheless courageous, even triumphant, trek from the East that the massacre had finally precipitated, eventually setting up Fort Walsh here in the hills; the 1880s when the buffalo were nearly all gone and the Indians were starving and camped out at the fort in the hope of getting food from the Mounties; Sitting Bull and his people on the run from the Bluecoats after the battle of Little Big Horn, looking for protection and then rations; it even has a graveyard — in the early 1880s it was a good-sized town. She finds that hard to believe: the stockaded fort with its whitewashed buildings never did have to fend off hostile Indian attacks; it's only a tourist attraction now, with an interpretative centre, costumed guides, and buses to the Farwell and Solomon posts where the massacre took place. Nobody lives there at all, the surrounding countryside is barely inhabited. And it's miles from anywhere. Resolutely, she whizzes past the entrance, begins the long descent to the plains below.

Eventually she turns west onto the Trans-Canada Highway, crosses the border into Alberta, and at Medicine Hat stops to stretch her legs. She's been gone from home about three hours; so far the way is familiar; she has made this hundred-and-fifty-mile trip a half-dozen times a year, mostly to shop. Even though she doesn't yet feel she has really gone anywhere, when she parks in the mall lot and goes inside, people seem to have a different look about them — people whose faces she has been looking at her whole life, whose work she knows as well as she knows the back of her own hand, whose voices she can hear in her head, are indeed the only voices she knows. Judging by the stetsons and boots they wear, mostly ranchers, their small sons dressed identically to them, their wives with lined faces from their outdoor lives and endless hard work; retired farmers, products of an older world with their fingers thick from work, their faces still darkened from sun and wind; city housewives, nondescript, absorbed in their errands. Yet today all of them look faintly alien. She tries hard to shake this perception and fails. It drives her to sit down on one of the hard plastic chairs in the noisy, falsely bright food court where she sips a cup of flavourless coffee and mulls over this bewildering observation.

At last she decides that it must be because she's going away, that the lifeline stretched between herself and these people and the farm miles back is stretching thinner and thinner the farther away she goes. A chill runs down her back. Should she turn back? But they're expecting her at Howard's, she has said goodbye to everyone, she has promised to find Lannie. She hurries out of the mall, gets back into her car, and heads west on a narrower road.

The countryside between Medicine Hat and Lethbridge is less dramatic; everything is closer together than the first part of her trip, and there are more buildings, more farms, and she knows later on in the season there'll be more variety in the crops growing in the fields than around her home: besides wheat, sugar beets, corn, potatoes. But this road is busy and, not used to so much traffic, she has to pay attention. She turns on the radio and drives to the accompaniment of country music: Randy Travis with his nasal, mellow voice, k.d. lang who comes from a town north of here.

This is the music of her country, and gazing out at the flat, cultivated landscape with that clean light spilling over it, Iris wonders whether its easy rhythms and nasalized sentiments are the right ones to express this place she calls home. She fiddles with the dial and stops, arrested between two stations by high-pitched, warbling cries that burst in through the ether to fill the car — behind the voices the insistent, hollow boom of drums. Goose bumps rise on her forearms, her hair prickles, a shiver races down her spine. At once unbearably sad and stirring, she recognizes aboriginal people's wild, thrilling music. She listens, fascinated, but at a curve in the road the sounds fade out as mysteriously as they came.

She drives on to Fort Macleod and the land opens up again, unfolding lazily on each side of the highway, the mountains sitting like a bank of clouds along the horizon that tilts upwards the farther west she goes. She should be getting tired, she has been on the road a long time, but apart from being ravenous, she is in no hurry to arrive at her destination. She finds there's an odd solace in driving alone like this, as if for the time being her grief and troubles were held in abeyance. And the countryside is so wide open, so visually stunning in its vastness, and so empty of people, although the signs of their presence are everywhere in the herds of cattle she sees spread out in the fields, and all the cultivated land.

She parks on a side street, goes into a café, finds a table, and sits down. It's just like the café in Chinook, chrome tables and chairs, the floor dirty with dried mud from the men's boots, it even smells the same — french fries, onions, beef. Half the tables are occupied, mostly by men in jeans, jean jackets, and ball caps, although there are a couple of stetsons too. The men all turned to look at Iris when she walked in, but she expected that; she's a stranger here after all.

The waitress is a plump woman her own age, her greying hair pulled back and tucked into place with shiny plastic combs.

"Welcome to the fort," she says, handing Iris a menu, then snapping out her order pad and pencil from her pocket. Iris remembers there's a fort here, she thinks it's one they called in school a "whisky" fort and the Mounties came and shut it down in the last century.

"Oh, Fort Whoop-Up, isn't it?" she asks, smiling, pleased with herself.

"Nope," the woman says. "Fort Whoop-Up's by Lethbridge. This is Fort Macleod. When the Mounties came out here in 18— " she hesitates, "1874, they built this fort. Named it after the head Mountie. Whoop-Up was a whisky fort, not like this one." Iris stares at her, the menu open in her hand. The waitress grins. "One of my kids is a university student, works at the fort in the summer. There's lots of history around here. If you came from east, you've been driving on the Red Coat Trail. That's what they call it now." Seeing

Iris is staring blankly up at her, she says, "The Mounties, you know? This is the trail they followed when they started up in the East. It was quite a trip." She taps her pencil on her pad and Iris sees she wants to get on with her work.

She says quickly, "A Denver sandwich and coffee, please." Now she remembers what she'd been told about the Mounties' trip out here. They'd ridden horses all the way, fed the horses the wrong grass, thinking the greener it was the richer it would be, when out here the best grass was the cured yellow grass — and they'd picked the wrong horses in the first place, they weren't nearly strong enough. And what else? Half the men couldn't ride a horse, either. But they came anyway, and did what they'd set out to do — brought law and order — and some of them were so brave, to this day people still tell their stories.

She heads out of Fort Macleod on the road that leads past the fort and soon turns north to run parallel to the jagged row of blue-grey mountains that line the western sky. This is a narrower, quieter road. Carefully, she consults the directions Mary Ann gave her and drives more slowly so as not to miss her turns. At one point two white-tail deer jump across the road in front of the car and Iris has to break hard to avoid hitting them, at the same time marvelling at their grace. At another, spotting movement in the field to one side, she sees a coyote running away from her on a diagonal path, stopping when she does to look back over his shoulder at her. It reminds her that she rarely sees coyotes on her own land any more, although deer still cross it. And antelope. Barney said you never used to see antelope off grassland, but now you do because there's so little grass left for them to graze. Or was it Luke? Luke, who has always hated her and she didn't even know it or, believing herself wholly blameless, refused to see it.

At last she spots the tall red-brick posts that support the open iron-grillwork gates she has been looking for. She drives through them and down a quarter-mile of paved asphalt road and stops in the driveway of the ranch where Howard is supposed to be working. The house takes her breath away. It's huge, three times the size of her own not-so-small frame house, and complicated; she can't quite make out what's what for a moment, all these rough stone facings, the gleaming sheets of slanted glass reflecting only darkness or clouds, and masses of flowers, tulips mostly, red and yellow, blooming everywhere. Behind the house, the grey and mauve mountains, their peaks still snow-covered, rise into a surreal blue sky.

Iris looks but can't see any way around this mansion to where the actual workings of the ranch should be. She's about to go on around the circular driveway and back out onto the road in search of another entrance when to the right off the flower-bordered, paved driveway she spots a lane that disappears between two more pillars, stone this time, that are themselves half-hidden by the branches of tall conifers. She knows it will lead to the stables, the hay sheds full of the best timothy hay for the racehorses, the offices, the tack room, and whatever else the breeders and trainers of racehorses require. And it's where she's sure she'll find Howard, about whom Luke always said, "Had a way with horses. Liked 'em." High praise, coming from Luke.

The spruces are parting on each side of her car; ahead and to her right sits a small log house. Rows of brilliant pink and white petunias bloom on each side of the sidewalk that leads up to the door of what she guesses will be Howard's home. Beside it, and straight ahead of her, is a long white stable trimmed with shiny red paint, and to her left, gleaming, white-painted corrals. Behind them, she catches a glimpse of a racetrack. She can hear Barney's voice: *What a set-up! Must've cost millions!*

There's activity in the corrals to the left. She can see heads bobbing, both men's and a horse, and the horse is whinnying. No, it's a louder, wilder cry than that, and although she has had little to do with horses, she knows a stallion's cry when she hears one. She hesitates, unable to decide if she should go there to look for Howard or try his house first. She opts for the house, needing the time it will take her to walk up the sidewalk and knock and wait; then maybe she'll be ready for him. She parks in front of the house, goes up the few feet of walk between the petunias, and knocks on the dark-stained plank door.

A pretty teenager wearing skintight jeans and a faded, too-tight western shirt unbuttoned to the cleft of her small, high breasts opens the door. Her hair is pale blonde, cut short, but curly. Iris's immediate reaction is disapproval — Howard is old enough to be her father. Then she realizes who this is.

"Misty?" she asks. The smell of brewed coffee wafts invitingly around them on the still afternoon air, and a shout echoes from the corrals on Iris's left.

"Yeah," the girl says brusquely, leaning against the door frame. She's wearing a silver and turquoise Navajo bracelet on her wrist and she twists it slowly with her other hand. She's not welcoming, she's not even polite.

"I'm Aunt Iris. I've come to see your father."

"Oh, yeah," she says, as if she's just remembered Iris is expected. A little taken aback by her rudeness, Iris can detect no hint of Lannie in her sister's face — Lannie's fairness, yes, but she hasn't Lannie's freckles, and there's a lushness to her face and body that is the opposite of Iris's memory of Lannie's thinness and fragility. She winces inwardly. "Come in," Misty says, softening. "Dad's out working with a stud, but he'll be in soon for coffee. Want some?"

The room is warmly dark, the log walls having darkened with age; she guesses the cabin was built before the turn of the century, probably was once the ranch house itself, and there are only a couple of rag rugs spread out to lighten the plank floor, and an orange-and-red Mexican blanket is thrown over the leather couch. Cowboy artifacts are everywhere: silver pistols mounted on the wall beside hand-forged iron spurs, and a plaited horsehair whip — Barney had one too, bought it or won it from an Indian on the reserve near the Christie ranch — and above that, a tanned diamondback rattler skin is tacked to the wall.

"Have a chair," Misty says, pointing to the chairs around the round wooden table that's covered with a brightly flowered plastic tablecloth. She turns back to the stove where a coffeepot hisses softly over a blue flame. Scarred thick brown mugs sit upside down on the table and a jam jar in the centre holds a cluster of spoons. Iris is reminded of the ranch houses Barney took her to before they were married: the wagon wheel chandeliers, the stiff furled ropes hanging among the coats by the door, and the rows of battered cowboy boots; at the brandings, the neighbours' brands cut into the piecrusts. Misty fills a mug for her, a few grounds spewing out with the still bubbling, smoky liquid.

"Are you still in school?" Iris asks. "I've lost track of how old you are."

"Naw," Misty says. "I quit a long time ago. I been married, but I'm not any more." She pulls out a chair roughly, gracelessly, and sits. "I work at the house, cleaning and sometimes in the kitchen." She pauses. "He likes me to serve when he has company. Guests." She says this last with special emphasis, as if she's been corrected, and didn't like it much. "I wear this dress, with this apron" — indicating it with her hands, and a faint, scornful smile. "Dad got me the job. I sort of look after him here," she adds, and shy pleasure creeps into her voice, quickly muted by a tension Iris takes an instant to see as uneasiness, if not fear.

"How lucky for him." Now she realizes Misty must be in her early twenties. "And Dillon?"

"He works here too. For now, anyway." Her voice has lightened a little, the shy note remaining. "I'll miss him if he goes. I might go back to Calgary, try to get a job there. Maybe . . ." Her voice trails off. The door opens behind Iris and a wedge of sunlight widens across the room. Iris stands and turns. Behind her, Misty stands up abruptly, noisily, and goes to the stove. With the light behind him Howard, a big man, looks about twelve feet tall and she can't make out his face. But she can smell him — sweat mostly, and horse — but some other odour too that makes her think of Barney, Howard, and Luke working together in Luke's big corral, and all the tensions that flowed among them, only half-concealed beneath the surface.

Now she remembers Barney climbing the corral, using his body to hide the dehorning of steers going on behind him. Afraid that if she saw the blood spurting ten feet from the animals' heads, if she had time to really hear the screams of the steers as Howard sawed off their horns, she would run away in horror, she would never marry him. The wind whooping around them mingling with the animals' cries, her glimpse of Howard's contemptuous half-smile that she thought then was meant for her and knows now was meant for Barney because he wanted a woman out of his class, would give up his manhood for her. And Luke, grimly determined to ignore it all. The fistfight the next day it took Barney years to tell her about. His black eye she'd seen herself. Luke knocked backwards into the manger. Howard packing his gear and leaving that night. And yet Luke forgave Howard for going, but not Barney.

"Hello there, Iris," Howard booms, advancing with his hand out. She takes it, overcome by his size, by the fact that she still can't see his face, and by the boisterous way he has chosen to greet her. As her hand touches his she knows his manner masks dislike. Like his father, she thinks.

"It's good to see you again," Iris says. "We hardly spoke at the funeral."

"Couldn't stay long," he's scraping out a chair and sprawling in it. Now Iris can make out his features, he has always been the handsomest of the Christie men, that dark, rough, all-man look, where Barney's features were more precise, less aggressively masculine, and in later years had been softened by excess flesh. "Whew! That bastard's something to handle," Howard says to Misty, whose laugh wavers between admiration and contempt, as if she's not sure which would be best. She fills his cup.

"Hungry?" she asks. He shakes his head, no, without looking at her. Misty hovers a moment at his shoulder, touches it so lightly Iris is sure he doesn't know she has. Iris is struck by how pretty she is, how curvaceous her small body. Certain men would be very attracted to her; Iris can see how tempting she is. Misty sets the coffeepot on the burner, then turns to face them, her back resting against the stove.

Howard says in a lazy drawl, "I'm surprised to see a lady like you in a place like this."

"I won't stay long," she replies too crisply, bristling at his comment. "I'm finding time a bit long on my hands now." She hesitates, then decides to plunge ahead. "I thought how much I'd like to see Lannie again. I miss her very much. But I don't have an address for her any more, and I thought you might."

"Hell, I coulda told you over the phone. You didn't have to come all the way out here."

"I was on my way to Calgary," Iris lies. "Anyway, I — to tell the truth the funeral sort of blurs in my mind, but I felt bad that I didn't talk to Barney's brother."

"Hell, Iris, I'm only Barney's half-brother," Howard says, falsely amiable, and again Iris sees his rage and wonders why he can't get over the grudge he bears all of them because he isn't Luke's full son.

"I'm sure Barney never thought of you as anything but his brother." She knows though, that Barney was Luke's favourite, even if he didn't know how to show it, even if Barney didn't know it himself. The two brothers, eyeing each other, vying for Luke's approval. She doesn't dare say that Howard's the only one who can't forgive Luke for not being his father. Howard is silent, then snorts as if he has just remembered something he didn't like much.

"The old man wants me to come back and take over the ranch." But his voice is quieter now, as if he no longer cares that she's here. "Now that Barney's — gone." He turns his head away toward the patch of blue in the small window above the sink.

"It would be good if you could," she says. "They're getting old and your mother suffers a lot with her arthritis. It'd be nice if she could move into town, at least for the winter — " Howard interrupts as if he can't stand to hear what she's saying.

"Yeah, I might have to do that." His eyes are dark and hard; they glint, but emit no light. *I raised your daughter for you*, she's thinking, although she'll never say it out loud. She thinks instead how ironic it is that tough old Luke succeeded in instilling his hardness in his stepson, but failed when he tried to do the same thing with Barney. How glad she is of his failure.

"I haven't seen Misty or Dillon in — it must be a dozen years. I didn't recognize her."

"Yeah," Howard says. "She grew up all right."

"You should see Dill," Misty says. "He's not as big as Dad, but he's . . ." She hesitates. "Really grown up." She keeps shifting between a sullen forty-year-old and an eager ten-year-old, Iris notes. Is that what not having a mother does to you?

"I haven't heard from my oldest in a long time," as if he can't bring himself to say Lannie's name.

"Years," Misty interjects. "I was about sixteen the last time she wrote me a letter. She was in Toronto. She said I could come and visit her there." Her voice sounds muffled, she might be going to cry. "But I never did."

"We don't know where she is," Howard says flatly, but there's a hint of something that makes Iris hesitate; she understands that one word from her would be all it would take to make him blow up.

"But when she left our place years ago, she said she was coming to see you. Didn't she find you?" As soon as she asks it Iris remembers that, of course, she did. Lannie wrote to them about it: *I stayed with him for a while.* "Do you think she's all right?" she asks Misty finally. "What was she doing in Toronto?"

"Receptionist in a doctor's office," Misty says. "Taking university classes at night — or something."

"How the hell should I know if she's okay or not?" Howard interrupts. "What am I supposed to do about it? You and Barney raised her." His anger frightens Iris and suddenly a matching anger at his unfairness rises in her: *We raised her because you refused to! You gave her away to us — you told her you'd come back for her!* She's about to respond, but Howard says, in a calmer tone, "Yeah, she found me. I was working in Kamloops. She stayed a while. Then she left." He's not looking at Iris at all.

Misty says, "She was living with a guy in Toronto. Tim, she said his name was."

"Oh, Tim!" Iris says, relieved to hear a name she recognizes and Howard looks quickly at her, would like to know who Tim is.

"She told me," Misty says, that sullenness suddenly reappearing, "when I was about ten or something, that she was going to come back and get me. Hah!" Iris wants to defend Lannie, but not even to write to her sister after she'd left the farm; this isn't excusable, and it shakes her.

"God knows what's become of her," she says abruptly. "I — "

"She's mad at *all* of us, I guess." The simple, glum way Howard says this makes Iris forget his unreasonable anger. She's warming to him a little. After all, she didn't treat Lannie with enough understanding either. And she can't help but think of Howard's intense grieving after

Dorothy's death, so that when she looks at him now, she feels her own expression soften. Surely he deserves a little sympathy too.

"She doesn't know Barney is — " she forces herself, "dead," her voice breaking a little.

"I still have that letter some place," Misty says.

"Do you? Could you get it? I want to find her now," she says, her resolve hardened. "Don't you worry. I'm going to find her," she repeats looking straight at Howard. He blinks and looks away.

"Come on," Misty says. Iris follows her through the door beside the stove into a short hall running parallel to the kitchen. Directly ahead is a cramped little bathroom, the white fixtures and white vinyl floor shining with cleanliness. There are doors on either side of the bathroom and Misty leads the way through the one on the right.

It's a small room too, the dark log walls rendering it gloomy, but there's a patchwork quilt, its bright colours faded with age, spread neatly on her single bed. The quilt is oddly familiar to Iris. Three teddy bears — white, grey, and a tawny gold — lean against each other on the pillow. The red curtains at the small high window have been there a long time judging by the way their folds are faded. Opposite the bed there's a shiny, dark brown, imitation-wood chest of drawers, and on the white-painted dresser that sits below the window Misty has arranged small glittering bottles and jars of cosmetics and perfume. A large poster of a rock star with spiky blue hair and a flaming guitar hangs on the wall between the bed and the dresser. Iris is swept through with pity for this lonely girl. A black-and-white snapshot sits on the dresser in an ornate gold-coloured plastic frame, a woman squinting into the sun. She doesn't have to look closer to know it's Misty's mother.

She opens the top drawer of the bureau and carefully lifts out a jewellery box of the kind Iris remembers seeing on her girlfriends' dressers when they were adolescents: cream-coloured imitation leather, gold trim stamped around its borders, fake red suede inside. Misty says, smiling, "It was Mom's. So was the quilt. Grandma Christie gave it to me, oh, years ago. She said Mom made it for me." She and Iris look down at the quilt in silence. Then Misty pulls out the chair in front of her vanity, sets the box on her lap and opens it gently. Handling it as if it were gold, Misty lifts out a letter, closes the lid, and sets the box on the vanity. Her cheeks are flushed pink, and Iris sees how she treasures it.

A flash of memory: Lannie's macramé book bag, the texts and notebooks spilled on the rug. Iris had unzipped the interior pocket and pulled out a mass of awkwardly folded paper, some written on paper from memo pads: *Meet me at four for coffee, A.* Or stick-it notes: *See you tonight at eight, Tim;* or on fragments of paper torn from notebooks, *the whiteness of your skin* — she'd not finished that one. *Cunt be there* a violent scrawl, his pen leaving a tear in the cardboard bar coaster, another one, naming a sexual act, a lewdness Iris won't remember. She hadn't shown them to anyone. She doesn't know what they mean. Nothing, she tells herself again. Nothing. Young girls alone in cities full of psychopaths and predators — But why did Lannie keep them?

"I would have looked for her myself. But I wrote to this address and the letter came back. Somebody wrote 'Not here' on it. And I didn't know what to do next. I was only a kid," Misty adds disparagingly. She gives the letter to Iris, whose heart flutters at the sight of Lannie's handwriting. She opens her purse, finds a pen and her address book and copies down the return address on the envelope. The postmark is unreadable.

"It came a long time ago," Misty says softly. But now the fact of Lannie's not having written to Misty, to any of them, seems more ominous than a mere failure of duty or love. The name of the city pictured on the postcard she'd sent Angela comes back to her: Iraklion, somewhere in Greece. For the first time she wonders if Lannie might be dead. Or in some terrible situation she can't get out of, not even to let them know.

"You can read it," Misty says.

"Oh, no," Iris says. "It's private. I don't want to . . ." She hands the letter back to Misty who shrugs, but lowers her head, as if she's trying to hide that she's glad Iris hasn't read it. She puts it carefully back in the box.

Then, as if she has forgotten Iris is there, she swings around on the chair, leans forward, peering into the mirror, uncaps a tube of pink lipstick and stretches her mouth to apply it. The shift in mood is so abrupt it's unsettling. She straightens the collar of her shirt, smoothing it where it opens to show cleavage, trying to make it sit neatly but revealingly against her small breasts. Iris is taken back a thousand years, to herself at that age — that pride in her young body. Wasn't she just like that once?

"I'm so sorry about your mother, Misty," Iris says. "About the way things have turned out — "

Misty lifts her head slowly, her eyes meeting Iris's in the mirror. The little girl is gone, she looks forty. Her voice is harsh. "It's too late to be sorry now."

For a second Iris can't think what she means, but then it comes rushing over her: *You should have taken me too, not just my sister.* Iris is aghast, she wants to defend herself. It was Howard's choice, not mine; what would I do with three children? Or even two? But then she sees the cruelty of splitting up the children, especially Lannie and Misty. Dorothy had used Lannie as Misty's substitute mother whenever she didn't feel like being a mother herself, which was pretty often, come to think of it. Dorothy was lazy. Or maybe she was depressed, Howard being such an awful man, an awful husband.

She remembers how smitten Howard was when he met Dorothy. He had loved her, at least at first. But there was something funny about Dorothy, some fuzziness, for lack of a better word, as if she'd never understood herself as capable of action, but only as someone always acted upon. Dorothy had been an orphan, she remembers, hadn't had a mother to raise her and show her how to be a full person.

That's what has happened to Lannie and Misty and probably to Dillon too. Everybody confused, nobody knowing what to do or how to do it. Mothers aren't supposed to die in the midst of raising three small kids. Her absence disrupted something vital inside each of them. Mothers, she thinks, but what does she know about mothers? She has never been one herself. She shivers a little as she sees that she has left something out of her life that would have transformed it in ways she can't quite imagine, but maybe would have been glad of.

Iris is afraid Misty is crying. She wants to go to her, put her arms around her, kiss her, offer to try to be her mother. But the knowledge that it's far too late, that Misty would push her away, makes her, finally, stand shakily and walk out of the room, back to the kitchen where Howard sits sipping his coffee.

"Find it?" he asks. Iris nods, unable to speak, sits again, more because her legs feel unsteady than because she wants to keep on talking to Howard. "She's a good kid," he says vaguely. "Keeps the place clean. Isn't a bad cook, neither." He's talking about his daughter as if she were his pet or a good servant. Angrily she stands to go, saying a brusque goodbye. Her newfound sense of urgency propels her too, and her dismay at Misty's accusation. At the open door she turns to Howard, whose face in the strong sunlight is suddenly clear. She sees a man whose once-crackling black hair has thinned and begun to grey, whose lined face, no longer handsome, bespeaks a kind of exhausted dissipation, whose opaque brown eyes have gone flat again, like a cat's.

"Your brother's dead," she says. "Both of your brothers are dead," her voice is tremulous with feeling. "You should take your children and go home. Your parents need you. What have you got here, working for some rich man?" A flash of surprise crosses Howard's face and is replaced by a glimmer of something that might be respect before it shuts down, stony. Iris has stepped back out through the door, too agitated to notice, much less care about her audacity. She's about to pull it shut, when she remembers why she has come here. In a voice that sounds more like her own, she says, "The moment I know anything I'll phone Mary Ann and tell her to let you know too." She hesitates, thinking about offering him money to help him relocate, but draws back in horror as she thinks of his reaction if she did. Instead, catching herself as much by surprise as she does Howard, she goes to him and bestows on his unresponsive shoulders an awkward hug before she turns away.

She pulls the door shut and steps outside into the sunshine, goes down the walk between pink and white petunias to her car and gets in. She sits for a second, filled with misery at not having seen Misty's, Dillon's, and Howard's needs all those years ago, instead of only her own, and then Lannie's. Finally, she starts the motor and, lifting her eyes, she realizes the man who's walking toward her must surely be Dillon.

She watches curiously through the windshield. A carbon copy of Howard all right, but shorter, slimmer, with a delicacy of bone unlike Howard's heaviness that she knows comes from his dead mother. He too is dressed in jeans, cowboy boots, a faded denim jacket over a denim shirt. Slowly she opens the door and gets out again.

"Dillon?"

"Aunt Iris?" he says, smiling, his hand out. Behind them, the mountains have lifted to hover mistily above the stables and barn. "Dad said you were coming. It's great to see you."

"It's been a long time," Iris says, and now she remembers that last, terrible visit when the cousins who'd raised them had brought both kids to visit Lannie on the farm. They'd been on their way to visit relatives in Manitoba. They'd refused even to stay overnight. And poor Lannie, hardly knowing what to say to her own brother and sister. And Dillon! Too big for his age, awkward and sullen — how has he transformed himself into this trim, apparently nice young man? "I'm glad to see you" is all she can think of to say.

"Yeah, well," he says, awkward now, kicking the ground. Iris is aware that Howard will be out any moment — she doesn't want to see him again.

"I'm trying to find Lannie," she says quickly. "The last address anybody has is Toronto. I'm going there to look for her."

"Oh?" he says, guarded now. His response surprises her.

"I met the man she was living with in Toronto," she says. "He came out to the farm once, years ago." Does he know? she wonders, why Tim came, why he stayed — those few awful days when Lannie — but no, she never even told Howard — why was that? She remembers vaguely that nobody was sure where he was — so Lannie's brother has no way of knowing about her suicide attempt — unless Luke —

"The last time I heard from her was a phone call," he says, but his manner has lost his easiness, it's as if he's ashamed, as if it's his fault Lannie is lost. "It was a long time ago." He clears his throat softly and looks away, off to the cabin.

She says with more certainty than she feels, "Don't worry. I'll find her."

"She was worried about Misty, when Misty got married. She was only sixteen. I tried to talk her out of it," he says, lowering his eyes, "but it was no use. He drank, ran around. Had this little place in the foothills. Misty wound up looking after the horses, feeding the cows. Dad went and brought her back." He lifts his eyes to Iris's, his mouth is twisted in a sour grin that reminds her of Howard. "Put the son of a bitch in the hospital." She doesn't have to ask if he means Howard or the husband.

"It's good he was looking out for her," she says lamely, although she's thinking of his failure to look out for Lannie. She doesn't understand why he would look after Misty and as good as discard his other daughter. When he doesn't answer her, Iris says again, "I'll phone you the minute I know anything."

She gets back in the car and drives away down the clearly marked road which she sees now she should have used when she came in. She's relieved that this meeting she dreaded is over. But something larger surfaces. These are the people who should care most about Lannie, who should have somehow saved her from whatever has happened to her. It's not that we don't care, she's thinking, even Howard cares in a way, it's just that — but she doesn't know what has brought them all to this. Selfishness? Or just indifference?

She will have to search out Tim Quennell in Toronto to see what he can tell her. That means flying from Calgary. Or she could go home and in a couple of days, when she's ready, drive to Regina and fly from there. But even though the thought of home tempts her strongly, she can only look longingly in that direction before she turns her car resolutely toward Calgary. No, she has come too far to turn back, and her small shiver of fear at the realization dissipates, replaced by a quickening of an emotion that just might be elation.

So lost in thought, she has driven miles before she begins to see the landscape again. She thinks then that there's not as much ranchland as there used to be, and twice she's surprised to see breaking ploughs at work in pastures. But what grassland there is looks in fairly good condition to her admittedly inexpert eye, and once again she notices how beautiful it is compared to the fields of stubble or summer-fallow, and also how much lusher than the fields of grass at home.

By the time she has relaxed again, she's near Calgary. The closer she gets to the city, the wealthier people seem to be. She's passing acreages, each with an elaborate new house on it and fenced with expensive board or stone or brick fences with two or three horses idly grazing behind them. The houses interest her for their architecture, although they all look as if they have nothing to do with the land they're sitting on, might have been dropped down there from Mars. Acreages in general arouse chiefly her scorn, she who has always lived on far more land. Some of the owners have allowed their horses to graze the grass right down to its roots; a few of the acreages look worse even than the worst overgrazed ranchland. Obviously the owners don't know the first thing about land, don't realize the damage they're doing. The farm girl in her is aware, too, that this is prime agricultural land taken out of use. And isn't it selfish for one family to take up so much room for no other reason than their own pleasure? Barney and I may own far more, but we put it to good use, she thinks smugly, and repeats the platitude: we grow food on it to feed the hungry around the world.

Now she can see the city rising out of the plains before her, a long blue shadow that as she draws nearer gradually extends itself up and out, separating itself into overlapping, many-sized rectangular shapes, the even blue metamorphosing into faded browns and creams, greens, mauves, and greys. In the years since she first came here as a child, Calgary has more than doubled in size and taken on a level of sophistication that has made her lose interest in it. She doesn't know what to do with so big a city, beyond shopping in it. It puzzles her where all these people rushing around on the jumble of freeways can be going, what it is they do with their lives.

Once, somewhere, high up in that confusion of shining towers, on a Christmas shopping expedition, she got lost and stumbled into a vast room noisy with water burbling through pipes and trickling into open troughs, and the hum of unseen machinery so powerful it made the floor quiver. It was the air in the room that attracted her: invitingly cool, moist, and fragrant. Thick cords of ivy climbed to the ceiling, greenery cascaded downward, a carpet of flowers overflowed into the paths. Here was an artificial, glass-walled, tropical garden, while below was frigid winter, the stink and roar of traffic, the crowds of shoppers, the banks of pock-marked, blackened snow, the billowing clouds of ice fog like some filmmaker's notion of hell. She was overcome by astonishment. What madness, what sheer, bald insanity — and yet, the perfumed air, the moist coolness, the stillness, such relief from the crowded, frantic mall. Although she'd tried on other trips, she'd never found the garden again.

She comes back to herself, realizing she has to make a decision immediately about where she's going; it's late afternoon, the rush hour will have begun. She has never driven in downtown traffic — Barney always did that — she has no idea where the airlines' ticket offices are. She decides to stay on the road she's on that she knows skirts the city, and go to the airport. She can buy her ticket there, and she knows from experience that there are hotels and motels nearby where she can spend the night.

Peering at signs, nervously changing lanes, then changing back again to the accompaniment of honking horns, having to circle around an extra time, she manages to find her way into the airport parkade. She parks, locks the car, and goes inside. She stands still, an island in the mass of people who part and stream around her while she searches for the counter where she can buy her ticket. After a couple of errors, she finds the right desk, buys a ticket on a morning flight to Toronto, goes out to her car, and drives away, stopping at the first hotel she comes to where she takes a room for the night.

It is small, stuffy, decorated in rusts, beiges, and browns that repel her, and in it she can hear the muted roar of planes taking off or landing. She's nervous about tomorrow's trip, apprehensive about finding Tim in a city she has never before been to. It occurs to her that she might try to phone him in Toronto; even if Lannie isn't there, he might still be. Her hand is already on the phone to call information, but — No, she thinks. If I don't reach him, I might not be able to go on, and if I don't — possibilities flit through her mind and she withdraws her hand from the phone as if it's hot. No, she doesn't want to find out over the phone. Instead, she calls Ramona.

"I made it to Calgary," she answers Ramona's abrupt "Hello?" There's a lot of thumping in the background, Cody and Ryan are roughhousing, she supposes. She tells Ramona where she has been, what she has found out, that she's going to Toronto in the morning. "I'm a bit scared," she confesses.

"Hey, kiddo," Ramona says. "You can do it." There's an eruption of loud, adolescent male laughter in the background. Ramona muffles the phone with her hand, says something sharp, then comes back on the line and says, "Oh, that guy, the one you said wanted to buy the place? He was back. Wanted to know where you are. Said he wants to make an offer. Had the paperwork done and everything." Iris's heart gives a little thud and she shifts the phone to the other ear. "I said we were renting. Had an agreement. He made me kinda mad. He said, 'Well, that's no problem,' like what we'd decided didn't matter. Asked us how to get ahold of you."

"Yes?" Iris asks, uneasy.

"Vance said he wasn't sure, thought you were in Alberta. Didn't know when you'd be back."

"If he — or anybody else, for that matter — shows up asking about the place, tell them I said it isn't for sale." Her own new firmness surprises her a little, but in a pleasurable way, as she hangs up the receiver.

She's not hungry, but she has a light supper in the hotel restaurant anyway, returns to her room, undresses, bathes, and gets into bed. Then she gets out again and reaches into her suitcase for her picture of Barney. He's sitting at the plank table, a can of beer in one hand, his ball cap pushed back at Ramona's command so there wouldn't be a shadow on his face, and he's grinning. He looks so at ease, and happy too, as if he didn't have a care in the world. She presses the cold glass to her lips, then sets the picture on the bedtable.

Lying in the darkness, unable to fall asleep, she thinks about the land deal. If everybody else sells and she doesn't, all her neighbours will be mad at her. After all, a lot of jobs would come with such a big enterprise, maybe she should sell. Then she thinks about what the jobs would be: secretaries in the offices, or housekeepers in the motels, or waitresses in the restaurants; for the men, feeding cattle in a feedlot, shovelling manure, driving trucks, fixing machinery — it seems to her that giving up the freedom and beauty of your farm for shovelling manure or washing strangers' dirty linen is a pretty poor trade-off.

And if she doesn't sell? She could rent the farm to somebody else when Vance quits. Or seed it back to grass and she and Vance could ranch together. The thought makes her smile — that'll be the day, she thinks.

Eventually she sleeps and finds herself standing on the patch of prairie that drops into the coulee that opens out and deepens as it winds its way downward to the small river. The sun is still below the horizon, although the distant purple hills to the east are haloed with pale yellow light. She walks through translucent violet shadows, setting her feet down lightly, and the earth, yielding and warm, cushions her steps.

At the coulee mouth she stops and lets her nightdress drop, brushing her breasts and thighs softly as it falls to the grass. Naked, barefoot, she makes her way down a deer trail until she reaches the cool green-gold water of the slough. It's like silver against her feet as she glides along its shallow edge, and the tall slough-grass brushes her thighs with raspy tongues. Smells rise up: damp clay, the water's tang, pungent sage, grass, cactus, the sweetness of wild roses, the fragrant yellow blossoms of the wolf willow that lines the coulee sides.

She walks on beyond the water to a waist-high grove of shrubs: dark green badger bushes and thorny greasewood, stunted, gnarled poplars, chokecherries, Saskatoon bushes, their plump, wine-coloured berries glistening with the weight of clear dew. Leaves caress her cheeks and twigs catch in her hair and release. It's cool down here in the animals' lair. Rabbits in their hiding places lift their noses to watch her pass by and a doe whistles softly to her white-spotted fawn curled in the underbrush, as her feet brush past. Small brown and yellow birds resting on green branches fix her, not unkindly, with tiny, unblinking black eyes.

Then she's out of the shrubbery, leaving behind the scent and the cool air for the hard-packed clay coulee where it levels out and widens before it deepens to continue its descent to the river. A coyote, her pups playing at her back, watches her from the mouth of her den along the sloping coulee wall; she can see her saffron eyes shining like beacons in the pale light and shadows, she can hear her breath — *hhahhh, hhahhh, hhahhh.*

The sun is nearer to the horizon now and a few stray rays escape its boundary to send out tendrils of rose light that flush the grasses growing up the coulee wall. At her feet stones of different sizes lie scattered against each other. Beige limestone or black granite or red sandstone, purple and white quartz or golden brown chert. Each carries a partial coat of lichen: orange, yellow, green, rust, black. The shards of light from the rising sun strike red and gold sparks in them.

At a patch of glistening white ground she bends to gather a little in her fingers, puts it to her lips to taste the salt tang of the earth. Three antelope stand alert to her left, the male sniffing the air, his head erect, his black horns precise against the background of glowing grass behind him. She walks on into the heat of the morning. Beside her the prickly pear cactus flowers bud and open to fragile yellow blooms, and the pincushion cactuses spread their small, spiky, fuchsia blooms.

She walks faster, the ground rises up under her feet to push her ahead with each footfall. Springing along, like an antelope or deer, a breeze swims along behind her, lifting her with gentle arms, then sets her down against a great, smooth, black-and-silver buffalo rubbing stone. She feels a weight and looks down. A thick, dull green snake has curled itself around her feet and ankles. As she watches, it writhes and bit by bit peels itself loose from its own skin to leave behind at her feet its transparent, crystal twin.

The new snake is a glowing, deep wine colour. It slides away to lose itself under the gnarled roots and limbs of an ancient sagebrush. When it is gone, Iris looks back to its discarded skin, but it has collapsed, lost its form, faded, and it disintegrates slowly into dust. But in the low distance she can see the dark red snake appearing and disappearing as it moves on past cactus and rocks and thorny, grey greasewood bushes. She turns to follow.

In the early morning she wakes, light streaming in around the curtains to remind her where she is. As she lies, not moving, her dream washes over her, perfect in its every detail. She's astonished by it, more than that, she's in awe; it's as if her body has opened and all her organs are dissolved in wonder. How she once conceived of the world has spread apart to reveal a dimension she'd never guessed at — whole, perfect, transcendently beautiful. For a long time she just lies there, contemplating her dream.

PART TWO

—◦◦◦—

Growing

Landraces

Somewhere in the walk through the sorghum stubble Lannie has lost the floppy green weed that she has been using as a switch to keep off the small blackflies. She holds on to her clipboard with one hand and bats them away with the other. Today they seem especially bad — or is it just that she's sick to death of them, never wants to feel another one crawling on her lips or landing on an eyelid? Years, years she has been tormented by the hideous little creatures; she'd like to kill every one of them. She stops, surprised and a little shocked at herself. It's just that today she feels lousy, and it's her luck to have lost her switch and not noticed. Dr. Abubech had told her to write down something Fatima had said, and when she stopped to do it, she'd dropped her pen and her shoulder bag had slid down and — Abubech is speaking to her again.

"She's invited us for the coffee ceremony." Lannie knows enough Amharic that sometimes she doesn't need a translation, but more often she's lost, can't get a single word. Amharic is a hard language with all its many inflections and, despite a few lessons years ago, she has never fully put her mind to trying to learn it, since most of the people she deals with nowadays speak at least a little English, and when they don't, Abubech translates for her. In the camps there had always been translators.

It has occurred to her more than once that rather than waiting for translations or instructions from Abubech before writing down what's going on, it would be simpler and probably more accurate to use a tape recorder. She rejects the idea though. Her position here with Dr. Abubech, she feels, is precarious and short term enough that she's afraid a tape recorder would make Abubech realize how superfluous she actually is. She can't bring herself to think about what would happen if she loses Abubech and her work. Where would she go? What would she do then?

Fatima stops and looks back at her son and daughter, barefoot children of about six and eight years, the six-year-old lugging a toddler, while three other little ones in their ragged and dirty clothing trail through the dust after them. They are herding the family's cattle, keeping the five or so cows from grazing up against the huts — the only fences are thorn hedges that enclose groups of huts — and from wandering too far away. She calls out to them in rapid Amharic — telling them to move the cattle back farther — turns, and goes toward her house.

The moisture situation is very poor right now, and Lannie hopes that when the major rainy season begins in June or July, it won't let them all down too, as the lighter period has. In this country there is no margin for error, no excess to cover nature's cruel vagaries. If there's once again no crop, or a poor one, Fatima will sell those bracelets that jangle on her arm, then their few skinny zibou and their goats will go, then they'll eat the seed they've kept for next year's crop. And after that, if it still does not rain, they'll have to go wherever someone will give them food. Lannie knows the sound of hundreds of feet trudging down a dusty road or through wind-driven dust sweeping across a naked, once-fruitful plain, no voices rising in conversation or song, just the steady, relentless slap and shuffle of feet, going to wherever there may be food.

Better just to pray for rain. *God is good*, Fatima will say, if she comments. But Lannie is tired; now she only listens, smiles, writes, does what Abubech tells her to do.

The other two have reached Fatima's *tukul* (*tukul* is not correct, Abubech had said severely, it is more properly called a *gojo*, but Lannie has never heard anybody call it that). In the distance the blue mountains dotted sparsely with trees make rough outlines against the cloudy sky, their deep clefts patches of indigo. Lower and closer to her are the yellow hills with their small scattering of single trees. It makes her sad to look at the bare slopes, all the trees gone so the peasants will have warmth, light, and fuel to cook their food. Too poor to buy kerosene, knowing exactly what they're doing but unable to do anything else, they destroy their own future. She thinks of her own treeless, grass-covered landscape, broken occasionally by deep, shrub-filled coulees where deer and rabbits lie in watchful silence, and for an instant she's gripped by homesickness.

She lowers her head to pick her way carefully over the uneven ground and is immediately engulfed in dizziness, so that she stumbles and almost drops her clipboard before the dusty stubblefield and the *tukul* at the edge of it right themselves again. The better part of seven years, off and on, in this country and she still gets ill regularly from food or water taken in villages. As if to emphasize that she's much too careless, her stomach lurches upwards in nausea. She clenches her teeth, managing to force it down, as she reaches Abubech who has paused to wait for her at the door of the hut.

"She says she hopes this year to have a little seed left over to trade for a certain kind of sorghum she likes — '*wotet-beguncle*,' she calls it — that's 'milk in my cheeks,'" Abubech says to Lannie. Absurdly, Lannie thinks of "winterfat," a grassland shrub at home desirable for its high protein content. "It's called that, she says, because it's good for her children. It has higher nutritional value than some of the other landraces. This I have proved in the laboratory." Abubech smiles with an edge of triumph at Lannie, her thesis — that farmers can teach much to scientists — confirmed once again. When she'd said this early on in her teaching of Lannie, Lannie had replied, "I wish North American scientists and government officials thought that. Instead, they think they are the experts and without them farmers would know nothing." Now, dutifully, without speaking, she writes down "*wotet-beguncle* — 'milk in my cheeks,'" then follows Abubech into the dwelling.

Windowless and dark inside, her eyes need to adjust after the bright light outside, and in the instant when she feels the cool air on her face and sees only blackness, she almost sinks to the ground with gratitude. How tired she is, always, these days. Even before this new bout of mild illness that at home she would have called flu, she has been feeling her energy, what little of it there is, leaking out of her body day by day. Sometimes in the middle of the day, seated at her desk transcribing her field notes, or typing Abubech's papers, she's overcome by exhaustion and wants only to lie down on the cool, rough grey rug and close her eyes.

And yet, when she first came to Ethiopia at the end of 1984 during the Great Famine, she would work all day and half the night and never really feel tired. And now — she sleeps eight and more often ten hours a night. She eats her small supper, reads a little, if you can call it that, and goes to bed to sink into a heavy slumber.

Books have stopped making sense. She can still read the symbols, and the words and the sentences and paragraphs. But she can't get a grip on what they mean, the simplest book seeming difficult and esoteric to her now. She's buffeted by life. Drowning in it. Books cease to make sense because they insist on their point of view, their opinions, their attitudes — and confused, trying to make sense of her own, she can't any longer let herself be engaged by the book for fear of accepting a formula, a proof for the way life is, the acceptance of which might allow her escape so that she would not doubt or question the incomprehensibilities of her own. Or perhaps it's only that she has no room left for what she finds in books.

It's clear something's wrong, it's been this way for months, and while it never gets worse, it never gets better either; maybe she just needs a vacation or something, she doesn't know what.

"Why don't you go home, go back to university there, get your own focus, if you want to be a documentalist?" Dr. Abubech had asked Lannie when she had gone to her office to ask for a job.

"I don't want to be a documentalist. I don't want to go home," Lannie had said. She considered adding, Addis is my home, but refrained because it would sound like the self-righteous lie she knows it to be. The fact is, she's a person who has an apartment in Addis Ababa where she lives, almost certainly temporarily, until something else happens that makes her move once more. Money, for instance, she has begun using the sum Barney deposited to her account so long ago and which for years she'd refused to touch, and it won't last forever, which means she won't be able to afford her new apartment on Bole Road for more than a year. Addis isn't a cheap city, not for expatriots anyway, and her apartment is the first decent place she has lived in since she came to this country. Well, she reminds herself, don't forget Dimitri's house in Dire Dawa — marble this and marble that — Dimitri was rich. And there was that delicious interlude in his house on Crete — but oh he was terrible, a terrible man, and she has to smile, not without a trace of bitterness, because he was exactly what she deserved. Until she'd had to leave him because even she could endure his rages no longer, what she'd always known was his contempt for her, his absolute refusal to see her as an individual, and not just a pretty girl to show off on his arm. Still, she'd had moments there of something close to happiness. She remembers sending Angela a postcard during one of them, and feels herself blush a little with chagrin at her own foolishness. Hope rearing its ugly head again.

"Unfortunately, my research grant leaves me no money to pay an assistant," Abubech said slowly. Lannie said hastily, "You don't have to pay me. I have my own money. I want to help, that's all." Abubech had looked steadily back at Lannie for a moment without saying anything. Lannie held herself rigid under the older woman's gaze, feeling herself colour, but forcing herself to look steadily back, although inside she felt no steadiness at all, only embarrassment and a kind of weary shame; after all these years, still that ineradicable shame at the bottom of everything. She knows, she has studied psychology, that she should dissect that shame, pull out every strand of it, examine it with a microscope in a good light until she makes it disappear. But whenever she thinks of this her weariness overcomes her: it's too hard, there is too much there, she can't possibly do the work, it's difficult enough just to keep it shoved down so it doesn't incapacitate her utterly.

"You do understand this project?" Abubech asked. Not knowing precisely what Abubech meant by this, Lannie had replied, "I come from a farm in Saskatchewan."

"That's good," Abubech said. "But don't confuse the two. This is a different kind of agriculture, with very different problems, and, in certain ways, different goals as well."

"I think I know that. I mean, these people have tiny plots of land and they do everything by hand, I've even seen them weeding their fields by hand."

"The difference is more acute than that," Abubech said severely, once again fixing those stern black eyes on Lannie so that she couldn't look away. "They farm almost entirely to feed their families, with a very little bit left over, if they're lucky, to trade or sell at the market. Your Great Plains agriculture has always been strictly for profit — for cash. My guess is that your family never ate one handful of its own seed."

"It's true," Lannie admitted. "Not since pioneer days. My aunt bought our flour in the grocery store." She sees Iris struggling through the kitchen door with bags of groceries, handing Lannie the milk, the butter, the cream, the vegetables to put in the fridge, the toilet paper and bath soap to run upstairs with: I don't know what I'd do without you, Iris would say, smiling down at her. And she would swell with little-girl pride on hearing that, even though she knew Iris was just trying to make her feel necessary and at home, never the burden she could not forget she really was. She shook herself, found the thread again. "My uncle sold every kernel he raised, just kept back enough seed for next year's crop. Some years he'd buy seed if he wanted to try a new variety, or if he'd been using hybrid seeds."

"So I can assume, by your use of the word 'hybrid' that you know what landraces are?" Lannie knew because she'd made it her business to find out before she'd come for the interview.

"I think so: natural seeds, not bred in laboratories, native to an area. Indigenous."

"Close. Some of them have been selected and improved by local farmers; some have improved themselves naturally over the centuries."

"I know your project is trying to keep Ethiopian agriculture from being taken over entirely by the new hybrid seeds we use in North America. And you're also trying to keep biodiversity alive by not letting the landraces vanish."

"We are indeed. But we are also trying to keep the small farmers on their land. What is there for them in cities but to starve? The women to become prostitutes." When she'd said "prostitutes," her shoulders jerked with the force with which she spat the word. "Biodiversity — Ethiopian landraces — are our most precious resource. Few realize how infinitely precious."

Abubech stood then, and walked to the window where a hibiscus tree flowered just outside, filling the space between the office building and its compound wall. Lannie knew Abubech probably didn't even see the flowers. But in her plain navy suit and with her dark hair pulled back in a bun and the coral blooms framing her, with her erect posture, her neatness, the air of quietly contained sorrow that she wore all the time, against the brilliance of the flowers, perfumeless as they were, made Lannie hold her breath at so much beauty. Moments like this she forgot Africa's cruelty, and this country's woes, thought of Africa as the lost Garden of Eden.

Abubech turned slowly to her. "For myself, I do this work because I am tired of seeing people dying of hunger. I am sick with it." She walked back to her desk and stood looking over Lannie's head across the room, glancing at her only occasionally as she spoke. "That is what this project will do: provide food security for the farmers. Improved landraces have high yields here in the country where over the centuries they've adapted, selecting themselves for optimum performance. Here they give a much better yield than the seeds you Europeans and North Americans use, and they give it without chemical fertilizers or herbicides or pesticides, none of which, for the most part, local farmers can afford. And which, in the end, do much damage to the soil, to water, and so on. And because of their genetic diversity, they are unlikely to all succumb to one disease or to certain adverse conditions. Unlike the hybrid seeds with their absolute genetic uniformity which are then completely destroyed by one scourge, landraces will not all die — something will be left to harvest. It is — it can be — a major contribution to food security in this famine-ridden country." She paused, smiled briefly at Lannie. "Forgive me, I am making a speech. I am perhaps too serious." Lannie murmured softly, "No, please. I want to hear."

Abubech sat down then, raised her eyes to Lannie's with a look so fixed, so clear-eyed, that in the face of it Lannie's mouth went dry. She wanted more desperately than she'd realized to be a part of this, if only because she wanted to be with this woman, to gain strength from her, or to float for a while in the steady wake of Abubech's fortitude.

"I'm tired out," she heard herself say. She would, bit by bit, when she knew Abubech better, tell her about her years as a relief worker doing whatever needed doing, checking out rumours, mixing batches of feed, weighing children; about watching people die of starvation, especially the children; about how angry the endless, hopeless poverty of the rural people made her, in a nation rich with mostly undeveloped resources; about her former disgust at the arrogance of the ruling class and their cruelty and their corruption and their negligence.

Knowing all the while that her deepest reason was that she needed to do something that, at the very least, would not add to her burden of shame, that would not waste what little strength she had left in worry over whether she was doing something to justify her very existence, her privileged, screwed-up, selfish existence. And Abubech and her agency had found something that seemed to Lannie to make clear, inarguable sense. Not that, in the beginning, there hadn't been plenty of arguments with government officials until they began to turn from dubious toward it to supporters of the project. The results already were speaking for themselves. And always, at back of all this, she did not want to leave Africa. She was in love with Africa.

"Yours is the only project I've ever heard about that makes any kind of long-term sense to me. I want to help. Please let me help." Abubech at first looked faintly surprised, then amused. She looked down at the papers in neat piles on her desk. After a moment, during which Lannie cursed herself for letting her own desperation leak into view, at the same time wondering if Abubech had a husband, children, a real life somewhere out in the ragged, tumultuous city around them, Abubech began speaking again as if Lannie hadn't said what she'd said.

"You know that Global 2000 is also present in this country?"

"I'm not sure what that is," Lannie said.

"It is an American initiative, with the backing of the World Bank. Introducing hybrid seeds and high technology, high input farming techniques like the ones you use in North America, here in Africa, because they get such high yields, as an answer to the problem of food shortages and famine. Former president Jimmy Carter and the Carter Center is behind it. I do not know who else."

"Like the Green Revolution?"

"It appears to be."

"That's ridiculous," Lannie said. "The Green Revolution got high yields at the expense of every single small farmer wherever it was introduced." At this, she saw new interest appear in Abubech's eyes.

Fatima has begun to roast the coffee beans and a rich, heavy scent, one that normally Lannie savours, is rising from them. Today it makes her sick. If she tells Abubech how she's feeling these days, Abubech will make her take a holiday. A holiday! The word makes her think of a Canadian family heading out in their overloaded mini-van for Banff or the Pacific, of the hordes of tourists she saw in Greece, Crete especially.

Crete — the warm blue Aegean, the welcome heat so strong it could melt muscle and bone, of Dimitri, his jealousy, his pride in her as if she were a racehorse he owned or a new sportscar. Sitting side by side in a taverna by the sea drinking the tawny Cretan wine, listening to musicians playing wild Greek music, the dancers snapping their fingers, their gleaming black boots — even dancing themselves sometimes. And Dimitri's friends with them, rich men like himself, with their gorgeous, long-limbed European girlfriends, their cultivated, wilful vapidity.

She shudders, and then she's lying, her palely freckled white limbs tangled with Dimitri's golden ones, in his big, square bed, the moonlight pouring in through the open terrace doors, spilling across the dark tiled floor, bathing them in its cool light. It's true that even as she hated him, she'd been in love with him; she'd stayed as long as she did for those endless nights in his moonlight-flushed bed.

And the long lazy days she spent on the terrace in the shade, lifting her head from her book now and then to stare out over the roofs of the whitewashed resort town clinging to the precipitous, rocky slopes of the island, running down its sides to meet the sun-sparkled Sea of Crete. She thinks now perhaps she had been happy then, steeping herself in *The Iliad* and *The Odyssey* and whatever other versions of the Greek myths she'd been able to find in translation.

Other times, while Dimitri slept or went off to do business in Athens, she took his car and drove to the ancient ruins which were everywhere on Crete, mixed in with bronze plaques telling of the horrors of the Second World War, whole villages of women, in preference to being raped and killed by the Germans, grasping hands and leaping off cliffs just as they had done three thousand years earlier. She could not imagine the women of Chinook joining hands and singing as they leaped off Chinook's clay cliffs to their deaths. Lying there on her blue-and-white canvas deck chair, she thought that without a history fraught with war, murder, blood, sacrifices, with gods and goddesses replete with human desires and passions, it was impossible to imagine any of these things except as insanity. She wondered if the people of Chinook, placid and smug as she remembers them, were better off without them or not. They were wealthier, but they were not better off.

Day after sweltering, dry day she parked Dimitri's car on the hard-packed dirt lots, paid her entrance fee and wandered through the palace at Knossos, the ruins of the ancient city of Gortyn, the wonders of the palace at Mali, the palace-city of Phaistos, the long-buried town of Gournia, and a dozen other sites whose names she'd forgotten. A whole universe of human desire and its fulfilment or failure existing before her own world had been dreamt of. It seemed to her then that if she could only sink into that city's or palace's life as it was three thousand years earlier, she would come to feel at home, because of all the things that counted, what could possibly be different?

She walked the ruins in the baking heat, her guidebook in one hand, her bottle of water in the crook of her arm, sliding slowly back into the Minoan world, then, hours later pulling herself out of it to get in Dimitri's car and drive herself back to the whitewashed villa set on the rocky cliff overlooking Homer's "wine-dark sea." And she would ponder what it all meant — she from a country without a past, at least not for her people, cut off irrevocably from her European ancestry. Not able to make a new world, try as they might, and the United States always with them, overshadowing their own possibilities even while sinking further and further into greed, violence, and corruption.

And yet the clean sweep of the prairie; it spoke to her sometimes in her dreams, whispering to her of its purity, of its power to sweep away history, to outlast all histories, to be stronger than the mightiest king, stronger even than any god — or perhaps, as the Native people said, it was itself a god. She thought that she had somehow fallen into the dreams of the pioneers, her own grandparents and great-grandparents who imagined the land as much as they saw it, and then set about creating that dream. Then her heart ached and she longed for the wind rushing through the grass, for its sweet and pungent fragrance in spring, for the liquid call of the meadowlark on a summer morning, for the lonesome melodics of a band of coyotes carolling from a windswept grassy hill to the star-ridden sky.

She thought — she thought a lot of things: that only land is more powerful than history, but only if it is not wholly transformed by the hands of human beings; that maybe some day she would be able to go home, followed, always, by the fear that the home she dreamt of was no longer there, the grass had been ploughed up, the buffalo were dead, there were fences everywhere, and the stink of diesel fuel and oil wells tainted the once-clean air.

Abubech is speaking to her. She comes to herself with a start, looks questioningly toward her, but Abubech has turned back to Fatima, they're laughing together. Pulled into her fatigue, she knows some kind of respite is needed, but she isn't sure what would help. With her money almost gone, she won't squander what's left on a holiday. When she has only enough left for a plane ticket home, will she buy one and go? Nausea grips her again.

"I have no past," she'd said to Rob Sargent as they sat together on the terrace of the café all the workers frequented in the town near their camp. "I renounce my personal history." And when he'd been angry with her, had shouted at her, causing the local men sitting against the back wall to swivel their heads and stare, she'd said, "In a country like Ethiopia what is the use of a personal history? A personal history is meaningless in Ethiopia." She had meant much more than merely that cut off from one's own country it became meaningless, or there was no one to share it with, but that was the significance Rob decided to take.

"Share it with me," he'd said. "I'll tell you mine." But she didn't want to hear Rob's history, it was too intimate, it would be more than she could bear. Nor did she want to know why he'd come to Ethiopia. If he told her, she was sure she would be able to read his weakness in what he said, and she didn't want to know in what way he was weak. It took all her energy to deal with her own, she had none left for anybody else's. It seemed to her that his red hair shot sparks in the light falling from the bulbs strung up against the back wall, his blue eyes darkened, boring into hers, searching, trying to fasten themselves to her.

"I will stay with you," he had said. "I will follow you everywhere. I will not let you keep me away." He had tried to break down her barriers thinking, she knew, that if he could, she would be able to love him. One night on the dark road to her house he had stopped walking, caught her wrist, and facing her, holding her by her upper arms, he had said from between clenched teeth, "I'll make you pregnant so you'll have to be with me." She couldn't move then, couldn't get her breath. She hadn't bled since the day she'd set foot in Ethiopia.

Rob had done his best but in the end, full of a bewildered, raw anger, he had given up and gone back to Canada without her. A year later a Canadian nurse who'd gone home on leave, then returned, had mentioned casually to Lannie that she'd run into him — he was married and his wife was pregnant.

Lannie had rushed outside and vomited, had managed to finish the day at work, but then she'd stayed in her darkened bedroom for three days, retching every time she tried to get up, until finally the sickness had worn itself out. Had she loved Rob? Or was it something to do with — she could hardly bring herself to think of it —

her abortion that she'd had so long ago? Even though she will always be grateful to Iris for making her have it, she is ashamed in some dark, unclear way that she will not examine.

Mornings now, when she rises, buttoning her blouse sometimes takes more strength than she can find. She has to sit down on her bed until moments later she notices her hands effortlessly fastening the buttons. Thinking it's her negligent eating habits, she has been trying to eat more, or better. But the same thing happens when she stands in the door of her kitchenette — she's too tired to cook a piece of meat or peel an orange or tear lettuce for a salad.

Or is she ill? She's had enough of doctors, wouldn't go to one even if she were covered with festering sores. Poking and prodding and asking stupid, cruel questions, and all the while she can see in their eyes that she's a failure, she's human refuse. But she doesn't know what's the matter with her — I'm a basket case, she tells herself. Maybe I should just go home.

Home. Which is where? Saskatoon where she lived for three years while she went to university? She remembers a moment: dancing, her body fitted against the slowly moving body of a man she has just met, she knows by some careful chemistry he's the one she'll go home with — the heat from the crowd, the flashing coloured lights, the racket of the guitars, saxophone, keyboard, drums, so loud it threads its way through her skin, laces itself around her molecules to lift her — no, she never wants to see that city again.

Iris and Barney's farm where her father left her that day so long ago without even asking them if they wanted to raise a half-raised child? She can't go back to them, begging them to take her back in when she's still a failure, a liar, and a betrayer —

Her childhood rises up before her: a trim little wooden house with a neat white picket fence around it, tiger lilies and dahlias along the sidewalk, lilac bushes and tall poplars in the backyard, and a brick barbecue pit her father built, stripped to the waist and sweat pouring off him, Dillon beside him asking question after question in his piping little boy's voice, while her mother sat on the back steps fanning herself with a magazine against the summer heat, her other hand rocking the carriage where Misty lay asleep.

Quickly she opens her eyes and shifts to a sitting position. Fatima has finished roasting the beans and, seated, is grinding them, the mortar and pestle in front of her. Fatima's baby begins to wail in a thin voice. It isn't healthy, Lannie has heard enough unhealthy babies to know. Immediately she sees a child lying on a pallet in the tent for the gravely ill. A girl about six years old, reduced to skin stretched over bone, barely conscious, in the last stages of starvation. Mariam. She wills herself to remember Mariam as she was the last time she saw her: healthy again, her plump cheeks, her shy dark eyes, her sweet smile — Fatima brings the child around from the nest in her shawl against her back and puts the baby against her breast. The whimpering stops.

After the camps she'd dreamt about the children every night for a year, would wake sweating, filled with a heavy, nameless dread. The endless, silent lines of people waiting patiently for rations that often gave out before everyone was fed, the children — "This is an old country," an Ethiopian doctor had said to her — "You've no idea how old it is, nor how complicated are the reasons for this, or that it will happen again and again and again, as it has in the past. How much good do you think you do, you NGOs with your tonnes of grain and your doctors and your nurses? You feed people today so they can die tomorrow. Tomorrow, if it isn't more starvation that kills them, it will be guerrilla fighters or government soldiers who shoot them. Or they will die under torture in the country's prisons. You don't know this country; you have no idea."

"Why are you here then?" she'd replied. And when he turned away she had, for a second, thought herself vindicated.

"Where else to be?" he said over his shoulder, smiling humourlessly. She was rocked by that remark, it expressed a sentiment she was beginning to understand. Where else indeed?

"Tell me how you got to this country, why you are here." Abubech had asked her this during that first interview almost a year ago now. She had been surprised by it, having already answered it a thousand times since her arrival; she'd told Europeans — nurses, doctors, reporters — she'd told Ethiopians — government officials, friends, strangers. She was about to give what she privately thought of as her short answer which she knew from experience satisfied, but stopped herself. It would not satisfy Abubech.

Involuntarily, her hand went up to her face, the heel pressed against her eyes, her fingers swept her hair back. "I came because it seemed to me imperative that I not turn away from such suffering, that I do what I could, no matter how little. I don't know why it seemed that way to me. I'd never felt like that before. It was as if I had suddenly found a way to — " She paused, unsure of what to say, chose finally the truth. "A way to either end my own suffering or to bury it in the greater suffering of others. I believe I thought it would save me." Then she'd laughed, appalled at what she'd said, dizzy with it.

Abubech said simply, "How did you get a visa?"

"I couldn't get a visa, I couldn't find a relief agency that would take me. So I wrote to some churches I knew about in Saskatchewan and Alberta. I offered to go to Ethiopia at my own expense to write about the relief effort. To find out what was happening to the grain they were sending here. I asked them to get me press credentials so I could get into the country. That's how I got here. And after I'd been here a while and had seen the relief camps, then I knew there were a dozen small ways I could help even though I wasn't a doctor or a nurse. So I worked in the camps through late 1984 and into 1985 until the people dispersed and went back home."

"And after that?" Abubech asked.

"I worked for development agencies. A couple of them, office work mostly. And I did other things. I left once. I went to Greece for a year. In '88 and '89." She doesn't mention — didn't even know it at the time, somehow Dimitri kept it from her — that while she had briefly escaped to his villa, Ethiopia was going through another drought and famine.

Abubech had not taken her eyes off Lannie's face while she made this reply, and there was perhaps the faintest hint of softening in its firm set as she gazed at her. It suddenly occurred to Lannie that Abubech already knew her short history in this country, someone had told her, or after Lannie had called for this interview, she had gone about finding out.

"You have to understand," Abubech told her, "that I talk only with the women, that my work is to document specifically the role of the women as farmers and to gather information on how they choose the seeds to be kept for seed for another year, why they choose them, and how they store them. We need that information because the women farmers are the only ones who have it and what they do is vital to the continuance of biodiversity. This has not been acknowledged or even noticed before. I gather that information, but I also take the opportunity to find out other things about their lives. It is a base of information that will one day be used to better their lot in life."

Yet Lannie had to admit, when Abubech had asked, that even in the relatively speaking prosperous farming community she knew in Canada, the women traditionally, and for the most part, worked harder than the men.

"The men work hard," she said, trying to be fair. "During seeding and harvesting they put in long hours, but the women have to look after the children and the house and grow a garden and look after the harvesting and preserving of it. Lots of them still sew clothing and wash and iron the clothes, and patch them if they need it. Of course, they have all kinds of labour-saving devices these days, not like these women, but still they put in longer days than the men. They do the grocery shopping and cook all the meals, and drive the kids to hockey practice and music lessons and do community work and have part-time jobs if they can find them, and most of them help in the fields and the corrals too: they drive grain trucks or ride horses or combine or bale hay. And when it's mealtime, they go into the house and the husband puts his feet up and reads the paper, and they go to the kitchen to start cooking."

"I thought North American women were supposed to be emancipated," Abubech had said.

"No women anywhere are fully emancipated," Lannie had replied emphatically. This is about the only subject she can think of on which she has no ambivalence. "But if there can be degrees of liberation, for the most part, farm women are at the bottom of the heap in North America too. But they'll never admit it. They're disgustingly pious about their lives. I don't know where they get that bilge from. Churches, maybe." When she got like this Abubech always gave her the same look, perplexed, questioning a little.

"What is bilge?"

"It means stupid talk," Lannie said. "In this case, pious untruths. All about a wife's duty and what makes a good wife and a good mother. All that — nonsense."

"When you marry — " Abubech began.

"I'll never marry." She was hard on men, she made them suffer. It killed her to see how she made them suffer, but she couldn't seem to act any other way. So she tries to stay away from men. Since Tim, since Rob Sargent — it seems the only course. And, of course, Dimitri. So rather than adding year after year, man after man, to the load of guilt she staggers under, since Dimitri, she has become a nun. That's what she is, a regular Mother Teresa.

In the end, Abubech had taken her on as a sort of apprentice and for a trial period only, which she eventually had made permanent when Lannie had made herself as useful as she possibly could, even setting up the slide projector for Abubech when she had a speech to make, even carrying her briefcase for her, even driving her sometimes, following her through field after dusty field under the hot sun into hut after shabby, empty hut, to wait silently, making herself invisible, while Abubech went about her work.

She is drifting into sleep and shakes herself awake. She has never fallen asleep before during one of these interviews; she's surprised at herself. The drone of Abubech's and Fatima's voices that has been background to her ruminations now seems to grow louder, to break into chunks of sound that she recognizes as speech that she should be listening to. She picks up her pen again and directs her attention to them, trying to concentrate. Abubech turns to Lannie, raising her voice a little.

"She says that she cares for the animals also. They have five goats and six cows. Did you get that?" Among other matters, in this survey they are counting the number of animals per household for which the women and their children are responsible. It's an endless load these women carry, Lannie and Abubech constantly shake their heads over it to each other — in bad years often while eating only one meal a day: hauling water and finding fuel and bringing it home consume many hours of the day, never mind the food preparation by the most primitive methods which take forever, so there's little time left for anything that might properly be called child-rearing. But most of all are the hours spent in the fields seeding, transplanting, weeding, watering, harvesting, and threshing. But nobody calls them farmers, only their husbands, who do less than half the work of farming are farmers.

"Two," Abubech says. "She's been very lucky. She's lost only two children." Fatima is pouring water over the ground coffee beans and setting the mixture on the fire. Lannie doesn't think she'll be able to drink any and that will be an insult. Why not just admit she's sick. But the thought of saying so makes her cringe. She's praying the nausea will go away as silently as it's come.

Watching Fatima work, Lannie wonders as she always does, if this woman has undergone the practice euphemistically known as female circumcision. It makes her skin crawl every time she thinks of it, but Abubech will approach the topic in each interview, and she has to write down the replies, if the woman will reply, and if, first of all, Abubech has judged this is a woman she can ask. And she will ask, too, if her girl children have undergone it, who did it to them, and if the mother requested it to be done, and worst of all, how extensive the operation had been. And if any of her children had died because of it.

Lannie's stomach turns over again and she measures the distance with her eyes from where she sits to the hut's entrance. If she has to, can she make it in time? She can tell by the smooth way their voices mingle and part that Fatima and Abubech are merely conversing in a friendly way now, that the interview is suspended. She relaxes, leans back and lets her head rest against the mud-and-stick wall.

She has been drowsing again, not even realizing it, when the powerful aroma of coffee is right under her nose and she sits up abruptly, nearly knocking the small cup out of Fatima's hand. What has she been thinking of? She's frightened, unaccountably she is drenched with perspiration.

"*Buna, buna*," Fatima, crouched in front of her, is crooning holding out the small cup and saucer.

"Oh, God, I'm sorry!" Lannie says, but Fatima is laughing, apparently not noticing how upset Lannie is, or maybe she just thinks this is how *ferenjis* wake. She's saying something else now, she has been calling gently to Lannie.

"She says, 'Wake up,'" Abubech says. Lannie takes the demitasse and saucer and, remembering to bow, says, "*Betam amesegnalehu*" — thank you very much — which now rolls off her tongue easily. As Fatima turns to go back to her seat and Abubech lowers her head to coo at the baby she is holding, Lannie tips a bit of the thick, black liquid onto the ground behind her leg. She finds her nausea at the odour is not so bad, though the *tukul* is redolent with the fragrance of coffee, her sensors for smell must be flattening out.

Abubech has decided that they will go up to Tigray. Their NGO has no project there, but the new government, Tigrayans themselves, are busy with reforestation projects, the terracing of fields — around two-thirds of the country's farmland is on slopes of twenty-five degrees or more — and dam building and irrigation projects. They are even closing off a few of the worst-damaged fields to people and animals, to give them a chance to recover from centuries of overuse. On the lookout for any innovative projects that might help to provide for future food security, they've expressed interest in the project of which Abubech represents only a part. The men who run the project — the administrators, plant geneticists, and field specialists — have already been up there. Now Lannie and Abubech will make a preliminary survey of the area and draw up a plan of attack.

"Data, always more data," Abubech said. "We can only hope it will eventually translate into some kind of action — beyond the preservation of biodiversity, I mean. Into respect for these women farmers who do most of the work; into concerns for their education, their health, their . . ."

But Lannie had stopped listening.

At least part of the reason Lannie stays with her is so she can study this hope of Abubech's, what it really is, how to get some herself. She has lost her own entirely, afraid what will happen if she cuts loose from Abubech's lifeline. She thinks again of Iris and Barney. Lately she has been thinking of sending them a letter or a postcard, just to let them know she isn't dead, but the thought of what to say makes that grinding weariness overcome her again, so that she can hardly support the weight of the cup and saucer.

She sets them on the sheepskin beside her and leans back, letting the soft voices of the two women, the occasional gurgle from the now contented baby, lull her. She knows she's drifting again, falling into sleep. She thinks of her work, of the answers she should be writing down, but she can't nudge herself into caring. Abubech will remember, or will write them down herself. Then she drops so deeply into sleep that even her dreams are pale layers far above the abyss into which she's sunk.

Holy Fire

Tim Quennell's apartment is on Spadina Avenue. Iris is just thinking that the neighbourhood looks pretty poor and rough when her taxi pulls up in front of a small grocery store with a handprinted sign in the window in Chinese characters.

"It's over there," the driver says, pointing at a door with the street number above it beside the store's entrance. She pays him, hesitating over the tip — too much? too little? — gets out, and goes up the sidewalk to the door. She's surprised to find it's unlocked, pushes it open and is confronted by a few feet of dingy hall and a steep, high flight of wooden steps. The walls are scarred and nicked and sport scrawls of faded graffiti, as if somebody had tried to scrub them off. A dusty spiderweb hangs from the ceiling and the ancient black rubber treads covering the wooden stairs have ragged pieces missing. Nervously, she creaks up the stairs to the upstairs hall where she walks slowly, stopping at the first of the two doors. She knocks.

The door opens and Tim Quennell stands there staring down at her.

"Iris!" he says, "I mean, Mrs. Christie." He's just as awkward as he was when she met him at least eight years earlier. No, ten. He looks a little older, but unmistakably the Tim she remembers sitting on the side of the bed in her guest room, his head in his hands, *I love her*, and Lannie unconscious in the hospital. "What are you doing here?" he asks. "Come in." He's smiling as he stands back to let her pass.

The room she enters is surprisingly bright and clean. A potted lemon tree stands in a corner, its precisely shaped, dark green leaves etched in the sunlight against the white-painted walls; a red and blue suncatcher revolves slowly in the upper part of the window that looks out over shabby rooftops, casting a shower of coloured light. Music is playing softly in the background, Bach — she recognizes it from long-ago, fruitless piano lessons. Two posters hang on the wall to Tim's left: a photograph of an Asian woman with long, straight hair playing a grand piano, with a Sold Out sign pasted across her back, and beside it, a faded, slightly tattered painting of a young, bright-faced Chinese man in a Mao jacket saluting, Chinese characters running down — or up — one side. The room is a kitchen and every surface — the table, the chairs, the counter — is covered with untidily stacked books, magazines, and papers.

"I'm looking for Lannie," she says abruptly, turning to him, tilting her face up to his, seeing again the thick, pale lashes, the unkempt, white-blond hair, the crookedly buttoned, rumpled shirt. He's looking intently at her. Even with the window closed the steady roar of traffic is audible behind the music.

"Lannie?" he says, taken aback.

"Yes," Iris says. "Do you know where she is?"

"Not here. She left here — I mean, Toronto — at least seven or eight years ago." He's obviously both puzzled and surprised to find Iris doesn't know where Lannie is.

"Where then?" Iris asks, in her anxiety and her confusion — the tumult of the airport, the ride downtown in the taxi, the huge hotel — forgetting mannerliness, forgetting Tim's feelings.

He's not smiling now. They stare at each other and Iris begins inwardly to crumble.

"Would you like some tea?" he asks, after a second. Iris turns away from him, momentarily at a loss. She wants Barney, and thinks, irrationally, just like him not to be around when I need him.

She sets her purse on the pile of books on a corner of the table and sits down hard on a yellow-painted wooden chair without being asked. He turns on a burner under the kettle and glances at her over his shoulder.

"Hasn't she been keeping in touch?" he asks finally. He occupies himself restacking books, lifting them from under her purse to pile them higher on a chair and setting two small, fragile blue-and-white

Chinese cups on the table. For the first time she notices the old manual typewriter beside her. The piece of paper rising from it has short lines of type on it, a poem. Below them and outside, a siren begins to wail. She waits till it passes before she tries to speak.

"It's been a long time, years, since we heard from her. Her uncle — Barney — is — he's — dead. Lannie doesn't even know." Tim is studying her with a gentle expression. He says softly, "I'm so sorry." Suddenly what she hears in the echo of his voice are the voices at Barney's funeral saying to her, over and over again, *Sorry for your loss, Sorry for your loss.* It confuses her and she says again, "Where is she?" hearing the quaver in her own voice.

"I don't know," he says simply. "When she left here — when she left me" — he corrects himself — "she didn't write to me either. When did you lose track of her?" He's curious now, looking off into space, his eyes sad. Visibly he shakes himself, and when he speaks his voice is crisp, efficient. "She thought the world of you and her uncle. It's hard to believe she wouldn't even write."

Iris is remembering the whole sorry mess, how Lannie had come home from university, pregnant, although Iris didn't know it, how she'd phoned Tim to come, that was when Iris guessed Tim must be the baby's father, her suicide attempt before Tim even arrived. Then, how happy Lannie seemed to be the day she left their home for good, the abortion over and done with, her future open to her. "She did keep in touch at first. She worked in Vancouver for a while, in a library and then — "

"Then she came to Saskatoon, where I was and we started living together. We came here, to Toronto." She waits for him to go on with his story, but he has fallen silent and is staring into space again, forgetful of her presence.

The kettle begins to whistle, he gets up slowly, more like an old man than one who can't be much over thirty — about the same age as Jay, she finds herself thinking. *I'm a poet,* he'd said to Barney, in a dogged, angry way — and pours the water into the blue-and-white teapot that matches the handleless cups, carries it back to the table, pushes aside some magazines, and sets it between them. The door at the end of the room opens slowly, Iris catches a glimpse of a shabby red sofa and a desk with stacks of neatly piled paper on it, and another young man enters, staring down at a book open in his hands. He's wearing a neatly pressed blue denim shirt and khaki pants and his lustreless black hair is perfectly barbered, she can see the teethmarks of his comb. He lifts his head — Iris sees he's partly Chinese — and seeing Iris there, looks surprised and then embarrassed.

"I made it, Allan," Tim says quietly. "Want a cup?"

"Uh, no," Allan says, and glances with some curiosity at Iris, but Tim makes no move to introduce her. The glance he and Tim exchange stuns Iris: not smiles exactly, but carrying a mute intimacy that puzzles her. Allan goes back into the living room without looking at her again, shutting the door quietly behind him.

"My roommate," Tim says. "We edit a poetry journal together. He works in there, I work in here." He laughs softly. "He's neater than I am. We drive each other crazy." Suddenly Iris wonders, are they a couple? But how can that be? She gives up the question as quickly as she has asked it.

Tim stares down into his teacup, deep in thought, or perhaps, Iris thinks, he's remembering Lannie, how she was in those days. When he spoke to her, fixing her clear yellow-brown eyes on him as if, until she heard his voice, she hadn't remembered he was there.

"We were happy, I guess. For a while, anyway. We both had Mcjobs" — Iris doesn't know what this means, but lets it pass — "And she was finishing up her degree at U of T, at night, you know? I was writing a lot then. I don't know, I just could write then." He falls silent again, Iris waits. "Then she started seeing pictures on TV, awful stuff. You must have seen them too. For a while there you couldn't avoid them, they were everywhere." Iris sorts through possibilities in her mind and gives up. "The famine in Africa," he says, as if he has realized she doesn't know what he's talking about. "In Ethiopia. You remember? It was in '84. Late in the year." Iris thinks, In 1986 we went to Expo in Vancouver. "At first she just looked at them, you know, like we all did. But then, after a while, it was all she talked about. It was like it haunted her. She was — she was obsessed." He's lost in his memory for a moment. "The shot that I think tipped her over the edge was of some aid workers loading babies — infants, orphans — into the back of a van to take them to an orphanage, I guess. Like they were so many cabbages. They were all crying and nobody was even trying to comfort them. Just loading them — it was the most awful thing." He pauses, visibly swallowing. "Anyway, she talked me into going to Ottawa with her to volunteer to go there — to Ethiopia — to help, as relief workers, you know?"

"What?" Iris says, surprised. She recalls Angela's postcard. "What about Iraklion?"

"What about it?" he replies. "I don't know anything about Iraklion." When Iris doesn't respond, he goes on. "Of course they turned us down, we couldn't do anything. We weren't nurses or doctors or nutritionists or whatever, and half of Canada was lined up to volunteer. And nobody knew how to do anything." He sighs again and puts his hand on his teacup, forgetting it's empty. Iris is frozen to her chair, the image of Lannie crouched in front of the TV, suffering anguish, when Iris had been picturing her happy at last, overwhelms her.

"We came back here, finally," he said. "She was okay for a while. I kept telling her, you did what you could, you give them half your money, you can't do anything else. But she wouldn't listen. She quit her job at this bookstore when we decided to go to Ottawa, and she couldn't get another one, or she didn't try. Things were going wrong for her. I could see it — she couldn't sleep, and she hardly ate anything. She'd get this look on her face — Then one morning I got up and she was gone. Note on kitchen table." He recites, "'Dear Tim, have gone to Africa. Love, Lannie.' End of note. End of life." But there's a wry note in his voice at this last, and Iris finds she's relieved to hear it. He's not quite so bare to fortune, is this Tim, as the one who sat in her guest bedroom and cried for Lannie.

Tim rouses himself and pours tea for both of them, slopping a little into Iris's saucer.

"You tried to find her — earlier, I mean?" he asks. Iris shakes her head no, and when she sees his look of surprise, she says, "Because — " Because why? She can't remember. Because Lannie was so smart and so capable, so full of hope when she left; because she didn't like people trying to get close to her; because, after all, it was her father she'd gone to, underlining that she and Barney were only stopgaps. She thinks of her own avoidance of the whole subject, not even being sure how long Lannie has been gone, her refusal to think clearly about Lannie's disappearance, to deal with it. She feels sure that whatever it was she did when she was raising Lannie had a lot to do with Lannie's going away and not coming back. She's afraid Tim can see right through her to her weaknesses, her shallowness, of which she's only beginning to catch an unwelcome glimpse herself.

"For a while there were letters. And phone calls. We sent her money. In fact," now it's coming back to her, how could she have forgotten? "In fact, Barney set up a bank account for her in Vancouver when she was there and put money in it. A lot of money," she says. "I wondered about it at the time, but he — got angry. He said he didn't want her having to beg, and he wanted to be sure she'd be okay. He said she'd never get any help from Howard. She'd find that out soon enough. So he put a lot of money in an account for her and he told me he didn't want to hear another word about it. As if I might try to stop him. I just didn't know why he did it, that was all. I just wanted to know why. It was my father's place after all, when you think about it, more mine than his — " She halts the rush of words, surely she'd never said such a thing to Barney himself. She hopes not. And she didn't mind the money, God knows they had more money than they knew what to do with, and she did love Lannie. It was just that he didn't even ask her. "That was the last time you heard from her?" He nods.

"I heard about her, though. I phoned Oxfam and CARE and a half a dozen relief agencies in Ottawa, you know, looking for the ones that sent people to Ethiopia during the famine. Finally I found somebody who remembered her name. She sent a message to somebody in the field and about six months later I got an answer. She was in Addis Ababa then. That was six, seven years ago or so. But where she went after that, I don't know." He pauses. "Or why." He laughs, humourlessly, lifting his eyes to Iris's, and momentarily forgetting her own guilt, she finds herself joining him. That was Lannie for you. Try as you might, you couldn't reach her. Did Barney reach her better than I did? she wonders, thinking again of the money. No, he was angry when he did it, not with Lannie, but with me. Did he blame me for the way she couldn't seem to right herself, or did he blame himself?

Tim yawns, and hands clasped, stretches his arms upward in a way that's almost contented, gazing out the window to the clutter of shabby rooftops and beyond them, to the blank-faced glass towers of the city. She thinks of Allan, sees with something close to envy that Tim has succeeded in putting Lannie behind him.

As she's standing in the door to say a final goodbye, Tim says, in a rush, "Why did she try to kill herself?" It feels to Iris as if the air between them has suddenly heated up so that it's hard to breathe. She's seeing the wild car ride, the way Lannie's long, reddish-gold hair bounced like a rag doll's as the car bumped over ruts with Barney clenching the wheel, trying to get to the hospital in Chinook before it was too late. Her face white as the sheets of her hospital bed and that look in her eyes, as if there was nobody there, nobody home at all, just a big hollow inside her. And Barney wouldn't come to the hospital, not for a couple of days, Lannie asking after him and Iris not knowing what to say. He did blame himself, she thinks, or else he felt responsible for his brother's failures as a father. Maybe it was his own life — he and Luke and Howard fighting all the time, never resolving anything, and Lannie the offspring of all that rage — so that he couldn't sort things out clearly either.

"You lived with her and she never told you?" she says. It's on the tip of her tongue to tell him Lannie was pregnant, but she stops herself. Lannie had never told her who the father was; Iris hadn't asked, assuming it was Tim since he was her boyfriend. No, if Lannie wouldn't, she can't tell him. At last she says, "It wasn't something that made sense, not then, not now." He studies her face and she holds it open to him, to let him see she's not hiding anything even though she is, and when he's finished his searching he seems relieved, although still baffled.

"Will you tell me where she is if you find her?" he asks. "I'd just like to know she's okay." He stares down at his slippers, his hands in his jeans pockets. "Sometimes I miss her," he says, and flushes, then shrugs.

It occurs to her that a picture of Lannie might help her in her search. "Do you have a picture of her I could borrow?" He's thought-ful for a second, then says, "Yeah, I do. Wait." He goes rapidly across the room, through the door into the living room, leaving it ajar. She hears a soft exchange of voices, the bang of a drawer, then Tim is back. "Here." It's a colour shot of Lannie sitting on the red sofa in the other room, the lamp on the table beside it lit so that one side of her face is clear and the other in shadow. She's smiling in that distant, bemused way she had, her eyes not on the camera, but off to one side, gazing at something not in the picture. Iris thanks Tim and tucks it away carefully in her purse.

"That person who told you she was in Ethiopia — what was her name? Maybe I could get more up-to-date information from her."

He hesitates, looks down at his feet in their worn embroidered silk slippers, incongruous on such big feet, and says, "I can't remember her name." He's silent for a second longer, thinking. "But she phoned some guy who'd just come back. He was actually the one who knew where she was. I talked to him on the phone. What was his name?" He stares into space over her head. "Sargent, that was it. Rob Sargent. In Ottawa."

"Ottawa," Iris repeats.

"He was an engineer, but he came back and started his own consulting business. Seemed like a nice guy. Said he'd run across her in the camps."

Iris quickly reopens her purse, takes out her address book, prints the name, and puts it back.

"You've been a big help, Tim. I'm sorry if I —" she hesitates, "opened old wounds. I mean — "

"No, no," he asssures her. "I've never stopped wondering about her. I'm glad you're looking for her."

She goes back down the hall and the steep stairs with the little piles of dirt and dead bugs in the corners, past the faded, illegible graffiti and the cobweb quivering gently in the still, dusty air, back out onto the street which hits her, with its noise and motion, like a physical blow. A taxi, its driver seeing her standing there at curbside in her smart suit, swerves out of the traffic and pulls up beside her. She gets in and names her hotel.

So many ideas are racing through her mind, Iris doesn't quite catch one before another has taken its place, and adding to the mental tumult is the muddle the cab is rushing her through: the streets thick with people of all races — at home there are only white faces — the incessant din and rush of the traffic, the signs everywhere demanding attention, the store windows, the contents of which she catches only glimpses, books, clothing, people sitting at tables in restaurants and coffee shops, dishes, furniture, computers, jewellery, shoes, paintings, posters, magazines. It's overwhelming. Then the taxi is swerving to the curb, slowing to a stop, and a man in a smart, navy pin-striped suit carrying a shiny leather briefcase is opening the door for her, not even looking at her, he wants her cab. She pays, clambers out, and pushes her way through the revolving glass doors of her hotel, hardly seeing where she's going.

She closes the door of her room behind her and leans her back against it as if she has been on the run from something and has found refuge. But the room, decorated in beiges and creams probably to soothe the weary traveller, oppresses her. She walks to the window, pulls back the curtain and looks out, but her window faces a wall of other windows, so she turns away again and begins to pace, trying to think what to do next.

Should she go to the airport and buy a ticket for Ethiopia? She thinks of Africa, what little she knows: wet green jungles, zebra and lions, drums, stately black men in colourful robes, poverty and mystery and — She's frightened, it's too far away, it's dangerous, the people there don't speak English. She should simply go to the airport, catch the first plane back home and start writing letters. But now she remembers herself the day she left home writing her name in the dust on the piano, as if to convince herself that in a Barney-less world she did still exist.

She imagines arriving home, starting over again with Barney gone and Lannie lost, somewhere: it's like having an itch you can't scratch; worse, it's like knowing there's something you have to do, but can't think what it is. And until you do, you can't go forward, and circumstances won't let you go back. It would be impossible to live like that for the rest of her life. No, it's clear she can't go home.

She kicks off her shoes and lies down on the bed, but her mind won't stop going round and round. Lannie might not be in Africa any more. If she isn't, how will she ever find out where she is? She supposes she'll have to go to Ottawa . . . Finally her eyelids drift shut, and she allows herself to sleep.

Everything is too large, too close to get a clear look at, too richly coloured. It's a country more real than the everyday one she inhabits. Howard moves around the log cabin beneath the blue mountains, Misty goes past, retreating toward a red barn, Jay bends over her, the torrent of black water in front of Barney's cabin swirls up around her and it's cold, it's tugging hard on her, trying to pull her under.

She opens her eyes slowly into the early evening shadows. Her dream has left her feeling weak, as if she has been ill. She waits for her strength to return, for colour to seep back into the room; it's too pale a world, this so-called real one.

She clicks on the bedside lamp and the room grows distinct, the dark wooden furniture taking on a richness of colour in the lamp's warm yellow glow, the cream walls turning apricot in its light. As she comes fully awake she sits up, her neck aching from lying awkwardly against the pillow, and tries to think what to do next. Beyond not going to Ethiopia she has no ideas. Oh, yes, Ottawa, but her head feels heavy and thick and she could cry with the disappointment of not finding Lannie here, in a Canadian city, where lost nieces ought to be. And yet, she tells herself, she had not really thought Lannie would be easy to find. Her own loneliness feels enlarged, room-size, and she wishes she were home, planting her garden, that Barney was inside, sitting at the kitchen table doing his books, or roaring his way across the field in his big tractor.

Or in bed with her. Her memory, always out to catch her off-guard, flashes back to the first year of their marriage, to the love they felt for each other that was so bound up with lovemaking that some mornings when she woke, Barney asleep against her, their legs entwined, she could hardly tell where her body ended and his began.

Their sex life had been good for all those years. But she won't think now about what had gone wrong.

She decides to see what Ramona has to say about what she should do, but the phone rings and rings into silence and finally Iris sets the receiver back on its cradle. The only person she knows in this whole city, other than Tim, is Jay Anselm. She locates the phone book, searches rapidly through it, and to her surprise and relief finds his number. Then she paces a bit, trying to decide whether she should phone him or not. He kissed me, she tells herself. I showed him my home, he should be willing to do the same for me. Even though she knows these are only excuses she's making up for doing something really because she wants to; carried on their reasonableness, she dials quickly, before she changes her mind.

"Iris!" he says, surprised. "What are you doing here?" Her body flushes with warmth at the sound of his voice, at his apparent delight at hearing hers.

"I have this niece," she says, "and she — I lost track of her years ago — her last address is here, in Toronto. I just made up my mind it was time to find her. Because, well — with Barney gone — " She falters.

"I understand," he interrupts. "And if I don't, you can fill me in. That is — are you alone? Where are you staying?" She tells him she's alone, knows no one in the city but him, gives him the name of her hotel.

"Nice place," he says. "I heard you're rich — a rich widow." She laughs nervously, embarrassed, a bit irritated. "I'll come and get you. Have you had dinner?"

"No," she says, feeling shy, wondering if she's supposed to say she has, but she knows that even if she had eaten she'd pretend she hadn't just to see him again. But all he says is, "I can be there in twenty minutes."

When she hangs up the phone, she sits for a minute, happy, then unsettled by this surge of elation, doubtful. He's almost half your age, she reminds herself, and Barney has hardly been gone two months. But then pleasure at seeing Jay again wells up, casting her uneasiness into shadow.

She hurries into the bathroom, washes her face, puts on fresh makeup, changes from her suit to a slightly wrinkled blue linen skirt and matching blouse, low-heeled summer shoes, and her light blue blazer. Studying herself in the mirror, she thinks she looks attractive, but casual enough that he won't think she's trying to impress him. Feeling like a teenager about to go out on a date, she is for a brief instant hurtled back through the years to pacing in her room waiting for her date's arrival, after an hour — no, she has to confess, it usually took her two hours — to complete her ritual bathing, plucking, brushing, perfuming, dressing, undressing, dressing again, preening in front of her mirror. And the moments when, snuggled against her date at the movies or in his car, his arm heavy around her shoulders, feeling low in her abdomen such lightness, such breathless possibility, not knowing what it was, but feeling its rightness, its — She pauses, thinking, And I still need a man, if not in the same way I did when I was a girl. The realization sobers her.

He's pushing open the big glass doors as she steps off the elevator; they spot each other at once. She halts, overcome with nervousness, and he strides toward her. He's wearing a black T-shirt today, under the same worn black sportscoat, and jeans and his cowboy boots, which she notices he has cleaned. What looked odd in Chinook is exactly right in this setting. He looks at ease, sophisticated, rakish. When he reaches her, he gives her a swift, brotherly hug that contains no hint of desire and she's left midway between disappointment and relief. He looks so young tonight, his eyes are such a clear, guileless brown; surely everyone will take him for her son.

"We can eat at this great little place I know — if you like Indian food." Without waiting for her answer he takes her arm and leads her away from the bank of polished-brass elevators, past the low blond wood table with its oversized vase of pink and white silk flowers and the overstuffed green sofas, and out onto the street. "How are you?" he asks. "Have you checked that address you had for her already? Or will you do it tomorrow? It's this way."

They cross the wide, busy street, Jay hurrying her, and turn down a narrower, quieter side street, walk a short distance past shuttered, dark brick buildings and enter a shabby café, brightly lit and full of chattering people seated at small tables crowded close together. The smell of curry and spices she can't identify weight the air. A young woman wearing a dark red sari leads them to a table. Iris doesn't try to answer Jay's question until they're seated and she has gone away. "I've been to that address. Her old boyfriend still lives there. He said she's gone from there a long time. He isn't sure where she is, but he gave me a lead." But then the woman returns with menus and glasses of water, Jay orders beer for himself, wine for her, accepts the menus, turns back to her. She tells him what Tim told her.

"Do you think I should go to Ethiopia?" She's hoping he'll tell her it would be a ridiculous thing to do.

"No," he says, after a moment's thought. "You'd better find that man he told you about. See if he can help you locate her. She could be in an entirely different country by now. She could be here in Canada for all you know."

"Never."

"Why not?" he asks. "What's she like?"

"It's the strangest thing," Iris says. "It's — at this minute, I feel as if she were only a dream, as if I don't know her, maybe never knew her at all. She was — withdrawn — " She looks up at him, frowning, needing to explain, for herself as much as him. "And I felt — no, I know it: I failed her. I was the grown-up, I should have known how to help her, and I didn't." He's silent, watching her.

"I think you're too hard on yourself. I'm sure you did your best for her," he tells her gently.

She thinks about how, through her adolescence, the pain during Lannie's periods was so bad that she would faint from it, that she insisted on suffering through those days without medication, she would not even tell Iris what was happening to her, but Iris would know, both by the calendar and by the way her face would lose all colour, her freckles standing out like tiny bruises. Or the cry that would finally escape her before she fainted and Iris would hear it, had been half-waiting for it, wherever she was in the house. Then Lannie would accept the doctor, the Demerol. Her refusal made no sense, not then, not now.

"Hey, Iris," Jay says softly. Iris touches her throat with her fingers, then puts down her hand. He's gazing at her with those beautiful, night-dark eyes of his. She puts her hand lightly on his slim wrist in thanks, and in something close to reverence at his physical beauty. She hears James's voice: *Your skin is so soft, it's like silk, your lashes are so thick . . .*

Sorrow stabs her because she's not beautiful any more. It shocks her to realize how important her beauty has been to her, that everything she is was grounded in it, that without it, she's at a loss, she doesn't know how to be. But how much of it can she have lost if this beautiful young man is with her? Reassured, at least momentarily, she smiles at Jay, who smiles back with a light in his eyes she knows. When she was young, all the men smiled at her with that light in their eyes.

The sari-clad young woman returns, and while Jay is talking to her, Iris looks around the café. All the diners appear to be younger than she is, they have strange haircuts and are dressed informally, the men and women the same in shirts and jackets and jeans. All of them have that air that country people don't, a sort of agreed-upon theatricality, a careful arranging of posture, gesture, and facial expressions.

"It was really nice of you to come out on this rescue mission," she tells him.

"I wanted to see you."

"I wanted to see you," she says ruefully, although she's trying to sound amusing, "I could practically be your mother." She's holding her breath, pretending not to be, as she fixes him with her smile. He blinks, looks away, then says, "Well, first, you'd had to have been about fourteen at the time. Secondly, so what?" Before she can answer, the food arrives: nothing Iris can name, or has tasted before, but she keeps silent, not wanting him to know. As naturally as if they took meals together every day, they both begin to eat.

After a while Iris realizes she's losing count of how many glasses of wine she has had and it worries her a little; she suspects she's a bit drunk. And yet, how long has it been since she felt relaxed and happy? The months when Barney was gone come back to her: the waiting, not sure if he would ever return — I deserve a little happiness, she thinks. Aren't widows ever allowed to be happy again?

"Have you decided what to do about your land yet?" Jay asks. She tells him about her arrangement with Vance and Ramona, about Jim Schiff and his offer to buy, about his company's plans, about her own uncertainty.

"Had any proposals?" he asks. "If I were a bachelor in your neighbourhood, I'd be courting you to get my hands on all that land." Iris laughs, and shakes her head, even thinks of telling him about her father's accusation that Barney had done that, when suddenly, she thinks, perhaps he was right. She's appalled at herself, Never! But her long-held resistance to such a cruel notion is beginning to crumble. So what if he did, she tells herself angrily. He made the farm his own with all those years of hard work and his faithfulness. If he did, she tells herself, I forgive him. Besides, if anybody schemed, it was me. Barney had been dating Alana Sproule, that barrel-racing cowgirl with her long, muscled legs — everybody thought they'd marry — when Iris decided she couldn't live without him, and smiled at him whenever she saw him, tried to be where he was, until he'd begun to understand she desired him. She still remembers that glitter that suddenly appeared in his eyes when he looked at her and she knew at that moment that she had him, he was hers. And before long he loved her — fully, passionately, completely.

When Jay speaks, it startles her. "I guess it's a big decision." Oh, yes, her land.

"I'm on the run from it," she says, trying to smile. "I'm on the lam. From my farm."

"No," he answers her. "It's only a little holiday, before you dig in." His eyes on her face are dark and gentle, and she cannot, does not want to look away.

"I'm very attracted to you," she says quietly, then stops, feeling her face — her whole body — getting hot, maybe it's only the wine, but sweat is even pooling between her breasts. Around them the other diners laugh and talk brightly, their blended voices retreating to a distant hum.

"I don't have to tell you how I feel," he says, not looking at her.

"Yes. Yes, you do."

"You're a very pretty woman." She doesn't know what to say to that other than an awkward "Thank you" — it isn't what she'd hoped to hear. She puts her hands up, her fingertips against her temples, then lowers them quickly. "What — Are you — I mean, I don't understand this. I don't know what this means," she says, meaning the two of them together here; she's trying to look into his face, but he won't let her.

"There's nothing to understand," he says. "We're attracted to each other. We're grown-ups. That's all." There's a long silence while she puzzles over this answer. *We're grown-ups.* That must mean that they're entitled to a sexual relationship if they want one. She feels an abrupt excitement mixed with dread, coming too fast for her to understand, leaving her trembling inside. "I like older women," he goes on in a light tone that makes her heart sink. "Because they're better at loving — I don't mean sex, although I suppose they're better at that too." He glances at her, then sobers. "I know most men my age see a long-legged nineteen-year-old as the most desirable woman" — Iris thinks of Lannie, although she is thirty now — "but that's just vanity." He taps his long fingers on the tablecloth.

Eventually, they finish eating and walk back the short distance to her hotel. All the way back she feels anticipation. Will he leave her at her door? But he doesn't, he enters the elevator with her, comes into her room, where he takes her in his arms and kisses her, then begins to slide off his jacket, and she knows then that she's about to make love to someone other than Barney, the first since James, who has been dead all these years. The excitement of being with a man, the two of them assessing each other, wanting each other, succumbing to each other, is as powerful tonight as it was when she was twenty-one.

They undress each other, stopping to kiss and touch, falling together onto the bed, then pulling apart to remove the last articles of clothing. As she slides her panties down off her thighs, past her knees, her ankles, it hits her suddenly that her body isn't what it used to be, that she's not the beautiful one any more.

He's reaching for her, but she can't respond. What if when he looks at her he finds her ugly? She turns back to him, aware of how strong her own desire is, she needs this. He is naked and she sees how slim he is, his chest, belly, and legs lightly dusted with dark hair that glints softly in the lamplight. He is gazing down at her, a long scrutiny, taking his time — she's afraid to breathe.

Pure physical sensation sweeps up the length of her body, removing every shred of uncertainty, as he kneels beside her, caressing her, then lies full length against her and above her, and enters. It is the joy of being female; something she has forgotten or lost, returning now in full force, carrying her away.

When Iris wakes, the room is filled with light, but there is no one in the bed beside her. Nor is there anyone else in the room. She calls softly, "Jay?" but no one answers. Maybe he has just gone out to get a paper or some coffee. She takes both pillows, pushes them behind her back and sits up, settling back against them. If he isn't back in a minute, surely he'll phone her. It worries her a bit that he's gone without saying goodbye. This isn't something she has done before, at least, not like this, in a hotel, or as a widow, and she isn't sure what the etiquette is for such occasions.

She looks across the room at the door leading into the hall, but the handle doesn't turn, there is no swift, soft knock on it. Then she notices that a hotel envelope is propped against the lamp on the desk. A word is scrawled across it in large, careless handwriting that, even though she can't read it from this distance, she knows is *Iris*. She gets out of bed, goes to the desk, and takes the envelope.

Her body feels different, some fluidity in her joints that wasn't there yesterday — or the day before; she can't remember the last time her body felt so relaxed, almost youthful in its ease of movement. Without looking at the envelope, she sits down on the bed and closes her eyes, lets herself go for a moment deep inside the memory of the night she has just passed, that warmth, that open mouth, that encompassing physical joy she experienced with Jay. Then embarrassment and delight sweep through her. When she opens her eyes the bedside clock tells her it's ten-thirty in the morning. She hasn't slept this late since she was a teenager.

She presses both hands to her chest, forgetting she's holding the letter, and then opens the sealed envelope.

Dear Iris,

 Sorry to sneak out without saying goodbye, but I have to get organized for my move and you were sleeping so peacefully I didn't want to wake you. It was a good night, wasn't it. Good luck finding your niece.

Jay

She lets her head fall back against the pillows, the letter onto her lap. He is gone. Her impulse is to burst into sobs like a schoolgirl, but instead, her eyes burn, a peculiar sensation that makes her blink rapidly. And her chest hurts, with each breath her lungs have begun to ache as if she's breathing in harsh cold air. She's struggling to get a grip on his dismissal of her. All she can think of is that she's fallen for a man who isn't Barney, that's she's slept with him, that he's walked out on her like some stupid romance novel or a soap opera. For a second, she's enraged that this misery could still happen to her. It isn't fair, she's thinking, at the same time, bitterly amused at the irony, I'm too old for this. I don't deserve it. He was only a boy, she tells herself, he was nothing to me. But the pain in her chest, the sense she has of absorbing a great blow, won't let her hold onto this belittling of him. I loved him, she says to herself, but no, it wasn't that. It was that I thought he would save me.

Then she feels strange, as if an illness is about to descend on her, or some disaster. A series of sensations rush through her body each barely registering before it departs: I'm hungry, I'm nauseous, I'm lonely, I'm exhausted, I'm depressed — but she can hardly tell the physical discomfort from the emotional unease, they express themselves in the same way — as dread. She sits up straight, waiting for it to pass.

Heat surges from a deep centre through her body, spreading outward and especially upward, expanding in size and intensity until it's pushing with all its burgeoning power against her physical boundaries — I can't stand it, she thinks, if it doesn't stop, I'm going to die. Then, at the instant when she feels she can't endure any more of this fire, it bursts through her skin, slowly transforming itself into a fine layer of perspiration. Then hot moisture — some pure, clear, odourless liquid forced from her cells — pooling in the creases of her neck, between her breasts, in the hollows behind her knees and along her forehead just below her hairline. It leaves her exhausted, as if she has been running for days.

Aware in the dim recesses of her brain of the implication of what is happening to her, now she feels her body's tremendous excessive heat not so much as illness or failure as a warning; it's as if a great hand, the hand of a goddess, has touched her with her immortal, incandescent finger, so that she is seared in the holy fire; she's the bush that burned and was not consumed. She would not speak at such a moment, or move, to escape notice, but a cry involuntarily escapes her as she recognizes the unrecognizable: Iris Christie. Widow. Crone.

Holy fire indeed, she thinks. Menopause is only sweat and stink, sleeplessness and growing old. And yet how jealous men must be of this, even while they're frightened and disgusted by it. This thing has such immediacy, she can't turn away from it. Her body is speaking and it gives her no choice but to listen.

At least you'll never again have to worry about whether blood is staining the back of your dress, never again have to fuss with sanitary pads or tampons or tell Barney you'd rather wait to have sex. All that nuisance and mess is over forever. It occurs to her to wonder how many years she's menstruated — something like forty years, month after month after month. The years have come and gone before she has had time to notice. I am approaching the end of my life, she thinks, with such bitter sadness. I am alone, facing my death.

Then it hits her at last, the degree of its intensity stuns her: it means you'll never have a child now. Never. She thinks of the child Lannie would have had. I could have raised her myself, she thinks.

I forced her to have an abortion. She was weak and I knew it; she couldn't even think rationally, and I said, "You must have an abortion," with that common sense I learned from my mother and that I thought was my greatest strength — I knew I was right. I! I didn't even think about it. Lannie wasn't mentally healthy enough to raise a child. She might have tried to kill herself again.

But maybe having a child would have saved Lannie. How do I know? *Not having a child didn't save me.* Save me from what? From life, she answers herself, but this only confuses her more, or upsets her, she doesn't know what to think. And looking back, she can't see that she could have done anything else. But what's the point of thinking about that now? For no matter how she twists and turns, she is alone in her silent hotel room, far from home and friends and family and Barney is dead, and James too, and now even Jay has gone.

She gets slowly up off the bed, and walks across the room. This is her, Iris, carrying on.

Then she sees her skirt and blouse she'd worn the night before lying smoothly over a chair. Jay must have placed them there before he left. And there are her shoes placed neatly together under the chair, and her underwear lying in a silky heap on the skirt. She goes to them and gathers them in both hands, her creamy half-slip, her lace-trimmed bra, her sheer panties, and holds them against her chest, inhaling last night's odours, cigarette smoke, perfume, that musky odour she recognizes as her own. She's thinking, what a fool you are, Iris. As if a man half your age might love you.

It's minutes before she can force herself to the bathroom. After she has bathed, she dresses in creased slacks, her yellow silk blouse, her cashmere jacket. She studies her face in the mirror; moving closer she makes herself look at the lines and wrinkles of her more than fifty years. Sadder but wiser, she thinks, and stares grimly at her reflection as she pulls the brush roughly through her hair.

She repacks her suitcase, checks out of the hotel and takes a cab to the airport. There are numerous flights to Ottawa, and she manages to get a seat on one leaving in under an hour. She's begun to suspect that the real reason Jay has left her is the simplest, age-old one: now that he's conquered her, he doesn't want her anymore. She phones Ramona and tells her what she has found out about Lannie.

"I might have to go to Africa myself," she says, to test how it sounds out loud. Ramona draws in a deep breath.

"Iris, don't do anything silly, eh? Remember us, we're here, waiting for you to come home."

"People go to Africa all the time," Iris says briskly. Ramona puts Vance on the line.

"Remember the land deal?" he asks. "Well, of course you do. Halvorsons and Wiebes have both signed. Not that they're saying anything, but you know how word leaks out. They've been back here twice, too. Just won't take no for an answer."

"Do people know yet where the money's coming from?" Iris asks.

"Some reporter's been here and he says the provincial government's trying to find that out before they'll let the deal go through. Maybe you should come home so's not to miss all the excitement," Vance says.

"No," she says firmly. "I haven't found her yet. And if I'm not there, they can't pressure me. Besides, Vance, we've got a deal, and I'm not backing down. Are you?" His answer is a snort that makes her laugh.

All the rest of the time, while she's boarding her plane, flying the short hop to Ottawa and checking into her hotel, she's thinking about Jay. His leaving her is such misery, she almost wonders if a night of lovemaking was worth it. Backtracking mentally, she tries to find the place where she might have stopped it before it began. No, she couldn't have stopped it. She wanted it all along, but she wanted to be in control of what happened between them, it didn't occur to her that he might have more power over it than she would.

She sets her suitcase down by the door of her new hotel room, which looks much like the one she just left, and goes straight to the phone, gets the book from the desk drawer and looks under "Sargent, Robert." She's about to dial the number when she realizes this must be his home phone number. She tries again under "Engineering" in the yellow pages, finds "Sargent, Bloom, and Atwater," and copies the address down on the notepad by the phone. As she did not phone Tim first in Toronto, she doesn't phone this company either. She'll only get some secretary who, she's sure, won't let her speak to him.

She hails a cab — how cosmopolitan she has become in a few short days — and it takes her quickly to her destination. As she waits in front of the office building for the driver to give her her change, she sees through the cab's window all the people hurrying up or down the high, wide steps. A couple of men pass by, their ties flapping over their shoulders in the wind, talking on cell phones. Women pull their spring coats tighter around them as they descend, and wave to friends hurrying up the stairs. Iris could weep for the ordinariness of it all.

"Rob Sargent," she tells the young receptionist who looks up from her computer when Iris enters the office. "Iris Christie to see him."

"Is he expecting you?" She's young enough to be Iris's daughter, younger even than Lannie would be now.

"Yes." She's nervous about this tack, but it gets her taken immediately into his office.

He turns out to be in his mid-thirties, a stocky, well-muscled redhead, the sleeves of his white shirt rolled to his elbows, his striped tie loosened. He looks up from his computer screen and sneezes, snuffles into a tissue, and apologizes, "Sorry, excuse me." His secretary goes out, closing the door behind her. Rob sneezes again, another apology, looks up inquiringly at her.

"You sound as if you should be at home in bed," Iris tells him. He agrees glumly, then offers her a chair across from his cluttered desk, and asks her what he can do for her.

"I'm looking for my niece," she says, and tells him the story briefly. "I understand you were there, in Ethiopia, during the famine of '84 and '85."

"Yeah, I was," he says, his voice is clogged, his tone heavy. "I was working for a relief agency doing engineering work — helping put up buildings, piping in water to the camps, that kind of thing. Got a picture of her?" Iris reaches into her purse, pulls out the snapshot Tim gave her, and hands it across the desk to him. He takes it, his swivel chair creaking loudly as he leans forward.

"Her name's Lannie, Lannie Stone." Before he even looks at the picture, his head jerks up, and a flush rushes across his face.

"Yeah," he says heavily. "I saw her. I remember her. Lannie. Lannie Stone." He tosses the picture back to Iris with a gesture of something: anger? dismissal?

"Where was she?" Iris asks. "Was she all right?"

"Harbu. And then I knew her in Addis and Korem and . . . there-abouts." Iris finds she has been holding her breath and lets it out quickly. "She moved around a bit," he says and sighs deeply, shifting in his chair, making it creak again, swivelling to look out the big window behind him which overlooks the downtown core, the Parliament Buildings, the river. "I met her at Harbu. She was running around, doing this and that. Working hard." He falls silent again, still looking out the window. After a moment, he lifts a tissue and blows his nose into it. "Sorry," he says. "This damn cold. I can't shake it. I've had it for weeks."

"You knew her," she says slowly, as if she isn't quite convinced.

"She was a little spaced-out, as we used to say, but who wouldn't be, after seeing what we both saw." Iris reflects on this as Sargent sits sunk into some glumness she can't read. "Her aunt, are you?" he asks finally. "She said her parents were dead, but I don't remember her mentioning an aunt." This startles Iris, but it could be he has just made a mistake about what Lannie said.

"Did she say where she was going? Was she coming home? Here, I mean?"

"Sometimes she'd be working on a story. We used to meet in Addis, after I left Harbu. I think she'd been in the south, too. I forget." He stares sombrely at his lap, then rises slowly and goes to stand looking out the window. She takes the opportunity to look around the room and notices a picture resting on a filing cabinet in front of a drooping plant. Probably his wife, and their three young children.

"Wait a minute," she says. "Working on a story? Is that what you said?"

"Yeah," he says. "She worked sometimes for some church magazines here in Canada. I don't remember their names. Doing stories and photos, you know?"

"But, I thought she went to do relief work."

"You couldn't just go there and help, you know, if you weren't a nurse. And when the agencies hired non-medical people, they hired locals, for obvious reasons." The reasons aren't at all obvious to Iris, but she lets it go. "Apparently she made a deal with a string of small church papers in the West that she'd go at her own expense if they'd get her a press card. That's how she got there. Then she just — made her opportunities. We . . . dated," he tells her. "As much as you could in a country like that, at a time like that. We were working eighteen, twenty hours a day. Then I came home. The worst was over — at least, that's how it looked — and I had a career to get started." He turns back to her. "She was a strange girl," he says. "Sorry, I forgot she's your niece." Iris says nothing. "There was a T-shirt people wore there then," he goes on. "It said, 'Check One: Missionary, Merce-nary, Masochist, Misfit.' I was number three: masochist. When I figured that out, I quit and came home."

"And Lannie?" Iris asks.

"Oh, number four. I was pretty disillusioned with the job. You think you're helping, but really — you're just propping up a violent, repressive regime."

"And Lannie? Did she come home too?" she asks.

"No. She didn't agree with me. She said no matter what, you can't let people starve." She sees the hint of a smile at the corners of his mouth, as if he's remembering the way Lannie spoke. Then he sighs. "She didn't say she was coming home. She said Africa was her home." Iris waits. It's as if he knows much more than he's saying, if only she could wrest it out of him.

At last she says, "I'm going to go there, to find her."

"Oh? It's funny, but I don't know how she got out of Addis. Maybe she stole a ride with a food convoy or something. They travelled at night, to avoid the bombing. She could have hidden in one. She never told me how she did that."

"Bombing! What do you mean — She had a passport, didn't she?"

"There was a war on," he says, surprised, lifting his head to look at her. "Didn't you know that? It was at its worst right about the time you're talking about. You could still get into the country, but you had to get a travel permit to move around and that could be pretty hard to do."

"I want to know about the war." He has been fiddling with a pen and at her question he swivels back toward her, tosses the pen down and tells her about the Emperor Haile Selassie.

"He wasn't any bigger than you are. Smaller, in fact. He was deposed in 1974 by the *Dergue*, that's Amharic for 'committee,' really the army. That happened because there was a major drought going on and thousands were starving, especially in the north, and the magnificent emperor — who later was strangled in his bed, there were rumours that in his last years he was sacrificing virgins — said there wasn't, and didn't help and didn't let anybody else help either. When word got out, he was finished. The *Dergue* took over the country."

He pauses, then, when he sees how intently she's listening, continues. "The *Dergue* was Marxist, allied with the Soviet Union. It nationalized all the land in the country, set up collective farms, and there was the Red Terror — "

"What?" Iris asks, but Rob only wipes his nose and stares at his desktop in silence for a minute, before he goes on.

"It was to stamp out all resistance. People were torn from their beds and never seen again. They were shot in the streets. They were tortured hideously." He pauses. "Mengistu's regime was harsh, terribly harsh, there were people who said they were better off under the emperor. Guerrilla movements began in separate parts of the country: Eritrea, Tigray, the Ogaden, and so on. That was the war." She nods, not taking her eyes off his face. "In 1991, Mengistu was overthrown and a new government took over the land, was promptly unnationalized, the province of Eritrea separated to become its own country, and the war was over."

"All those years she was living in the middle of war?"

"There was danger," he admits. "Early on some relief workers were killed, but on the whole, as long as you did what you were told, you were reasonably safe."

"The war is over?"

"More or less," he says. "The new government is pretty stable." She reflects.

"I don't speak Ethiopian. How will I find her?"

"You mean Amharic. It's the official language — or was, until the new government took over. It's probably Tigrayan now. Anyway, a lot of people speak a little English. They learn it in school. If they go to school." At this last he turns his head away from her in a quick movement that fails to hide — anger, she thinks. "Maybe you should let her be." Iris isn't sure she has heard him correctly, she's about to ask when he says, "Not everybody can be saved." A deathly silence envelops them as Iris understands his remark. "Not everybody *deserves* to be saved," he says, and the unexpected passion in his voice brings Iris to her feet.

"You're wrong," she says quietly, firmly. "She deserves a normal, happy life as much as you or I. I am going to bring her home."

Addis Ababa

In years to come she will never be able to say what was going on with her during the month she spent in Ottawa waiting for her passport and visa and having her immunizations, for when she should have been full of grief, when she should have been dying with loneliness, and eaten up with fear, she wasn't. She didn't worry about Barney's or even Jay's abrupt departure except distantly, as if she were the one who had died and crossed an impermeable border from them, and although she could see them in the distance, their shapes were muted, she felt little when she thought of them.

Her hotel room was not beautiful, but it was large and comfortable, and when she went inside and locked the door she was safe from all demands on her; she could be purely herself. She hadn't known she wanted to be free of demands, or maybe it was only that she'd never before been alone and a complete stranger in a strange place, and she experienced it as oddly pleasurable, a kind of surprising, agreeable suspension in time and space.

Night after night she dreamt vivid dreams of stunning beauty so that when she woke every morning she found it necessary to lie in bed rehearsing them in her mind until she had managed to cross the border from them into the everyday world of Ottawa in early summer, and Barney's absence, and Jay's defection, and her own quiet solitude that she found herself savouring.

Occasionally she dreamt her now familiar water dreams: the darkness of an unending night — no, a world where there seemed to be only night, a nightworld, and herself in dark water swimming, or in a mysterious ferry as a passenger, the other passengers silent and hooded, heading for a distant shore where lights flickered, but no detail was revealed of the city there or its inhabitants. In these dreams she was not afraid, although her struggles were desperate, her chances of gaining that shore seeming slight, and there was no one to help her.

Other nights she dreamt about the wild grasslands of her home as she remembered them from her childhood, or as she remembered them through her parents' and her grandparents' stories: *When people first came to this valley the grass was so high it brushed your stirrups when you rode through it, you could set down your mower anywhere and cut, and there weren't no fences at all.* She was back in her childhood walking with her grandmother to the old farmhouse on the prairie above the deep coulee, or she was in the coulee climbing its rough, crumbling clay side past a coyote's den and a golden eagle's nest while the eagle soared, screaming above her; or she was rolling in the grass, her face buried in its pungent sweetness, and lifting her head a little, she surprised a sparrow hiding out of the wind between two small rocks, and saw tiny holes in the light brown soil where the smallest insects lived, and the minute tracings of their comings and goings. After those dreams, she woke filled with longing, the fragrance of sage, sweetgrass, wolf willow, and wild roses still scenting the drab air of her room, the clear prairie light slowly being subsumed by the hazy eastern sunlight fighting its way through the room's grubby windows.

One night, the silent woman came to her: that open, direct gaze held her transfixed, a look that penetrated through her skin, her flesh, her bones. This time, instead of the white gown, she wore black robes, not the dead black of nuns' gowns, but a rich black that shimmered with hints of other colours. Iris woke and realized that this was her wise woman, her guide.

She began her series of shots at a medical clinic: hepatitis, meningitis, typhoid, polio, diphtheria and tetanus, yellow fever, which made her think of diseases, of soldiers and rape and murder, of plane crashes, and lonely deaths in desert or mountain wilderness.

"I believe I'll be all right," she told Ramona carefully, when Ramona called to express concern at her intention to go to Africa, as if Iris had thought it all over and on balance felt she would come out of this adventure alive, when in fact, something well beyond rationality was driving her.

"Want me to put your garden in for you?" Ramona asked. Iris had forgotten about her garden. She opened her mouth to say no, she'd do without a garden this year. What did she need a garden for with Barney gone? But in that instant's pause she smelled the fresh earth in sunshine; she was catapulted back into that moment when, gardening, she forgot her everyday self and her borders became the borders of the garden, and she moved in rhythm with it and with the wind and the songbirds and the seeds she held in her palm and dropped solemnly, one by one, into the earth. She was overcome with longing for the pleasure of her garden. When Ramona said, "Iris?" into the silence, she heard herself make a small, odd sound of regret before she said, "Oh, don't bother, Ramona. I'll put it in myself when I get back." And was grateful to have remembered, both for Ramona's sake and her own, that she would be coming back.

"You'd better stay at the Hilton," the nurse at the clinic told her. "If you can afford it. Failing that, the Ghion. You have to worry about being robbed otherwise and my guess is you'd prefer comforts if you can get them." She'd worked in Ethiopia for an NGO, "That's a non-government organization," she explained, "like the U.N., or Save the Children, or Oxfam," during the '87 famine, that was how she knew what to suggest to Iris. "And don't forget to take your malaria pill once a week," she'd lectured her sternly. "You should be safe in Addis because it's so high — over seven thousand feet — so there aren't supposed to be mosquitoes there, but personally, I wouldn't take the chance."

Iris wanted to ask the nurse many more questions, but she couldn't clearly form them. Instead, she went to a bookstore and asked for books about Ethiopia. The store had only two, both published by the Ethiopian government and full of practical information about currency, banking, the climate, public holidays, taxi and bus service within Addis Ababa. Mostly they were made up of brightly coloured photos of the city taken from a distance, the buildings interspersed with greenery, some of it palm trees, or of cathedrals and mosques, hotels and government buildings, or of silver jewellery displayed on black velvet which might be bought in Addis Ababa, or pottery, or woven straw basketry, and of pretty young women dancing in nightclubs wearing red-trimmed white gowns while behind them men beat with their palms conical drums hanging by straps from their shoulders. In the photos all the people looked well fed and happy. Remembering what Rob Sargent told her, she recognized this as government propaganda.

One morning she woke and it was the day she was to board her plane to Europe. She bathed, dressed, ate breakfast, collected her suitcase packed with the new, more appropriate clothes she'd bought for her trip — she'd mailed home to Ramona the things she didn't need — checked out of her hotel, and took a cab to the airport where she boarded her plane. She felt a little as if she were sleepwalking through the world of her dreams.

But then, a day later, after changing planes in Frankfurt, even her anxiety dissipated; she'd grown too tired to worry, hadn't any energy left for it. Instead of changing to a little propeller-driven plane, the engine missing, the doors tied shut with baling wire, flown by a fast-talking African pilot with maybe two other sorry-looking, mysterious passengers, as she'd half imagined, she was flying Lufthansa in a huge, sparkling-clean jet, every seat taken, and more of the passengers looking just like herself — Caucasian, Western — than dark-skinned, and Arab or African in colourful robes and hats and veils. A few of the passengers with their video cameras and waistpacks were clearly tourists. It seemed that, after all, one could go to Africa without a pith helmet and machete. And the view of the countries they were crossing over down below was so marvellous that her awe squeezed out any fear. When the pilot told them they'd be following the Nile for the next while and she looked out the window and saw a tiny silver river snaking south through limitless warm brown desert, she felt breathless with excitement.

She had flown out of time, that was what she'd done, and no rules applied any more, no ideas, no facts. Staring down at the world as she moved through space faster than time itself, past and future vanished; she was grounded in the moment, a wholly new experience. The world is real, she thought, and in her excitement, her pure, unadulterated joy, heard herself make a small noise somewhere between a sob and laugh. Then they were landing in Addis Ababa.

The realness of the place stuns her: the clouds of evil-smelling black exhaust all the vehicles spew — vans, buses, taxis, cars, Land Rovers, and trucks; the crowds of people on foot — the women in Western clothing or in ankle-length robes and cotton shawls that cover their heads and shoulders, mostly white, but sometimes in bright pinks or faded pastels, at whom she stares drinking in the grace and drama of their clothing, and who look back at her out of dark, mildly curious but not unfriendly eyes as she rushes past them; the men, some in Arab-like garb with big turbans on their heads, or knots of slender young ones, mostly in Western clothing, lounging on street corners or in front of shops. She stares at the small three-sided, roofed shops made of corrugated iron with quarters of raw red meat hanging in them, or bunches of yellow bananas, or colourful straw baskets and dishes, or items she hasn't time to identify before they whip past; the shockingly potholed city streets, and the close, lush blue-green hills. She feels it all invading her body like a disease, intensifying her sense of herself as a small woman riding in a bouncing taxi through the beauty and squalor all around her. It is at once as fully magical as it seemed to her before she'd even seen it, and as real and ordinary as anything she has ever known.

This Addis is a small town, but one that's spread out for miles in every direction, all haphazardly treed, no city planners here. Or maybe she hasn't been paying attention, fragmented as her attention is by the traffic, the — she almost can't believe it — the cattle and donkeys, and the sheep and goats so underfed they're the size of dogs, nonchalantly grazing the narrow boulevard and sauntering among the cars waiting at the traffic lights. And the beggars who stand mournfully at her car window every time they pause, their hands outstretched. There is something very wrong with this boy who has thrust his hands too near to the closed window. They are huge, gargantuan, it's as if for a joke some god stuck hands the size of Luke's on the frail arms of this perhaps ten-year-old child. She turns her head away from him quickly, but a wretchedly thin woman with a face that's horribly twisted — an accident? a birth defect? is peering in the window with her hands cupped chest-high toward Iris. Iris begins to fumble in her purse, but the light has changed and the driver pulls away leaving the beggars behind in the traffic. She keeps staring out the window as they whiz past buildings and people and trees and animals.

They slow in a bottleneck and she sees that something is very wrong with that donkey standing against the wall. Its dull, shaggy, reddish-brown hair covers his thin ribs in patches, it's falling out, his ears droop and his head hangs as he stands motionless in the midst of the people passing around him. The donkey is clearly dying and no one cares.

The taxi enters a large square with a long block of viewing stands down one side. The street, obviously a major thoroughfare, is lane-less and the cars and trucks advance in a clump, every which way, easing in front of each other or switching from one side of the street to the other by dint of honking, rushing, then slowing, then edging into the stream of vehicles in such a way that Iris is sure they should hit each other, although they never seem to. At least nobody's driving too fast in this jumble. Apparently the light is red because the driver pulls to a stop in what seems to be the middle of the square.

He turns to her, "See? Over there?" She hadn't realized he spoke English and responds eagerly to his pointing finger. "That is where Mengistu made his speeches." One of her books had been published in the eighties and had a picture of Mengistu. The driver is pointing to a railed platform to their right, a sort of viewing stand painted a flat, military grey, with wide steps leading up each side. She sees above the stand the faded outline where a large star had once been. "He would stand there and all the people would fill the square and stand over there." He points to the rows of bleachers on their left. "Used to be Revolutionary Square, but now is Maskal Square."

"Maskal?" Iris tries out the word.

"It is — cross," he says. "For the day the True Cross was found."

The True Cross? Does this mean these people are Christians, as she is? Her eye is caught by a tall, strong-looking woman standing on the sidewalk only a few feet away. She's wearing an ankle-length cloaklike garment in a pattern too small for Iris to make out but that blurs into a hazy, attractive blue-orange design. As Iris watches, a man comes up to the woman who smiles broadly at him, yet with what seems to Iris to be a touch of deference or even shyness. As he stops to speak to her she lifts her head and Iris sees that all the skin of her neck from the underside of her chin to where the garment touches the base of her throat is covered with small blue tattoos. More, the woman is show-ing them off deliberately as if she thinks they're beautiful. They seem wonderful to Iris, both the fact of them and the fact the woman is proud of them — this is the first she's seen of the Africa of her imag-ination — they're tribal markings, she guesses. No, she thinks, they're adornment, that's all. She winces at the thought of the pain the woman must have endured to acquire them.

This scene barely has time to register when the driver steps on the gas, jerking Iris back in the seat, and in a second the square is lost behind them in the uneven flow of Land Rovers, small trucks and cars, and blue and white vanlike vehicles that seem to be buses, all packed with three times the number of people they were built to hold, all spewing a smoky black fog from their exhausts. Everyone honks, everyone manoeuvres; it's a miracle they aren't all dead.

They arrive at the Hilton, although from the street outside it's impossible to tell if the walls contain an embassy, a mansion, or a used-car lot. Inside the compound — she finds herself dredging up the word *compound* from forgotten depths of girlhood reading — she finds parked cars around the edges of a smoothly paved lot, no potholes here, and a doorman and a couple of traffic policemen, and palm trees slapping their fronds against each other lazily in a light wind that Iris hadn't noticed before. It's like a movie set, she thinks, and here I am: Iris Christie, world traveller. For a moment she's forgotten why she has come. In her delight she has even forgotten the beggars and the woman with the blue tattoos and the dying donkey.

She'd changed some traveller's cheques for birr before she left the airport as the nurse at the clinic told her to do. The nurse had warned her to be sure to get a government taxi and not one of the ones wait-ing in the parking lot outside the airport compound, so she knows in advance what the fare will be and how much to tip. Now he opens the cab door for her, hands her her single suitcase, bows gravely when she pays him.

Inside the hotel Iris gets herself a room from the clerk, an Ethiopian male who also bows, but with such grace she feels her cheeks heating up with surprise at such an extreme degree of etiquette. He inquires as to whether she would like to check her valuables in the hotel safe, but all she has in the way of valuables beside her passport is her money and she decides to keep it with her. He is so pleasant and gracious that she has an impulse to ask him for advice on her search for Lannie, but she is too shy.

She thanks the clerk and makes her way out of the lobby through a horde of tourists, all speaking loudly in German, cameras hanging from straps around their necks or carrying video cameras in the crooks of their arms, guidebooks in their hands, waistpacks securely fastened around their ample middles. She skirts an Arab man and his wife whose abundant, heavy gold jewellery and gold-trimmed, white robes speak of wealth so vast she can't comprehend it. She finds her room. She's sure she's far too excited and exhausted by her two-day trip and too eager to find Lannie, who can't be far away now, to sleep, but she lies down on her bed anyway.

Stretched out on the rust-coloured bedspread, propped against her pillows, she's more than a little surprised that, despite the elegant lobby, even the Hilton isn't particularly new or luxurious. There's an air-conditioning unit against the wall, but the room isn't hot. Otherwise, it's anonymous: bed, desk, single chair, bureau, lamp, bedside table — she could be anywhere. Staring at the slightly grimy ceiling she tries to marshal her thoughts.

As the day of her departure for Ethiopia approached, she'd found herself thinking about the moment, finally, when she and Lannie would meet face to face. She'd tried out various scenarios: throwing their arms around each other and crying with joy; careful handshakes and the brushing of cheeks; a quarrel — Why not? Would she be able to stop herself from accusing Lannie of neglecting her family and friends in Canada, who were worrying and wondering what had become of her? Would Lannie be angry Iris had come chasing after her? Angry about whatever it was that made her stop writing to them? Or will she be indifferent, not caring that Iris has come so far, not interested in seeing her?

When she'd told the nurse she didn't know where to start looking when she arrived in Ethiopia, she had given her the name of a woman at CIDA — "Canadian International Development Agency," she explained. "She still goes there to oversee projects and she was there in 1985, and she knows everybody. Talk to her."

Iris phoned the woman at once, Celia was her name. When Iris arrived at her Ottawa office it turned out she'd already located the phone numbers in Addis Ababa of the agencies she'd thought were the best bets to locate Lannie.

"And if they don't know her themselves, they'll know where to send you to find her — if she's still in the country." Iris asked for street addresses, but Celia warned her, "Addis has no street addresses. For the most part the streets aren't even named. One finds one's way about using landmarks." When Iris asked why, Celia explained grimly that the people had taken the signs down during the Red Terror, to make it harder for the soldiers and police to find anyone. And now, here she is in the maze of Addis Ababa.

She searches through her new leather folder that contains her money, traveller's cheques, passport, and visa. There the numbers are, tucked away in a small compartment. Agitated, she goes to her window and looks out over the hotel grounds without seeing a thing. If she hadn't had the imperative of the phone calls hovering over her, she would succumb to the wave of homesickness now engulfing her. But she forces herself back around the bed to the phone, the slip of paper on which Celia scrawled the agency names and phone numbers quivering in her hand, and dials the first number. When a man answers in a peremptory tone, she takes a deep breath and explains who she is and what she wants.

"I do not know her," he says roughly, and then is silent. She can hear paper rustling. She wavers between anxiety and slamming the phone down at his rudeness, but in the end merely says, "Thank you," and hangs up. This encounter emboldens rather than weakens her, and when she consults her paper for the next number, it doesn't tremble in her fingers any more.

But no one answers at the second number, and her third call is answered by a young-sounding woman speaking in a bored, vague manner, as if she has other, more important things on her mind than this conversation. Iris has to tell her twice what it is she wants.

"No, I think not so," the voice says. "No, this person, I do not know. She is not here." Iris suspects the young woman of just not wanting to be bothered, so she puts a tick beside that number too, as she has with the second one where no one answered, meaning, call again tomorrow.

She has two numbers left. She dials the first carefully, consulting her paper twice to make sure she gets it right. The phone rings and rings and nobody answers. Puzzled, Iris looks at her watch which she's been carefully adjusting as she passes through time zone after time zone. It's past five o'clock. All the offices must be closed. What if I never find her? She has to give herself a pep talk: How upset would you be if you were in Canada? You'd just wait till morning and try then.

She thinks again that she should try to sleep, but it seems to her that every nerve in her body, every sense receptor has been on full alert from the moment she left Ottawa two days before and she's utterly, totally exhausted at the same time as she feels herself wound up to such a pitch that rest is unimaginable. She goes back to the window where this time the view comes into focus and she sees the clear azure water of a swimming pool in which a couple of heads bob, and people, Europeans, sitting with drinks at poolside tables. All of this is surrounded by palms and trees flowering in vivid colours, it's as if she's flown out of the world and landed in some impossible paradise. She decides to go down for a quiet drink before she looks for the hotel restaurant.

She makes her way downstairs and out the lobby doors to the garden where between a wall of greenery and the pool a cluster of glass-topped, white wrought-iron tables and chairs sit under colour-ful umbrellas. She sits down at a table, orders a gin and tonic, and takes a good look around. How peaceful and beautiful it is here, so quiet after the din of the city outside the garden walls.

Now she notices a woman sitting by herself at the table next to hers. The woman's blonde hair is swept up and tucked into an elegant roll at the back of her head. She's dressed in a long, full-skirted white cotton sundress, with a matching jacket thrown over her shoulders. An empty carafe and wineglass sit in front of her. She has a book in one hand, but she's not reading it, she's looking straight at Iris in a frank, friendly way out of large grey-blue eyes. Startled at being stared at — so she's not invisible after all — Iris says awkwardly, "Hi."

"Hi there," the woman says. "Just arrived?" Iris nods, feeling a bit shy, but glad to speak at last to anyone who isn't a taxi driver, customs agent, clerk, or other functionary. This woman is middle-aged too, although it's hard to be sure since her tan is so dark that from the distance of a few feet it hides what might be wrinkles.

"Your husband still making arrangements?" the woman asks, with an ironic hint in her voice that Iris doesn't understand.

"I'm alone," Iris says. She looks out to the swimming pool where now no one is swimming. The water laps gently against its blue concrete sides and a woman who has been lounging in a deck chair rises, gathers her things, and goes slowly away between the trees that burst with red, coral, and orange blossoms. Iris can't name them — bougainvillea? The woman sitting across from her says, "Never been here before?" Iris shakes her head no and smiles with lips that unexpectedly wobble a little. She drops her head to hide this.

"Oh, dear," the woman says. She stands, takes a step, overbalances slightly so that she has to put her hand on the back of the chair kitty-corner from Iris at Iris's table to catch herself, and says, "May I?"

"Please," Iris says, wondering at the stumble, then thinking of the empty carafe sitting on the woman's table.

"Betty Chamberlain." They touch hands politely. "I'm American," she says. "My husband works here — he's in the diplomatic community — so I live here. Have for two years now." She says this last failing to hide a flash of something that might be anger. "I hope you don't think it too forward of me to speak to you. I thought I detected distress, if you'll forgive me for saying so."

"No, no, you're right," Iris says. "I'm just tired from the flight." As she reaches the end of her brief recitation, her search for Lannie, she manages to smile in a way that she hopes is something like her normal self. "So for the time being, all I can do is wait, but I'm hoping to track her down first thing in the morning." The waiter arrives with her drink, bows, and goes away.

Betty Chamberlain, who is Iris's physical opposite — tall, angular, and sinewy — puts out a slender, tanned arm on which a narrow gold bracelet shines discreetly and lets it rest on the table by her book, which Iris sees has "Ethiopia" in its title and is by someone named Pankhurst.

"It's an interesting country," Betty says. Her tone is weighted with knowledge that appears to trouble her. She looks off across the pool to the hotel's huge blank windows, on the other side of which Iris knows are comfortable sofas and low tables where hotel guests are lounging or chatting quietly. She sighs, in a way that's somewhere between weary and irritated, then turns back to Iris, smiles briefly, as if she's just remembered that smiling is required here, pauses a moment, then says brightly, "Too bad to be alone your first night. I'll soon have to run. My driver's probably waiting already. But you're better off resting anyway. This city hits you like a blow in the face the first time you see it — if you haven't been in a Third World country before. You must understand that this is one of the very poorest countries in the world. You are not likely to see worse than you will see here."

"The roads," Iris says, wanting to say more, "and people every-where walking! Everybody's walking! And the beggars!"

It's not that she hasn't seen such poverty on television; it's only that its living, breathing texture — its true enormity — cannot, she sees now, begin to be conveyed by television. Yet, when she thinks of the beggars, what she feels isn't chiefly pity, it is instead a kind of active suspension in her mind, as if, if she just thinks hard enough she will find a comfortable place for them in a scheme of things which would relieve the burden of being upset about them. Forgetting Betty, gazing out over the pool's turquoise water, she thinks that just maybe this is only her inability, or worse, her refusal, to accept that people do suffer like this, not just for an hour or a day, but for their entire lives. The realization makes her ashamed.

"Well, Addis isn't Ethiopia," Betty says. "You should try to get out into the countryside, see some of the antiquities while you're here. They're really magnificent, you know. Absolutely unexpected, and completely . . . unspoiled," and gives a short laugh as if the word "unspoiled" in the context of Ethiopia is a bit of a sour joke. "You see those people over there?" She nods toward a middle-aged couple seated on the far side of the pool. "Brits," the woman says. "They've hired a Land Rover and a driver and they're off to the hot springs at Sodere tomorrow. Then they're going on to Awash National Park for a couple of days of looking at the wildlife. Cars and drivers are always available for a price. You'd be safe with one of them."

"If it turns out I have to wait for Lannie," Iris says, "maybe I'll take your advice," not that she can imagine herself doing any such thing. And what does she mean, safe? In the taxi Iris had felt perfectly safe, indeed, knew no reason not to. Safe from what? she wonders, but doesn't ask.

"I'm here for part of most days. It's about the only escape possible in this city from all that *ferenji* stuff." She explains — foreigner. "You probably haven't been here long enough to see how people stare at you, think you're rich, ask things of you." She sighs. "People are always at you. I used to come only when I couldn't stand it any more, but now" — she shrugs — "now that our tour is close to ending, I give myself a couple of hours here almost every day. It keeps me sane." She stands awkwardly, smoothing down her skirt, and picks up her book from the table. "I'm sorry, but I have to go. If you need any advice or help, you know where to find me."

As she walks stiffly away between the trees and through the glass doors into the lobby, Iris feels a brief pang of longing for a driver and a home and a husband waiting for her somewhere not far away. But tomorrow, surely, she will see Lannie again, and in the meantime, now that she has talked to someone who lives comfortably here, her nervousness is allayed. And she's perfectly safe here in this walled compound, doesn't have to leave it until she hears from Lannie.

She sips her drink, and when she finishes it, goes off to look for the hotel restaurant. It turns out there are three of them and she picks the most informal where she refuses an Ethiopian meal in favour of North American-style chicken and pasta, which she finds quite good.

After dinner she goes to her room and, even though it's early, goes to bed and falls asleep, and into her other world.

It is night and very dark — no moon or stars — it's raining lightly, she's hurrying down a city street trying to catch up with a small, dark-haired little girl who clacks down the cobbled surface, past puddles of black water, a half a city block ahead of her. The little girl holds a woman's hand, her mother's, and although they are walking steadily, purposefully, not hurrying, Iris can't catch up to them. She hurries, slipping on the wet stones, but the little girl and her mother remain an even distance ahead of her. If she doesn't hurry, she'll lose them in the darkness, and she wants desperately to reach the little girl.

The dream shifts to the farm kitchen at home, and Barney is sitting at the table drinking coffee. Lannie, a small girl with her strawberry-blonde hair plaited in two shining braids, asks Barney to buy her a pony and Barney is saying, *No, no, there'll be no ponies on this farm. I have no pasture.* Then Iris looks out the window that has appeared in the wall behind the table where there was no window a moment before. She sees open grassy yellow fields, and in the distance a herd of horses — greys, browns, blacks, roans — run, their golden manes and tails rippling.

She wakes then, it's only three in the morning by her bedside clock. In the shadows, her head full of the long gentle fields of tawny grass, she can't think where she is. When she remembers, she feels her heart will break with longing for home.

She falls back to sleep and the dreams tumbling through her head are of beggars and donkeys and streets so decayed they are hardly more than heaps of rubble. Soldiers march by carrying guns, tanks rumble past, fire leaps up from wooden shacks consuming them, and cars and trucks rush down the main road from the Addis Ababa airport, past crowds of plodding, white-gowned people, toward Maskal Square at the heart of this shabby, breathtaking city.

The next time she wakes it's to someone rapping hard on her door. She stumbles out of bed, her heart pounding with fear and surprise, and seeing it's noon, dismay at the lateness of the hour. Her dressing gown pulled tightly around her, she opens the door to find a maid standing there, her cleaning equipment on a cart behind her.

"I clean?" the woman asks. Trying to collect herself, Iris says, "Soon," holding up a finger. She closes the door. It's her second day in Ethiopia and she has accomplished nothing. This thought makes her rush to the bathroom, hurry through her ablutions, dress, and then she can't decide whether to eat something first, she's starving, or start phoning again. She decides to begin by phoning.

She repeats her calls to the two numbers where no one answered yesterday. Both voices on the other end of the line claim never to have heard of Lannie Stone. She's about to retry the number where the young woman answered and Iris felt sure she simply didn't want to be bothered with Iris, but the maid appears at her door again and Iris, although exasperated at a further delay, bows to the inevitable, leaving her to clean while she goes downstairs to find some breakfast.

It's almost an hour later when she returns to her now pristine room. Although she's beginning to wonder if she shouldn't just go by taxi from agency to agency, consulting her piece of paper, she tries the number where she felt she'd been summarily treated the day before. The phone rings and rings before the same vague young woman answers again.

"May I speak to the director, please," she says. There's a silence, then, "One moment." Nervously she waits.

"Alec Martin here," a voice says. Iris lets her breath out slowly, then she starts in again with her story. "Lannie Stone," the man says thoughtfully. "Maybe she's not stationed in Addis," he says. "Save the Children have compounds in several other towns. If she's with them, she could be in Weldiya or — wherever." Iris is fighting for composure. How can she go to strange towns when she doesn't even have phone numbers or any contacts or — "Or it could just be I haven't run into her. I've only been here about seven months. I came here from India," he tells her.

"But what shall I do?" Iris asks, hearing panic creeping into her voice. He tells her he'll get his assistant to give her more phone numbers. "And if she's not at any Addis offices, we can find phone numbers for you in some of the towns where she might be." She thanks him, but she's thinking longingly of the airport, of her return ticket tucked safely away in her purse. "If she's in the country, we'll track her down. Which reminds me, you can try the Canadian Consulate too." He gives her that number himself.

She's on the phone another half-hour while the lackadaisical young woman bit by bit gives her the names and phone numbers for further possibilities, taking breaks every few minutes to have chats with other people who wander by her desk. Once, she sets the phone down and goes away. She's gone so long Iris thinks the connection is broken and is about to hang up when she comes back on the line. Iris feels like asking to speak to the director again and telling him he should fire this incompetent, but of course, she doesn't, and anyway, the girl isn't exactly rude or even brusque, she just doesn't seem to understand how thoroughly unbusinesslike she is.

When she finally gets off the line, Iris stares at the long list of phone numbers, some with notes she has written to herself — "Tuesdays only" "Everyone in field" "Employs only Ethiopians" — and thinks she'll be at this the rest of her life, she'll never find Lannie, she'll never get out of this country. She almost tosses her new list into the wastepaper basket in her despair, but stops herself. Instead, she picks up her purse and walks back downstairs and out to the garden again where the white wrought-iron tables sit under the flowering trees. She's looking for Betty Chamberlain. A few minutes of normal conversation, she's telling herself, someone from home, and I'll be all right.

But Betty isn't seated at one of the tables, nor is she one of the heads bobbing in the swimming pool. She's not in the hotel lounge either or in the lobby or in one of the gift shops that line the lobby's mall. Iris gives up and goes back to her room. On the way up in the elevator it suddenly occurs to her that there was one more number at the bottom of her original list, the one she brought with her from Canada. She hadn't called it yesterday because it had grown too late. She glances hurriedly at her wristwatch. It's past four o'clock, closer to five really. This day has flown by, and she's no further ahead than when she left Ottawa.

Back in her room she dials. It rings and rings and Iris would hang up but if nobody's there what does it matter how long she lets it ring? She's not even listening any more, when finally she hears the phone being picked up and a woman answers, first naming her agency and then saying gravely, "Mrs. Samuels here." Her accent is British overlaid on some other, unidentifiable accent, but her voice is rich and warm and sounds as if she has all the time in the world. Iris takes a deep breath and explains again.

"Well, to tell you the truth," Mrs. Samuels says without a moment's hesitation, "she doesn't really work for us. She's a volunteer, she isn't on our staff." She pauses and Iris hears papers close to the phone. She's holding the phone so tight her hand hurts, and she loosens her grip, waiting for the woman to go on. "And at the moment, I'm not sure if she's here in Addis or if she's out in the field with Dr. Abubech. That is, Dr. Abubech Tefera is out working in the Kombolcha area where we have some plots." Plots? Oh, yes, this agency runs agricultural programs. "I'm not sure if Miss Stone is with her or not." There's a pause. "Although I expect she is. Wherever Dr. Abubech goes, Lannie is never far behind. Lannie adores Abubech. We all do."

Iris has broken out in a sweat all over her body. She can't hear what the woman on the other end of the line is saying.

"Are you there?" the woman says in a kindly way.

"Yes," she says. "It's a shock — I can't thank you enough. I — "

"Nothing to thank me for," the woman says. "I'm happy to help. I'm sure Lannie will be very glad to see you."

"But," Iris says, beginning to tremble again, "but — what shall I do? I mean — "

"You've just arrived?" she asks. Her nonchalance is replaced by a certain careful concern.

"Yes. And I've never been in a — a country like this before and I really want to see my niece. Her uncle died — "

The woman interrupts. "You're at the Hilton?"

"Yes," Iris says. She gives her room number.

"I'll do some checking, see what I can find out, and I'll call you back. Now the only problem is that it's late, in fact, this office is closed — you've reached me by accident, I am not the usual telephone-answerer. I may not be able to find anything out before morning."

"I can wait till morning," Iris interrupts.

"Yes, it's only a matter of time till you speak to her face to face. You go have dinner, have a shower, get some sleep. I will call you promptly at ten tomorrow morning, sooner if I locate her here in Addis — although I think that's unlikely," she adds quickly.

Iris puts the phone down and then can't remember if she'd thanked the woman or not. She puts her hands to her head and holds it, then slowly lowers them to her lap and sits that way gazing into space, barely breathing, her body filled with trembling.

The ringing of the phone wakes her from a deep sleep and Iris is startled to see that it's ten o'clock — she isn't over her jet lag yet. Fumbling in her haste, she picks up the receiver. Her heart is already pounding. It might even be Lannie herself.

"It seems that Miss Stone is in the field with Dr. Abubech," Mrs. Samuels tells Iris. "They've gone to Kombolcha and aren't expected back before the end of the week, although they could be delayed longer." Her heart, which has begun to slow, now sinks. A whole week, if not longer! "You could go up to Kombolcha if you choose to. They always stay at Afewerk's Inn. They come in every evening. You could meet your niece there," she suggests.

"Is it far?" she asks. Mrs. Samuels explains it's to the north and east of Addis, that Afewerk's Inn is clean and comfortable, that Iris can fly to Kombolcha with Ethiopian Airlines if she wants to, or that she can hire a driver and a car, in which case it will take the better part of a day to get there.

"It isn't far, but the roads aren't good and there's a lot of traffic. Seven or eight hours, I believe. But then," she adds, her voice picking up enthusiasm, "if you go by car, you'll see something of the country. Your niece won't return to the inn from the countryside before evening." She pauses. When Iris says nothing, her brain busy with all these alternatives, she goes on, "Or you could just wait in Addis until she returns."

That settles it. Iris has already travelled too far, waited too long, gone through too much, to simply sit and wait some more. She will hire a car and a driver and go to Kombolcha, for indeed, when she has nothing to do but wait for Lannie, what would be the point of flying? If she's lucky, by tonight she'll be eating dinner with her. Her heart lurches, whether from joy or fear she can't tell, because even while she finds she's smiling like a fool into the receiver, one part of her is worrying suddenly that Lannie may refuse to see her, and yet another has faltered, crying out, *Not yet!*

By noon the next day, Iris is riding in the passenger seat of a fairly new Land Rover, driving north up a paved, but impossibly potholed road with a young Ethiopian male in the driver's seat. Giyorgis is in his mid-twenties, and is courteous but warm, by turns boyish and grave, and she thinks she sees in his eyes a gentleness that reassures her.

She'd gone to the desk clerk to inquire about hiring someone to take her to Kombolcha. The clerk and the two other men working behind the counter had held a brief discussion in a language Iris knew must be Amharic; in fact, there seemed to be a brief, suppressed argument. The first man dialled the phone and spoke into it also in Amharic. In a moment he'd set the receiver down and said to her, "Your driver will be here in an hour." When Iris had asked if he was with the Ethiopian Tourism Agency, or whatever it was called, he'd replied, "He is private. But he is very experienced. He was once a driver for the United Nations." It had occurred to Iris to wonder if he was perhaps a relative of the desk clerk, but she hadn't asked, concluding that it didn't matter since the clerk had said that his rates were the same as the official agency. It flashed through her mind to wonder how safe she'd be with him if he wasn't official, but couldn't see, beyond thieves, what there was to be afraid of anyway. And surely having driven for the U.N. was credentials enough.

Giyorgis had arrived in under an hour, medium height, strong-looking instead of fine-boned and tall as most Ethiopians seem to be, freshly shaven, smelling faintly of soap and dressed in neatly pressed khaki trousers and a clean short-sleeved blue shirt with a beige windbreaker over it. He had bowed over each of her shoulders when they were introduced in the way Iris now recognized as Ethiopian. How formal they are, she thought, shy at being the object of actual bowing.

It's taking them a good half-hour to make their way from the Hilton's parking lot with its Mercedes, new Land Rovers, and other expensive cars, along the busy city streets, always climbing, it seems to her, until they finally reach the outskirts, the road levels out, and they slowly leave the jumble of Addis Ababa behind. At first she and Giyorgis make polite conversation. She asks him how long he has been a driver, and from what part of Ethiopia he has come.

"I am from here, Addis," he tells her. "As my father, too. I began to be a driver after I finished school." She wonders if this means university, and decides if he had meant that, he would have said so. She remembers there has been a long war, and thinks how it must surely have disrupted lives even here in Addis. He asks her how long has she been in Ethiopia, is it her first trip, what does she think of it?

"It's a very beautiful landscape, what I've seen of it," Iris says, a careful reply to his last question. The landscape they are travelling through is a relatively flat plain, but every once in a while far off to the east they catch glimpses of a great, deep, blue-shadowed valley dotted with those flat-topped African trees, the valley lined with low mountains, and the bottom and terraced sides divided into small, square fields. "It's very different from Canada."

"Canada is a new country," he remarks. Abruptly he turns the wheel to hug the edge of the road as a huge truck pulling a box behind it as big as the first one squeezes past them, going north, the same direction they are. She thinks the truck with its double load is what Barney would have called a "B-train."

"I know Ethiopia is old," Iris says, "but not how old."

"Ah," Giyorgis says, "I will tell you. Is book *Kebra Nagast*. It means 'Glory of Kings.' In it is told the story about how old is Ethiopia." He pauses and by the eagerness of his expression she knows he's dying to tell her the story. Out of politeness, she asks him to tell her what *Kebra Nagast* says.

"The Queen of Sheba was Ethiopian woman," he begins, taking his eyes from the road for a second to gauge her reaction to this news.

"Her name Makeda. She went to Jerusalem to visit King Solomon. There she became pregnant. She gave birth to son named Menelik who became," here his voice rises, grows emphatic, "the first Ethiopian king — Menelik I. That was a thousand years before Christos. So Ethiopia is three thousand years. Is one of oldest countries in world." He turns to her, his eyes lit up with wonder at his own story. "There is more?" he says. She sees that he means, does she want to hear the rest?

In fact, the story does interest her, and she feels sure, by his soberness and the care with which he's telling it, that this is more than some tale concocted for tourists.

"What else?"

"Menelik was born here — in Ethiopia, but when he was twenty years he went to Jerusalem to meet his father, King Solomon. He stayed there for a little while," his pronounciation of "little" is deliciously precise, "but when he came back to Ethiopia, he and his friends brought back — " he pauses dramatically, "the Ark of the Covenant! And it is here in Ethiopia now!" Iris looks at him in some surprise, remembering vaguely that it was a box that Moses built, that — that God was in it? That worked miracles. Something very holy and powerful. She can feel him waiting for her reaction. By the look on his face, she knows Giyorgis believes this utterly.

"Yes, here!" he says, nodding his head vigorously as if she has commented. "At Aksum. But no one may see it." Iris exhales noisily expressing wonder, since she can think of absolutely nothing to say, and she knows better than to voice doubt.

"Amazing!" she says finally.

"All Ethiopians know this," Giyorgis says calmly.

In a kind of weary awe, Iris begins to see how much there is to learn about Ethiopia. It's more than she can hope to deal with, and she knows there's no story in all of Canada that could even begin to be held up against this one. If a thousand years pass and Canada remains a country, will some national story explaining its existence have sprung up? She can't imagine what it would be.

"What crops will they plant?" she asks, taking refuge in the view out the window, pointing to the farmers' fields they're passing.

"Sorghum," Giyorgis says. "You know sorghum?"

"We don't grow it in Saskatchewan — where I come from. Too short a growing season or too cold or not enough moisture or — something." And people everywhere, walking down the side of the road, working in the fields, riding donkeys or driving them, herding cattle or ponies or sheep and goats. The people wear leather-thong sandals or no shoes at all, and their clothes are at best nondescript, at worst, rags. Suddenly she thinks of the crowds of people she saw on the streets of Addis Ababa; at least half, maybe even more, had been young men.

"Why are there so many men on the streets in Addis Ababa? Don't they have jobs?"

"No jobs, no. And they are soldiers, you know? After war they are not soldiers and they have no jobs so they come to Addis and they wait." He shrugs. Now she notices that many of the people on this road are children.

"Aren't the children in school? Is it a holiday?"

"Some go to school," he says vaguely.

Iris contents herself for a while watching the scenery they're passing through. It is a landscape stunning in its strange beauty, its — compared to her own vast, spread-out landscape — small-scale ruggedness. Now she can see clearly where most of the trees have been cut off the mountainsides, she guesses by the smell in the air which she'd noticed filling the air in Addis Ababa this morning too, for firewood. She asks Giyorgis.

"They cut all the trees," Giyorgis says. "All. They have no fuel, so the trees — they go." He shrugs his shoulders in a way that conveys regret. "And the government, it bring eucalyptus trees here, where no eucalyptus grows. Because if you cut, it grows back fast."

After a while they pass three tall, skinny pack camels being led down the side of the road. She has never seen camels before in her life and her delighted exclamation makes Giyorgis laugh. The farther they go, the more Iris relaxes and begins to enjoy herself, especially since her driver is friendly without being forward, solicitous of her comfort.

They stop for a break at Debre Berhans, which Giyorgis tells her means, "Mountain of Light," but all Iris sees is poverty everywhere. It's hard to tell how big the town is since much of it is out of sight behind or below trees, or disappears behind hills. The houses she does see are small and shabby, made of a muddy-looking plaster with sheets of corrugated iron for roofs, and, in fact, she isn't sure which are houses and which are businesses or offices. But the people seem cheerful — the children follow her giggling, one little girl shyly taking her hand, until Giyorgis speaks loudly to them in Amharic and they fall back and drift away.

"They beg," he says angrily, and she sees he's embarrassed. They had been saying, "Give me pen. I stu-dent," and "Give money," and rubbing their stomachs in a woeful way that Iris recognizes as bad acting, but some of them are so thin and ragged she suspects that though the begging may be a performance, the need is real. To these she gives out her few coins, the denominations of which are so small they're worth practically nothing in Canadian money. Following Giyorgis's lead, she ignores the few adult beggars whose absolute destitution appals her no less than when she first saw it. And, of course, there are the maimed and crippled ones, their condition so shocking that it upsets her. How could Lannie have lived with this all these years? The town itself looks as if it is teetering on the edge of total decay.

Giyorgis says, "In sixteenth century Ahmad Ibn Gran stopped here to get ready for more war." Iris doesn't know who Ahmad Ibn Gran is or what war Giyorgis is referring to. It occurs to her that she could ask, that she has spent a lot of her life not asking questions because answers only complicate life. She wonders, Is that why I turned away from university? She thinks of a girl in her Grade Twelve class from a Christian fundamentalist home who'd turned down a scholarship to university, explaining that she was afraid university would make her lose her faith. What was *I* afraid of? Iris wonders. She turns to Giyorgis.

"Who was Ahmad Gran?" she asks. "What war are you talking about?" He stops walking, turns to look directly down at her, taking note of her interest. She doesn't look away.

"He was Muslim," he says, opening the door of the café he's

picked out for them to snack in. "He invade Ethiopia and destroy many, many things. Books, churches. Killed many people. Ethiopia was Christian since fourth century. But Gran, he destroyed Aksum. Everything. But not all obelisks. Some still lie there." He indicates the ground with his hand.

"Aksum?" Iris asks.

"Where Ethiopia begin," he says, as if he's amazed she doesn't know this. "North. Is now Tigray. Aksum was powerful kingdom. Was a city, Aksum, too. Gran destroyed." He clearly wants to tell her more, but is hindered both by his inadequate command of English and some other, interior control he seems to have placed on himself. Maybe someone has told him that too much history bores *ferenjis*.

Lunch consists of a greyish, rolled flatbread which Giyorgis tells her is *injera*, and meat in a highly spiced gravy which apparently is supposed to be mopped up with the bread, using one's fingers. Iris tries valiantly to eat, but tears spring to her eyes and she wheezes for a moment when she swallows what must be a piece of crushed chili, if chilies grow in Ethiopia, and Giyorgis laughs, then commiserates. The owner of the restaurant brings her a fork.

Then they are off again toward Kombolcha through country slightly more intriguing and various than before. At one point, the great valley Iris had spotted earlier off to the east reaches to within a half-kilometre of the roadside and she gets a closer look at the ruggedness of its terrain. She has the feeling that they're climbing higher too, although the road runs up no obviously steep hills. Every few kilometres Giyorgis has to slow down and honk so that people herding cows or goats or a few small donkeys can get themselves and their animals out of the way of their vehicle.

At one point he laughs out loud and, turning to her, says, "Do you know this story? Once a donkey, a goat, and a dog each went for a ride in a — a — " he fumbles for an English word, "contract — taxi. The donkey paid his fare, so he owns the road. That is why he does not move off it when I go by. But the goat, he did not pay. That is why he runs away each time. The dog, he paid, but the taxi driver ran away with his change." He pauses for drama, grinning. "And that is why the dog barks when I go by."

It is a charming story, Iris thinks; it pleases her that Giyorgis would tell her this folktale.

But this road is also in a scandalous state of disrepair; her bottom is getting sore from so much jarring, and she has to change position often to keep her back from aching. When she remarks on the state of the road, Giyorgis explains that the Italians built it during the Second World War. "For five, six years they were here," he says. "Before we drove them out." Oh, that's why the waiter offered me spaghetti, Iris thinks.

By the time they reach Kombolcha it's after six and dark, and Iris is tired. Giyorgis apparently knows the town well because without hesitation he leaves the main street with its streetlights and drives directly down street after bumpy, unpaved, and unlit street until they arrive at the end of a road tucked into a dark corner of the town. The inn gate opens, Iris catches a glimpse of the two men in long robes, one of them with something — a rifle? — slung over his shoulder, who've opened it. Giyorgis drives through, and the men close it behind them.

The Land Rover's headlights reveal a long, single-storey, white-painted building with a veranda running its length at the level of the parking lot. Iris has a strange feeling in her stomach, a kind of tingling, from the sight of that gun — if it was a gun. She does not know what it is to protect them from, has so far seen nothing of which to be frightened. But then, she thinks, I suppose the only way to keep those who have so little from trying to take more for themselves is with guns. It is a sobering thought.

They park, get out, stretch, and go inside. Branches laden with scarlet blooms brush Iris's hair as she enters the inn behind her driver. In her exhaustion she'd forgotten until this minute that behind this wall Lannie may be eating dinner, or lying asleep in a bed, or sitting studying, as she used to do at home on the farm in Saskatchewan, her books spread out before her, her long, fine hair glinting red in the desk lamp's light. She begins to tremble, and her stomach goes queasy before she wills it to stop.

Yes, Lannie Stone and Dr. Abubech Tefera have rooms here. The middle-aged woman who tells them this is tall and big-boned, dressed in a plain wool skirt, a white blouse with a shawl draped loosely over it that also covers her hair. She speaks surprisingly colloquial English. But, she goes on, they are not presently in, they have flown up to Tigray for a few days and are expected back on the weekend. But of course there are rooms here for Giyorgis and Mrs. Christie, and the dining room remains open until ten. She's very polite, but casually so, in an unEthiopian way. When Iris congratulates her on her English, she replies that she had an aunt and uncle in the United States and as a girl visited there often, once staying almost two years. "After the war my uncle has come home, here."

Giyorgis, ever-mindful of his duty to Iris, begins to explain about the war, but Iris, tired as she is, interrupts. "I remember. The Tigrayan freedom fighters fought Mengistu and the Dergue and won. In 1991," she adds.

"Indeed, it is so," Giyorgis says. The woman says proudly, "I am Tigrayan."

Iris notices that Giyorgis is looking at his shoes. She remembers Giyorgis isn't Tigrayan, and she wonders what has just passed between them that she hasn't understood.

"Under the Dergue our country was Communist," the woman remarks. "Communists!" she says, as if the word means some kind of terrifying, disgusting plague. Which reminds Iris of the many red stars, rusting and broken, or just the faded outline of ones that had been removed, over gateways or on public buildings, she saw both from the taxi, and today as they drove through Addis.

As if she's remembering her manners, the innkeeper says, "I am the widow of Afewerk." She gives her own name too, but it has too many syllables, and Iris fails to catch it and doesn't like to ask the woman to repeat it. "I'm pleased to have you as a guest here."

Iris thanks her, warmed by the kindness of this greeting, but the fact that once again she has missed Lannie and has no choice but to stay here or go back to Addis and wait there is slowly sinking in. Giyorgis is waiting for her to make a decision. So is the woman who stands with them in the room which can't properly be called an office but serves as one. Iris is getting used to the poverty of Ethiopia and finds she doesn't even miss the fake-wood counter, the computer humming insistently in the background, the swimming pool in the room next door to the office, or the polite indifference of the desk clerks.

She teeters a little and Giyorgis steadies her carefully by putting his arm gingerly around her shoulders and stepping close to her so she can lean on him if she needs to. She is grateful to him.

"Of course, you must stay at least until morning comes," the innkeeper says to her. "Then you can make your decision whether to wait in Kombolcha or not." She calls into the next room and another, older woman, wearing a white shawl over a cotton house-dress, an employee, a housekeeper, enters from a back room carrying a handful of keys. Afewerk's widow speaks to her in another language, then says, to Iris and Giyorgis, "Hagosa will look after you. Good night." She goes out.

Giyorgis says, "We meet at seven for dinner, here," pointing to a dining room Iris now sees through an open door on her left. The housekeeper hands him a key, he goes out of the room and disappears down the corridor. She says to Iris, "Come," and Iris follows her down a hall in the opposite direction.

"You are waiting for your niece?" she asks Iris, over her shoulder. Had she been listening through the door? She is more forward than Afewerk's widow seems to be, or curious maybe, about Iris, the *ferenji*. "You will go back to Addis in the morning?"

"I don't know what to do," Iris replies. They have reached her room around a bend in the corridor and the woman unlocks the door, goes in ahead of Iris, and puts on the light by pulling a string hanging from a bare bulb in the centre of the ceiling.

"Dr. Abubech will bring her in three, four days. You wait here," Hagosa suggests, holding up fingers in case her English is wrong. The room is clean, but so dismal with the poor light and the shabby, insufficient furniture, that the thought of staying here for any time longer than she absolutely has to chills Iris.

"Maybe I could go to Tigray?" she appeals to Hagosa.

"But where in Tigray?" Hagosa asks dubiously. "Is long way." Seeing the dismay on her face, Hagosa says, "Or you could visit our country. The rock churches at Lalibela very famous, the castles at

Gondar, the obelisks at Aksum. Obelisks very famous." When Iris says nothing, she goes on. "Some have fallen, they are broken. They have words on them, history, from kings and priests. They are very, very old." Iris thinks wearily, What does it matter to me what I visit?

"How far is Aksum?"

"Is far," she admits. "Two, three days by road. Gondar — is best to go by airplane to Gondar. Lalibela is closest — six, seven hours drive. Rock churches there."

"Rock churches are at Lalibela? What are they?"

"I have not seen," Hagosa admits. "Churches carved out of rock long ago. When King Lalibela rule. Very beautiful. Are still used."

At dinner — Giyorgis has *injera wat*, and Iris has spaghetti — Iris questions Giyorgis about going to Lalibela.

"Yes, yes." He nods vigorously. "It is good place to go. I myself go there many times when I was driver for U.N. The churches are most beautiful."

"Is there a hotel there?" Iris asks, still uncertain.

"Oh, yes. Was Hilton before. Is very good hotel."

After she has returned to her drab little room and is lying in her bed in the dark, her mind drifts. She finds herself back in the cabin, Barney's body stretched out on the couch, the moment when she knew he was dead. She has to pull back before its full weight hits her again, his image then replaced with Jay, stretched out beside her on her hotel bed in Toronto, the way the fine black hair on his stomach glinted faintly, his eyes with their long, thick lashes closed.

She thinks of Lannie lying unconscious on her bed at home, the way Iris had found her that morning, her reddish hair spread out like a wound against the white sheets. She tries to form Lannie's face in her mind's eye, but in spite of that one explosion of memory in the Hilton in Addis, it eludes her. Will I even know her when I see her? she thinks. Maybe this woman people here call Lannie is somebody else, not the one she and Barney drove frantically to the hospital, her stomach full of James Springer's sleeping pills. Or the one Iris took to the hospital in Swift Current to have an abortion.

She thinks again of Lannie's years of silence— of her joy the day she left Chinook to find her father, and how happy for her she and

Barney had been, that she had at last gained the strength to take control of her life. And yet, from that much-desired beginning Lannie became even more lost, so much so that here I am searching for her in the most distant and foreign of countries.

Did I never do more than wait for her to speak to me because I was afraid of what would come out when she did open up? Is that why I didn't even try to make her speak? She must have been full of — of what? Terror, Iris thinks, absolute terror for what would happen next to her life, and rage at what had already happened. And I didn't want to hear it because I would have had to face what I am facing now — that there are not solutions to every problem, that there are not always happy endings to stories. And I thought that if Lannie never spoke, I would not have to hear what I couldn't bear to know.

Lalibela

The road heading more or less north out of Kombolcha toward Dessie, Weldiya, and eventually Lalibela, winds around mountain-sides revealing views of more low mountains, mostly having just enough trees left here and there to indicate to Iris that they must once have been covered with forests, and in level or gently sloping areas between or below them, those same small, square fields. Now and then they come around curves to find precipitous drop-offs to valleys far below. Even here on this narrow mountain road, although they are considerably fewer, people are walking, herding donkeys, cattle, sheep, and goats, or occasionally riding a donkey or a horse.

Frequently their vehicle is squeezed to the side of the road by huge trucks pulling a second, equally big box behind the first, both loaded with full burlap sacks. It occurs to her that they were passed by quite a few of these big trucks yesterday, too, on their way north to Kombolcha from Addis Ababa.

"What's in those bags?" she asks Giyorgis. It seems the urge to ask questions, once succumbed to, is habit-forming.

"Grain," he says, "going north to Tigray."

"Oh," Iris says, remembering the pictures Tim spoke of on television in the early eighties of starving people that had brought Lannie to this country. "Is there another drought up there?" Giyorgis looks as if he's about to speak, thinks better of it, then says, "Maybe, I don't know. They store it. Is always drought in this country. Each truck carries four hundred and fifty quintals."

"How much is a quintal?" she asks.

"It is . . ." he says slowly. "Ah, yes! I think — is a hundred kilos."

Iris makes an attempt at the mental arithmetic, but gives it up without solving it. A lot, that's how much it is, a whole lot of grain. Especially when truck after truck squeezes past them, all heading north.

Is there or isn't there a drought in Tigray? She ponders what she knows. As a result of too much starvation, too much neglect by the central government, both under the emperor and then the *Dergue*, the Tigrayan guerrilla movement had at last overthrown it and itself become the central government. Doubtless the Tigrayans had vowed that as the new government their own people would never starve again. She's sure if she were in that position she'd do exactly the same thing.

Three hours later they've reached Weldiya where Giyorgis searches out a suitable place for Iris to eat lunch — suitable because the cleanest and most modern, at least from the exterior. Over what Iris is learning to view as the inevitable *injera* and a meat sauce, he tells her that from here they'll travel for a while on "the Chinese Road."

"The Chinese build it," he says. "When Mengistu was here. I admire them for it. Chinese died building it. It is a good road." As they're about to leave Iris asks him to inquire where the ladies' bathroom is and she's led outside, across a courtyard and into a small, tiled, none-too-clean cubicle within which there is a wastepaper basket, a bucket of water, and a hole in the floor. Lord, she thinks. How could Lannie stand to live like this year after year?

The Chinese Road is indeed a better road, even if it is only gravel. For the first time since they left Addis they're able to travel at fifty miles an hour. But it too curves precipitously as they climb higher and higher. In places they're so high and the drop-off on one side or the other is so deep, she's reminded of driving between Banff and Jasper, although the mountains here aren't as high or as craggy, nor are their peaks snow-covered. In the distance, though, she can see a rugged blue range which Giyorgis tells her is the Simien Mountains where Ras Dashan, the highest mountain in Ethiopia, is. "Over four thousand metres, the fourth highest mountain in Africa." The Simiens look like the Rockies.

This road is a little easier on Iris's posterior and she loses herself in the constant surprises of the landscape that open to viewing around each of the bends and spread out below each rise. The lower hillsides all look as if they were once tree-covered, but nothing is left now but low green shrubs here and there, and as for grass, there's very little of it. At one point they come upon two men on foot driving a herd of more than fifty young camels, and she wishes she had a camera. They arrive at a fork in the road and Giyorgis says, "From here seventy-seven kilometres to Lalibela."

The track they turn onto from the splendour of the Chinese Road is a narrow, dusty trail that reminds her of the road at home that runs through the back of Cypress Hills Park to Fort Walsh, bearing the sign Impassable When Wet. Giyorgis tells her that soon, during the rainy season, Lalibela will be unreachable by road. She isn't surprised. This hardly deserves the name "road," dusty, rocky, and unmaintained as it is. But although they've had to slow to about twenty-five or fewer miles per hour and more than once in low spots they drive through streams that have spread across the track, Iris doesn't worry. She's used to roads like this, and she keeps reminding herself that under the mud holes and the long stretches of loose dirt, unlike at home, here the bottom is rock, so that getting stuck is unlikely, even if they weren't in a four-wheel drive. And she trusts her careful driver Giyorgis.

As they leave behind all vestiges of cities or towns or even large villages, the countryside appears wilder, the mountains closer and more rugged. It initially appears empty of people. Yet even without villages or people on the road now, it quickly becomes evident that the countryside is populated. Every hundred yards or so they see above on the mountainside or along the sides of the road another child herding the family's five or six cows, or few stunted goats and sheep. She thinks how at home, around where she lives, she could drive for two hours or more and not see another living soul, not even meet or pass another vehicle.

The children all wave and shout and grin when Iris waves back. Some of them run to keep abreast of the car for a little way. Iris wonders where they live, and now and then she sees high above them on the sloping mountainside a cluster of two or three of the thatched-roof, conical houses. The walls seem to be made of some sturdy but narrow vertical poles which must somehow be woven together and then plastered with mud.

"Sometimes they build with sorghum stalks," Giyorgis explains. "That is why they grow very tall sorghum. And, also, it is firewood." The huts blend so completely into the low shrubbery and stony earth of the hillside that she really has to look to find them.

And the children! When they slow to go around a rocky, rising curve, she gets a close look at a little girl standing about ten feet above their vehicle. She is barefoot and filthy, but then, who wouldn't be in this dirt, Iris reminds herself, and she's wearing what was once a dress, but is now better described as a rag, faded to a no-colour, torn or worn through in places. Worst of all, the child is perhaps four years old.

"They don't go to school?" she whispers, meaning, Don't they play? Don't they have childhoods?

"No, too poor," he says. "Or, there is no school." He keeps both hands on the wheel and looks straight ahead so she knows he's upset by this too, maybe ashamed or sorrowful for the state his country is in, or for his own helplessness. She even thinks this would be bearable if it were only one child, or only one four-year-old child, but the children are everywhere she looks. A four-year-old herder is commonplace.

Two hours have passed since they started out on this road and Iris's back is beginning to ache from the constant jolting, and her tailbone is sore from two days of sitting. She would complain, but it wouldn't do any good, so she keeps silent.

At last they see a village ahead. Village is perhaps too grandiose a word for this collection of eight or ten of those conical African huts with the thatched roofs, but as they draw closer they see a crowd of people gathered on the dusty track running between the huts their Land Rover is travelling down. Iris is apprehensive as Giyorgis slows their vehicle and, just short of the crowd, pulls to a stop at the side of the track. There are perhaps twenty people, nearly all adults, the men wearing what she guesses must be traditional garb, a short-skirted — well above the knees — togalike garment of natural-colour cotton, one long end brought up from the back to hang loosely down over one shoulder, the women wearing layered, dresslike garments, worn and dirty, and held together at the waist with cords.

One of the women who must not have seen their approach is still wailing loudly and turning in circles in a movement that is like, but seems not to be quite, a dance. As their vehicle stops, she stops too, her wailing cut off in mid-cry.

So quickly Iris doesn't see it happen, their vehicle is surrounded by villagers. They press up against the car, their faces within inches of hers and Giyorgis's, she couldn't open the door if she wanted to for their bodies, and Iris, aware of her rudeness, hastily rolls up the window she'd just rolled down. She feels acutely that there is only one thin layer of glass between her and these strangers. What puzzles her even as it frightens her is that all those faces three and four deep crowding in on her, staring at her, are not threatening. They are, instead, blank. Just, it seems to her, carefully, wilfully, blank.

Iris's heart is pounding, her mouth has gone dry. Is this where she's going to meet her death? Here, in this godforsaken corner of the earth, far from home and family and people who speak her own language? Will they soon drag her from the car and — she's trembling through and through, about to say — no, to order — Giyorgis to put the vehicle in gear, his foot on the gas, they can at least try to escape, when she glances quickly at him. He's speaking to one of the villagers, a man dressed in the traditional garment carrying a tall staff who towers over the others. Giyorgis turns to her and says calmly, "It is a funeral."

"What? Where?" Now she sees at the far side of the crowd, a half-dozen men lifting a long, narrow pallet to their shoulders. Whatever is on the pallet is shrouded in cotton, but it takes Iris only a second to realize that the cotton covers a body.

"It is him," Giyorgis says. When he gestures and she turns her head quickly to look, the people pushing up against her side of the car turn their heads to look too. Giyorgis says quietly to her, "It is only that they wonder. They are curious." She recognizes that he understands how frightened she has been.

Now, from behind the huts two horses and their riders come into view, moving slowly to the track behind the Land Rover, going in the direction Iris and Giyorgis have just come from. The riders are men wearing robes and wide white turbans; Iris notices the horses are small but strong-looking, and both are covered to their knees in gold-trimmed, green brocade ceremonial blankets that fasten at their chests and from which their tails protrude. Even while Iris is trying desperately to see everything, her heart still pounding from the fright she has had, the splendour of the horses' blankets beside the people's rags is not lost on her.

At the appearance of the horses and riders the people who've been crowding around the Land Rover move slowly away without looking back. The men bearing the body move into place behind the horses, the villagers crowd around the pallet-bearers, and the procession begins to recede slowly. At once the wailing starts up again, although Iris can't see the women making the noise. As Giyorgis puts their vehicle in gear and they drive on slowly past the rest of the huts, the keening fades away behind them. They drive on around a rising curve and a mountainside imposes itself between them and the procession.

"I was afraid," Iris admits.

"Few strangers go down this road," he says, explaining the villagers' reaction to her. But what puzzles Iris most is that blankness on the people's faces. She has seen enough Ethiopians now to know that they are normally as vivacious as any Canadians. She can't think why they would wipe away all expression — the crowding she can understand if they were merely curious — but — could it be that mixed in with their curiosity was fear? Fear that she and Giyorgis were police or maybe government officials who might cause them trouble? Wouldn't they just run away instead? She would like to ask Giyorgis what he thinks about this, but when she reflects, she remembers that he seemed not even to notice it. And he has had to explain the peculiarities of his country to her so many times since she got into his vehicle, more than once she felt her questions about the sad and ugly things she has observed have humiliated him, that she feels she will let this one pass.

They drive on in silence a few more miles, and Iris notices that the countryside is not only far more rugged than that which she saw farther to the south yesterday, but that there is also much less vegetation and what there is appears parched, in need of rain. And the dust! The farther they go into the mountains and north toward the famous town of Lalibela, the drier and dustier it gets. On curves rising up a mountainside once or twice Giyorgis, having to drive very slowly because of the extruding rocks on the road, actually spins out, the layer of dry, loose dirt is so thick. He has to back up a little until his wheels find a place to grip, and then inch slowly upward again. Were it not for a lifetime as a country girl driving at least once a year somewhere in conditions like this — and don't forget driving through blizzards in winter, she reminds herself — Iris would be alarmed, might even want to turn back.

Suddenly they round another curve and there it is: on the flat top of a mountain two mountains beyond, shining white in the afternoon sun, sits the magical town, Lalibela. Giyorgis, smiling proudly and with a touch of wonder of his own, slows so she can take a good look.

She has come all this way to Africa, braved this godforsaken road to ride for days by herself with only a stranger for a companion and, just when she's afraid she's approaching the limits of her endurance, there is her destination shining in the sun like some magnificent, lost, mythical city.

The child herders, the beggars, the armed gatekeeper, the funeral, her fear at the people crowding around the car pale and disappear. She has begun to tremble. She's a *voyageur*, an Indiana Jones, and now, at last, after a cautious and smug lifetime, she understands what drives such people — the Henry Kelseys, Alexander Mackenzies, even the Irish soldier, Palliser, of her home landscape. Surely it is for moments like this that they yearn, that repay them a thousand times over for the hardships of the journey, for the terrors, for the suffering, for even the loved ones left behind — yes, the love abandoned, done without. Barney should be here too, but the thought vanishes as quickly as it comes. It is enough to be here herself.

They keep advancing, still climbing, the town appearing and disappearing with the twists in the road, and just when Iris thinks Lalibela is surely just over the next rise, instead of climbing they drop a long way to cross a wide valley. They're just in time to see a large silver plane circling above them — a plane? Here? Who on earth could be on board?

Then she sees that far to their left there is a wide landing strip, and next to it, another, apparently even bigger one being built. Iris keeps her eyes on the shining dot that is the circling plane, half thinking she's imagining it, even though she knows she's not. It's just that a plane, especially one of such size and modernity breaks her reverie of being intrepid, trail-blazing, struggling into wilderness and beyond it into the land of the mythical. Abruptly, the ordinary world she has forgotten intrudes, breaking the spell.

They slow to a crawl. Iris sees a couple of yellow bulldozers, but mostly the work appears to be being done with pick and shovel in clouds of dust by a legion of tall, extremely slender men wearing that long piece of discoloured cotton that they wrap around themselves to make a shawl and headcovering — Giyorgis finally tells her it's a *shamma* — which they wear over their worn jackets and shirts, and below that, trousers or shorts or a sort of skirt formed with another length of cotton. On their feet they wear leather-thong sandals. The incongruity of the malnourished, inadequately clad men with their picks and shovels and the airplane circling above drives her into silence.

They begin to climb again as Iris catches a glimpse of the plane descending to land, while on their right a rickety, aged bus leaves the parking area, lumbers across the road behind them and, kicking up a trail of dust, heads down a track toward the landing strip.

"Tourists," Giyorgis says.

"What?" Iris says, although she has heard him perfectly well. She thinks of the two days of driving she has endured, today especially over nearly impassable trails, when she might have flown to the very doorstep of the rock churches. She finds she wouldn't have missed the drive; it has made Lalibela only more precious.

Behind the flat mountaintop on which the town sits glinting in the sunshine is a distant, high, blue mountain range, and further ranges disappear into the blue of the sky behind it, as if for all the rest of the world, to its faraway, mythical edge, there are only uninhabited, rugged mountains. Giyorgis points to a distinctive, high mountain with a flat-topped mountain in front of it to the northeast of the town and says, "Is called Abuna Yosef. Is more than four thousand metres. Lalibela is twenty-five hundred metres." Automatically, she converts to feet, more than eight thousand.

The loose dirt and dust they're driving through has taken on a red hue, and as they drive up the final road to the edge of the town meeting ragged, barefoot women bent almost double under enormous loads of firewood they're carrying on their backs down the mountain, she sees that the town's gleaming whiteness was an illusion. This town is red: red stone, red dust, red bricks.

Giyorgis is ready with the facts: "Volcanic rock. Red tufa."

It's like a town in the Arizona desert, it's so dry. There are many dusty green trees but beneath them grows not a blade of grass, not a forb or a sedge or a lovely flowering shrub. Just rose-coloured or pink-tinted dirt, and dust inches thick, everywhere she looks. And what she thought was a city turns out to be only a town, its buildings strewn haphazardly up the sides and on flat spaces of this mountain which, within the general flatness, turns out to have short, but steep rises and narrow, dramatic clefts. She sees too that here the houses, still the familiar conical ones with the thatched roofs, are built of unpolished wine-coloured stone and that some are, surprisingly, two storeys high.

Immediately on their left is a handsome new-looking hotel built of red stone blocks. It occupies its own flat-topped rise, really the top of a cliff, and has the usual wide gate and fence, although here the fence is only barbed wire and shrubbery, not an actual concrete-block wall as she saw in Addis and Kombolcha. A valley inserts itself between this building and the first buildings of the town isolating the hotel. The dusty road dips and rises again, before it curves out of sight behind trees, another small hill, and the town proper.

"This is the Hilton," Giyorgis tells her, "but the name is called 'Roha,'" he adds. "Is the name of this town before King Lalibela came and built his churches."

Iris says, "I wonder what the deal is? That Hilton would build it and the Ethiopian government run it? Or did the government just take it over?" Vaguely, she recognizes this as not the sort of question — having to do with politics and government — that in the past she would have thought to ask. Giyorgis shrugs. They drive past what she now knows are the inevitable guards. It occurs to her to wonder who it is, in a place as remote as this, the guards are here to keep out. The poor again, she supposes. Giyorgis greets them and they call back a greeting, he parks their vehicle in the small, empty paved lot — there's no sign of the bus from the landing strip yet — and, walking stiffly, Iris has trouble straightening up, they go inside to register.

The interior has that tropical-country look that Iris recognizes from the travel channel on television and from magazines: low ceilings, carpeted stone floors, a few wide steps leading to different levels, and Ethiopian rugs, wall hangings, and posters decorating the thick supporting pillars.

With a tentative expression, Giyorgis taps a sign posted on the wall near the desk informing guests that there is running, cold water only, for an hour each evening and each morning, and electricity only from six to eleven in the evenings. Iris is taken aback but then shrugs. A small matter. It will soon be dark, already it's dusky in the lobby, and she's famished and tired out and aching in every joint and not about to quibble over niggling matters like running water and electricity.

By the time she and Giyorgis meet in the bar, it is full of the tourists from the plane. Most of them are middle-aged, the men with big stomachs, the women nondescript, grey-haired, tweedy. They all look wealthy though, and are speaking German. In another corner a smaller but louder contingent is speaking French. She and Giyorgis eat dinner in the elegant dining room, served by dignified local waiters, but without choice — there is only one meal being served. On their left at a long banquet table the Germans and their guide talk quietly as they eat and drink, and at another table at the back of the big, high-ceilinged room, laughter from the French tourists rises above the drone of voices. The only other guests are four people sharing a table behind Iris and Giyorgis. In a lull in the general buzz, Iris thinks she hears British accents. Aside from the waiters, Giyorgis is the only Ethiopian in the room.

By ten o'clock they are in their beds in rooms side by side. Iris is so tired that the night passes rapidly, dreamlessly; she doesn't even have hot flashes, or if she does, she doesn't wake during them. At dawn she is up in order to take advantage of the water supply, which comes gurgling and banging, and after a quick, light breakfast, which she and her driver have alone in the empty dining room — real tourists apparently sleep later than this — they head out in the Land Rover to visit, at last, the churches they've come so far to see.

They hire a guide, a slender, handsome young man, whose grasp of English is better than Giyorgis's. He turns out to be not a professional guide but a friend of Giyorgis's, who got to know him during his trips to Lalibela during the famine years of the late eighties. When Iris wonders if they shouldn't have a professional guide, one is waiting eagerly at the hotel gate, Giyorgis explains to her in a careful way, as if it is important that she understand this, that Yared, who is seventeen or eighteen years old, is a student. He wants to go to university in Addis, but he is very poor, he needs to earn money. He's neatly dressed in a clean, short-sleeved white shirt and navy trousers, although he's wearing the leather sandals of the poor on his bare feet. He smiles tensely at her, and reluctantly Iris agrees to hire him. Delighted, he jumps quickly into the back seat.

The churches, Yared explains as they drive, are in three separate clusters short distances apart, although the third location has only one church, St. George's, the famous cross-shaped church. He seems to think Iris already knows at least this much about them, when actually, although she doesn't say so, she heard of them for the first time in her life only last night. It might be as much as a mile from the hotel gate to the first cluster of churches, none of which can be seen from a distance.

Yared leads them through the rituals necessary to get them past the courtyard of the first and main church. This involves courteously asking the beggars, both children and adults in their colourless rags, to move back, and trying to shield Iris without appearing to, from the emaciated young men selling handcrafted items and crosses which they claim are solid silver, but which, by the men's very surreptitiousness Iris suspects aren't, and further, might be stolen. Or maybe it's just that they don't want the handful of priests seated on a stone bench across the courtyard to see what they're up to. He shields her too from the children, who merely want to get close to stare, giggle, and possibly touch the *ferenji*. She has to pay a hundred-birr entrance fee, about twenty dollars, which seems high to Iris, but in a country so poor, how can she complain?

Two old beggar women follow her as she descends the stone steps following Yared and Giyorgis into the courtyard of the first group of churches. The steps are so old that their contours are worn to smooth concavity.

"*Christos, Christos,*" the beggar women say, or, "*Sela Selassie,*" and although "Christos" is plain enough, and she knows they're asking for alms, she has to ask Yared for a translation of the other.

"Selassie is the trinity," he explains. "Haile Selassie is the power of the trinity." She gives them each a birr.

These two old women are so thin that they might well be dying of starvation. At the bottom of the stairs, when she turns to look back, she has to look twice before she can separate them from the stone walls they lean against. Their skin colour from a lifetime out of doors, and the stony grey-beige of their aged, dirty rags, are the same colour as the rocks. It is as if they are wraiths, rock-ghosts, that detach themselves from the walls at sunrise and at nightfall meld silently back into them. She has never seen human beings this destitute. In an undertone she asks Yared how old he thinks the women might be. He says, "Maybe in their forties."

Before they enter the first church Yared lectures her, and she has to stifle a smile because he is so grave and intent and yet so young. He tells her there are eleven churches and names them with a mixture of pride and care, in case he forgets or gets the list wrong: "Beta Madhane Alam, that is in English, House of the Redeemer of the World; Beta Maryam — 'beta' is 'house'; Church of Emmanuel, Church of Mercurious, Church of Abba Libanos — is a saint; Church of the Archangel — that is, St. Gabriel's; St. George's, St. Michael's, Golgotha, the Cross — that is Maskal; and Denaghel — the House of the Virgins." They are seamless, he tells her, like giant sculptures which can be lived in and used, and are to this very day. She nods politely, smiles her encouragement. Yared goes on, lifting an arm to gesture, spreading his hands, pointing, shifting his weight, doing his best to convey with his entire body the miracle of the churches' construction.

The early builders simply stood on the top of the rock, he tells her, the way she had been a moment before, and started carving downward, hacking each church out from the top down, sculpting the exteriors to look as they would if they'd been constructed of stone blocks and wood, and then chipping out the interiors to make rooms. "All had to be planned ahead, every window, every decoration. It is truly wonderful." Especially, he says, when the biggest have three storeys of rooms, and stand perhaps forty feet from bottom to top. Then he points out that the churches within each group are built successively lower, so that when she comes out of one into its courtyard, she'll be standing on the roof of the next.

"You see, they had to think of drainage for *keremt*, the main rainy season." He stops, his face lit from the interior, his expression full of pride. "All the churches, the roofs, the ledges, the courtyards, slant precisely so for drainage."

When Iris asks for a date, he says, "Their age is not known. Some used to think they go back to 1000 B.C., to when the Queen of Sheba visited Jerusalem. But others say that after the Muslims made it impossible for Christians to go on pilgrimages to Jerusalem, these were built to make a New Jerusalem. That was in the thirteenth century. So — at least eight hundred years old."

Iris looks slowly around her. Off to her left, thirty feet or so away, three or four of the inevitable young men in tidy Western clothes, their hands in their pockets, lounge against a rock wall silently watching her. To her right and slightly behind her the two old beggar women stand shyly beside some stairs, not speaking or moving, looking as if they might take flight if one of the men so much as glances at them. Behind them a few child beggars have appeared — boys, she sees. They watch her, too, in grave silence.

How quiet it is, she thinks, unnaturally so, and lifts her head to the pale blue African sky, and the white sun casting its rays down over this centuries-old courtyard hewn of living rock. She listens. There is no sound, not of wind, nor motors, nor distant voices, nor airplanes, barking dogs, nor anything else. Just this hush, this still-ness, as if here the whole world comes to a stop. Slowly she turns back to Yared, to find him watching her with what she interprets as an apprehensive or a puzzled frown. She smiles, lifts a hand, palm up.

"Please, go on."

"Ahhh, now, listen," he says, lifting a finger to emphasize the seri-ousness of what comes next. His voice alters slightly, goes lower and is softer. "It was prophesied when he was born that Lalibela would be king, so his half-brother, who was king, tried many times to kill him. On one of these occasions when Lalibela was a young man, an attempt to poison him caused him to lie unconscious for three days. During those days Lalibela went to heaven and there God spoke to him. God told him he would rule one day, and that when he came to power he must build these churches. Then God gave him the dimensions of the churches and told him how to build them." He pauses, lifts his head and gazes up at the walls soaring upward around them as if he hasn't seen them before either. "It is not known how long it took — maybe twenty years — or how many people worked at it, although it is said that angels worked alongside the builders during the day and then alone at night."

He lowers his eyes to hers. She can't tell if he believes this story or not, but his expression is serious, so she controls her face carefully, making sure not a twitch gives away her desire to smile, not that the smile she's stifling would be of disbelief as much as it would be of delight.

But he is finished at last with his orientation lecture. He leads her toward the first church, with Giyorgis following Iris. Walking down the stone passages Iris exclaims over the beauty of the worn pink rock faces with their many shades from black through wines, browns, and corals to red, and at the doves cooing softly as she passes from their nests in the cracks and fissures of the rock walls. She sees too, that the tool marks from eight hundred years earlier are still visible on them. She can touch them with her fingers.

She is thinking how, when she approached Lalibela, if she hadn't known the churches were here she would not have guessed it, as they are hidden from view, have to be discovered — a secret world of precious stone structures beneath this African town. She finds herself wondering, Is there something in the Ethiopian character that made them choose to carve the churches out of standing stone, downward into the earth, rather than to quarry the stone and build their churches upward, reaching for the sky, as the Europeans did? Or was it history that made them do it this way? If they were hidden, it would keep them safe from those who would destroy them.

As they're about to enter the first church, Giyorgis touches her arm and points to her shoes.

"You must take them off," he says, doing so himself. When she looks questioningly at him, he says, smiling, "It is said because such holy places have many angels in them and you might tread on them." She bends and slips out of her walking sandals, leaving them at the door, next to Yared's flimsy sandals and Giyorgis's neatly polished, worn, black oxfords.

Madhane Alam, at roughly one hundred feet long and sixty feet wide, is the largest of all the churches. Here the carvers left stone behind to form four rows of widely spaced pillars as might be found in the interior of a traditionally built cathedral. Narrow bars of light streaming in through the high, small windows show this church's lack of decoration — only a few designs carved at the top of the pillars, as if the builders thought that the church's size was impressive enough in itself. Large rugs in brown, cream, and black, characteristic Ethiopian rugs, Yared informs her, are spread on its stone floors.

Four or five drums of various sizes and shapes — Iris guesses they're made out of animal hides because of their natural brown and beige tones — sit on one of the rugs in the centre of the church. The priest whose church this is, noticing Iris looking at them, goes to them and strikes a large, conical one, not hard, with his hand. The sound the light, flat-palmed blow produces is deep and loud, so unexpectedly resonant she's startled. It bounces off the rock walls and ceiling in such a marvellous way that it jars something loose inside Iris, an odd sensation that starts at her womb and floods upward through her body. What if the priests played all these drums at once? How the different tones would reverberate off the stone interior, the echoes themselves repeating the drums' different timbres and rhythms, the very church would become a musical instrument, dissolving the rock walls, the shadows under the ceiling, setting the angels Giyorgis told her of dancing. Transfixed, she imagines the doves flying up out of their niches, adding the whirr of their pale wings to the sound. Such a noise would jar people's very souls into their mouths, and they would dance and sing, for who could resist such music?

The priest has gone. Yared is moving toward the entrance where Iris sees a pair of beggars, one on each side of the rectangle of intense bright light, peering into the darkness where she and Giyorgis stand.

"Come," Giyorgis says gently, touching her arm. As they move together to the door, the beggars slowly retreat and Iris sees that behind the women a few more adult beggars have gathered.

One of the churches — is it St. George's, the cross-shaped church? — has a wider courtyard than most of the others, and she walks the short length of it. And when in one of the many cavelike openings in the courtyard walls, whether natural or man-made, she doesn't know, a face appears, she stops abruptly and, thinking it a trick of light, an illusion, looks again. The cave's diameter is maybe four feet, and half sitting, half lying in it is a man who appears to be very old, simply skin and bone. He's wrapped in a shawl-like garment of a dazzling white, and he stares, curious and innocent-eyed, back at her.

"He is a hermit," her guide explains, amused at the look on her face. When Iris's heart stops pounding so hard, she nods politely at the hermit, although she doesn't say anything, not sure if you should speak to a hermit, nor does he speak to her. He simply looks, bright-eyed, back at her.

She walks on a few feet farther to the next cave, preparing herself to see another face staring out at her. But instead, her horror growing as she makes sense of what she sees, she recognizes a partly mummified corpse, the skull resting crookedly on one of the lean, golden-brown, leathery shins, its grin tipped lopsided. Her hand goes up to cover her mouth, she swivels, and then, before Yared or

Giyorgis notice how upset she is by what they seem to take for granted — not even warning her — she scurries back the length of the courtyard and leans against the church wall, shading her eyes from the sun that's suddenly dazzling.

Yared comes up to her and peers carefully into her face.

"You are well?" he asks.

"Oh, yes, certainly," Iris says quickly, dropping her hand, pushing herself away from the wall and smiling. Yared gazes an instant longer, then, satisfied, eager to continue, he explains to her that there are tombs in all the walls, that the caves often are burial sites, that there are places in this labyrinth no non-Ethiopian has ever been allowed to enter, or even knows are there.

"Even many of the priests may not enter Selassie Chapel. It is by Golgotha Church, where the tomb of King Lalibela is," he adds. He pauses, scuffs the ground with his toe, considering. "It is said, too, that Adam's tomb is in Golgotha." He doesn't look up to see how she's taking this. For a second she can't think who Adam is; the fact that all of this is Christian, as she is, dumbfounds her.

"Wait!" she says. "Isn't Ethiopia the place where they dug up Lucy? The first woman, I mean? Or was it Kenya?" Yared is grinning delightedly at her.

"Yes, yes," he says. "It was here, in Ethiopia. She is in National Archeological Museum in Addis. Ethiopians call her *Dinkinesh* — it means, 'it is wonderful.' She is three and half million years. But," he says, solemn again, "It is another kind of history." He looks at his sandalled feet, troubled, as if he knows he'll never be able to explain this to her, or else it's that he doesn't understand it himself.

Iris looks down the length of the roughly hewn stone courtyard to the faces peering back at her from around corners or from shadowy niches, or from those who lean against the walls flattened by the clear white light. Nobody moves, all those dark eyes, so full of intelligence, watching her. She's slowly comprehending that Ethiopians believe Ethiopia is the first nation in the world, the cradle of humanity, in more than merely one way.

She catches a glimpse of how, just maybe, the history she learned in school shades off too at its thinning edges into mystery and myth and — *the holy* — like these stone churches — into a place where fact is no longer separable from fiction, or the separation even relevant to truth. It isn't just suffering, as she'd thought at first, that has made these people as they are. It is history — they are anchored by the weight of history. Ethiopia is the only African nation that has never been wholly conquered and occupied, Giyorgis told her, and she had said nothing, not understanding what he so plainly took as a matter of great pride.

What happens to a people when somebody tries to destroy their history as Ahmad Ibn Gran tried to do? she asks herself. Isn't that the first thing that all conquerors do? A people whose history is destroyed don't know who they are any more; they get lost, they wander, they can be pushed whatever way by others, because they don't have a sense of their own relevance and — and they can't see a future because they have no past.

She thinks of the Great Plains of North America. We have no history to anchor us. She tries to see how this has shaped her own people. All that comes to mind are the protests about clear-cutting the forests in B.C., the ploughing up all the grass and driving all the country people off their land and into poverty in the cities, as if all of this never happened anywhere else before. All land means to us is money. But surely it's something more than that? We lack awe, she thinks. We don't approve of it. That's because we lack a sense of the past — we really believe we're in control, when all around us all the time is evidence that we aren't.

But the Indians — she thinks of the stone circles on her land, of her grandfather destroying them, her father wanting to, and Barney also, and she and her mother stopping them, but only when there was nothing but a bare reminder left of the civilization that was once there.

She is growing confused, her mind can't absorb all this, and the contrast between the sun's brightness and heat when she steps outside and the chilly darkness in the churches, sounds deepened and magnified by the stone, intensifies her confusion.

Yared shows her the cave in which the church beggars spend the night. Iris goes to the entrance, hesitates, then steps inside. It is completely empty. There is not a pack of any kind, not a bedroll, not a tin pot or a lamp. And she's seen the beggars — none of them carry anything but a walking staff. She comes back out, stunned further into a heavy silence.

As they've walked, climbed stairs and once a ladder, crouched to go through tunnels and low stone doorways, twice finding the Land Rover and driving a few hundred feet to the next set of churches, Iris has become more and more disoriented. She no longer has any idea how the churches relate geographically to each other, or to their parked vehicle, or to the hotel — if there really is a hotel somewhere outside this rocky universe.

She finds herself standing in the courtyard of — she has to ask Yared twice for its name — St. Mary's Church, where a flight of steps leads upward to a large, deep stone pool.

"For baptism," Yared says. "Although sometimes people go in for their health."

"I see," Iris says, although her attention has been caught by the beggars again. There must be a dozen there now, or is she mistaken, and there've been more for a while.

"Come," Yared gestures to her as she pauses. There are more young men in this courtyard too.

As usual, a priest greets them as they enter, then retreats backward into the shadows and Iris half notices that, as with each of the other priests, he's putting on liturgical robes over his cotton pants and shirt, and mounting his church's bronze cross onto a shoulder-high processional staff. While he is doing this, Yared clicks on a flashlight to focus slowly over the remains of the rich decorations on the ceiling and walls: wall paintings and bas-reliefs which seem to have been originally colourfully painted.

He halts the light on the ceiling vaulting for some moments on a chipped and faded painting of what Iris slowly recognizes as the Virgin Mary being given the news that she is with child. The virgin is seated, spinning, and she draws the red thread upward with her left hand. She has large dark eyes, dark hair, and golden skin, and Iris is surprised. All the Madonnas she remembers have blue eyes and blonde hair. She stares up at the painting until her neck begins to hurt and she has to lower her head.

The flashlight catches a square pillar in the centre of the church wrapped tightly from top to bottom in a cotton cloth discoloured with age. She's about to ask Yared for an explanation when the priest who has joined them begins to speak in Amharic. Yared listens respectfully, and when the priest is finished he bows and turns to Iris.

"It is the only pillar in Ethiopia like this," he says. "It is called, 'the Pillar of Unity in the Faith.'" His voice is filled with awe; it's almost as if he's afraid to say what he knows, but after a second he continues. "The priest says, no one may look. He says that God touched that pillar with his hand, and on this pillar is written," he turns then to look straight at her, "'All the past and all the future of the world.'"

Iris takes an involuntary step backward. The priest looks off into the distance, his black eyes catching what light there is and glittering, his tightly wound white turban emphasizing the deep lines in his golden-brown face. He is not so much stern as detached and patient. In the stillness it seems to Iris that she can hear her own heart beating, its steady tripping small hammers in her ears. She looks up to where the top of the pillar is lost in the shadows under the heavy stone ceiling. It looks as if it might go on forever, soaring all the way up to heaven.

She senses that she has flown out of time and into *now*. Every step of her way from her farm outside Chinook to this mountain village on the other side of the globe has been leading her out of her personal history, her family's history, her country's history — into this alien one that she has discovered as an explorer discovers a continent or a river. How little she has understood about anything. She feels as if she has been struck on the head — she's losing track of things: Barney doesn't matter, nor Jay's leaving her, nor her mother, nor — any of that. And Lannie? Her search for Lannie has become a part of this labyrinthine world she has flown into. She stares at the pillar, her eyes following its length from where it rises out of the uneven stone floor upward, losing itself in darkness.

Beams of light break through the small windows carved high in the thick layers of stone, descending slantwise to the floor. There are angels dancing there, she thinks, fierce, bright flecks of God's heart, whirling between the dust motes that sail down the shafts of light;

they are in the shadows too, under the vaulted ceiling and behind the
stone altar, and waiting in the stiff, gleaming folds of the priest's
robe. I am breathing in angels, she thinks, and in the stillness she can
almost hear them dancing through the rushing of blood in her ears.

She imagines herself reaching out to touch the pillar, knows they
would stop her at once; if she tried to pull the cloth away they might
kill her. Something like fear strikes her and she lowers her head and
stands motionless, as if she's praying.

After what feels like a very long time, but may have been only a
moment, she shakes her head slowly and looks around. The three
men say nothing, as if they're used to this silence from visitors. She
wants to see more, to ask more questions, but the darkness, the walls
blackened and worn smooth in places from centuries of bodies
brushing past, the overwhelming press of poverty outside the door,
all of these prevent her. She leaves the priest an offering and Yared
and Giyorgis lead her back outside into the courtyard at the far end
of which the beggars stand quietly.

Yared says, "I will go ahead to find the priest so he may unlock the
door of the next church." Before Iris can answer, he disappears around
a corner. She turns to Giyorgis, but, unaccountably, he too seems to
have vanished. She doesn't like standing here by herself so she goes
around the corner of the church intending to follow Yared, but on the
far side of the church there is only a narrow passage from which other
passages branch off, and she doesn't know which one to choose.

How hot it is, how dry. She stops to rest and leans against a rough
rock wall, regarding, without meaning to, the beggars who've
followed her even here, into this maze. They stare silently back at her,
their eyes following her every move, with what she reads as a mixture
of shyness and curiosity. She tilts her head upward trying to catch a
glimpse of the sky above this passageway she's halted in, but stone
blocks her way. What she sees instead is the sunlight on the beggars'
dirty rags, the gleam of their greyed-ebony skin.

She closes her eyes, but isn't that the rustling of their garments she
hears? their bare feet brushing over the stones? the hissing of their
breaths? or are they whispering to her, trying to tell her something?
Or is it the beating of the doves' wings she hears around her head and

chest? She tries to stir herself to move away, but her body won't respond.

And her mouth is full of dust, dust clogs her nostrils; she can't breathe, black shadows are blossoming there behind her eyelids, growing larger, enveloping her, blotting her out. Here in this infinite darkness all is in motion, disintegrating. She's a dust speck herself, she's gone, become one with the rocks and the heat and the dust, whirling giddily through cavernous blackness.

A weight descends on her shoulder, bringing her rushing back from wherever it is she's been. The beggars! Her eyes fly open — but it is Giyorgis, peering into her face, his heavy, warm hand firm on her shoulder, anchoring her, as if she has been falling and he has caught her.

"You are ill?" She rubs her hand across her face, squinting against the sudden brightness.

"I was just — resting a minute." She looks about for the beggars, but they are gone.

"He will come soon," Giyorgis says. Who? Iris wonders. Oh, their guide, Yared. They stand side by side in silence, Iris trying desperately to calm herself, Giyorgis facing her, but looking down at his shoes. "It is hot," Giyorgis says.

It was only the heat, she supposes. As they wait, her heart slowing to its normal rhythm, her sense of herself settling back more firmly, she sees that her shoes are coated with a layer of fine pink dust. She hasn't the energy to brush them off.

Yared appears suddenly in a passageway up ahead and beckons silently. She and Giyorgis move forward together. Without looking back, Iris knows that the beggars have returned, she can feel them back there, a solid, breathing band of bodies, shuffling noiselessly forward too.

Having been through seven or eight churches now — she long ago lost count or got confused what with the caves, chapels, ramps, and passageways — and also the cave where King Lalibela was supposed to have stabled his horses and sometimes slept himself, and the cave where the beggars live, she is aware that her feet are sore, her back is aching, in fact, she's so tired she can hardly move. She thinks, maybe it's the altitude.

But the truth is, she's as much exhausted by the effort to understand and absorb the continuing marvel of the churches, the *meaning* of all this, as she is by stooping her way through rock tunnels, climbing up ladders or precipitous stone stairs and down them, and stumbling across uneven stone floors. It is too much for any human to take in during one visit. She's disoriented, in pain, almost angry at the churches for being more than she can deal with.

"I just can't climb another set of stairs — I can't stagger through another church — I'm completely exhausted," she tells Giyorgis. Both Yared and Giyorgis try politely to persuade her to go on, they're disappointed in her, or maybe Yared is afraid he'll be paid less, but Iris pleads with them. "You're both young men. You're strong, but I'm old, I don't have your strength." She is amazed at herself, declaring herself old in this unexpected way.

Giyorgis makes his way back slowly to the Land Rover while Iris stops with Yared to pay him. It is more of that touching Ethiopian courtesy on Giyorgis's part she knows, not to embarrass his friend by watching him be paid. She hands him the agreed-upon ten birr, says, "Thank you," and is about to add, "Goodbye," but he touches her arm lightly, withdrawing his hand immediately and says, "Wait, please." He rushes back into the church they've just emerged from. Iris stands uncertainly, shading her eyes with her hand, watching him go. Giyorgis has climbed out of sight. Beggars are again coming toward her; she isn't sure if this is a different pack or the same one that's been following them, but she doesn't know whether to wait as Yared has requested or to abandon him and hurry after Giyorgis before she loses her purse containing her money, passport, and visa.

But here comes Yared trotting toward her, holding something small out in front of him. She sees that he means to give it to her, and she protests, "But I have no more small birr."

"No," he says, shaking his head vehemently. "I do not wish money. I wish to give you this — " He pauses as if he can't think how to say what he wants to say, or perhaps is having trouble bringing himself to say it. He lifts his chin and looks into her eyes with those dark, troubled eyes of his. In them she suddenly sees all the ages of Ethiopian history, the thousands of years of suffering and darkness and sorrow and tribulation. And also its beauty and the dignity of its people. She finds she can't move, although she wants to but she can't look away either. He says slowly and distinctly, "I am giving you this so that you will remember me."

She accepts it then, touched. When he tries to bow over each of her shoulders, Iris resists and touches her cheek to his, which, by the look on his face, distresses him. She wonders if she's made some sort of terrible blunder, touching him so informally. But he backs away, bowing, that look still in his eyes, saying, "Do not forget me."

Iris hurries to catch up with Giyorgis, holding the object, which turns out to be an ornate cross carved out of wood and stained a dark brown, threaded onto a narrow brown thong.

"See?" she says to Giyorgis. "Yared gave me this." Giyorgis is surprised. He examines it closely.

"Ahh," he says. "The priests used to make these and sell them. What did he ask for this?"

"He wouldn't take money. He said he gave it to me so I will remember him." Iris watches him as he carefully masks his expression before she can interpret it.

When they return to the hotel so Iris can rest, Giyorgis tells her he'll take her shopping to the two or three small souvenir shops in the town. Back in her room, Iris lies down on her bed. For a long time she lies motionless, too tired to move, staring at the ceiling. She closes her eyes and sees the white doves nesting in pink fissures in the rocks, sees the jumbled yellow bones of the mummified corpse, the glittering, fathomless eyes of priest after priest, as they stand motionless in the interior shadows of the stone churches.

All the past and all the future of the world. She cannot imagine what this might be, she does not think she would know even if she'd been allowed to see what was under the cloth, she does not even know what such a concept might entail. Nor did she know if it was true in either sense — the Lucy sense or the Adam sense — that Ethiopians might be the oldest people in the world. They may be the same in the end —

both mysteries, both legends. Three and a half million years is older than the Old Testament, she thinks, but strange, the Old Testament seems older to her. Maybe because it is a length of time she can grasp, as the other is not. She thinks of the graveyard at Chinook. There isn't a grave there before 1900. Her head won't stop going around.

There is something very unsettling about this place, she thinks. There's some dark secret here and everyone knows it, even maybe Giyorgis, but I don't. The air is tainted with their unhappiness, their — something — fear? Is it that those ancient churches drag them down? Or maybe it's the mystery of the angels who helped build them, or of the great King Lalibela who was also a saint, who made the people build them. Or that pillar, there every day of your life, the knowledge it has kept a secret from you. Maybe at night when people are sleeping what it knows seeps into their dreams. Maybe these people know things no one else knows.

Or is it something simpler: their distance from the rest of the world here on their mountaintop, the sheer difficulty of getting from here to anywhere else. Or the drought right now. Or the war that went on for twenty or thirty years, and the Great Famine in which hundreds, maybe even thousands of their friends and families died — and all the famines before and since. Three thousand years of living under dictators. Is this what it does to a people? Makes them silent, gives them a grave courtesy, carrying around all those thousands of years in the darkness in the back of their eyes. Iris's chest feels heavy with these thoughts; she feels suspended, as if what she knows now is too cumbrous for her body, as if her heart and her lungs can hardly work under the weight of them.

An hour later Giyorgis knocks with polite firmness on her door. He drives her to a tiny souvenir shop, a three-sided corrugated-iron shelter squeezed in between two others. As they park she sees, a hundred feet or so down the road, a pair of tourists have lined up three little girls and are taking a picture of them with a camera mounted on a tripod. The little girls stand shyly together, not quite smiling, barefoot in the dust, their pathetic rags that do for dresses looking picturesque. The man taking the photo and his tall, slender wife in the pale khaki safari suit with the shoulder-length, silvery-blonde hair, which somehow only wealthy women seem to have, are both smiling warmly at the little girls. A stab of pity goes right through Iris's chest when she sees this and, feeling herself helpless in the face of this obtuseness, this cruelty, she twists away from the sight.

"I hope they paid them well," she says to Giyorgis, who doesn't reply. Iris is sure very little if any money will change hands, even though she knows it isn't fair to assume this. Still, she wants the Europeans' evil to be total. She doesn't want to have to partly forgive them. But — isn't she a rich tourist too?

A gang of boys about ten or eleven years old have been following her ever since they stopped their Land Rover in front of the shop and got out. She and Giyorgis go inside the shop and with Giyorgis interpreting for her, although the young shopkeeper speaks a little English, she buys a small, handwoven rug and a Lalibela cross. She doesn't really want either one and she refuses to bargain. Everyone here is so poor, it seems to her that to try to get the price lowered or not to buy anything would be criminal.

Bowing and thanking them, she and Giyorgis leave the shopkeeper and his two helpers and walk back to their vehicle, the band of boys still following, chattering and giggling with each other in the way of small boys everywhere. A handful of men squat in the dirt along the wall, apparently with nothing to do, nowhere to go.

As she gets back into the vehicle, she's distracted by a sudden racket from the boys. Two of them seem to be fighting. But when she pauses to look, she sees that one boy is abusing another. Although they're about the same size, the stronger boy is wearing trousers, a shirt, and actually has on shoes, so Iris thinks of him as the rich boy. The other one, whose arm is being twisted so that he falls down in the dust, tears streaking down his dirty face, has the beggars' no-colour, dresslike rags wrapped around him, he's barefoot, carrying a staff, and his arms and legs are thin as sticks.

She shouts at the rich boy, "Leave him alone!" for the beggar child has sunk to the ground wailing under the pressure the other boy is exerting on his arm. Too weak from hunger and malnutrition to fight back, Iris thinks, but the rich boy calls back to her, grinning, "Sister, he is very bad boy!" Iris is so enraged she's almost crying herself. She feels Giyorgis standing helpless by her side, wanting to silence her, caught between her anger, his need to placate her, and whatever demands this community will make on him that she doesn't know about or understand.

"It doesn't look that way to me!" she shouts, holding back the accusation, *You hideous little bully,* out of deference to Giyorgis, out of not understanding anything that is going on here, out of not being in her own country. Giyorgis calls something in Amharic to one of the men lounging against the rough shop wall and pretty soon three or four other men join in and a loud conversation among the men is going on, nobody looking at the two boys or at Iris, while the beggar child sits on the ground crying and the bully stands above him, still grinning at all the adults who ignore him.

Iris refuses to look at any of the men, just sits staring straight ahead through the windshield while the words fall around her. Giyorgis doesn't interpret any of what they are calling back and forth to her. She doesn't even want to know what the men are saying to each other. It doesn't matter. She hears a placatory note in Giyorgis's rapid Amharic; she has put him on the spot, they probably all think she should just mind her own rich Western woman's business, what does she know of their struggles and their suffering and the reason why a little beggar child has to lie crying in the dust, too thin and weak to defend himself?

"Take me to the hotel," she says. Tears stream down her cheeks; she wipes her face furiously. Giyorgis says nothing, does something funny with his face, wiping away emotion; he starts the vehicle and inches away; Mrs. Rich White Woman having a tantrum. What is she doing in this terrible country anyway?

Lannie, she reminds herself. You've come for Lannie. But she finds she can't remember who Lannie is or why she so badly wants her to come home. For one bewildering second she almost asks Giyorgis.

Alone again in her room, waiting for dinner, she throws herself back on her bed. But she's too upset even to close her eyes or lie still. Every time she does she sees the corpse in the hole in the rock wall lying there like a cast-off shoe, she sees the forty-year-old beggars who look seventy, she sees the beggar child's tears and the sticks that are his arms and legs, she sees the men, how thin they all are — and dust and dirt everywhere, not a blade of grass.

She would tell herself, *It's no use thinking about it, there's nothing you can do.* But turning away no longer works, she can't let this pass. If she does, she is indeed the fool she's always suspected deep down that she is. She knows now finally, two-thirds of the way through her life, that she's responsible for these people. And she will never turn away again.

When Giyorgis knocks to let her know it's dinnertime, she gets up, combs her hair, puts on a fresh blouse, and goes out to meet him. All through dinner, in the midst of the laughter and multilingual chatter of the other tourists, she and Giyorgis sit in silence eating, or make polite conversation about the food, about going back to Kombolcha in the morning. And all the while she sees the little girls smiling in the dust, the barefoot infants herding animals on the rocky mountain slopes, the women bent double under their loads of water or firewood.

After dinner there is folk dancing and singing. This isn't arranged by the hotel — first a thin young man comes around to each table and asks the tourists if they will pay to watch the dancers. Iris doesn't care, but she opens her purse and pays what he asks. The dancers are a troupe of local men and women, and they give a rousing performance full of the vigour and the sense of fun of the non-professional. They are accompanied by drums and by stringed instruments, which Giyorgis says are called a *kirar*, which is like a small guitar, and a *masinko*, which has only one string.

As the program goes on, the men, laughing at their own exertions and at each other, are clearly trying to outdo each other in the display of finesse and speed with which they dance. Grinning, they snap their heads in unison to the left and to the right, knees wide apart and bent, hands on their waists, their torsos tilted back and rippling effortlessly. The women advance, shaking their shoulders, their small breasts bouncing in a way that at home would be considered provocative, but that here has a beauty and a clarity of meaning that Iris recognizes as the frank joy of being female.

Despite the shouting, the drums, the clapping and cries from the watching tourists, after a while Iris finds she can't concentrate on the display before her. She can only think of all she has seen, of the reason she has come here, and finds herself sitting among strangers in this shameful, counterfeit palace. The noises fade, the swaying, red-banded white skirts, the full white cotton trousers, the golden arms and hands and faces of the dancers blur.

In the shadows around them she sees Lannie's face, but finds she's no longer sure that the woman she has been scurrying after really is the child she and Barney raised. For the first time it occurs to her that if Lannie had wanted to be found, she'd have written; if she needed help and wanted it from Iris and Barney, she'd have asked for it; if she'd wanted her brother and sister and her father, she'd have stayed with them. What Lannie? Who is she?

Now, in the cacophony of voices, a singing that sounds to Iris more like wailing, in the insistent, high-pitched jingle of the sistrum and the unrelenting rhythmic boom of the drums, she feels herself transported, removed. It's as if she's sitting here at her table in front of the performers, while at the same time part of her is viewing the scene from above and beyond it. And suddenly, hovering above, she understands clearly that when Barney died, he did not love her.

Sitting here in this remote dust heap of a town, she can hide it from herself no longer. He wanted children, he wanted us to have babies of our own. He said so, but I couldn't hear him; I wouldn't hear him.

Abruptly, a huge weight has descended on her. It is the weight of knowing her own selfishness finally destroyed Barney's last shred of love for her. She can't move, she can't stand up, she can't breathe.

And I came all this way, she marvels at herself while in front of her the dancers shake their shoulders in frenzy, the drummers drum frantically, the singers keen in an eery, minor timbre that makes her want to throw herself on the ground and wail along with them, *I came all this way, all the way to the dark side of the world, to this ancient, stony kingdom so I wouldn't have to face myself.*

Cock's Crow

Iris sleeps badly, fitfully, waking over and over again to a noise she thinks is an intruder or to some dreaming imperative that vanishes when she opens her eyes to find herself in her dark room, the stone of the hotel absorbing and deadening all sound so that it's as quiet as a night back on the farm. She has been dreaming, she knows, but what the dreams are about she can't remember, only a veil of figures, pale green and blue, soldiers maybe, but what they were doing she can't bring back.

At first light she gives up, extricates herself from her knotted bedcovers, and begins to get out of bed, but her body is stiff and aching, her eyes feel grainy, her mind buzzes stupidly; her head fills with recurring images, as if in a film projector gone mad. She puts both hands up and rubs her face hard.

Her old life shines in that space behind her eyelids. This morning it appears as one of those small glass domes inside of which a plastic scene is anchored, Bethlehem on Christmas Eve, plastic snow drifting downward to glitter on the village rooftops. The farm, her own village, hovers there for an instant before it slowly dissolves and vanishes. A confection, a falsity, a foolish dream.

There's still no water, so without washing she pulls on yesterday's clothes. There's no electricity either, and it's so early the room is still deep in shadows. She feels claustrophobic, in need of fresh air and space to wash away the night's accumulated woes. And she has to wait for Giyorgis to get up before they can leave. She pockets her key, opens her door quietly, and, concentrating on holding it so it will shut noiselessly, steps into the hall.

"Sister," someone whispers loudly near her ear. She spins around, taking in her breath sharply, stifling an exclamation. A tall, very thin man she guesses to be in his forties is standing behind her, one hand raised as if he meant to touch her shoulder and then thought better of it. "I must speak to you," he whispers urgently to her startled face. "I wait here — all night," he says, "so I may speak to you." Then, while she's still getting over the fright he has given her, he walks a couple of steps down the hall, going in the opposite direction from the lobby, stops and looks back. "Come," he whispers, his eyes glittering, when he sees she's not following.

Iris hesitates, reluctant to follow a total stranger in this strange place, thinking of the benefits to him of kidnapping a *ferenji*, but then she reminds herself that she's in a modern hotel inside a guarded compound, that on three sides there is a sheer drop of twenty feet or more. Probably the grounds are patrolled regularly too. All she has to do is scream and people will come running from all directions.

He says again, "Come, sister, please." The way he says it, in a tone more imploring then commanding, and all the things she saw yesterday — especially all of that — overcome her caution. She follows him in a way that's almost angry, nevertheless rising onto her toes so as not to make a sound on the stone floor. They turn the corner and walk a few feet to an exit leading into the hotel garden, but where an angle of the building shields them from the view of the guards at the compound entrance. He holds the door open for her, then follows her as she goes through.

It is going to be another cloudless, bright day, but this early there are still shadows in the clefts of the mountains around the town and high up the sky is still a deep night blue. The air is chilly and she shivers. The man stops and faces her. He is darker skinned than most Ethiopians she has met and she guesses from this he is a farmer. Or is he a priest, who apparently are also farmers? Does he perhaps look a bit familiar? Maybe she saw him yesterday in one of the rock churches, or leaning with his companions against the wall in one of the passages.

"Yes?" she says uncertainly, staring up into his eyes. He bends his head toward her and stoops a little from his shoulders to better compel her attention.

"I ask you, sister. We have no food."

"What?" she says, although she has heard him perfectly well.

"Sister, you must tell the NGOs to come." He's treating her as if she's his last hope in the world, as if she absolutely must understand him. As the import of his message strikes her at last, she takes in her breath sharply. "The NGOs," he repeats urgently. "You must tell them to come. You are Canadian — we need Canadian grain." How does he know she's Canadian? Oh, yes, her passport presented at the desk. She wonders suddenly if the hotel guards let him come in. Or is he, maybe, one of them? Still perplexed, she asks, "But — but won't the government help you? I saw all those truckloads of grain going up to Tigray — " Abruptly he drops his eyes from hers.

"We cannot get government grain," he mutters, as if he is ashamed to say this, or afraid. After a second's hesitation Iris says, "What?" again, thinking she couldn't have heard him right. Aware she's frowning, thinking out loud, she says, "But they're building that new air strip — " meaning that if they can build a new air strip, surely they have the money and the means to transport food here? He shrugs and looks over the barbed-wire fence to where the distant mountain Giyorgis told her is Abuna Yosef is flooding with the clear, pale light of the rising sun.

I suppose the answer is too complicated for him to tell me, Iris thinks. I suppose I wouldn't understand anyway, or it wouldn't make the slightest difference. Or he doesn't dare tell me for fear of — she stops here, not knowing what: the police? the army? the government? Then she thinks, I'm a stranger — how can I judge? I can only refuse him or accept what he says.

She stares into his eyes as he looks gravely down at her, trying hard to see whatever it is there that contains the answers to her questions. No, she cannot read that darkness; she does not speak that language, she from a country created only yesterday, from a people who believe that by crossing a mere ocean, they've escaped the weight of history. She takes in a deep, slow breath.

"I will tell people you need food," she says. "I'm going back today to Addis and I will tell the NGOs. And when I get home, soon, I will tell the people back in Canada." She imagines the truckloads of grain rushing up the winding mountain road, or maybe the NGOs will ship the food in using the new airstrip. Then she wonders whom in Canada she can tell and whether anyone will listen to her if she does. Lannie! she thinks. Lannie will know where to find the right people to tell. And I can call that woman in Addis who helped me find her — Mrs. Samuels.

He lifts his head abruptly, looking off in the distance before he brings his eyes back to meet hers. It's as if he's searching as deep inside her as he can go, looking perhaps for some promise he can trust. Then, he bows.

"Thank you, sister," he says, and disappears around the corner.

While they've been talking, the sun has risen to bathe the countryside's rough peaks and valleys, the flat-topped buttes Giyorgis says are called *ambas*, its dusty roads, its distant, dark-red, round, two-storey dwellings. Such a busy landscape, she thinks, with its ups and downs and ins and outs, its varied palette, it tires her this morning to look at it. She thinks of her own country with its long, gently sloping lines, unbroken for miles by buildings or people, its pale yellows and tans and dusty blue-greens, and its enormous sky that's both a steady question and its own unreadable answer.

A motorized vehicle is roaring down the road on the far side of the hotel and Iris recognizes that the world is stirring at last. It occurs to her to wonder why, in a hotel full of tourists, this man has come to her, but she knows the answer. The other tourists travel with guides from their own countries and have the blessing of the government because of the money they bring. To disturb them would surely bring harsh penalties to the local people. And because she's alone, travelling with an Ethiopian who isn't an official guide, because she speaks English, not French or German, like the other tourists.

Thinking hard about what she will do, she goes back to her room, where she quickly packs her few things and takes her suitcase through the lobby to the desk to check out. People are about now, mostly hotel staff, but even though she studies the faces of the several men who are standing in the lobby or passing through, none of them is the stranger who spoke to her. She says hesitantly, carefully to the desk clerk, "I see you're having a drought here." He nods, handing her back her passport, then speaks slowly, in a soft voice so that she has to strain to hear him. "Yes. There has been a crop failure. And there is no rain."

He looks down at the stack of papers he's filling out, no computers here — of course not, there's no power — and Iris notices that his collar, the collar of the desk clerk in what was once a Hilton Hotel, is frayed almost through to the stiffening beneath the cloth. Whoever is paying him isn't giving him enough money, she thinks. He shuffles his papers without looking at her while he waits for her to finish signing her traveller's cheques, and she thinks it's as if he'd like to say something more to her, but keeps changing his mind.

As she hands him the cheques, Iris sees Giyorgis coming across the lobby, carrying his bag.

"Are you well this morning?" he asks. His voice is gentle. There must be signs in her face of her sleepless night, nor has she bothered with makeup or teased her thick hair into a coiffure, just pulled it back and tied it with a scarf at the nape of her neck. She supposes she looks terrible; she finds she doesn't care.

Giyorgis loads their bags, they drive slowly out of the hotel compound, waving to the guards whose faces Iris doesn't recognize, and turn down the dusty road that will lead them to the Chinese Road, then to Weldiya, Dessie, Kombolcha, and, she hopes, to Lannie. Iris leaves the town with no regrets, and yet with an absence of relief.

The words of the stranger in the hotel corridor continue to sound in her ears, and she is determined to act, although she is still not sure what she'll do. If she tells people, she's afraid no one will believe her. She expects she'll be viewed as naive, as a silly tourist who, on seeing the standard poverty of the Third World for the first time, has mistaken the commonplace for a crisis. She can't think how she'll overcome that. Perhaps she can't.

In any case, she thinks, she will at least try her very best to convey to someone in authority that the people here are desperate enough to have asked her for help. After a while she turns to Giyorgis and asks him bluntly, "Why won't the government give them food?"

He starts to, then doesn't reply, only shrugs and grasps the steering wheel more firmly. She would press him to get him to speak to her, but she's anxious not to put him in a bad position. But when she sees some country people walking up the mountain road to the town, she makes Giyorgis stop and ask them about the food situation, which he does without apparent reluctance.

"They say they have no food," he tells her. "They say there was a crop failure last year, and a poor crop the year before that, and if the rains don't come," he gestures to the clear blue sky, "there'll be another one this year and they will starve. They will have to go away to find food."

Twice more, with several kilometres between each group, she makes him stop to ask the same question of different bands of people walking along the road or crossing the fields with loads of firewood on their backs. Each time Giyorgis tells her, "They have only firewood, they have no food." The second group has also asked them to send the NGOs.

All the way as they head south from Weldiya to Dessie to Kombolcha they meet truck after truck loaded with grain and heading north. Now she and Giyorgis don't even mention them, Giyorgis poker-faced, Iris staring grimly at them, knowing that none of these trucks are turning off at Weldiya to take grain to the hungry people at Lalibela. *A relatively stable government*, they'd said in Canada, *a step toward democracy.* Why would they say that if it isn't true? They know things about this country you haven't even dreamt of, she reminds herself.

It is late afternoon when they finally reach Kombolcha. Iris notices that the people here are thin too, although not as thin as those in Lalibela, and some of them laugh and talk as they walk along, which she didn't notice people doing in or around Lalibela. There they were mostly silent and grim as they trudged along the road with their burdens or chased their animals, at least, that's how she remembers it.

They drive through the gates of Afewerk's Inn. How is it that nothing has changed here, the flowers are still blooming red and orange, the guard who opens the gate is the same impassive, tall man, swathed now as evening approaches in a thick wool *shamma*. In silence they park, get out, and walk with stiffened joints, inside. Hagosa, still wearing her patterned cotton housedress over her bulky figure, her white *shamma* loosely draped over her black hair and sturdy shoulders, greets them at the door to the threadbare reception room.

"You return," she says, beaming shyly at Iris. Then she directs her gaze to Iris's rumpled, dusty clothing, her uncombed hair that's escaping the scarf she'd tied around in the morning. "You have been travelling," she remarks. She seems concerned.

Iris says, "Yes, to Lalibela." She'd say more, but Hagosa claps her hands together and holds them under her chin.

"How very good!" she declares, her black eyes shining. "You like?"

"Oh, yes, very much. The churches were wonderful." The door at the back of the room opens and Afewerk's widow enters. Although she too wears a *shamma* over her head and shoulders, her straight gabardine skirt and neat flowered blouse are, as before, North American in style and in her way of wearing them. She and Giyorgis greet each other with stiff bows.

"You're back," she says, smiling down at Iris, although with less ardour than Hagosa had. Iris had forgotten how tall she is, and big-boned — a strong-looking woman. Behind her, Hagosa hurries silently out. "Two rooms?" the innkeeper asks in her slightly bored manner. Iris nods. Hagosa had apparently gone to get keys, because now she returns and hands a pair of them to the innkeeper who takes them, glancing at Iris who stands tiredly, waiting to be shown to her room. "You were out sightseeing?" she asks politely. Hagosa has vanished again.

"We went to Lalibela to see the rock churches." Afewerk's widow — how embarrassing it is not to be able to remember the woman's name — literally takes a step back. Her clear brown eyes widen. Giyorgis moves back to lean against a narrow table set against the wall as if he's tired or bored, or recognizes this conversation has nothing to do with him. Or is it something else?

"Lalibela?" the woman says. She's thinking, her eyes fixed on Iris's face. "How did you go there?" she asks. "Did you fly from here?" Iris shakes her head, no, they drove, she tells her, but the look on the woman's face puzzles, even alarms her a little. It's as if she and

Giyorgis had violated some rule by going there. Bewildered, Iris reminds herself that, after all, Ethiopia is not a free country in the way that Canada is free.

She hesitates, then says in a tone that she hopes sounds innocent, "I had to wait for my niece, so I thought it was the perfect opportunity to see a little of the country. And I did want to see the rock churches. They're practically the eighth wonder of the world." She doesn't mention that she hadn't heard of them herself until three days ago. Afewerk's widow is still staring disconcertingly at Iris. She looks away, then asks slowly, "What are the churches like? I've never been there," she adds as if it's an afterthought, and Iris feels pretty sure the woman is lying, or else she wants to find something else out from Iris without Iris knowing she's doing it. She must be careful not to mention the hunger of the people.

"Oh, really quite amazing," she says brightly. "There are ten or eleven of them — I didn't see them all because I just got too tired. It's the altitude, I think. But — " The woman is staring at the floor, Iris sees worry in her face.

"What are they like?" she persists. "Tell me about them." Is it that she wants to be sure that's where Iris went? Maybe there was something along the way, in Lalibela itself, that she wasn't supposed to see. So she tells her how the churches were carved from the top down and are forty feet or so deep and other details of their construction.

"And did you take pictures?" The question is so careful that Iris does her best not to show any hesitation.

"I wish I could have, but there's no electricity so the churches are too dark inside for pictures. And anyway, I forgot to bring a camera." Is she imagining it, or does Afewerk's widow relax perceptibly? "I'm sorry that I don't have one," she adds. "I would have liked to take home pictures of them they're so remarkable."

"They are remarkable," the woman agrees quickly, apparently forgetting she has just said she hasn't seen them. There's a brief silence during which Iris considers, then risks asking her about the situation in Lalibela. She's thinking, I'm a Canadian, they wouldn't dare do anything to me.

"Did you know," she begins carefully, "that there's been no rain there? That there's been a crop failure and now the fields are bare and it's no use planting without moisture?" She waits.

Afewerk's widow says angrily, "Hah! They are stupid up there! They don't know anything about conservation, they farm all the wrong way. If they don't have grain stored, it's their own fault!" Her answer is so vehement, so full of contempt, that Iris is shaken. She does her best not to show it. Giyorgis changes his position against the table and yawns audibly. Is he trying to warn her? She glances back, but he's studying his shoes, doesn't appear to be listening at all. Still, Iris thinks, she'd be wise to pretend she's satisfied.

"Oh, I see," she says after a moment, her voice softer than she intended, and clears her throat. As if starvation were only what those people deserved because of their stupidity, their improvidence — which she doesn't believe in anyway. Again she is assailed by the beggar child crying in the dirt, she hears the farmers saying they have nothing to eat, and the stranger saying, "We can't get government food."

"Oh, I see," she says again, as if already the subject bores her. She will tell Lannie when she comes; after so many years in this country Lannie will know what to do. Or her agency will. Maybe it will send grain. "Well," she says, turning away and passing a hand across her face. "I'm hungry and I'm dying for a shower."

"Yes, it is a long way and the roads are not good. You must be very tired — " Her tone is soothing, but she's interrupted by the door behind Iris opening, and Iris sees her break into a smile, as if she has forgotten what she has just been talking about. Giyorgis straightens and takes a step forward. Afewerk's widow makes a gesture with her hand and nods her head toward the door. Puzzled, a bit apprehensive, Iris turns.

A rather beautiful, tall, stern-looking middle-aged Ethiopian woman is standing in the doorway, one arm around the shoulders of a second woman, as if she's comforting or supporting her. The second woman is slender and very pale in the harsh light from the unshaded overhead bulb, which also makes her long, drab hair shine dully, and although she is warmly dressed in faded jeans and a bulky, dark red sweater, she's shivering in the evening chill. It's her niece, Lannie.

"Oh," Iris says, as she takes a step toward her; the day Howard left ten-year-old Lannie alone in the middle of Iris's kitchen is flooding back over her. Lannie looks just the same way now: not quite seeming to see or to register that it is her aunt Iris standing in front of her. Iris has begun to tremble, she feels as if the room has grown brighter, as if this new light is flooding through her as well as over her. How Lannie's white skin shines in the light. How frighteningly real she is finally.

Lannie sighs, her eyes roll upward, her eyelids slowly close, her knees give way, and she slides, unconscious, to the floor.

Time stops. They are all — Afewerk's widow, Giyorgis, Iris, the Ethiopian woman — frozen where they stand, then all moving at once, voices mingling — someone has cried out — hands reach toward the prostrate girl, people crouch beside her, touching her. Giyorgis, the only man present, says something in a commanding tone that gets everyone's attention. The women move back, he bends, slides an arm under Lannie's head, another under her knees, and gently, carefully, with visible effort, lifts her slowly from the floor.

The innkeeper looks at the keys in her hands and rushes from the room, plainly expecting them all to follow. Lannie is making whimpering noises now and moving her head back and forth without opening her eyes. The Ethiopian woman, whom Iris realizes must be Dr. Abubech Tefera, pushes her way past Iris and Giyorgis to catch up with the innkeeper. She hands her a key she has taken from her jacket pocket. They hurry on around the corner, Iris last. At the door to what must be Lannie's room, everyone stops while the innkeeper unlocks and opens it.

"I didn't mean to startle her," Iris says, wringing her hands. "I never thought she'd be so upset to see me." Giyorgis crosses the few feet to the nearer of the two single beds with their faded flowered covers and gently sets Lannie down. Iris goes to Lannie's side, shakes out the folded blanket she finds at its foot and spreads it carefully over her. Giyorgis, Dr. Abubech, and Afewerk's widow stand in the open door carrying on a brisk conversation in Amharic, ignoring Iris.

How pale she is, how smooth and transparently bluish are her eyelids, her lips colourless and chapped; Iris wants to soothe her rough lips with salve, to brush her lustreless hair and make it beautiful again, to bathe those fragile limbs. She holds Lannie's hand in hers, icy to her touch and weightless, and yet she thinks she detects a faint quiver.

"We'll put your suitcase in your room," the innkeeper says, startling Iris. The tableau in the doorway is breaking up; Giyorgis has already gone. "Your key is here." The innkeeper sets it on the table by the door and vanishes down the corridor, leaving only Lannie's companion with Iris.

"She is going to call a doctor and get some medicine," Dr. Abubech explains in her low-pitched, steady voice. "Giyorgis will go and bring it back." She moves the same way she speaks, with a deliberateness that Iris finds reassuring, to stand with her looking down at Lannie. Iris notices the streak of grey in her smoothly coiffed black hair, and notes that she's probably at least Iris's age, maybe even older. Lannie moves her legs under the blanket, pulls her hand jerkily out of Iris's grasp, and grimaces. Abubech puts a palm gently on her forehead. "She has a fever." She removes her hand and turns to Iris. "I am Abubech Tefera. Lannie works with me."

Iris introduces herself. They shake hands and Abubech does the inevitable Ethiopian bowing, first one side, then the other, then again. Iris hardly notices. "I'm so sorry I startled her. I should have given her some warning. It never occurred to me — "

"It wasn't surprise at seeing you that made her faint," Abubech interrupts. "I phoned the office yesterday and was told you were here, and I told Lannie. But she hasn't been feeling well all week and today she became ill. The way she is shivering, it has to be her malaria back." Lannie's eyelids have begun to flutter. "Somewhere along the way she didn't take her malaria drugs, I'm sure of it. She contracted malaria several years ago when she was staying in the lowlands, and now this."

"But," Iris begins, "surely they can treat it? It can't be too bad?" Abubech swings her head back to fasten her stern black eyes on Iris's face.

"I'm afraid that people die of it," she replies. "It can be very serious." For a second Iris is too shocked to speak.

"Then we have to get her to a hospital right now," she says. "Is the doctor on his way?"

"Perhaps," Abubech says. "But the hospital is not a good idea."

"Why not?" Iris asks, stunned.

In an undertone, Abubech says, "There is too much AIDS." Somewhere outside, far away in the perfumed darkness a rooster is crowing, out of sync with the world. The sound strikes terror into Iris's heart and involuntarily she moves a step closer to Abubech. Abubech says, "We must get her to Addis. In Addis she can see a doctor I know. She will get good care there."

"She looks too ill to travel," Iris says doubtfully, "doesn't she?" turning to Abubech for verification as if in this strange country she can't trust her own instincts any more. Now she too puts her hand on Lannie's forehead, and in a flash before she closes off the picture, remembers touching Barney's cold, set face, as if with her own abundant warmth and energy she might bring him back to life.

Lannie opens her eyes. Something like alarm crosses her face, is replaced instantly by a frown, she turns her head away, then brings it back again to stare up into Iris's face with those dark gold eyes that now have gone nearly black with whatever it is she's seeing.

"Iris," she says, and her mouth goes tremulous, then firms itself. "Aunt Iris? Is it you?"

"Yes, yes, it's me," Iris tells her softly. Lannie stares up at her, her lips trembling faintly. She seems unable to find any more words, and to fill the gap of her surprise and whatever other emotion is rendering her speechless, Iris continues, trying to sound light and cheerful, "You fainted. I thought it was because you were so surprised to see me." Then emotion overcomes her and she takes Lannie's hand back in both her own and holds it tightly. "I've found you at last. I'm so glad — "

"No, no," Lannie says. She wobbles her head from side to side on the pillow, then stops, wincing, as if the movement has hurt her or made her nauseous.

"I will leave you two," Abubech says. "When Giyorgis returns with the medicine, I will bring it to you. In the meantime, I will be in my room if you need me." She bows again and goes out. As she pulls the door shut Iris turns back to Lannie, who whispers, "Did you come all this way to find me?" Iris nods, now she's the one not able to speak.

Hungrily she studies the once-again familiar face, the narrow, red-gold eyebrows she remembers so well, the delicate, pale mouth, the fine-grained skin of her face and neck. She is overcome with love for the girl in the bed, for the little, lost child she'd fed and clothed and tried to be a mother to. She bends toward her, intending to gather her in her arms and press her against her bosom, to make her well again with her own lavish health.

In a sudden, harsh movement, Lannie turns her face away. Iris falters, stopped in her forward movement.

"I should put on my nightgown. I'm pretty tired." Lannie doesn't look at her as she murmurs this, but then she turns slowly back to Iris, smiles in a troubled way that holds perhaps shyness, and lifts an arm so that Iris understands she's asking for her help to sit up. Relieved to be helping her, Iris supports her while she sits and moves her legs over the side of the bed. Then Lannie waits quietly, not moving, while Iris rummages for her nightgown in the suitcase she finds leaning against the wall. "That's it," Lannie tells her. It's only an old pink cotton T-shirt, faded, with a tear in the shoulder. At the sight of it tenderness again floods Iris, and she finds her eyes filling with tears as she glances over her shoulder at Lannie sitting on the side of the bed.

Lannie's eyes are fixed on her with so strange an expression that Iris, crouched over the suitcase, the T-shirt pressed against her chest, can only stare back until with visible effort Lannie breaks her gaze. She wonders, What was it Lannie was seeing? Something in me? Or something in her own life that my presence has reminded her of? Sobs of relief threaten her precarious composure, but she struggles and succeeds in stifling them. She pats her eyes dry with the T-shirt, not noticing she is, then goes to Lannie.

They don't speak as Iris helps her take off her jeans and sweater, pulls the nightgown over her head, fluffs the two thin pillows and puts them back. Lannie has always been slender, but now she is bone thin, her body pale as snow, her small breasts with their pink nipples like two delicate flowers against her chest, her long, exquisitely shaped, palely freckled legs thin too. Iris is moved by the beauty of her young body, which she had forgotten, or perhaps had never known. Lannie is shivering as she gets back into bed. Iris pulls the blankets up around her neck and tucks them securely into place.

"I'm so happy to see you," Iris tells her. "You're not angry with me for coming?"

Lannie has closed her eyes, but she opens them and says, in a tone Iris can't identify, "I never thought you'd come." She pauses. "But I should have known you would."

"Why didn't you tell us where you were?" Iris asks, then wishes that she hadn't, thinking this is no time to accuse her. She will have to find a way to tell Lannie that Barney is dead, and decides she'll wait until Lannie feels better. She rests her palm gently against her cheek. Lannie shivers violently at her touch, as if Iris's hand is too cold to bear.

"I meant to tell you, but the longer I didn't write, the harder it was," she says. "It was just that — " She falls silent. "I — didn't have anything — to tell you."

"It doesn't matter now," Iris says briskly.

"Where's Barney? Didn't he come with you?"

"He — couldn't come." Her voice catches.

"You came all this way alone." The look on Lannie's face puzzles Iris, as if she has done something miraculously difficult. She is ashamed; she's done so little, and so very late.

"I visited your father," she tells Lannie. "And I saw Misty and Dillon."

"Is Misty all right?"

"They're both living with your father."

Lannie, who has again turned her head away, turns back rapidly to look at Iris when she hears this, and then closes both eyes.

"I'm going to throw up." She's pushing back the bedcovers. Iris grabs the only container she can see in the room, a black clay pitcher sitting on the table. Lannie retches violently into it, but her stomach is empty; this isn't the first time she has vomited. There's a brief knock and Abubech enters carrying vials of pills. The expression on her face, neutral when she entered, changes to concern when she sees Lannie holding the pitcher.

"Vomiting again? Get some water," she says to Iris in an easy, polite way that shows she's used to giving commands, knows they'll be obeyed. Iris goes into the bathroom where she finds a bottle of water, a plastic glass, and a towel and brings them back to the bedside.

When Lannie's nausea passes, she takes the pills with sips of water and then falls back against the pillows. Abubech says in an undertone, "I think early in the morning we will start back for Addis with her. What is your vehicle?"

"I have a Land Rover. Are you sure she's all right to travel?"

"Good," Abubech says, ignoring the question. "I have only a small truck and there is not room for all." They look back at Lannie whose eyes are closed. Abubech says softly, "She will sleep now. Come with me and we will have dinner."

"Yes, go with her, Aunt Iris," Lannie says. "I'll sleep now. These relapses only last a few days. I'll be better in the morning."

Abubech and Iris walk the corridors together to the hotel restaurant, a small, plaster-walled room with a few cloth-covered tables and straight-backed wooden chairs set around them. A row of windows at the far end open onto the veranda. Giyorgis, the only other occupant, is sitting by himself at a table for four eating a plate of spaghetti. He stands when they come in.

"She is — well?" he asks.

"The medicine will make a difference," Iris says. "Thank you for your help. Without you — " She gestures helplessly. He smiles, a boy's grin of shy pleasure at praise, and bows gravely.

"You will fly her back to Addis?" he asks. Surprised, Iris turns to Abubech.

"It is not a good idea," Abubech replies. "The plane does not always leave on time. I have waited a full day for it. Better to drive, I think."

It's agreed they'll leave in the morning as early as possible, that Abubech will follow in her small truck. Abubech speaks to Giyorgis in Amharic, ending with a smile. He sits down again and as Iris is about to join him, Abubech touches her arm and takes her to a table on the far side of the room.

"We will talk," she says. Iris can only hope Giyorgis isn't insulted. She thinks of him now as a friend, then realizes Abubech must have explained her intentions to him.

"Hagosa tells me you went to Lalibela," Abubech says, as they wait for the small, silent boy who took their order to bring their food.

"Oh, yes, and it was wonderful — and terrible," Iris says. She tells Abubech everything she saw, ending with the stranger who accosted her in the hotel corridor. "He said — I'm sure it's what he said — 'We can't get government food.' And yet I saw those trucks loaded with grain going north on the highway. Is there a drought in Tigray?"

"There may be, there often is. It is a very dry place." There's something in her manner that suggests to Iris she's carefully formulating her thoughts before she says them out loud. Their food comes. When the boy is finished serving them and leaves, she turns back to Abubech and tries again.

"Did you know they're building a new airport there? It's for tourists, I suppose, although the strip that's already there seems to work well enough. I saw a planeload of European tourists come in and land on the old one." When Abubech still says nothing, she goes on. "It seems very strange to me to spend all that money on a new landing strip when the people in the area have no shoes, when they have nothing to eat." Abubech shrugs.

"It gives people jobs for a while," she points out. "Tourists bring money into the area. It helps a little." She sighs. "And the government needs the foreign currency the tourists bring." They are sitting close together and speaking softly, Iris is sure even Giyorgis can't hear them. At this point he leaves his table, bows silently from across the room to them, and goes out, stifling a yawn with his hand.

"All the tourists at the hotel looked wealthy," she admits. She remembers the row of ragged little girls standing in the dust and the couple photographing them. Iris has so far barely touched her food and now the sight of it makes her feel ill. Abubech is eating a mouthful of her spaghetti, chewing slowly, thoughtfully. "I have to know what's going on there. I can't stand not knowing and I can't just forget what I saw. Why did that man come to me in secret if he had nothing to be afraid of? Why did he tell me what he did if it isn't true? Won't the government feed its own people?" Abubech chews doggedly, refusing to look at Iris. Iris waits. When it appears that she will not speak at all, she moves impatiently, intending to go on, but Abubech interrupts.

"Mrs. Christie." She sets her fork down neatly, lifts her face to Iris's. For the first time Iris sees there a cold formality. "I can tell you nothing." She says this slowly, deliberately, looking straight into her eyes. "My project is everything to me. It is the only thing I can do that will eventually make a difference to the hunger my people endure. I will not jeopardize it." Iris wants to take Abubech by the shoulders and shake the truth out of her.

"Are you telling me that if you tell me what the problem is, and I go away and tell my government, or the press, somebody — the government, maybe — will stop your project?" Abubech lifts her fork again. Just when Iris thinks she will not speak at all, she does.

"I know nothing about it." She pauses. "However, you may be assured that the government knows the people have no food. Also, there are NGOs in the area. They will see that the people do not starve. As well, you should understand that in Ethiopia, when one locality has no food, the people traditionally walk to a locality where there is food. There, other Ethiopians will feed them. They will not starve. You are upset for nothing." She begins to eat again, but Iris feels her exuding an unwilling restraint, a huge sorrow. Abubech keeps eating. The silence extends itself through the gloomy room with its uneven, discoloured plaster walls, its shabby tablecloths, its two bare light bulbs. The curtains stir in a breath of air, and out in the night behind compound walls the rooster crows again, an elongated, many-syllabled, minor-keyed cry.

Abubech speaks. It is as if her voice is part of the night that has fallen over the town, part of the wide, soft breeze that moves the curtains softly in and out; it's as if she has always been speaking and Iris has just begun to hear her.

"Ethiopia is a very ancient country. Much goes on here — has gone on here in the past — that someone like you cannot hope to know or to understand. It is better that you take your niece and go home to North America." Abubech has bent her head to toy with her fork and spoon and, watching her closely, Iris sees a faint sheen of sweat on the golden skin of her neck and the underside of her chin. She must dare the question again.

"Why won't the government feed those people?"

Abubech lifts her eyes to the far wall. "In Ethiopia we do not have so good governments."

"In Canada they told me this new government is good. They said it is closer to democracy. They said — "

Abubech interrupts.

"Mengistu dragged people off the streets in the daytime, from the middle of crowds, so everyone knew the evil he did. He killed my brother, he killed my father. But this government, it does it secretly, at night, so no one knows, no one believes — "

Iris is finally silenced. She wipes her damp cheeks again with her paper napkin. Her palms are damp and when she tries to pick up her fork, she fumbles, drops it, picks it up again.

"Forgive me. I'm sorry."

"We will not talk of it. I beg you to forget what I have said. I was mistaken."

Iris draws in a quivering breath, forces a smile. "With your education you could live in North America. You could teach at a university. You wouldn't have to look at this terrible poverty every day of your life."

"Yes, it is hard to go day after day into the field, into people's houses and see how little they have. See the poverty, the disease. The women dying in childbirth, half the children dead before they are four years old." Abubech's eyes have clouded with tears. She turns to Iris, suddenly fierce, "You have to be strong." Ashamed, Iris struggles to stop the moisture from welling up and running down her cheeks.

They finish their meal in silence, Abubech chewing each mouthful carefully, as if to remind herself that one should not spurn food if one is lucky enough to have it. Seeing this Iris tries to eat, but her stomach will not allow her. Abubech doesn't look at Iris's plate.

"Do you think she'll be all right?" Iris asks. "I mean, how soon will she be able to — " She pauses because she has just realized that she has always taken it for granted that Lannie will return to Canada with her. "I mean, I'd like her to come home with me — if she wants to."

"Lannie is free," Abubech says. "She is not my employee. As far as her health is concerned — a week or so, and she should be well enough to travel. Now it is late. We must go to bed." They rise together and go out of the dining room and down separate halls to their rooms.

Iris, intending to sleep in the second bed in Lannie's room in case Lannie needs her in the night, goes first to her own room to get her nightgown and toiletries. As she comes down the hall she's surprised to find her door slightly ajar. Thinking that Hagosa or Giyorgis must have failed to close it, she pushes it open. Someone is bending over her suitcase that's open on the bed. It is the innkeeper, Afewerk's widow. Suddenly Iris remembers her name. It is Asegedetch.

The woman turns around, a flicker of guilt or shock crosses her face, then she smiles and says smoothly, "I thought you'd need your things."

Iris hears herself say calmly, politely, "I was just coming for them."

Without meeting her eyes or looking at her the woman comes to her, hands Iris her things, and slides past her out the open door. She pauses in the hall and says, "Call me if you need anything, or if your niece gets worse. I hope you don't think I was . . . in this country hostesses serve their guests."

"It is very kind of you," Iris says.

"I am concerned that your niece is so ill. Malaria is very dangerous." The woman is still standing there, as if she's trying to think of what else she can say to reassure Iris that she wasn't up to no good.

"I do very much appreciate your help. Really," Iris says, trying to sound warm and natural.

The woman regards her for a moment more, then says, "So . . . excuse me," and bustles off down the hall.

Iris thinks, I *did* see something I wasn't supposed to see. Suddenly she's genuinely frightened.

But she doesn't have any paper in her suitcase, she hasn't written anything down anyway, and she was telling the truth when she said she had no camera. That must have been what the woman was looking for: for a camera and film that might have recorded the images she wasn't supposed to see, or a piece of paper that has written on it what she saw, a letter maybe, or a report to a newspaper, or a foreign government. Thinking back over their few, brief conversations, Iris is sure she gave no hint of her concerns, just a traveller's observations, as if she didn't understand their implications. She's safe, if she's just very careful until she leaves this inn.

Lying in the narrow bed across from Lannie asleep, the child she'd lived with all those years comes back in easy, vivid pictures: cooking her breakfast egg just the way she liked it, walking her to the driveway to wait for the school bus, handing her her shiny yellow lunch kit with the sandwiches in it she'd so lovingly made, sitting in her classroom admiring her childish paintings and her neat schoolbooks while the teacher spoke of Lannie's successes, waiting eagerly for her as Lannie walked across the schoolgrounds to the car. She remembers how quickly she had grown to love her, and how deeply. She remembers her now. And she feels the first uneasy stirring of some new emotion that she can't quite identify, that she's afraid might be, but hopes is not, anger.

The Underworld

The baby in her arms is so thin she can count each tiny rib, his yellow-brown arms and legs are twigs, his abdomen round and hard, his face a ghastly triangle with no flesh between the skin and the delicate bones of his skull. She feeds him, spooning in something that looks like pablum, but it dribbles out of his mouth again, or runs out his ears and nose, or from his rectum, and he wails in that high-pitched, hopeless voice, hideous music rising up out of darkness, a discordant jangle. She spoons in the food desperately, but the child is dying in her arms, withering to a tiny yellow bird with eyes that are two small black holes in his head. It hops away, chittering, out of her horrified grasp, then turns to shriek at her raucously, crowlike: *Caw! Caw! Caw!* She's to blame for the trouble; it's all her fault; and the harsh cries so strident that they fill her head, the pain is so bad —

"Drink this, Lannie. You must drink this."

"I'm cold," Lannie whispers. "I'm freezing. Get me some blankets, please, Auntie. Cover me." Her eyes are closed, the words, forced as they are through cracked, quivering lips, are hard to make out.

"Sshh, dear, yes, here are more blankets," Iris says, although she isn't moving from Lannie's bedside, because there's nothing left in the small apartment to add to the pile of blankets that she's already buried under. Still Lannie's teeth are knocking together, her body shivering violently. Iris has never in her life seen anybody so ill in such a strange, frightening way.

Once in a while Lannie stops shaking and drifts into sleep that can last for hours, giving Iris respite that at first she welcomes. But then Lannie throws off the blankets, pulls herself to a sitting position with the unexpected strength of the delirious, sweat gleaming on her face and neck, to stare wild-eyed and unseeing, muttering frantically. Now that she's seen Lalibela Iris has an inkling of what it is that causes Lannie's panic. How many children have died in her arms? How many bodies has she laid out for burial? Or God knows, maybe even buried herself?

"A recurrence of malaria," the doctor Abubech brought has agreed, instructing Iris to keep her warm, to make her drink fluids against the serious danger of dehydration, and to give her the several kinds of pills he has brought. "In these cases, nursing care is everything." He is a short, thin man, with narrow bones, wrists like a girl's, and large, dark Ethiopian eyes, but there's a hard, penetrating glint in them as he tells her, "There is no cure for this scourge," and leaves, shaking his head, promising to return if Lannie doesn't improve. But Iris thinks he was not unduly alarmed by Lannie's condition, and she vows that if nursing care is everything, Lannie will be well soon, and she'll take her home.

Lannie's apartment is small for two. Besides the bedroom, it has a walk-through kitchen with a little window at the end facing the street, a bathroom with the first bathtub Iris has seen since she left the hotel in Lalibela where there'd been no water with which to fill it, and a living room with glass doors that keep the room well lit during the daylight hours, opening onto a small balcony from which it's possible to watch the busy road below.

There isn't a personal item of Lannie's — a comb, keys, cosmetics, a wallet, a scarf, an open paperback — to be seen on any of the surfaces where people normally leave such things. It's as if she has spent no time here or else, Iris thinks, perplexed, she had no personal existence. There's a shortage of furniture too. The several small, sturdy tables are tightly woven out of straw dyed red and yellow, and the bookcase is built of the standard college-student bricks and unpainted boards. Instead of a sofa there are a half-dozen large floor cushions covered in brightly printed cotton that Iris is forced to use for a bed. She doesn't find them easy to get up out of, although they're comfortable enough once she arranges them.

Everything is covered with a layer of dust, spiders have made cobwebs in all the corners, but the electricity is reasonably steady, and water runs from the taps even though Iris has to boil and cool it before she dares to drink it. She's comforted to find that Lannie has been living reasonably well, at least, when she's in Addis.

She spends much of the first couple of days cleaning up vomit that Lannie can't always contain until she reaches the bathroom or the bowl Iris holds out for her. And her diarrhoea, in the first day or two before the medication begins to ease it and before Abubech brings a bedpan, is so violent she doesn't always make it to the toilet either. Not only does Iris have to bathe Lannie almost hourly to wash away the sweat, vomit, and excrement, and the bathroom floor and toilet, she also has to change the soiled sheets and wash them by hand. It's like caring for an infant, all spit-up and faeces. All the while she's cleaning, she's listening for the slightest sound from Lannie that will bring her from her knees, running, to her bedside.

It reminds her of the times when Lannie was sick as a child. Iris would sit by her bed and play endless games of Go Fish or checkers with her, or read stories to her. And that makes her think of other times: waiting with the mothers at the rink while Lannie and the other little girls had figure-skating lessons, or at poolside while the lifeguard taught them swimming, and Iris feeling proudly one of them, like a true parent. It surprises her that she didn't realize then that she was happy.

After the first two days the medication begins to take effect; Lannie stops vomiting and her diarrhoea lessens considerably. Iris occupies herself, when she's not nursing Lannie, with cleaning the apartment. She washes all the dishes, even the clean ones from inside the cupboard; she scrubs the bedroom, kitchen and bathroom floors; she stands on a chair to knock down cobwebs and to polish the cheap plastic light fixtures; she picks by hand every speck of lint off the living-room carpets and, sweating and puffing, drags them out to hang them over the balcony railing to hit the dust out of them with a broom. Then she uses a damp cloth to clean the wooden floor under the carpets. She scrubs the windows and polishes them until the world outside grows brighter and more distinct. She washes walls, paying minute attention to the smudges and fingerprints, and then she washes the doors too.

Standing in the hall outside the open apartment door, wiping the exterior while Lannie lies quietly in the bedroom, she notices that the apartment door across the hall is ajar an inch. She can't see anyone, or hear a voice anywhere in the building, but she has the uncanny feeling that someone is standing just on the other side of it watching her. The feeling is so strong that the hairs on the back of her neck prickle. She reminds herself, I'm a Canadian, they can't do anything to me. She doesn't know who "they" are or what "anything" means, but she does a cursory job of cleaning, the sooner to be able to step back into the apartment and lock the door.

She knows there's not a lot of sense to all this cleaning, as they'll leave as soon as Lannie is well enough to travel, in a few days. But it gives her a peculiar satisfaction to leave a shiny, blank place where before her vigorous wiping there were grimy smudges, dead insects, and cobwebs. She scrubs harder, rinses twice, scrubs again. Her hands have grown rough and red from constant immersion in hot water and the strong cleaning fluids she found under the sink, and her nails are broken and ragged. At last there's nothing left to clean.

Then, during the spells when Lannie is sleeping, or at least is still and silent, Iris takes the one wooden chair out onto the balcony and sits staring down at the heavy traffic passing by on the way to or from the airport, exhaust fumes rising to further taint the air already heavy with the odour of burning wood. The traffic din is horrendous and unending, but she isn't much bothered by it. She sits in her own silence, a frown creasing her forehead, a cup of cold coffee balanced on her lap, and considers what has brought her into this tumultuous, horrifying, challenging new world. She thinks, laughing wryly to herself, that she's in an Ethiopia of the mind too.

It occurs to her that during these lulls she might use the time to write home to Ramona or to her mother, but whenever she thinks of this, the notion drifts away as loosely as it arrived; it is too much trouble, what would she say anyway, since she can't possibly describe — at least not yet — Ethiopia, or what has happened to her here. Besides, she thinks, I'll be home before a letter would arrive.

So she sits on the balcony staring down at the traffic and off across the rooftops and the trees to the low wooded mountains that in the early mornings and evenings fade to a misty blue-green in the haze of smoke from cooking fires, or are partially obscured by the black and oily effluent from the nearby factories. Her thoughts are interrupted when she hears the bed springs creak or when Lannie calls out in a high, thin voice or, in a deeper one, makes gutteral sounds that might be words. Iris doesn't recognize either voice, and this adds to her sense of all of this as a bad dream, an underworld she has inadvertently fallen into and can't climb out of. Yet she feels curiously alive, her senses sharpened.

The second morning when she moves her wooden chair out onto the cramped balcony to watch the crowds of people walking up and down the road on their way to school or to their jobs, it occurs to her that a man leaning against a fruitstand on the far side of the street was also there the morning before. Her eyes swing back to him and she catches him looking up toward the building and she thinks, with a tinge of fear, Is he watching me? She wants to dismiss this notion, she's plainly becoming paranoid, reminded of the old joke that just because you're paranoid doesn't mean somebody isn't watching you. But she's more than half convinced now that she knows something the government doesn't want her to know. From then on, whenever she thinks of it, she goes to the small kitchen window and peeks out to the street below. He is always there.

Iris is thinking a lot about her mother too, because every time she rushes to cover Lannie, or to wipe her face with a damp cloth, to give her sips of water or pills, or to talk soothingly to her when she cries out, she feels the shadow of her mother dogging her. All her life she admired her mother's coolness in the face of illness, the firm way she could take charge and clean up blood or vomit as if they were nothing more than spilled flour, the way her very assurance, her calm, made whoever was ill feel less frightened. She finds that she has adopted that air of her mother's and that pleases her.

But she also hates this feeling of having become like her mother, to hear her mother's voice in every word she says, to see her face when she looks in the mirror, to recognize her mother's gestures when she moves her hands, to see her body that was young, shapely, soft, thickening as her mother's had, the graceful silhouette dissolving, the skin sagging. No matter how hard she tries to will away the illusion, it refuses to go. It makes her wonder if far away in Swift Current, Saskatchewan, in that nursing home where Iris too casually relegated her years ago — she thinks this with shame — if her mother hasn't died and come to haunt her for her cruelty.

If it's true she's dead, what could she do about it anyway now? She doesn't want to even try to telephone to find out; she can't grieve right now, her head is too full, her heart won't settle down into some steady pattern, but keeps fluttering breathlessly, and she's constantly in a cold sweat, her body clammy, she perpetually feels she needs a bath. She can't deal right now with the fear that her mother's dead.

When she gets back to Saskatchewan, she'll go to that old people's lodge and take her home. That big house with only Iris in it — now she has seen Ethiopia, she knows it's a scandal. Her mother deserves better and always has. She wills Lannie to get well so she can go home and take proper care of her mother.

Two more days pass. Lannie shows no signs of improving; in fact, Iris is beginning to think she's getting worse. She is always either in a sleep so deep Iris fears it is really a coma, or else she's trying to get out of bed, raving and grimacing until Iris is afraid that if she ever does get physically well, she will never find her way back to sanity. What if she dies? What if everyone dies?

She runs through an immense field of ripe, shining wheat. The beards of the stalks catch at her, tangling in her skirt, scratching her legs until they bleed, she leaves a scarlet trail behind her. She's searching for her mother who's gone away, but she isn't far, Lannie knows if she just keeps running she'll catch up with her, she's just over that next rise. She stumbles and falls, the rich aroma of dirt fills her nostrils, the wheat scratches her cheeks so they bleed, and she's calling, *Mother, Mother*, but she's too far ahead, running through the damp, faded native grass, Lannie can't see her, the wheat catching at her, hissing as it tries to hold her back. Running again, her legs are so heavy she can hardly move them forward and her lungs feel on fire, sweat pours down her face and neck and chest, her heart knocks so hard it's as if everything she is has coalesced into a great thumping ball in her chest: "Mother!" she cries, "Mother! Mother!"

Iris comes quickly, stopping to refill the basin with cool water, rushing to push Lannie back against the pillows. She calls, "Lannie, it's all right." Lannie settles back, mumbling and twitching and reaching toward Iris with flailing gestures that make Iris despair. She holds Lannie's face gently between her palms for a long time, in hopes that her warmth will seem to Lannie like her real mother's touch.

For the first time Iris accepts that Lannie might die. She brings a few of the floor cushions into her room and sleeps on the rug by her bed so as to be there instantly, the minute she rouses. Whenever she goes into the kitchen she looks out the window to see if her watcher is still there. He is, although it isn't always the same man. She senses, when she looks down at him, that he has to hold himself back from saluting her.

Her own dreams are troubled and broken now and there are interludes when she's caring for Lannie in a state somewhere in that borderland that's neither sleep nor wakefulness, so that in the morning she isn't sure how many times she got up with Lannie and how many times, when she thought she was up, she was dreaming it.

She dreams of Jay: he's come to see her, he bends over her as she lies sleeping in her bed at home, and puts his open mouth on hers and kisses her with such passion that his kiss travels right through her, and all her woman's parts from her knees to her breasts grow fluid and ache with it. When she wakes and sees his shadow dwindling from her as she reaches out for him, she feels a desperate grief, and catches herself calling out loud "Jay!" as Lannie in her sickness calls for her mother.

Then she sobs and rocks, seated on the floor cushions, and blames herself for being such a fool. Because, no matter what, she shouldn't have fallen in love with Jay, she shouldn't have fallen for his beautiful eyes or his long-fingered gentle hands, for his silences heavy with pain that it seemed to her so matched her own. She can see as clearly as she can see Addis Ababa through the glass of the balcony door that women fall in love with him all the time.

The doctor comes again, spends a half-hour with Lannie, while Iris and Abubech stand together at the foot of her bed.

"I didn't think it would come to this," he says, pursing his lips in an annoyed way, putting his stethoscope back in his black doctor's bag, clicking the bag shut. His hands are small, his movements precise. He questions Iris closely about Lannie's fluid intake and output, whether she swallows her pills or not.

"I crush them," Iris says. "I sit by her side and put them into her mouth with a teaspoon. I stay until they are all inside her. I do." The doctor looks even more closely at her, and Abubech touches her arm gently.

"We know how well you care for her," Abubech says softly. The doctor moves his feet impatiently, as if this whole situation is intensely irritating to him.

"I will set up an I.V. for her," he says. "She is not very dehydrated, but — it is protection for the possibility. I will teach you to look after it." When he has finished doing this, and Iris has learned to check the I.V. by counting the drops per minute, to watch to be sure the needle doesn't come out of the vein, he stands back. "If you have to disconnect it, or if it disconnects itself, do not try to start it again. I will come tomorrow." He studies her again. "Wait until I come," he cautions. She follows him to the door, trembling, trying to hide it.

"You remember I told you nursing care was everything? Do you wish to hire a professional nurse?"

"No, no!" Iris says, shaking her head fiercely.

"Perhaps you are tired. Perhaps the I.V. worries you?"

"No!" Iris says, adamant. The doctor considers briefly, then shrugs and goes away. Abubech stays a little longer, but eventually she has to leave too. As if the doctor's mere presence has helped, for a few hours Lannie sleeps quietly, and Iris takes advantage of this respite to collapse on the floor cushions in the living room and try to sleep. But she is consumed with the fear that Lannie is dying. Now in between trips to Lannie's side she paces the apartment crying, talking to herself, wringing her hands. Sometimes the crying turns into wails and moans. She hears the sound she's making distantly, as if it may be coming from someone else. The sound interests her, that she could make such noises, but she doesn't try to stifle it, knowing no one can hear her over the racket of the traffic in the street below, knowing no one would care if they did hear her.

Precisely when it's time for Lannie to take pills, Iris rises from her burrowing among the pillows, wipes her face and blows her nose, and goes to sit by Lannie's side, making her take sips of water or fruit juice in which Iris has dissolved her medication. Sometimes it takes a half-hour or more, and during the whole time tears pour from Iris's eyes to run down her face and drip off her chin, as they did, it seems months ago, when she came back to Kombolcha from Lalibela.

One night she cuts her finger deeply with a paring knife while she's peeling an orange Abubech brought in a basket of groceries. When she welcomes the stab of pain, and the dark blood trickling down her hand and arm, she sees, with exhausted clarity, that she has just made a miniature suicide attempt.

After this Iris begins to have quiet spells during which she falls asleep and dreams vivid, chaotic dreams which she can't remember when she wakes. Except for one: she's lying on her side, curled foetus-like on the floor of her bathroom at home. The floor opens and she is sucked out into empty, absolute silence and stillness. Stars gleam coldly eons away, giving no light. Nothing moves, nothing is alive. She floats, weightless and alone, through the boundaryless caverns of space.

She wakes, bathed in the sweat of pure terror, gasping for breath, and clings to Lannie's hand as a drowning victim clings to her rescuer. Long minutes pass before she is able to assure herself of the untruth of the dream — she is alive, she is not alone in the cosmos, there are walls around her, a ceiling overhead.

In the darkness of the apartment she hears the warbling yip and bark of coyotes, and she rises, setting Lannie's hand back on the cool bedclothes, and follows the sound into the living room where it grows louder. Coyotes, a troop of them, are calling her with their wild, lonely cries from the night-dark range of hills just beyond the pile of floor cushions. The moon shines down, illuminating the long, sloping silhouette of the hills on the edge of her farm at home. The coyotes' lament rises to fill her head, piercing her heart with its passion, its ancient, unkempt wisdom, its unending grief. The coyotes are calling her: to the west they bark like a pack of unruly dogs, fast and in different keys, their voices tumbling over each other's; to the east one yodels repeatedly, while above it, another raises her voice to a clear high note and holds it. Farther back in the hills, faintly, a whole chorus sings.

She is standing in a rock circle in the moon's silver half-light; it is just enough for her to make out the rocks' planes, their jagged rims, the quick sparkle of gold or silver, the flat gleam of quartz. A mouse crouches in the dark, matted grass at the base of a rock and stares, motionless, up at her out of bright, frightened eyes.

Her brothers and sisters have sung her into their skin. Her mouth is full of wildness, her entrails surge with it, her heart roars as if it would burst with it. She paws the ground, brushes it with her thick tail, lolls her long tongue out and pants, saliva dripping off her ivory teeth. Her wild coyote heart is pounding against her furry chest, she blinks her yellow coyote eyes and stretches around to nuzzle her flank, while a coyote chorus encompasses her, swelling, soaring and falling and ascending again. She opens her jaws and gives an experimental answering bark, and then puts all her considerable strength into a full-throated tenor cry of mingled supplication, defiance and joy. It fills the silver-edged, night-black air, it soars upward to the crystal stars, descends to fill every coulee and draw, every hole and den and animal's hiding place in the distant, glowing hills.

Abubech comes. Iris opens the door and when Abubech gets a good look at her, her face changes and she says gravely, "She is very ill, I know it. The doctor will return today, but there really is nothing more that can be done. You are taking the best care for her. No one could do better." By Abubech's expression Iris realizes that she has let herself go. It scares her a little: she hasn't even noticed that her hair is a rat's nest, she has that musty smell of the unwashed, and her clothes are wrinkled and soiled. She wants to explain to Abubech that if only Lannie would get well, or if that man who's watching her would go away, Iris would stop being so crazy. But she says nothing, obeys when Abubech makes her bathe and wash her hair while she watches Lannie.

After she has dressed in clean clothes, she finds Abubech has made coffee and wants her to sit with her on the cushions in the front room.

"Do you have children?" Abubech asks her. This is a surprising question coming from an Ethiopian with their exquisite courtesy, but after a second Iris recognizes that Abubech is trying to bring her back to normalcy.

"No, we had no children of our own," she tells her politely, conversationally, as if what seems like only moments ago she hadn't been on her knees banging her head against the floor. Then she says, "My husband died a few months ago," and it's as if she'd forgotten, because there's this bang in her chest and things slip sideways, and she has to blink and blink again before they right themselves. And in that instant it is clear to her that she has been mourning Barney.

She can smell the faint residue of the cleaning fluid she'd been using. The factory down the road must be spewing that oily smoke again, because she can smell it in the air too. Sunlight breaks through the glass doors to spill across the floor and lie warm on her bare toes. The room is small and clean and anonymous; it is the residence of someone who does not want to live.

Iris clears her throat, swallows, and continues. "I realized I needed to tell Lannie. I needed to find her. She — we lost touch with her a few years ago," and is embarrassed again at having to admit that for so long she didn't even try to find her. She moistens her lips with her tongue, swallows again, before she goes on. "Lannie was very troubled, because of her mother's death, you know. And then her father — her father left her with us, and took her brother and sister to live with other relatives in the city." She pauses to listen, but there is no sound from the bedroom. "I was just as glad to have her gone. More than once I wondered if Barney hadn't begun to love her more than he did me. Mostly, though, I had become so afraid of what was inside her." In the ensuing silence it surprises Iris a little that she didn't just admit this to herself a long time ago, instead of all the excuses she'd thought up for why Lannie should stay lost. "If she let it — her real emotions — out, I thought it would destroy us — her, Barney, me."

Time has stopped; nothing moves; all is silenced. Then horns honk on the street below, and the familiar roar of traffic rushing by returns. Tiredness, pure exhaustion, sweeps slowly and fully through Iris's body.

When Abubech speaks finally, the timbre of her voice hasn't changed at all; it's as if Iris hasn't just voiced these shattering things.

"You are a farmer?" she asks gently. Iris nods, opens her mouth and waits to see if she can still speak. Amazingly, the voice that comes is as calm as Abubech's.

"I was born there, but I didn't do the actual farming myself. My father did it, and then my husband. But now I'm the one who has to make the decisions about it. Maybe I'll have to learn how to farm myself, I guess."

"I believe Lannie said it's a big farm?"

"It's the biggest in the district. Everyone is after it now that Barney's — gone." Abubech is carrying on with her own thoughts, and a vibrancy that wasn't there before has entered her voice.

"What a wonderful thing that is," she says. "A woman with much land. What power! How good it is to think of a woman with power."

Iris says, with a rueful laugh, "Power? I'm helpless. I need a man to run the place for me." Abubech gives her a stare so grim Iris has to look away.

"Land is power," she tells Iris firmly, deliberately. "If you were a woman in this country, you would know it. Men will try to take it from you, but you must hold on to it. You must use it to make changes."

"But no one wants to steal it, they want to buy or rent . . . or marry it."

"But you see, no one wants you to have it, am I right? Men don't like a woman having land, especially not a lot of land. They think all land is theirs." When Iris says nothing, Abubech goes on. "In this country someone will take the land away from a woman, even if it is hers legally. If her husband dies, the land will go back to her husband's family and she will be turned out. Or to stay she will have to marry the husband's brother. If she has no children, or no son, she'll be divorced and driven away." She's looking hard at Iris, compelling her to listen, to understand. "If women have no enforceable rights to land, they will never have any power, they will continue to be beaten and starved. Did you know that most of the people who died during the famine, even in the relief camps, were women and children? They were more undernourished to start with and so they died sooner. Even most refugees are men. And women will continue to be circumcised — it may be women who perform the operation, but they do it for men who believe that if women feel no sexual pleasure, they will not be unfaithful. They tell them that the way God made women's bodies is dirty and ugly."

She is growing fierce, Iris is a little frightened of her, but most of all, she's aghast at what she's hearing. Recognizing that this is more than Iris can handle, Abubech breathes deeply several times. "Forgive me — I talk too much. It is my failing. But — you must think hard about what you have and how to use it."

After a moment she tells Abubech about the company trying to buy up all the land around Chinook, how she isn't sure what to do and is giving herself a year to make a final decision.

"It is greed," Abubech says simply. "Greed for wealth, greed for power that begins with the ownership of land. They are harassing and stealing and undercutting people all over the world to get control of their farmland. Here in Africa it is especially bad. Or if they don't want to own the land outright, they want to put the farmer in such debt for his chemical fertilizers, his pesticides and herbicides, even his hybrid seeds — in your country for his machinery — that they don't need to own the land because they have control of it anyway." Looking away from Iris, she says "There is evil in the world."

From the other room comes a loud cry in a timbre so strange that Iris's skin prickles. Both she and Abubech start; they scramble to their feet and run the few steps into the bedroom. Lannie is trying to sit up, her eyes are huge and liquid, searching.

"Where, where?" Lannie asks them, lifting her head from her pillows. "I need — I want — " and then her words break apart into meaningless sounds. Abubech waits at the foot of the bed while Iris, speaking soothingly to Lannie, wipes her face with the cloth she keeps by the bed, and smooths her forehead with one hand while she pulls her pillows into place with the other. At last Lannie relaxes visibly and her eyelids drop shut. Iris checks to make sure the intravenous needle hasn't come out of her wrist and that the fluid is running as it's supposed to.

Abubech says, "It's late. I'll come back tomorrow."

Iris sits beside Lannie with a basin of cool water, wiping away her sweat, now and then moistening her lips, and despite the I.V., dropping water with a teaspoon into her parched mouth. Lannie is moaning and tossing again, and Iris moves the basin out of the way before Lannie tips it. She talks to her quietly, "It's all right. Everything's fine. You're going to be fine," all the time stroking her face or her shoulders or holding Lannie's hand, so thin now she can see through the bluish skin. Eventually Lannie quiets again, and Iris resumes stroking her face.

She thinks of the men she has loved. She wonders if she really loved Jay. I desired him, she tells herself, and I felt something very strong for him that I thought — that seems to me even now — was love. It puzzles her. I loved James Springer, because he was so full of passion and Barney and I in all our years together never experienced that kind of physical passion for each other. I loved Barney, first because he was a romantic figure — handsome and remote — then I loved him as if he were part of me, as if there was no separation between us. But there was.

Lannie's always transparent skin is shiny now, stretched tight over the delicate bones of her face. She's so beautiful, Iris thinks, and I never really noticed it before. I've been such a coward, and yet so fierce and desperate, I would not let anything disturb my little paradise — not Lannie's anguish, not Barney's struggles, not even my own, unlived life, my Self that was begging to get out. She thinks again of her mother, lets her mind slide back over the years to the picnics the two of them used to have on the grass overlooking the deep coulee, the way her mother changed when she was there, a peace settled over her that used to extend itself to Iris so that she moved inside it too. Her mother would kneel and smell the grasses, she would separate the stalks gently and say to Iris, "See? This one is called speargrass, and this one is bluejoint." How she loved that land. When we were there, her love of it was in every line of her body, every footstep, every breath she took.

She thinks of her father's announcement at his birthday dinner: *Your mother and I are moving to town so you two can have the place to yourselves.* Her father did not love the land, no. But her mother did. I drove her out, as surely as if I'd locked the door against her. She prays that she is still alive, so that she, Iris, may admit to her crime, ask forgiveness, and at last try to, in some way, make it up to her mother.

She walks through a palace or a cathedral somewhere in the heart of Ethiopia; this is a building she should recognize, she learned about it in the camps, but she can't call its name to mind. The building is vast, an endless labyrinth of ruined and half-ruined rooms, some with arches still standing, but no walls on either side, some with walls standing but only raw-edged openings torn in the piled rocks instead of doorways. An icy wind howls through it, moaning some message she can't quite understand. She keeps walking, stumbling and falling over rocks, cutting herself on their sharp edges, she's bleeding from her knees and shins and hands. Every step leads her farther down toward the dark centre of the building, which is also a monument, although she doesn't know what it commemorates.

Now the stones ooze a stinking tarlike liquid; they menace her with their evil. She's panicky with fear, but she can go only forward, farther down, the way behind her obliterated as she passes, until at last she reaches the centre. Here, in the blackest of all the rooms, an obelisk towers over her, both its zenith and its foundation erased in impenetrable darkness. Its four sides are intricately carved with symbols, interspersed with strange birds and animals. One has the head of a lion, the outspread wings of a great bird, the tail of a lizard. A line of elephants marches nose to tail, a badger flings up dirt, an eagle soars over craggy mountaintops, a giant fish roils a vast, inky sea. The sun sends its burning rays earthward, the moon moves through its stages, all the myriad stars in the sky send out steady beams of crystal light.

As she stares in awe up at the obelisk, the symbols break apart into words, the words dissolve into pictures, the pictures come to life. Armies swarm, roaring, swords clash, guns boom and crash, fountains of blood spout with heavy, sickening splashes across its surface. Kings, queens, sultans, and emperors pass by, the fringe of their red and purple processional umbrellas swaying over jewelled thrones carried by crews of scarred, naked slaves. Floodwaters pour over cities drowning them, fires consume them before her eyes, hurricanes push up walls of water to swamp flotillas of ships bobbing between mountainous walls of water, avalanches roar down mountainsides to crush screaming villagers. Women, children, soldiers, old people die, swords plunged into their chests, hanging from gallows, blood streaming from bullet wounds, contorted in torture chambers: headless, armless, limbless, begging for food, for mercy, for life.

It is the history of the world; history is a monster.

Lannie cries out wildly, and Iris leaps up from her bed of cushions, getting tangled in the one blanket she's allotted herself, and clutches Lannie who has managed to stand and seems to be trying to climb up the wall. Iris pulls her down.

"Lannie, Lannie! Stop it, Lannie! Stop it!" She's at her wits' end, she doesn't know what to do. When she has Lannie lying down and covered, the I.V. dangling uselessly at her bedside, out of her need to do something, anything, she takes Lannie's pulse. For an instant, she can't find it, and then at Iris's fingertips laid against her wrist-bone, a tiny bird seems to be struggling: a weak flutter of wings, a pause, another flurry, longer this time, and then a pause so long that Iris is rising from her chair before she feels the quiver of its wings again.

It can't go on like this for many more hours. Impulses rush through Iris: to run screaming into the street, to lift Lannie into her arms and drag her onto a plane for Canada, to fall, weeping in despair, over her body. To have come all this way to find her, only to have her die in her arms. Because it's perfectly clear to her at this moment that Lannie is dying.

She will not panic. Instead, she washes Lannie's face with fresh warm water, rinses it clean of soap and pats it dry. She does the same with her hands, then places her arms carefully by her sides under the bedclothes. She draws up the sheets and blankets, smooths them, and folds them down neatly under Lannie's chin. She kneels to say a prayer for Lannie's recovery, the first formal prayer she has said outside of church in years. She is sitting vigil now, the job of women and priests.

As she waits quietly by Lannie's bedside, Barney's funeral begins to march past her eyes. She lets it come, watching as if she hadn't been there at the time. The gathering in the church vestibule as the funeral director organized the mourners into rows according to closeness to the departed, Iris last, with Howard at her side, behind Barney's mother and father, his sister Fay and her husband, their four children, Barney's aunts and uncles and cousins, Iris's relatives, and ahead of the other relations, Ramona and Vance and their family. How cold the church had been, as the house had been earlier that morning. Even though the sun shone in the open doors of the vestibule, she shivered with the cold.

She and Howard make their way past the people who'd come too late to find seats and who stood in the back, down the wide aisle past crowded pew after crowded pew. There is no one on the side reserved for Iris's oldest child. It was rightfully Lannie's place, and Iris feels her absence acutely; she feels naked on that side. Even though Howard walks beside her, supporting her, he has hardly spoken to her. He looks grim, angry even, although his eyes are red. She remembers how on that interminable walk up the aisle Wesley's funeral came back to her — nobody in the echoing church but a dozen family members, no choir, no banks of flowers. As if his life had been meaningless, his death unimportant. She remembers thinking then that her heart would break over poor Wesley.

As she makes the turn into the first pew under the pulpit, she glances past the rows of family, looking for Ramona. There she is, halfway back, wiping her eyes. In that second, behind Ramona's family, Iris sees a row of strangers, which puzzles her until she realizes they're the Castle family — the old man, his son, and his daughter Daisy. It amazes her that she could notice these things with one part of her mind while the other is hollow with the fact of Barney's death. As she seats herself, the organist begins to play a lugubrious, tuneless noise and Barney's funeral begins.

She sits crushed against Howard's bulky arm, not moving away, partly because the row is crowded with the immediate family, and partly because she doesn't want to leave the safety of his body. On her other side Mary Ann sobs audibly and Luke takes deep, slow breaths that quiver slightly and that everyone can hear. Iris doesn't cry, although she wants to. Howard doesn't turn to look at her or to comfort her. She can feel the whole time the strength of whatever it is he's holding in, she doesn't know what it is, she doesn't want to know. She feels small and isolated and half-frozen without Barney there beside her while the twins boys, Barney's distant relatives, their faces polished to a shine, sing two cowboy hymns in thin, unmusical voices, and Barney's uncle Len, then the skip of his curling team, and finally Vance Norman give brief eulogies, which Iris can't remember, only that Vance's was terse, delivered through tight lips. The people stand to sing or pray, then sit with much rustling of garments, thumps, and coughs.

All the while, just ahead and to her right, she can see the expensive oak casket Ramona picked. She can see the hump of his knuckles where the undertaker had folded Barney's hands on his chest. She knows Barney is wearing the navy blue pin-striped suit she picked for him, the white silk shirt, the dark red silk tie. She knows he looks perfect, if not the Barney she has been married to all those years.

When it is finally over, she tries to stand, but Howard has to put his hand under her elbow before she can get up. Behind her, she hears the creaks of the mourners getting to their feet. She takes three steps to Barney's side. Howard and the funeral director stand discreetly nearby, ready to catch her if she falls or tries to get into the coffin with her husband. It seems to her that a wind is blowing through the church with a high, whining noise, engulfing her in its cold breath. She remembers how she put her hand out to touch him, to take his hands in hers, how she bent to put her face against his mouth one last time, but Howard and the funeral director each took an arm and moved her back. She knows that somebody is closing the coffin, but she doesn't look up, and she doesn't lift her head as she moves down the aisle behind it. She doesn't see the pallbearers lift it down the church steps or put it in the back of the limousine. She doesn't know if she cried or not. She thinks perhaps she didn't. She remembers how heavy the pain in her chest was, that she could hardly move because of it.

They are at the open grave high above the town, overlooking the whole valley. She remembers how from up there she could see the pockets of snow still resting in the clefts of the hills, and the returning hawks circling on the wind drafts above the river.

Then she is at the reception, seated at the centre of one side of a long table with Luke on her left and Mary Ann on her right. There is a babble of voices all around her and much laughter from those more distant from the family's table. Howard stands before very long and walks among the tables, shaking hands and talking to this man and that. Luke doesn't move, and Fay and Mary Ann speak in low voices to each other and, red-eyed, hand each other tissues. When everyone has eaten their fill of small, triangular sandwiches provided by the church ladies and the cakes shiny with icing, and drunk two cups each of tea or coffee, they form a long line to the table where the family sits.

That is the part Iris dreads most. She stands up, the better to speed the process. One by one the faces of the people of her community confront hers: lined faces, rough faces, faces dark with years in the sun and the wind, faces pale with illness or old age and, startled by grief into clairvoyance, she recognizes immanent death lurking there; she sees the bright inquisitive eyes of the young searching for explanations of this day, for news of the world; she locks eyes with those deepened with mute suffering and finds in those few humble ones mutual recognition, perhaps even comfort; she sees eyes with no shadows behind them, no depth at all, so that she wonders if those people are truly alive or any different from the deer hiding in shrubs or the badger digging a burrow into the earth, or if perhaps that blankness is evil. She shakes hands briefly with each person, tilting her head to receive polite kisses on her cheek, says, "Thank you," over and over again, until the line dwindles and ends. She does not cry. Then Fay and Barry drive her home to the farm where relatives are waiting, having gone ahead, or, following in their own vehicles, are soon to arrive.

What she cannot forget is leaving Barney behind in his coffin in that hole in the frozen ground. They could drape it with all the fake green blankets they liked, it was still a hole in the ground and she had gone away and left Barney there. And she had not gone back, not even once. When a tombstone-maker had sent her his advertising material, she had thrown it in the garbage without reading it. She sees now that as soon as she gets home it will be necessary to get him a headstone, the most beautiful marble headstone she can find.

And then she understands that Barney is really dead.

Lannie is quiet, her chest rising and falling evenly, and Iris sits by her bedside and cries quietly. When she gets home she will fold Barney's jackets and trousers and sweaters, shirts and underwear into boxes; she will empty the bathroom cabinet of his shaving lotion, his razors, his deodorant and toothpaste and toothbrush; she will clean out the drawers of his bedside table and throw away all those useless odds and ends he would toss into it every evening for want of a better place. She will keep his picture and his curling trophies; she will give his coin collection to his nephew Quinn whom he had tried and failed to make his son; she will give his framed high school diploma back to Mary Ann and Luke; to Fay she will give — she can't think what is precious enough to give to the sister he'd stood by through all the vicissitudes of her unhappy life. Maybe the worn leather desk set Fay had given him as a teenager and that he'd used all these years. And his two silver pens.

The vast, rubble-strewn city is utterly silent; the night smothers its motion and noise. In the soothing ambience of this room closed off from the grim reality of the city, she finds something that is, if not exoneration, close to forgiveness of herself for all her many follies and sillinesses, her cruelties, her selfishness. It is, at least, a rueful acceptance of the woman she now recognizes as herself.

The room has grown peaceful, the flow of calm so strong it is tangible. It is something beyond the furniture, the damp and wrinkled sheets and blankets, beyond the unconscious woman, beyond even the shadows in the corners, the dusky ceiling. In this miraculous calm

Iris feels herself clearly: her toes, one by one, her fingers — their tips, their sinews, the flesh of her palms — the muscles in her thighs and calves and arms, the bones of her ankles and wrists, her womb, her breasts, the pulse in her chest and throat, each hair on her head. With relief, flushed with the rich warmth of her own blood, and with simple joy at the shock, the *rightness* of it, she settles down, at last, into her own body.

Some time later she comes awake with a start, lifting her head, trying to identify a distant keening that she knows is not from Lannie. As she listens, it comes again. It is the muezzin calling before sunrise his ancient, lamenting cry from the mosque whose minaret she can just see from the balcony. *Rise up for prayer*, Abubech had translated for her, *There is no God but God*. The sound drifts away into the darkness. Lannie is lying on the bed beside her, her chest rising and falling in the long, slow breaths of someone peacefully asleep, a faint flush of pink colouring her cheeks.

PART THREE

Harvesting

The Lilies of the Field

After having stood in at least six line-ups, after having their passports checked and rechecked, their hand luggage searched and the money in their purses counted, after having stepped behind a curtain to endure a body search conducted by a couple of women, Lannie and Iris finally board the plane for Frankfurt and settle into their seats.

As the plane taxis down the runway, then lifts off into the night sky, Lannie looks out the window at the city where she has lived for so long as it recedes below. Its myriad small lights are random dots in the blackness mapping its disordered sprawl, its haphazard scatter down the bushy hillsides, the patches of darkness ravines, streambeds, precipitous slopes, or the electricityless slums crowded together on low areas.

The fact of her leaving still surprises her. She wonders if she has always known at some level that she would eventually leave, even though she told herself countless times she would not. Her heart rises into her throat with the plane's lift-off and she feels regret. And sadness. And fear, fear of what lies ahead.

It amazes her that Iris should have simply taken it for granted that she would come home with her. It was as if she had not conceived of Lannie's life in Ethiopia as a real life, one with purpose and direction. Lannie suspects that to Iris her ten years away from the farm and Chinook were only as a long dream, or an error that could be easily scrubbed away. She wonders now, in fact, if they were a mistake.

She thinks about Abubech, who came with them to the airport as far as the compound gate where the sentry stood and through which she couldn't pass without a ticket. For a moment in the dull single light bulb over the sentry's box, Lannie had seen Abubech's face lose its severity when she bowed formally to her, still stiff after a year of constant companionship, then lifted a hand, her fingers bent, to brush Lannie's cheek.

"I shall miss you," she'd said. "I shall not forget you."

When Lannie had told her she was going, her voice faltering in mid-sentence as she realized what it was she was saying, Abubech had stared into her eyes. "Do what you feel you have to do," she'd said. "But don't go because you think I do not need you." This had so shocked Lannie that she'd had to lower her head to contemplate the sudden possibility of staying.

Abubech had said then, "Forgive me. I do not wish for you to change your plans. I wish you only to understand that you have been a gift to me." Lannie had looked up at her again, feeling her face grow warm, and Abubech had laughed gently. "Always mistrustful. Never able to believe you make a difference — at least, not for the better. You are quite able to believe that you make a difference for the worse." Yes, Abubech and her work is the only reason to stay in Ethiopia. And yet, here she is, leaving with Iris the moment Iris arrives, as if she has no will of her own, no sense of where she should be.

It's true, she doesn't know where she should be. She's drifting, has been for years, as if the part of her that is her will, her sense of who she is, has disengaged from the rest of her. She's going home because — she moves her head back and forth against the seat's headrest — because one morning soon I will wake up and I won't be able to will myself out of bed; because I'm at the end of my tether, and Iris, somehow knowing it, has arrived in the nick of time to rescue me.

Her own brush with death interests her, although she can't remember much about it, just how terribly cold she was, how she ached in every fibre of her body. The pills she swallowed — that time too when she woke up, she had no memory of where she'd been. I am almost the age my mother was when she died, she thinks for the thousandth time: Will I make it past my thirty-third birthday?

She glances speculatively at Iris, noticing that she has lost that adolescent-like plumpness she always carried, a delicate extra layer of flesh to protect her from life's blows, and that she's pale, too.

What a shock Ethiopia must have been to her, pampered as she has always been. And me so sick. Yet Iris seems more sure of herself than Lannie remembers, as if with that layer of protective fat gone, she has bumped up hard against the world. Of course, she reminds herself, Uncle Barney's dead; she has to manage on her own now, how hard that must be for her. But her sympathy is detached, remote from the reality of Iris's loss.

Ever since Iris finally told her about his death, a couple of days after she'd begun to mend, she's been trying to stir up some feeling about it. But his death seems far away, a long distance from wherever her heart is. What heart, she thinks, I can't even mourn Uncle Barney. Since Mother died — but she doesn't want to go down that road again. Or is it that I was plunged into mourning with my mother's death when I was only ten and I've never been released from it? But this failure too exhausts her too much to think about. Everything exhausts her. The truth is, she's barely out of the woods. If Abubech had had her way, she and Iris wouldn't leave for at least another couple of weeks. It was Iris who had insisted, and the doctor had agreed that it would probably be safe for Lannie to travel home, although he'd pointed out that she'd need months of recuperation.

"Her system is most depleted," he'd explained gravely to Iris. "She is fragile. You must care well for her." Abubech had given Lannie's landlord notice that Lannie was vacating and then had moved them both out of the grim, noisy little apartment, abandoning Lannie's bits of furniture to the next tenant, and into her own home, a pleasant, fairly modern bungalow set in a garden behind its compound wall, with its own hired guard. They'd stayed there for the few days before their plane, which came only once a week, was to depart. Those few days are pretty much a faded dream. She'd slept most of the time, often in a chaise longue under a tree in the garden. She's still so weak she has to be supported to walk more than a few feet.

She's growing drowsy again. Below them now there is only velvety darkness as they fly swiftly on, droning their way across the Red Sea. She leans back from the window and closes her eyes.

*

Even two hours since it happened Iris's heart is still beating fast. The taxi had dropped them at the narrow entrance to the airport compound with the sentry standing guard. Hanging clumsily on to their suitcases, their passports and tickets in their free hands, they'd joined the crowd of passengers squeezing one by one through the gate. In the poor light the sentry had scrutinized Lannie's passport, looking from it to her face and back again several times. Iris had noticed how Lannie hadn't glanced even once at him, just waited with the detached patience of somebody who has been through this a lot of times, until he let her through.

Iris was about to step forward when a woman, heavily swaddled in traditional garments and clutching several bags, pushed her way in ahead of her. The guard looked carefully at her face and passport, let her through, and then it was Iris's turn. She moved forward, passport ready, when abruptly a khaki-uniformed policeman stepped from her right out of nowhere and, facing her but looking over her head, leaned past her to the sentry. Iris had barely time to register a prick of fear. She stopped, her hand holding the passport frozen in the air, the guard ignoring it.

She waited, it seemed interminably, but was less than a second, time only for the policeman to say one quick, unintelligible word in Amharic to the sentry before he bobbed back out of sight. Then the sentry took her passport, glanced at her picture or appeared to, it happened so quickly, but she's pretty sure he didn't even look at her, that she doesn't see how he could have known if the passport was hers or not, handed it back to her, and let her pass. She doesn't know if the policeman's appearance had anything to do with her, although it was certainly strange how the guard didn't really check her passport after that, when he'd checked everyone else's with such care.

She believes that she has been saved from an ugly fate in this country. This is why she'd insisted on leaving the instant Lannie was well enough to go, despite the doctor's warning and her own misgivings. Her only thought was to get out of Ethiopia as fast as she could, to get Lannie home to safety. Now her relief is great, even though she won't tell anyone about the instant at the sentry box, as she doubts she'd be believed. She isn't sure herself that anything happened.

Despite her concern for Lannie, the line-ups, the hours waiting in the crowded lounge after that were nothing. But it brings back to her with force the people at Lalibela and their plight, that she'd almost forgotten during her illness. She is about to correct herself, she means, Lannie's illness, but the word is apt to describe what she has been through during those couple of weeks locked up in Lannie's apartment. The memory of her own anguish, far deeper than she'd guessed or even imagined, amazes her and she approaches it as warily as a traveller approaching an abyss — astounded by its depth and wildness, respectful, even awed.

She keeps wondering what to do with what she saw at Lalibela, with what the people told her, and what she thinks is going on there. Should she call the United Nations? Amnesty International? Or someone else? Who? The manner of her finding this out — her, of all people — is so purely coincidental that she can't help but view it as fate, maybe even as a test of her humanity, although she has the grace to be a bit embarrassed at the grandiosity of the thought.

Lannie has tucked a pillow against the window and Iris, seeing she's going to sleep, takes the folded blanket from the seat beside her and drapes it over her. She's wide awake herself, can't imagine sleeping, thinks that she'll sleep again when she's safely home in her own bed in her own house.

"We meet again," a woman's voice says above her. Iris looks up and sees a tall handsome woman smiling down at her. It's a face that's familiar — this is the woman she met weeks ago in the garden of the Hilton Hotel, the woman who said she was the wife of an American working in Addis. "Betty Chamberlain," the woman goes on. "We met in — "

"I remember," Iris interrupts, pleased Betty has spoken to her. "It's so nice to see you again."

Betty says, "I saw you from a distance in the waiting area. I seem to be quite unable to sleep." Observing Iris's glance at Lannie, she lowers her voice. "There's an empty seat beside me." Iris unsnaps her seat belt, follows Betty up a few rows and sits beside her.

"I remember you said you'd soon be leaving for good."

"Indeed. My husband is due to follow in a few weeks. Is that your niece with you?" Iris nods. "Pretty girl," Betty says. "I take it it's been a successful trip?"

"What a time I've had since I met you," Iris says. "I swear you wouldn't believe it." Iris notices that her tan has faded and, this close, she sees by the fine lines around her eyes and mouth that she's Iris's age. The flight attendant bends over them, asking if they'd like something to drink. Betty takes a glass of white wine from her tray and Iris, following her lead, does the same. When she's gone, Betty says, "What happened to you that was so extraordinary?"

"I hope you've got time for this," Iris says. "It's a long story." The lights have been lowered in the cabin and all around them is the drowsy murmur of voices broken now and then by quiet laughter or a muted cough.

"My dear, I'm a captive audience," Betty says, and there's a note in her voice that makes Iris wonder suddenly if she has been drinking. She hesitates, then decides it doesn't matter. Betty knows the country; maybe she'll be able to explain things.

She takes a deep breath and begins: "After I left you, I found my niece had gone with her employer to Kombolcha, so I hired a car and a driver to follow her there." She goes on, not looking at Betty. As she speaks she loses herself in her own story, sees the herd of pack camels sauntering down the road ahead of her, a pair of red birds like over-grown swallows swooping past the windshield, the barren yellow hills, conical in shape instead of the long, sloping silhouettes she's used to, and behind them low mountains appear and behind them another ridge of blue mountains and then another all the way back to the sky. Men walk past her carrying tall wooden staffs, driving donkeys, goats, and thin zibou, calling cheerfully to each other. The red rock churches rise up around her again, the beggar child cries in the dust, and the strange man in the hotel corridor bends toward her with desperate courtesy. She stops talking because she feels strange, as if there's something in the air like a thunderstorm about to break, or the rising rumble of the earth before a quake.

She breathes deeply again, passengers' voices rise up around her. She turns to Betty, but Betty is leaning back against her seat, looking off into the distance as if she has forgotten Iris is there. But the look in her eyes — her eyes have changed colour, grown from that faded blue-grey to a more intense blue.

"They are Amharas, those hungry people," she says quietly.

"What? What does that mean?" Iris asks. Betty stirs, pulls herself into a more upright sitting position, and turns to Iris.

"You know the Tigrayans won the war? That Mengistu was an Amhara?" Iris nods. "It is a Tigrayan-led government now ruling the country."

"I thought everyone was happy with the new government, that it wasn't a dictatorship any more." Betty shrugs.

"They've suppressed some dissension. They fired all the Amhara university professors, replaced them with Egyptians. Not just at the university — they replaced certain newspaper journalists with Tigrayans. Other positions of importance too."

"But why?" Iris asks. "What difference does it make?"

"Let me give you some background. The ancient kingdom of Aksum, the true heart of old Ethiopia, the founding region, is in Tigray. Those obelisks the woman told you about, they lie in the ancient capital of that kingdom. They record the earliest history of what became Ethiopia. Ullendorff, he wrote a classic book called *The Ethiopians*, says that the people who speak Tigrinya are the authentic carriers of the historic and cultural traditions of ancient Abyssinia. But they — the Aksumite kingdom — the true descendants of Menelik, the son of the Queen of Sheba and King Solomon who became the first king, lost power somewhere in the sixth century A.D. or so to a usurper dynasty called the Zagwe dynasty — your king Lalibela was one of them, not of the Solomonic line — and they didn't regain power until the thirteenth century. The new king, Yekuno Amalak — "

"Wait," Iris says. "How do you know all this?" A woman, a housewife. Uneasily, she remembers abandoning university and coming home, her father's indifference, the look on her mother's face, as if Iris were a stranger, or someone she didn't like much, although she'd said nothing. She feels vaguely ashamed, but Betty laughs.

"I have a master's degree in American history," she says, "acquired before my marriage. When I came here I had no job, my children were grown and living in California and France. I had nothing to do. So I took to drinking wine to pass the time. And I read Ethiopian history." She pauses. "Am I boring you?"

"Never!" Iris says. "I'm beginning to see that I need to know what happened in the past to understand what I saw." Satisfied, Betty goes on. The lines of her face grow cleaner and more taut with the effort of her thought and the obvious pleasure it gives her. Iris is humbled.

"The new king's family had been south, in Shoa, for generations and so his language had become Amharic. He moved his capital from Aksum to Shoa and it is said he made Amharic the official language of the realm." She turns to Iris. "Tigrayans speak their own languages." Iris nods mutely. "In the first part of the sixteenth century the Muslims under Gran overran Aksum and destroyed it. As far as I know, Tigray was never powerful again, until today." She turns to Iris questioningly. "I suppose the Tigrayans feel that at last they've recovered what was always rightfully theirs. I don't know. I'm only guessing."

"I think it's wonderful that you know so much." Betty laughs.

"You could do it too," she tells Iris.

"I did go to university for a year," Iris says. "I just — all I could think about was this boy — " This boy, Barney, who is dead now. Betty makes a noise, a delicate snort.

"Sorry," she says. "I know all about it."

"But you got an education."

"My boyfriend couldn't have an uneducated wife for the career he'd picked out for himself. He encouraged me to get my master's. But not my doctorate. That wasn't necessary. That was overdoing it." The attendant appears and refills Betty's glass. Iris stands, looks back to where Lannie sits, eyes closed, head lolling against the window, and sits again.

"Go on, please. I want to hear it all."

Betty sets her already half-empty wineglass down on her tray.

"For the last hundred and fifty or more years Amharas have ruled Ethiopia. Of course, they made enemies. And now the Tigrayans are in control. Maybe they're getting even for things we don't even know about. Things that maybe aren't even recorded anywhere, that are remembered by word of mouth alone, in councils where no *ferenjis* are allowed to go." She pauses to sip her wine.

"But would the Tigrayans deliberately starve Amharas?" Betty snorts again, less delicately.

"If my research is right, the Amharas starved a few Tigrayans in their day. Oh, don't quote me. I'm not sure that's true." Iris wonders why Betty is suddenly backtracking. But if what she thinks she knows does indeed add up to a deliberate policy — and what little information she has points directly to this and to no place else — What if a strong people has the means, but refuses to feed another, weaker people? The reason must be to further weaken them, maybe to displace them — land again — or to make them die.

"Are you — are you talking about — genocide?" And when she says it, there's a kind of rushing in her head, as if the word has come hurtling towards her out of some ancient place, a rocky darkness where dwells all that is terrible in the human heart accelerating through all the eons since Creation. She's terrified she has hit on the truth.

Betty starts, puts both slender, long-fingered hands to her face, covering it, rubs her eyes with her fingertips, then lowers her hands to rest loosely around the stem of her empty glass.

"I would not say that word myself," she says. "It is true though that the Tigrayans occupied Lalibela for a time during the war." She pauses. "But, really — I know nothing about it."

Iris is silenced by this sudden change in Betty's certainty.

Finally she says, choosing her words carefully, "If it were true — just suppose that I had absolute proof of it — I don't, but imagine that I did. What could I do about it?"

"I suppose you could go back to Canada and tell people."

Iris is afraid no one will believe her. She is afraid she is wrong. She is about to ask Betty exactly whom she should tell, when Betty abruptly shifts in her seat so that her tray bounces and she has to rescue her glass. She says, sounding unwilling or exasperated, Iris can't tell what exactly, "I'll ask my husband when he phones. He'll know what to do."

Relief floods through Iris.

"I'm grateful to you," she says.

"It's nothing," Betty says sharply. "It's less than nothing. First of all, you may be sure that if those people are hungry, the government is well aware of it." She stops, as if thinking better of what she's saying. "He'll probably tell me to mind my own business. He'll say that's Ethiopian business, that we can't know what has happened there, that someone else is looking after it, that the Tigrayan government is the best government the country has had in two thousand years and we mustn't expect too much. Leave it with me. I'll do what I can. The usual thing one does in such a situation is go to the press. But if you do that, you have to have photos, some kind of documents that constitute proof, and you don't have any such thing. You could call an aid agency that's in the area. But you said you didn't see any? Right?" She doesn't wait for Iris to answer. "But there are aid agencies working nearby, and if they know about it, they will do something. Obviously, the government isn't going to want the rest of the world to know what they're up to. There's also Amnesty International. They have observers in the country. They'd be able to apply pressure — if they could get proof."

Iris rubs her temples with her fingertips. It's all beginning to seem hopeless; no one will believe her.

Sister, we have no food. His voice repeats itself in her ears, above the whisper of the motors, the murmur of voices, above the thudding of her pulse in her ears. *Sister, help us.*

"I have to try," she says.

At Frankfurt there's a long wait between planes. Iris and Lannie barely speak to each other; one or the other of them is slouched, asleep in her chair, or Lannie watches the hand luggage while Iris stretches her legs by strolling around the shops lining the waiting area, or Iris helps Lannie use the bathroom. Finally, they board the plane that will eventually land in Calgary. They both sleep through most of this flight too.

Over thirty hours have passed by the time they land on a balmy, late summer morning at Calgary and whisk through Customs and into the luggage-retrieval area. Lannie hasn't been out of Ethiopia for something like three years and in the shine of the bright lights on the smooth floors, the steady noise of the public address system, agents calling flights or passengers, the click and hum of the loaded escalator, muffled bells dinging out of sync here and there, the roar of air conditioners and other unseen machinery, in her weakened state she's disoriented, faintly frightened.

She is back in Canada. She tells herself this over and over again as if she's in danger of forgetting, or maybe she'll whirr off in bits and pieces into the noises and lights if she doesn't hang on to something. Canada. Canada. But she can't grasp its meaning. She feels sweat breaking out on her forehead and down her backbone, her breath is coming quick and hard, dizziness is making the shining, hard floor slant. Ahead of her the luggage conveyor belt clanks and jerk to a start. People mill around brushing against her. She is going to be sick or faint.

"Sit here," Iris says into her ear in a firm, sharp voice. She pushes Lannie down into a hard plastic chair in a row of backless chairs fastened to the wall. Behind her people lean over the chest-high barrier and wave or call to people gathering their luggage. Iris has vanished back into the crowd. Lannie gasps, leans forward, and puts her head over her knees, her hands over her ears.

In the darkness and silence she has made for herself, her dizziness and nausea slowly retreat. She sits straight again, her eyes closed, her hands loose on her lap. She knows what this is: the suppressed urge to run. And run again. And again. She sees Vancouver, Toronto, Ottawa, Greece, Ethiopia. She has run as far as she can go and all the time it has been a circle, bringing her back to where she started from. She opens her eyes and looks around the concourse where the crowd is slowly thinning as people find their luggage, locate their waiting relatives, and leave through the sliding-glass doors. But already the doors on the other side of the conveyor belts are sliding open to the entrance of another planeload of people. And when they're gone, another plane will land. She takes what comfort she can from this, and waits, motionless, for Iris's return.

Iris is stunned by what she had once taken for granted: the splendour of the airport building, the casual wealth of the crowd — all these unwitting, smug travellers, wearing blue jeans she knows cost more than fifty dollars a pair, jackets that cost more than a hundred, the three-hundred-dollar shoes, the thousand-dollar suits. Now she sees it all for what it is: an abominable excess, a crime against those who have to scrabble every day to get enough to eat to carry them into the next.

But she goes straight to the bank of pay phones where she calls Ramona, leaving a message with Ryan that she and Lannie will be home by nightfall. Then she phones the nursing home in Swift Current.

"Your mother is much as usual," the voice at the other end of the line tells her, and at this news Iris's knees threaten to give way with relief. As she hangs up, the luggage conveyor belt for their flight begins to move, people are crowding forward, and she is trying to remember where in the parkade she left her car. Abubech had faxed a colleague at the university some time ago and asked him to call the airport parking authority to tell them she hadn't abandoned it. She hopes they haven't already towed it away.

She turns and moves into the crowd, making her way past designer suitcases and shiny leather purses with gold-chain straps, through the odours of perfume, cosmetics, hairspray and aftershave lotion, past women with golden tans, elegant and thin with dieting, past young people wearing headphones, plastic tape players thrust in their pockets, and men carrying two-thousand-dollar miniature computers.

She doesn't know if she will be able to carry on with her old life; she knows she cannot. Pressed between well-fed strangers shoving toward their luggage, she cries inwardly: *I must not forget; I will not forget.*

At a turn-off just past Medicine Hat, Lannie says, "Can we go home on the back roads?" It's the country Lannie wants now, she has no energy for anything else. She needs to see her own countryside again, to find out if it still draws her as it used to. Because if it doesn't . . . She doesn't want to think about that possibility. She watches, frowning, out the side window as they head south, rising to the top of the road past the park, then beginning the long descent onto the plains below the southern slope of the hills.

The Sweetgrass Hills come into view southeast of them, a short blue range that as they draw closer becomes three hills rising mistily against the sky. She keeps her eyes on the hills and the surrounding plains until, eventually, they turn west to cross the border into Saskatchewan.

At Mallard she asks Iris to go still farther south. She's taking them at least thirty miles out of their way; Iris looks faintly perplexed as she glances at Lannie, but Lannie doesn't care. At the high curve running around the edge of the Old Man on His Back Hills, Lannie says, loudly this time, "Stop here. Please." Iris brakes, but the car is still not quite stopped when Lannie has the door open and is stepping shakily out onto the narrow, bumpy, asphalt-topped road. She stands still, looking out.

Squares of farmland interspersed with rectangles of grass fall away to the west and south for thirty miles in each direction. She thinks of the tiny Ethiopian fields, of drought and hunger. But the clean hot wind whoops over the plain from the west, bending the yellow grass and the nearly ripened, golden crops, pushing, pushing all the way from the Rocky Mountains a hundred and fifty miles behind it to howl around the precipitous slope of the hill, rocking the car gently, blowing Lannie's hair out straight behind her. It's whipping away Ethiopia, the famine camps, the dead children, the poverty.

She wants to fly out over the prairie like an eagle, like a hawk. She wants to scream into the wind out of joy at all this empty land laid out before her all the way south to the purple line of the Bear Paw Mountains in Montana. She turns a half circle and sees the square fields of growing grain, more of it than grass, although even she, young as she is, can remember when to the west it was almost all grass. Now she picks out the motionless black dots that are grazing cattle.

Spread out before her is the New World, and she thinks she's feeling what the first settlers must have felt looking out over it for the first time, seeing all that grass, all that sky, and believing it was theirs, a new land that matched the size of their desire — knowing, but not caring that they were driving out the true owners.

She thinks that what they wanted was to embrace this vast land-scape, to become one with it. But the only thing they knew to do to satisfy their longing was to plough it up, seed it to grains, wrest it into the shape of their own choosing, trying to make it theirs that way. She knows this, because she wants the same thing. She wants to be a hawk soaring over it, a rabbit burrowing into it, a sage hen nesting in its woolly grass, a stone resting on a hillside, growing, slowly, over the centuries, a russet coat of lichen. She thinks of Caroline, all those years ago, in a moment of despair telling her to go home before she had no home to go to. I am a westerner, she thinks, a prairie girl. I belong here. And now she knows one thing about the shape of her own soul.

The fiery sun beats down on her head, the hot wind blows harder, nearly lifts her off her feet and whirls her away into that vast wilderness of sky. But Iris is calling in her ear, "Lannie! You'll make yourself sick again." She comes back to herself with a start and obediently, shivering although it must be ninety degrees, gets back into the car.

"Is it good to be back?" Iris asks.

Lannie nods, murmurs a faint, "Yes." After a moment she asks, "How did you find me?" Until now she has never been curious.

"I saw Tim in Toronto. He told me you might be in Africa."

"How was he?" she asks, keeping her voice neutral, although her heart is tripping a little faster.

"He seemed fine. He had a roommate. I forget his name." Lannie looks at Iris, a little surprised by this, but she says nothing. "He said they edit a poetry journal."

"How did you track me down to Ethiopia?"

"In Ottawa I found somebody who knew you when he worked in Ethiopia."

"Who?"

"Rob Sargent." Lannie closes her eyes.

Iris sees something she reads as dismay cross Lannie's face and she remembers what she'd forgotten, how it always is with Lannie, how careful you have to be with what you say — not to pry, not to upset her, that secret, subterranean life of Lannie's that no one was allowed to trespass. And her own inability to understand it, her frustration with it. Finally, she is angry. Through clenched teeth she says, "I swear if you are going to be like that again, you can just turn around and go right back to Africa, because I will not stand for it any more. I will not."

The air in the car is thick with Iris's fury and Lannie's shock. But she isn't done yet. "Ten years!" Iris says. "Ten bloody years and you hadn't the grace, the courtesy, the gratitude, to even keep in touch with us. Not me, not even your grandmother, not even Misty. I am so *angry* with you." Her chest is painful from the effort of not shouting, of squeezing this speech out, her tongue feeling like a viper in her mouth: quick and precise. She doesn't care.

Lannie, trying not to cry, feels more as if she's waking up from a long sleep. As Iris watches her, she turns her head away for a moment and brings it back again to stare at her as if she hasn't noticed before what she looks like, and there is some terrible darkness in her eyes that Iris can barely look at.

"You want me to tell you what's inside me?" Iris doesn't speak or turn away. "You don't want to know," Lannie says. "You do not want to know."

"Why not?" Iris cries. "Why the hell not? I lived every day with it — How do you think that felt? How do you think it felt to love you and look after you and never, not once, have you say one word except thank you in that tiny little voice of yours that I *knew* wasn't your real voice at all! Where the hell were you all those years? Where were you?" In her frustration Iris hits the steering wheel with her fist.

Lannie opens her mouth; she is trying to speak, she makes a noise, tries again, and says, "I don't know." The words tumble out, slowing gradually as Lannie finds she can speak after all, "The world seemed so fragile to me. So easy to lose everything. I was afraid if I moved too fast or spoke too loud the world — would crack apart and — kill us all."

An instant follows without movement or sound. Then she looks at Iris and gives a faint, mirthless laugh before she turns away.

Iris is sobered and humbled and ashamed.

"Forgive me," she mutters into the steering wheel.

Lannie sighs, a heavy, shuddering sound. Nobody could tell her what it was she had done to deserve to be abandoned by her own parents. Nobody knew. Maybe even God didn't know.

"No, forgive me," she says at last, bowing her head. And when, after an instant, Iris reaches for and clasps her hand, Lannie moves and finds herself gratefully pressing her forehead against Iris's warm shoulder.

They drive the last thirty miles to Chinook in silence. The closer they get to the town the farther Lannie's thoughts retreat from it — avoidance, she knows it, but still, she keeps thinking of Iraklion. How she loved that city, its clutter, its noise. Dimitri insisting she wear the cream-coloured linen dress, or the pink he'd bought for her instead of jeans, whenever they went into the city. Sitting in the outdoor café across from him, tall and handsome in his linen slacks and pale linen shirt, his gold necklace gleaming against his dark skin, knowing everyone around them saw them as the idle rich, the jet-setters who stayed in the private villas and the expensive hotels on Mirabello Bay. Hating Dimitri for his wealth bought at the expense of Ethiopian peasants, knowing he got all the profit from the coffee plantations they worked, hating herself more for living off their labour too.

But there Chinook is, spread out below them, looking barely different from what it was ten years before. Crete vanishes. She stares and stares as they descend the last curving hill, cross the railway tracks, and reach the first small frame buildings — houses, shops. After Ethiopia they seem less shabby and banal than she remembers. And the familiar, tall old poplars, planted by the settlers seventy years earlier, still spread their branches protectively above the streets and buildings. But now she finds these neat, freshly painted little boxes with their white picket fences and their squares of flower-bordered, immaculate, cropped green lawns insular, unbearably smug.

Hysteria strikes, and for an instant she almost leaps from the moving car to run screaming back down the road they've arrived on, that all those years of her absence this hideous little town was still sitting here, people walking around in it, remembering things. She puts a clenched fist up against her forehead, her eyes shut tight against the sight, then quickly lowers it and opens her eyes.

"Drive past the house, Iris." She trembles to ask it. Iris points the car to the west side of town where it still sits, shingles missing from the roof, the screen door hanging from one hinge, the boards covering the windows splitting with the weather and coming away to reveal the brooding darkness behind them. The yard is untended, full of weeds and other people's garbage. Lannie gazes at it, remembering how for years she had avoided even driving down this street, as if by never seeing it, the house where she was raised might be erased from history. Now, as she stares at it, the world settles down with a crash that makes her vision shift.

They drive past one of the town's oldest houses, a two-storey, rambling frame house. It sits on a corner lot bordered by ancient poplars, some with their upper branches sawed off to accommodate power lines. The house has been freshly painted pale blue with white trim, and she recognizes it as having belonged to James and Aurora Springer. Children's toys litter the big, grassy yard and an overturned tricycle blocks the path to the house.

"Angela and Orland bought it," Iris says, not looking at Lannie, as if she divines what Lannie is thinking. "They live there now."

"Oh," Lannie says, in as noncommittal a tone as she can muster, but she's remembering picking up James's vial of sleeping pills from the table by his bed when she was supposed to be helping Iris clean, slipping them into her pocket.

God, she's weary. Weary right through her bones. But the small wooden house of her childhood sits right there, and with it come voices, pictures, smells, and sounds. She can hardly believe how much she has pushed aside, buried, not forgotten exactly, but managed not to think about for such a long time. She'd almost succeeded in convincing herself of what she'd claimed to Rob, that she had no history. Now it's settling on her; weightless for years, she feels herself growing denser, heavier, by the second. She makes an effort to fight it, but she can't, not anymore.

Panic strikes her, bringing moisture out onto her palms and her upper lip, and she wipes her mouth and rubs her hands on her jeans to dry them. Now that she has thought this — that she'll have to face all of it — she wants to stop it at once, but she's terrified she can't, that she can't go back to the way she was.

It's evening when they finally arrive on the farm. The high late summer sky is deepening, not a cloud mars its brilliance, and the violent wind has died, as it often does in the evening. The air will be perfectly still for a couple of hours. Iris recognizes the habits of her own climate with a mixture of weary satisfaction and annoyance. It's good to be back, but as they come up the gravel road toward the place that has been her home almost her entire life, it seems not so inevitable as it always has, not so unquestionably right. And this new view of it, instead of worrying her, makes her feel alert, critical. She regrets the loss of her own certainty even as she's glad of it.

How much more bitter is the pang she feels now for Barney, that he isn't inside waiting to greet her, that tonight his side of the bed will be empty, that she will never see him again. But the car has to be put in the garage, the luggage taken inside, a snack has to be made and eaten. Humbly, she sets herself to these tasks.

Lily is napping in her wheelchair in front of the television set in the common room off the entrance when Iris and Lannie enter the nursing home. It is Iris's second visit since her return, but Lannie's first.

"Mother," Iris says softly, placing her hand lightly on her mother's arm. Under its thin covering of flesh the bone seems even narrower and less solid than before. Her mother wakes with a little start.

"You're back," she says, and smiles. "Did you find her?" she asks, as Iris kisses her cheek and straightens. Iris nods, unsurprised by her mother's forgetfulness, turning toward Lannie who waits beside her. "I am so glad to see you," her mother says, lifting her hand to Lannie. Lannie takes it, smiles, nods with a touch of embarrassment, but doesn't speak.

"Let's go to your room, Mom," Iris says. Lannie falls in beside her as she pushes the wheelchair down the hall. In Lily's room she helps Iris move her mother onto the lounge chair and cover her with the afghan. When she and Lannie have pulled up chairs, one on each side of her, her mother says to Iris, "I've been hanging on, waiting for your return." She speaks to Iris, but then she pats Lannie's hand where it rests at the edge of the afghan.

"Lannie's been sick," Iris tells her again. "She's still far from well, she's going to need a couple more months of rest, but — "

"But I made it all the way back from Ethiopia," Lannie says mildly. "So an afternoon trip here is easy beside that."

"I wanted to see you both again, before . . . " Lily doesn't finish her thought, shifts her gaze to the wall, and sighs almost imperceptibly. "Especially you," she says to Lannie. "You'd be surprised how little you've changed since you used to come to my house for Sunday supper when you were a little girl."

"I liked going to your house," Lannie says softly. "You used to tell me stories — I'd forgotten that."

"Now, listen," Lily says. "Listen to me. Do something with that farm." When she says nothing more, Iris and Lannie glance in puzzlement at each other, then back to Lily. She has closed her eyes, but her lips move as if she's talking to herself and her eyes dart behind her eyelids.

"When I was a child it was a beautiful place." They have to lean close to hear her. "Flocks of snowbirds and horned larks and blackbirds — and the meadowlarks! Singing everywhere . . . Nights, the fields were full of rabbits . . . swift foxes . . . coyotes sang to us all night and in the morning their tracks were all around the house. There were even prairie wolves, and before that — before my time — but not so long ago at all, they say there were grizzlies in the hills, and the buffalo! Millions of them swarmed across the prairie . . ." She opens her eyes, and looks into some memory-laden space between the two women listening intently to her. "The world was wild once, the air was rich with it. The prairie grass was so thick — it looked like it had been stirred with a stick, and all these little, sweet-smelling flowering grasses — full of birds' nests in the spring. And over above the coulee there were burrowing owls, popping up from their holes to stare at you when you went by. And a great horned owl nested in the loft in the barn." She pauses, her eyes lose their distant look and she drops them, gazing down at the afghan that years ago she'd crocheted herself.

Iris is growing more and more upset. She interrupts, "Mother — "

"No," her mother says. "No." She lifts her eyes to Iris's, then to Lannie's. "Put that place back the way it was." Iris draws back. "You do what you're told, Iris," Lily says, as if she knows what Iris is thinking, can see right into her.

Iris's mind is whirring, trying to get a grip on what her mother is saying. It's a stunning idea, but she's wondering, Is that even possible? Abruptly Lannie stirs.

"I think — " Lannie sits up straight. "The land," she says, about to go on, but Iris's mother interrupts.

"The men are gone," she says. "It's in our hands at last."

Lannie says urgently, "It can be done, Iris. There are people who know how. There are places where it's been done." Iris is about to question her, but her mother is speaking again. Her words hang in the air like the peals of small bells: "'Therefore I tell you, do not be anxious about your life, what you shall eat or what you shall drink, nor about your body, what you shall put on. Is not life more than food, and the body more than clothing? . . . Consider the lilies of the field, how they grow; they neither toil nor spin . . .'"

Iris suddenly remembers the moment her father announced that her parents would move to town: her mother turning away from Iris, turning her face into the shadows, sorrow settling forever into its lines. Never forgetting the betrayal of an uncomprehending — a fierce-willed, selfish young Iris. Never speaking of it to her. But I knew it, Iris thinks. Behind my sweet face — my *little-girl face* that Luke accused me of having — I was as cruel and as implacable as any force of nature. I knew what I was doing and I did it anyway. Because I was young, because I thought the world belonged to me, that anything I wanted I should have: the farm, the land. Not truly loving it herself, she had stolen it away from her mother.

Lannie makes a faint mewing sound, like a kitten. Tears spill down her cheeks; she makes no attempt to wipe them away. It is only when Iris sees the tears that she remembers Lannie never cries, never did even as a child, not even after her mother's death. She stares in surprise, a warm flush starting in her abdomen and rising up through her chest. She recognizes it as hope.

The Great Plains

They are having a barbecue. The picnic table is set under a grove of poplars in a sea of shin-high native grass beside Vance and Ramona's dilapidated old two-storey frame house. Ramona and Vance, Iris and Lannie, are still sitting on the benches across the table from each other, the dishes with the remains of their hamburgers and cobs of corn are pushed to one end, mugs of hot coffee sit in front of each of them. Off to one side the Norman sons are playing scrub with two of the grandchildren, Kayla and Jason, and a couple of their friends. Every once in a while the crack of the bat hitting the ball rises over the birdsong, accompanied by shouts. Faintly, floating over a rise, they hear a cow bellowing, and sometimes the insistent bleat of a bull. The fire in the stone barbecue behind them has died down to glowing coals. Ramona says, "I guess we should get these dishes into the house."

"Couple of hours still till dark," Vance says. "Let the kids play." There's a long comfortable silence while Ramona and Vance stare out at Jason who's running the makeshift bases and Ryan in the outfield, who's throwing to one of the neighbour's kids on second. A pair of nighthawks swoop over the picnic table, their cry like the creak of rusty hinges. Iris is thinking of Barney, of that last barbecue their two families had together on Iris and Barney's deck the previous summer. He hadn't bought his ranch yet, he hadn't left her, he hadn't died. But the signs were there: the signs of the high blood pressure that would kill him, the signs of his discontent. Only I couldn't see them, I wouldn't see them, she thinks sadly.

"That land agent been over yet?" Vance asks.

"Maybe he doesn't know I'm back yet. It's only been ten days."

"Hah!" Ramona says. She and Iris exchange a glance that starts out wry and then fills with warmth. How I've missed her, Iris thinks, and she doesn't just mean during her trip; she means since they were in high school together and best friends. "I'm so glad you're home," Ramona says to her as if the two of them are alone. "I was scared to death you'd never come back."

"I was scared to death myself," Iris tells her.

"And you, Lannie," Ramona says. "When she got back and you were with her, I just jumped up and yelled. I hope you don't go running off again the minute you get better."

"I'm not planning to go anywhere." Lannie is embarrassed.

"I got something to tell you," Vance is speaking to Iris. "I made a deal — Ramona and me — we made a deal with that nature organization." He waits for her to say something and when she doesn't, he goes on. "Either I sold to that Schiff, or he paid off my note at the bank and took me over. My back was shoved against the wall and — "

"And I found this ad in a magazine," Ramona tells her. "About saving the landscape? And Vance wasn't home — " She looks at him, grinning, and he grins too. "And I just up and phoned 'em."

Vance says, "Fact is, Iris, that we don't own this place any more — "

Ramona interrupts Iris's gasp, "We never did own it. The bank owned it."

"That nature group — it bought the place and left it in our hands to run it as long as we're alive — run it the way we always run it."

"Because we — and Vance's dad before him — took such good care of the grass, we don't have to change anything."

"Just keep running it the same way, and when we're too old, they'll take over."

"Our note's paid off and we still got the place — "

"But what about the kids?" Iris asks uncertainly.

"Shawna and Debbie are married and gone," Vance points out. "And Crystal's going to marry Dave Gallant. They got a big place that'll be his one day. Cody wants to be a vet, and Ryan — " He turns his head, his grin gone, to look across the wide space of grass to where Ryan is chasing a fly ball. "Lord knows I woulda liked him to have this place. He'd like it too, but the way things are going in agriculture — They may let him stay on and run it when we're gone. But we gotta face some truths and better he know now he's got to find his own way to live. It was this or nothing, Iris," he says, turning back to her. "He isn't the only country boy getting kicked off the land these days."

"At least he'll have his childhood here to remember all his life," Ramona says.

Iris contemplates what it must have cost them to finally make this renunciation, what sorrow it will cost their son, in the years to come, how he will have to make his reconciliation with his loss. It's a minute before she can say "Good for you two!" knowing they do not want her commiserations. And Lannie joins in with "Congratulations." For the first time this evening she's showing signs of genuine interest.

"I've got something to tell you too," Iris says. "Mother wants us to put our land back the way it was. That's what she said." She and Lannie glance at each other. "And I've been thinking that — maybe I will."

"You mean seed it back to native prairie?" Ramona asks.

"Take this crop off, and then seed it all to grass," Iris says, nodding.

"What?" Vance says. "Where did you get that notion?"

"You're the one who taught me, Vance," she says, although it wasn't just Vance, it was her mother, it was Barney, it was Lannie, and especially Abubech. She doesn't think she has ever seen Vance so at a loss, and she's mightily pleased with herself, although, she tells herself, she'd do this even if he disapproved. Ramona exclaims, "You're full of surprises too!"

"You still got that land buyer breathing down your neck," Vance warns her. She ignores him.

"Lannie and I have been talking about whether we could do it and how we'd do it."

"That's the problem," Lannie explains. "It would take a lot of expertise — "

"I know! Talk to the nature people who took over this place. They'd know how," Ramona interrupts.

"Maybe sell to 'em?" Vance suggests.

"I won't sell," Iris says, more sharply than she meant to.

"It's called restoration — prairie restoration," Lannie says. "There are plenty of experts around, and lots of literature, not to mention that there are projects all over the grasslands, although I believe mostly in tallgrass prairie." Vance and Ramona stare at her and she colours faintly. "It was part of my job to help Abubech keep up on the literature about preserving biodiversity around the world: the temple grounds in Bangladesh, the cemeteries in the American West — that sort of thing. And there are all kinds of private individuals who are saving seeds and replanting parts of their own land."

"Just a minute here," Vance says. "What about money? If you do that, where will you get an income, Iris? And you can't forget that land buyer. I'm telling you, he's after your land and I don't know how you're going to stop him. And people are selling now, at least he says they are, and that means if you fight him, you'll be fighting the whole community too. Ramona and me — our place is along the riverbank — we aren't vital to the deal the way you are. Can you take the pressure?" He stops, out of breath, he has never spoken so much, and when Iris starts to answer, he interrupts her. "Don't get me wrong. There's nothing I'd like better than to see all them acres back in native grass, but it ain't going to be easy, that's all."

"Putting all your land in grass — you don't want to leave yourself broke in your old age." Ramona speaks softly, regretfully.

"If I never got another crop," Iris replies, "I could get along just fine. In Ethiopia — " and then, sobering even more, she says, "I won't say I don't like my comforts, but three TV sets and a house big enough for twenty people with only two in it . . . I've spent my whole life taking. It's time to do a little giving."

"Not that your neighbours will be grateful to you," Vance says. "You can trust me on that," and Iris knows he has had to take plenty of criticism for selling to the feared conservationists.

"If you can just get people to listen," Ramona says. "We tell 'em and tell 'em this is the most threatened landscape in the country, but they just don't seem to get it."

"Thoreau said," Lannie quotes, "'in wildness is the preservation of the world.' All of us came out of wildness; wildness is the source of life — not chemistry laboratories. And if we kill off all our wilderness, we kill off *wildness*. When that happens, we won't be human any more. We'll be robots, mechanical creatures in a perfect, clockwork world."

The others stare at her. She colours, but doesn't look away. All of them look out over the field of wild grass where the kids' game of scrub has dissolved into a shouting game of tag.

She can put it off no longer. It's time to start phoning the agencies Betty Chamberlain suggested to her would be appropriate to tell about what she saw in Lalibela. She has held off until she has been home a couple of weeks, out of jet lag — she wanted to have her wits about her to answer questions — out of her reluctance to face the ridicule she's expecting, out of her own growing certainty that nothing she can do will make a difference. It takes all her courage to dial the first number.

The voice at Amnesty International, after he has listened to Iris's long story, tells her he'll speak with his sources and get back to her. She has to make three phone calls before she finds a development agency with offices nearest to Lalibela, only to find that it isn't run by a Canadian branch, but by a branch out of England, which runs independently from the Canadian or U.S. branches. She tells her story again. The woman on the phone says she'll check it out and get back to her. She calls a reporter at a major newspaper. The reporter says, "If this is true, it's a big story. The victory of the Tigrayans over Mengistu was seen as the victory of right over evil. The whole world celebrated their courage." Iris is no longer sure it's true herself. She closes her eyes and remembers the scene: the dust, the drawn looks on the people's faces and their silence, the farmers saying, *We have nothing to eat*, the grave, tall man bending toward her in the hotel corridor. The reporter goes on, "It seems to me that not long ago the newspapers in Scotland were full of claims like these from a Scottish nurse who'd worked in the south. She smuggled out photos of mutilated bodies lying in fields, and transcripts of tapes of people — I think it was Oromos — telling stories of disappearances and torture and murder. In fact, there've been a few scattered reports like yours coming out." She says she'll go to her sources, see what she can find out to verify Iris's story.

It's late afternoon when Iris gets off the phone and she feels exhausted. She's about to fall on the couch in the living room, when she hears car tires crunching over gravel and goes to the window to look out. As soon as she sees the car, a luminous silvery grey, and big, she knows who it is and says "Damn" under her breath at the timing, as Lannie has gone to town to meet the bus that will bring home her sister Misty. She goes out onto the deck, shutting the door firmly behind her.

The car stops opposite the steps. Immediately the driver's door opens, and she sees it's the same man who came to her weeks ago: Jim Schiff, from the company that wants to buy her land.

"Welcome back, Mrs. Christie," he calls up to her. "Was it a good trip?" Iris studies him, not replying.

"You have a new car, I see," she says in a measured, not-unfriendly way.

"It is a beauty," he says. "May I come up and talk to you?"

"No, I don't think so," she says. He has already come around the car and put his foot on the first stair. He stops, frozen in mid-step, then puts his foot back down on the gravel.

"I beg your pardon?" he says, smiling uncertainly.

"No, it isn't any use," she says. "My place is not for sale. Not now. Not ever." He stands looking up at her; she can see him trying to figure out what he ought to say to her now. "You may as well go," she says, and smiles in what she hopes is a pleasant way. In the back of her mind it registers that the countryside she can see from her deck is beginning to look dry, it's been almost a month, Vance told her, since the last rain, and that was barely half an inch. She frowns without noticing she is, wondering about the crop. The old dust bowl black humour passes through her: *Remember in the Bible when it rained forty days and forty nights? Yeah? Well, Chinook got a tenth.*

"I'd just like to talk to you a little," he says softly. "No pressure, just to make sure you know what our offer is. I'll be happy to tell you what your neighbours are thinking, so that you can evaluate your position." A magpie lands on the deck railing and struts self-importantly a few steps in their direction, its glossy black feathers gleaming an iridescent purple and turquoise.

"I appreciate that," Iris says gravely, "but it makes no difference. I've decided not to sell." He lowers his head to stare at the ground in front of his scuffed brown oxfords. She notices that his hair is thinning at the crown of his head, and he seems tired or — suddenly she wonders if this is a ploy, that she should feel sorry for him so that she'll let him into her house and then —

"Maybe you don't understand," he says at last, raising his head, looking first down the deck to where the magpie has fixed him with a glassy, one-eyed stare, and then up to Iris. "We will have all this land. We will have every farm from the other side of you to town. You'll be isolated, you'll have no neighbours." He stops, as if he thinks he's gone far enough for now.

"That's not true," she replies calmly. "You won't have the Normans' place either."

"Hah!" he says abruptly. Suddenly she knows that he is not merely an agent: he's the real buyer. The magpie screeches, flies up into a poplar branch and sits there, bobbing up and down. "The Normans have no choice. They're heavily in debt. We'll buy their note from the bank and take the place over. We've done it before." His tone is faintly amused.

"I believe you're too late for that," she says comfortably. "It's owned by a conservation organization now." If he's dismayed, he doesn't show it, but he's silent for a moment, gazing around the yard and out beyond it to the dusty fields of ripening crops. At last he says, as if he's innocently curious, "Why are you so determined not to sell?"

"I don't like your plans," she says. "I don't like what you want to do to us."

"Your community can only benefit," he replies, surprised. "Think of the jobs we'll provide for local people." The magpie squawks again and Iris glances at it, bemused, before she speaks.

"Where will they live if you've taken their land?"

"We'll build new houses in Chinook for everybody who works for us. The social and cultural life in town will flourish again. It will be the way it was in the twenties, that time you prairie folk are constantly mourning."

"People owned their own places then," Iris says. "What you're proposing sounds like England during the Industrial Revolution, or like Ethiopia under Haile Selassie when all the land in the country belonged to him, and the people worked twice as hard so they could pay their taxes. And mistreated their land just so there'd be something left over for their families. And still they went hungry." He goes on again as if she hasn't spoken, and she wonders why she's still standing here listening when what she wants to do is go inside and lock the doors. But that would look like weakness, so she doesn't.

"With computerization and satellite link-ups we can do our business from Chinook. In time we'll use robot tractors and combines. It's called 'precision farming' and it's the coming thing. We'll build huge greenhouses and laboratories with our own plant-breeders to do up-to-the-minute experiments to produce new crops as well as improve the old ones. We'll own the very seeds you plant," he tells her. "We'll own those dandelions out there, we'll own the carrots in your garden."

His voice is mild enough, but his look is one that in the old days would have frozen her, or sent her running into Barney's arms, but now she says, reasonably enough, "You have no faith in the people at all, do you? You think none of us will object, that we'll just let you turn us into slaves, into serfs and peons? People who came here three generations ago and knew nothing but hardship until the middle of this century — " She thinks of the Indians whose land they'd stolen, and she hesitates for just an instant, hopes he hasn't noticed. "You think we'll give up our land that easily?"

"Money talks," he says. "Everybody has his price."

Something is rising in Iris. She feels dizzy, disoriented, the inner chaos distracting her from the breeze, the birdsong, the smell of crops in the fields.

Then she thinks, Barney died for something. When he left me — it was leaving me, even if he didn't know it himself — it was to go to the land; he left me for the land. He was telling me something, but I couldn't understand it, I was so caught up in myself that I couldn't even hear it. I suppose he didn't really understand it himself. Her hands, her face, her chest feel hot, as if she might be glowing, and looking down at him, she begins to feel big, as if she's gaining a foot or two in height, and expanding in breadth. As if she has, in her travels, acquired something — something that might be power.

"I think you are evil," she says. "Get off my land." And when she says *my land* it seems to her that the entire countryside comes to a halt, the wind ceases its murmur, the moving grass stands still, the birds halt in mid-song.

The phone rings, but Iris has been sleeping only lightly and she snaps on the bedside lamp and answers it on the second ring.

"Betty Chamberlain," a voice says. Iris is alert at once. Her clock says it's three in the morning.

"What did you find out?" she asks, forgetting even to say hello. Betty laughs, and there's something in the sound, some imprecision that tells Iris Betty has been drinking. What time is it in California? she wonders. After midnight, at least. She sits up and lifts the phone from the bedtable onto her lap.

"I talked to Frank," Betty says.

"Yes?"

"Grain has gone in," she says. "One of the NGOs took in a truck-load." When Iris hears that what she'd wanted has finally happened, it no longer seems like a solution or even much help. A truckload of grain for all those people?

"But what about," it's hard for her to say it even now, "the question of — genocide." In the small pause that ensues Iris thinks she can hear Betty breathing, the sound too deep, muffled, or as if she were cupping her hand around the receiver.

"Iris," Betty says, "listen. What happened to you happens to first-time visitors to Third World countries all the time. It's an old story. It doesn't mean anything. Forget it."

"I won't forget it," Iris says determined. "I think every time people hear something like that, they hear the truth. Some kind of truth. There is so much evil in the world." She can hear Betty draw in a long breath, not wearily, but as if she's letting some emotion go.

She says a long "Mmmmm" glumly, and then, as if she's reciting, "They're fixing the roads, probably for the first time since the war; they're allowing dissenting newspapers to be published in Addis; they're trying not to interfere in tribal politics — "

"They're taking care of Tigrayans," Iris says.

"I don't know," Betty says, in a defeated tone. "People are always trying to kill each other somewhere." Iris sees how easy it would be to forget the man in the hotel corridor, the beggar child crying in the dirt, the women walking slowly up the road bent double under their burdens, even Abubech and her courage and dignity.

"I spoke to a newspaper journalist about it; I called Amnesty, and an aid agency that has a branch near there. They've all called me back and told me to forget it, that I was wrong. One of their so-called sources even said that the Amharas and the Tigrayans love each other." Her emotion is so strong that she has raised her voice without meaning to.

"Let me tell you," Betty says, "that if you insist on making a fuss about this," her voice is louder now, "people will be killed. They will stop that project you told me about, if you're associated with it. Are you willing to risk that? Do you want that responsibility?"

"What about my responsibility to the people who said they are starving?" she asks Betty. "What about to those who claim people are being imprisoned and tortured and killed in secret? What about their right to a better government, to go about their legitimate business in dignity and without fear, the way we do?" Betty doesn't say anything and then Iris hears a faint clink, and knows Betty is drinking.

"Some choice," Betty says finally, but it's as if Iris has been talking about whether to wear the blue dress or the red. Again, more loudly this time, Iris hears the ringing of the wineglass's rim against the receiver.

She doesn't understand why nobody will listen to her, why nobody wants to help. Is it because after a Communist regime, an apparently more democratic government willing to align itself with the West has to be supported, its flaws ignored? Why? Because that's how governments work? They're incapable of subtlety? They're stupid? Because any improvement at all is at least an improvement? And as for the Ethiopians — the amount of aid money going in there from countries like Canada must be enormous. And Ethiopia can't do without it. But it was the press who started the rebellions that got rid of Haile Selassie and then of Mengistu, by telling the truth about what was happening.

What if I'm wrong? she asks herself. What if I've misunderstood, overreacted, what if all of them are right and what I thought was an emergency was really a commonplace? But she knows what she has seen.

She thinks of Abubech who has surely weighed a few thousand starving people against the endless good her project can do, and has chosen her project, because as Betty said, people are always trying to kill each other somewhere. The killings will go on regardless, but the work with the indigenous seeds will slowly, year by year, improve the lot of the Ethiopian peasant. This is it, she thinks. I, who have never seen such suffering am weighing my perceptions over the perceptions of a woman who has lived her whole life in the certain, horrific knowledge of it. How do I dare?

It occurs to her to wonder if the word "genocide" carries political implications she doesn't understand. Is there some international law like the Geneva Convention or something, that, if it is proven to be going on, forces actions no government wants to take? Is it a word aid agencies are warned never to use without a pile of bodies in front of them? Without maybe having to run for their own lives? Is that why I'm so quickly dismissed?

Here she is, sitting up in bed in her own house in safe, comfortable Canada, and she's breathing in and out, her heart is pumping blood through her veins just as it always has, and down the road in Chinook children will soon be walking to school and the grocery store will open, the cash register will ring, somebody will pump gas at the co-op, and nobody in the whole town is starving or being tortured or murdered. Doesn't that mean something against the darkness? Isn't that a reason to go on?

In the silence while Betty drinks again, Iris understands at last that there is nothing she can do.

"Betty," she says, "isn't it time to get that Ph.D.?" Betty laughs.
"Is that advice?"

"Yes, I believe it is." When Betty doesn't say anything more, Iris says, "Thanks for at least trying to find out if I was right or not." She waits for Betty to speak again, but she doesn't, and finally Iris hangs the phone up gently, quietly.

She leans over to replace the phone on the bedtable beside the lamp. As she sets it down, she notices something glint in the light on the corner of the bedtable farthest from her, behind the lamp's wide crystal base. She reaches for it and pulls it over to her.

It is the carved wooden cross that the young guide Yared gave her. She remembers him looking hard, straight into her eyes with an expression she couldn't even begin to read. He'd spoken slowly, emphasizing each word: *I am giving you this so that you will remember me.* She stares down at the small wooden cross on its leather thong lying in her open palm. After a moment she lifts it on over her head, straightens it against her throat and chest, then leaves it to rest lightly there between her breasts.

Ramona and Vance, Iris, Lannie and Misty are seated in the town hall in the midst of row upon row of friends and neighbours. Every chair is taken and people are lined up three deep along the back wall and halfway up the sides. As Iris entered Henry Swan, standing with a group of men at the door, had turned to her and said formally, pointedly, "Good evening, Iris," while the men he'd been standing with, people she'd known all her life either would not meet her eyes, said nothing, or were unusually jovial in their hellos, so that she knew they were angry with her. When she saw Luke standing with a knot of older ranchers on the far side of the hall, she felt his hard blue eyes penetrating right through her, and she pretended not to have noticed his stare. When she led Lannie and the others to their seats down this row, she'd noticed Marie Chapuis, Ardath Richards, and Mavis Miller sitting together two rows ahead. In the general rustle at her arrival, they turned to stare, returning her greeting with brief, guarded smiles. She was hardly surprised, had squelched her hurt feelings, having resolved to stand up to everyone's complaints without giving in, or breaking down, or revealing any anger of her own.

But what she's really feeling right now is fear; she's quaking with it. She's going to have to speak in front of all these people, she's going to have to explain, defend herself, be persuasive, truthful. She has to lock her hands together to keep them from trembling, her jaw is clenched so tightly it hurts. Schiff has delivered an ultimatum: everyone has to sign by the end of the month or the whole deal is off. Some are convinced it's a bluff, others aren't so sure; all of them know if the deal's to go through, Iris Christie has to agree to it. The crowd is unusually quiet, a sign of the seriousness of the situation that has brought them here.

Seated at a long table facing the crowd is a row of men: the reeve of the municipality in his western clothes, Chinook's mayor in his sports coat and jeans and boots, a couple of politicians in shirts and ties, both of them men Iris went to school with, Jim Schiff the land buyer, a government land agent dressed the same way as the men in the crowd, the director of Vance's conservation organization wearing the hiking boots that instantly give him away to the crowd as not one of them, and the head of a hunters' lobby group. Behind them is an easel with a professional-looking flow chart on it that Iris recognizes as Jim Schiff's company plan.

People shift positions noisily, begin to whisper to one another as the mayor, the reeve, the government agent, the hunters' lobbyist each speak briefly about the problem as they see it and how it should be handled. The crowd is waiting to hear from Jim Schiff and from the representative of the conservation organization — no, Iris thinks, they're waiting for their chance to tackle Vance and me. She can hardly believe she's going to have to stand against her entire community, when she has spent her life accepting and accommodating herself to its beliefs and standards and way of doing things. Her palms are wet and she unclasps her hands to wipe them surreptitiously on her thighs.

The room is deathly silent as Jim Schiff lays out his plans once again. He ends by telling them in an amiable, almost condescending, way that he and his people are prepared to take their money and their project to another site they've already selected if the signatures aren't forthcoming by the thirtieth of the month. Iris had been told the meeting was "a chance to clear the air," and "to clarify the situation." Maybe. But now she sees clearly that as far as Schiff is concerned, its sole purpose is to get her to sell. She sees that he thinks she won't be able to withstand her community's pressure. For a second, she wavers. He's right: there's no way she'll be able to hold firm.

What does she want the worry of all that land for, anyway? Why does she want to complicate her life when Barney isn't here to help and support her? Could she possibly live here among people she has been friends with her whole life if they all hate her? She knows what they can do to people if they turn against them, she has seen it: nobody speaking to the offender, shutting the door in his face, hanging up if she phones, turning away at public events, leaving him to sit alone, throwing rotten tomatoes at her house, spray-painting graffiti on his fence; in the countryside putting sugar in fuel tanks, leaving gates open, spooking cattle and horses so they run away, or turning them into crops to destroy them, tearing up fence posts or disputing established land boundaries, dumping garbage in fields, even setting crop or grass or building fires. To be the object of so much hate — she won't be able to endure it.

The conservationist is speaking. He's a handsome, youngish man, dark-haired, short, wearing round, gold-framed glasses that keep sliding down his nose, dressed in the inevitable plaid shirt, jeans, and those hiking boots as if he strode here all the way from downtown Vancouver, or wherever he's from.

"Together Mrs. Christie and Mr. and Mrs. Norman own over twelve thousand acres. The Normans have sold to us. As you know, Mrs. Christie is considering making an arrangement with us to turn her land into a grass conservation area." Iris dares to glance at Vance, who's staring unblinkingly straight ahead, his jaw firmly set. "Given the size and the drastic nature of Mr. Schiff's proposal, somebody has to represent those of us who think that enough of the grassland of this region has been ploughed up, enough of it is in the hands of larger and larger entities, driving out the true family farmer and displacing or threatening the existence of too much wildlife, and killing off biodiversity, both plant and animal."

"Consider the future of your children if we just left the logging companies to take all the trees, the fishermen to fish out the ocean, the farmers to wipe out every last shred of grassland biodiversity. There'll be no future for your kids then — no clean air to breathe, or water, or new medicines, no — "

Somebody is booing him. From three or four places around the hall voices are rising to challenge him.

"You got no respect for us!" The chairman recognizes the loudest voice, although Iris doesn't recognize the speaker. "You got no respect for what we've accomplished here, not for what we've suffered, or what we want — you don't care what happens to us. Our lives aren't worth anything to you." He punches his arm toward the young man with each phrase, and voices rise up around him in angry agreement.

"It's no skin off your nose when we get shoved out of our jobs or off our land and can't look after our own families any more. You don't have to live with the shame of being on welfare. Or all the bad things that happen when a family falls apart — drinking, wife abuse, kids going delinquent because they can't see a life that makes any sense any more. When they got no future and no place to call home. When you think about it, that's what happened to the Indians when we came — only a thousand times worse."

A woman, again Iris can't see who it is, shouts, "If a kid's got scurvy, or he's in jail, it don't make much difference to him if he's breathing clean air or not."

The room is getting rowdier, people are talking out loud to each other, or shouting across the hall. The chairman is calling for order but nobody's listening. The uproar in the hall swirls around Iris. She's thinking of all the farm meetings she's been to over the years: over drought, over the dismantling of the Crow rate, over the government's desire to take exclusive jurisdiction over the sale of certain grains from the Wheat Board. Each time they were filled with fear, seeing one more blow that might be the one that would finally fell them, but she never saw them as agitated as they are tonight.

She remembers something Vance said, "Our branch line's gone, our elevators are going. It's the end of an era and everybody knows it. If you aren't willing to go the way of the big boys, they'll drive you out — market forces will drive you out. If all you really want is to stay on your own farm and listen to the birds sing in the morning and smell the fresh air and watch the sunset, you'll fight any force that tries to take it away. You won't care what side of the fence it's coming from."

It's Schiff's turn now, an old rancher is challenging him, questioning him closely, objecting to what he's told them he wants to do.

"Globalization!" he shouts. "That's just another word for turning all of us out onto the streets to starve while you get rich. Ain't you never heard about the camel going through the eye of the needle?" Then he declares belligerently that he'd take the environmentalists any day over the Jim Schiffs of this world. Iris is glad to hear she and Vance aren't entirely alone after all, that apparently they will have some allies.

But as they shout at each other, argue and debate, she has begun to think about the dust rising off her land, the wind carrying away the topsoil, and the weeds Vance has fought all summer and can barely keep ahead of, she's thinking about that handful of soil he held in his hand months ago to show her, how it trickled through his fingers like water, no organic matter left in it at all. Dead. Then a face rises up before her eyes: beautiful, stern, clear-eyed, an age of suffering far older than the face itself written in its lines. It is Abubech.

Iris is standing before she quite realizes she is, and when people see her on her feet they hush each other until the hall is silent.

"I know you'll think it's easy for me to say, but we'll all be better off in the long run if we refuse to deal with Mr. Schiff."

"Louder," a couple of people call. "We can't hear you, Iris." She takes a deep breath, touches the back of the chair in front of her with her fingertips to steady herself. She wants to tell them what she saw in Ethiopia, but knows they wouldn't listen and, anyway, there's so much to say she wouldn't know where to begin. "He represents — for all of us out here on the land — the return of the feudal system, where his company owns all the land and we'd work for him, and he can hire us or fire us and pay us what he wants. But it's worse than that. He doesn't just want to own all the land, he wants to own all the seeds too, so that every time we want to plant anything at all, we'd have to buy the seeds from him. He could starve us if he wanted to, make us do what he wants, hungry people will do anything for food. So I'm not selling to him, not now, not ever. And if that means the whole deal falls through, I'm sorry to upset people's plans, but that's the way it is." She sits down into a heavy silence. Ramona squeezes her hand, then lets go. People begin to stir now, to shift their positions, turning to mutter to each other. Someone boos her, someone else hisses at the boo.

A nasal voice she recognizes as Hank Osbourne's, a man she dated as a girl, long before Barney, calls from somewhere near the door, "Easy for you, Iris. We ain't all rich, you know, get to do whatever we want with our places." His voice vibrates with anger. Heads swivel, embarrassed grins on a few faces. Mavis and Ardath, Iris notes with some satisfaction, drop their eyes after they've located the speaker, as if they feel distaste for his words.

Royce Cummings, a small farmer whose place is just outside town, gets the chairman's attention. "I just want to say that I'm one of them wants to sell. All I got for retirement is the price my place will bring and Mr. Schiff here, he's offering real money. I won't get that much any place else. I might not even be able to find another buyer the way things are going." Heads nod, there's general agreement on this point.

Iris lowers her head, clasps her moist hands together and squeezes them. She knows what Royce says is true; she knows she will be responsible for his and Ruth's poverty if she refuses to change her mind. Yet, how can she change her mind? In the face of this, how can she carry on with her plans? She thinks of the poverty she saw in Ethiopia. Compared to that, everyone in this room is wealthy. Not that they could be persuaded to see things that way. And what right has she to make the judgement for them? Her mind is so busy that she doesn't notice somebody has asked her a question until Ramona nudges her and the chairman asks that the question be repeated.

"What would this 'conservation area' be all about?" She's surprised to see it's Angela's husband, Orland, until she remembers that Lannie, who has renewed her friendship with Angela, told her that he'd just inherited a half-section of his grandparents' land. Angela isn't with him, probably at home with the children. She stands again.

"We're a long way from having all our project clear yet," she says. "We plan to fence off a few acres and just leave them to see what comes up, how long it takes it to go back to its original state, although none of us will be alive to see it. Some we're going to seed to the original prairie grasses, try to get them in the right proportion, and so on. And what we want to do is bring people back to live on the prairie. Remember when every quarter had a family living on it and the towns were thriving, not dying or dead like they are now?" She has everyone's attention now, the hall is silent as she speaks.

Then somebody shouts, "Pie in the sky!" And someone else calls, "You never seeded a square inch in your life, woman. You never ploughed a field, you never ran a combine. Who the hell are you to tell us what to do with our land!" But she knows that voice too. It's Hanford McKinley, so right wing in his views that most of the community — who are themselves right wing and conservative enough — regard him as too influenced by prevalent attitudes in the American West where his family came from, if not slightly addled, to be paid much attention to.

"What you say is true," she says, humbly enough. "But I've lived on the land my whole life. I'm from a farm family and a farming community. I don't know any other way of life. And if I don't know how to run the John Deere or the combine, I *do* know what the issues are as well as you do."

"The thing of it is, Iris," it's Oskar Halvorsen, a neighbour who is rumoured to have already made a deal with Schiff, "you're making this decision for all of us. Don't think you got that right."

Iris is nonplussed. Oskar is a good man, a friend, if not a close one. People are staring at her, waiting for her answer.

"I don't mean to be doing that," she says slowly. "But look, Oskar, isn't the opposite just as true? If I don't do what I want to do, it will be because *you're* making *my* decision for me — " She hesitates, hears a few chuckles, is vaguely ashamed, feels she's falling into silly quibbling. "I mean, it's really Mr. Schiff, isn't it? He's the one who's trying to run the show. He's the one who's turning us against each other. He's got the money and the power and a dream of his own he's trying to make happen by using all of us — our lives, our farms, our — "

She stops, but she can't think how else to put it, or what other argument she could make. Slowly, heavily, she sits down, thinking: the hatred has started now. Now I'm an outsider to my own community.

The chairman recognizes the old rancher who made the angry comment about globalization earlier. He's an old bachelor from the western side of the district, where there's more ranchland.

"Seems to me we still don't know what Mrs. Christie's got in mind for us. I'd like to hear what she and Vance are up to." Iris glances down the row at Vance, but he's stubbornly staring straight ahead and she knows he wants her to respond, believing she can speak better than he can. She wants to ask him to stand up and talk himself, but everyone is staring at her, the chairman has already said, "Mrs. Christie?" She rises slowly and begins to speak.

"The thing is, it's all an experiment. We have to learn as we go, but we heard of a project in Kansas that is trying to find ways to bring people back to fill up the land, and we're going to visit it as soon as we can. You all know that the bigger the farms get, the fewer people there are living on the land. And you know as well as I do that aside from the Indians we're the only ones left who really know anything about how nature works: scientists only know about their own speciality." She paused. "Now they've got something called ecology, but country people have always been ecologists, until machinery got so big. If we don't keep people out here, the government will stop maintaining our grid roads and we'll lose them, and then they'll make power so expensive that we'll have to have our own power plants, and we'll wind up back on radio phones, or something, instead of being connected to the phone grid. That's partly why repopulating the countryside is so important. But mostly it's because . . . "

She turns to look at all the people seated in the rows radiating out around her, at those leaning against the wall, at the row of men seated at the front of the hall. She's not quaking with fear any more. She's feeling that force again, the one that gave her the courage to refuse Jim Schiff when he last came to her house. And she's hearing the wind in the grass, seeing the moving cloud shadows on the long grassy hills, smelling the prairie on the air. "We belong to nature. Because every single time we kill off a species or plough up or pave

over another piece of ground, a little piece of our humanity dies too."
She sits down firmly, hearing the ringing of her own voice still hanging on the air in the hall. Mavis Miller has turned to watch her. Now
she gives Iris a bright stare before she swivels her head back toward
the chairman. In it Iris reads new respect.

When they go outside, it's after midnight and a warm rain is
falling on the asphalt parking lot, and under the streetlights the
leaves of the trees along the border gleam and slope downward with
the rain's welcome weight. Iris pauses. The rain falls lightly on her
hair and trickles down her face. She's thinking about that moment in
the hall when she felt power flowing through her again and she
wonders where it came from. Since Barney's death, she knows, the
world has become infinitely larger and also endlessly deep, yet richer
than she had ever dreamt. She has found herself, that's what has
happened, and precious and miraculous as it turns out to be, she
could nevertheless weep for all that its finding has cost.

The Inconsolable

She is wearing Iris's leather gardening gloves and they're stiff with old dirt so that her fingers feel numb as she grasps the piece of soggy cardboard buried in the tall weeds under the front window. A half-ton comes down the street, slowing as its driver sees her scrabbling in the grass and weeds at the front of the house she called home when she was a child. She doesn't lift her head or turn toward the vehicle. After a second she can hear it accelerate down the street. This too is expiation — the curiosity of the villagers, word spreading like wildfire that the crazy Stone girl is back, searching around in the yard of her father's house. Or perhaps expiation is the wrong word. Not so much penance as expurgation, a cleansing process; at least, she hopes that's what it will be.

Ever since her return she has dreamt every night about this house, scenes from her childhood. She couldn't tell if she'd imagined them or if they'd really happened: her mother buttering toast for herself, Dillon and Misty as they sat around the rickety kitchen table, the radio playing country and western in the background, her and Dillon's schoolbooks piled crookedly on the counter by the door; her father's heavy boots making the floor creak as he stomped across it to slam the door behind him, his truck roaring to life in the driveway, her mother crying as she ran up the stairs; Dillon scooting his toy trucks and cars back and forth across the worn linoleum floor in the living room, while Misty babbled cheerfully in her playpen, clapping her fat little hands together and bouncing wobbily on her diapered bottom. Sometimes they're eating hamburgers at a picnic table in the backyard, her father standing at the fence talking to a stranger in a half-ton while her mother watches uneasily, squinting into the sunlight; in the front yard, Lannie in her flowered dress, white ankle socks, and freshly polished white shoes, leaving with her mother to go to church while her father stands in the doorway holding Misty; or her father, back from somewhere, in the cramped little hallway, picking her up and swinging her around, setting her down abruptly and walking away. Always, every night, the house.

Until finally she'd asked Iris who owned the house now and Iris had told her it had gone back to the town for unpaid taxes. "Buy it for me," Lannie had mumbled, "Please, I mean — "

"Never mind," Iris said, meaning she needed no explanations, no apologies, nor would she listen when Lannie tried to tell her that one day she'd pay her back.

"If you're not my daughter, I don't know who is," Iris had said firmly, as if she were angry, making them both laugh in embarrassment.

Which has brought Lannie here, this morning, to begin the job of cleaning up the yard and then restoring the house to liveability. Not that she intends to live in it — or does she? One step at a time, she reassures herself at the mixture of distaste and fear that stir when she thinks about the possibility. She is not unaware of the metaphor she has consented to — the cleaning up of her past — it amuses her, yet she's dogged. Hasn't she tried everything else? Including eight years on the far side of the world, which she thinks of now with something close to tenderness.

She picks up two tin cans that have been in the yard so long weeds have grown through the holes rusted in them. She thrusts them into the plastic garbage bag she's dragging, along with two pop bottles, a broken beer bottle, and some sticks of wood. When she has the yard completely cleaned of refuse, she'll have the weed-ridden topsoil scraped away and fresh soil brought in before she seeds a new lawn.

On the third morning, just as she's thinking of taking a break and pouring herself a cup of coffee from the thermos she filled before she left the farm, she hears someone say her name. A shiver runs down her spine. She knows that voice.

He's standing on the sidewalk in front of Barney's truck that she has parked at the curb, his own pulled up behind it, scowling at her.

She almost says "Dad!" before she remembers that she has vowed not to call him that any more. So she straightens and stands where she is by the driveway near the living-room window and stares back at him. He comes toward her, slowly, trying to smile, but she sees he's studying her, he's trying to figure something out. She's beginning to tremble, and then she remembers the last time she saw him.

He was working for a construction company in Kamloops. She didn't know which one and had to try three companies before she found him nailing cedar shingles on the roof of a new house on a quiet suburban boulevard. She recognized him by the long, thick black hair and his size compared to the boy working beside him. From up there he must have had a marvellous view of the valley and she wondered if he'd noticed it. Instead of calling to him, she waited in her car parked in the shade across the street until she saw him descend the ladder, his helper following him down, and go to the cab of the new half-ton parked to one side of the house. She got out of her car, crossed the street, and walked nervously up to where he was sitting with his lunch on the grass in the shade of a row of spruces.

All she could think of to say was "Hi — Dad." He'd already begun to look up at her, and she saw he didn't look any different from the day he'd dropped her off at Iris and Barney's and said he'd be back for her.

Slowly, then, he rose to his feet, dusting off the back of his jeans with the flat of his hand, then rubbing the hand on his thigh as if to clean it before he shook hands with her. She held back, refused him her hand.

"It's me, Lannie."

"I know," he said. She could see he'd forgotten her, and she almost wilted and gave up, staring back at him. Then he let air out through his nostrils as if he'd been holding his breath a long time, ever since she'd come up to him.

"You better sit down." She hesitated a long moment, then, shrugging her shoulders, sat down facing him in the cool shadows under the line of spruces. "I don't have much time," he said.

She kept looking at him, drinking in his face, his hair, the length of his arms and legs, his powerful shoulders.

"I've missed you," she said, but her voice came out choked and too soft, as if she hadn't spoken for a week, which she practically hadn't. Not since she'd stopped off in Calgary to visit her brother and sister. She cleared her throat. She could see him trying to say that he'd missed her too, but she could tell he couldn't make himself say the words. And anyway, he hadn't missed her, she was pretty sure of that. "I came to find you," she said. "I wanted to see you again." He grinned at her, easy, as if she were a potential girlfriend. She hated him for it. "I . . . I — " but she couldn't say out loud what she really wanted from him.

"How're the other two doing?" he asked, and when she stared at him in astonishment at this question — the other two — she thought she saw a flush cross his tanned face. "I haven't seen 'em either for a while."

"They're okay," she said finally. "Dick and Marie look after them."

"I send them money," he said, looking straight into her face so that she had to drop her eyes. He'd never sent any money to Iris and Barney, but then, there'd been no need to.

"They said you wrote to them sometimes." She tried to say this neutrally, but in her own ears she sounded accusatory and she ducked her head, embarrassed.

"Yeah," he said. "I wondered who it was in that car."

"I — " she faltered again, struggling. She had to make her case, quickly, before he went away again. "Dad," he was carefully looking away from her, toward the backyard now, and the view of the mountains. "I need you," she said quietly. "A girl needs a father," she added, trying to sound lighthearted, to lift the burden of her need from him. He turned his head quickly back toward her, his face filled with anger, and she was frightened, remembering suddenly shouting, broken furniture.

"I drink too much," he told her, pointing to his chest. "I got no money. I got nothing for you." Yet she didn't really think he was trying to get rid of her, at least not yet.

"I'm not asking for much," she said. This, of course, was a lie. "I have money."

"Yeah," he said.

"Can I stay with you?" When he didn't reply, she added quickly, "I mean, just for a while, a few days, that's all." She felt disarmed by him, a whining child again.

"You won't like my place much. You won't like how I live."

"I don't care," she said. He thought for a moment, his uneaten sandwich in his hand.

"Listen," he said. "I'll give you the address. You can go there now. No use waiting for me here." It was the way he said it that made her suspect him; plenty of time for her to look around, see what kind of man he was, that she didn't want him for a father. He told her the address and how to find the house.

Walking away from him, knowing his eyes were probably on her as she retreated from his shady refuge under the trees, she was beginning to feel sick. But she forced herself to walk evenly, as if she weren't in any hurry or under any particular stress, to get in her car and drive slowly away.

She was startled by how much his house looked like the one in Chinook they'd lived in when they were a family: a small frame structure needing paint, with a brown-tinged lawn and a few big trees in the backyard. She parked the car in front and went slowly up the sidewalk, onto the sagging wooden porch and inside. Someone was standing in the doorway at the end of the hall and she was so startled she almost shrieked. But then a woman's voice asked, "Who are you?" and moving closer to her so that Lannie began to make out her face and figure: medium height, plump, her light brown hair pulled back in a short ponytail, her face neither pretty nor plain. An ordinary-looking woman.

"I didn't know there was anybody here," she said. "Dad said to come here to wait for him — "

"Dad?" the woman said, then in a different tone, tired, as if she might have known, "Dad." The woman was wearing a pale pink shirt and slacks — a nurse's uniform.

"Howard Stone. He's my father." The woman laughed a short bark, then said, "Come in."

As she led the way into the kitchen, she said over her shoulder, "I'm Dierdre." She stopped with her back to the sink and asked across the expanse of shining grey formica table that stood between them, "What's your name?"

"Lannie."

"I just made some lemonade — unless you'd rather have beer?" She went to the fridge, an old one, from the sixties or earlier with a rounded front, that stood humming noisily in the corner.

"Lemonade, please," Lannie said. She'd only just realized how thirsty she was. "It's hot out there."

"Un-bear-able," the woman said. "But it's not too bad in here. The big trees help." She opened the fridge door and reached inside bringing out a pitcher. "He never mentioned kids to me. But I sort of knew it, I guess. How many more?"

"Two," Lannie said. "I'm the oldest."

"Where's the rest of 'em?" she asked, setting the lemonade on the table. "Are they gonna show up on our doorstep too?"

"They're both still in Calgary with the people who raised them," she said. "Our mother died."

"That I knew," Dierdre said, setting out two glasses and filling them from the pitcher. "Sit. You might as well." Lannie slowly pulled out a chair and sat down. Dierdre sat down too.

The small kitchen was spotless, scrubbed to a sterile shine. Even the plain white walls shone. It made Lannie think of T.S. Eliot, "We are the hollow men . . ." It seemed to her that her mother had been a poor housekeeper; in her memory there were always piles of things around and jam and egg yolk stuck to the table. How Lannie hated hyper-clean, white-walled houses like this one. And yet, in Saskatoon, she had kept her apartment just like this.

"How long have you — been together?" When she thought to look, she saw that Dierdre wore no wedding ring. In fact, she wasn't a lot older than Lannie herself, but she had an air of weariness about her, as if she'd been around.

"Not long," she said. "A year pretty soon." Lannie thought six months, I bet. Dierdre looked up at the clock that hung on the wall high above the window over the sink. "I have to go to work. You're welcome to stay till he gets home. Stay the night," she added. "You're his daughter, after all," and she laughed again, that half-snort, filled with surprise. "The spare room's off the stairs on the right. The bed's made up. Make yourself at home. I gotta go to work." She stood, set her empty glass in the sink, picked up her purse from the counter, and went slowly out into the hall. The screen door slapped shut behind her.

Lannie sat on in the kitchen listening to the clock tick. Eventually she stood and walked quietly through the house, room after room, downstairs and up. It didn't take very long. Her father's boots in a neat row in the bedroom closet beside Dierdre's high heels and extra pair of nurse's shoes. Why did this cleanliness, this order, this silence oppress her so? The father she remembered had been loud and violent — she'd seen him strike her mother more than once, even though she'd tried not to remember it. And now this, this — emptiness.

At six o'clock he still hadn't returned. At seven she turned on the television set. The next thing she knew, Dierdre was leaning over her, saying her name.

"It's after midnight, you might as well go up to bed. He isn't coming home tonight."

Very early on the morning of the third day, when Howard and Dierdre were both still sleeping, she'd packed her things and gone quietly away. She tried to leave them a note, but in the end, she found she had nothing to say, so she left the pencil beside the blank sheet of paper on the kitchen table. As she walked out of the house to her car, she felt hollow, light, as if she were filled with air.

"What are you doing here?" he asks her. "What are you up to?" Not even hello, she notes. She has stopped trembling.

"Cleaning up the place," she says crisply. "I own it. I bought it." He smiles sourly.

"You mean Iris bought it."

"Yes."

"You planning to move back in?" he asks, with a touch of uncertainty, and she sees it's an attempt at a joke.

"Yes," she says again, not knowing if she means it or not. He stops in surprise, then his face darkens and twists with anger. It's a look she knows well; she's been seeing it all these years in her dreams.

"You're shaming me," he says. "Right here in public. You're sham-ing me, aren't you." He's still coming toward her. She has the urge to run, and her mother's face as she backed away from him comes back to her, but she stands where she is.

"If I am," she says evenly, "it isn't intentional."

"I want you to stop. Just get back in that truck and drive away. I'll burn this damn dump down!" She knows he won't. He'll go get drunk, maybe beat somebody up, that's what he'll do. Or he'll run. She tries not to let him see the contempt she's suddenly flooded with, because it is for herself as much as it's for him. Hasn't she been running all these years, too?

"What are *you* doing here?" she asks him instead, coldly. He stops again, as if she's caught him by surprise. She can tell his first reaction is to yell at her, to work himself up to some action — a blow, a kick, a hole in the wall made with his fist. But he seems puzzled, as if he's warning himself not to do any of those things, but doesn't have any other alternatives. "Sit down," she commands him. "Have a cup of coffee with me." She walks away without waiting for an answer.

When she returns from the half-ton with the thermos and a mug, he's sitting on the steps. She fills the mug and hands it to him, then fills the thermos cup and sets the thermos down on the ground. She crouches, facing him, in a patch of ragged wild grass she's cleared of weeds, holding the thermos cup in both hands.

"I brought Dillon," he says. "He's coming down to Iris's tonight, so you two can visit."

"Are you staying?" She doesn't look up, but she can feel him shrug-ging. She supposes that means yes.

"I quit," he says. "I can do that same work for Luke — pay's not as good, but — " He shrugs. She knows he almost said, *But at least I'm home*. He shifts, looks off down the street and back to her again. "What's it like inside? A mess, I bet." She clears her throat and drops her head. "I haven't gone in yet." She can feel his involuntary twitch of surprise.

She looks up at him to find him staring down the street, past the trees and the neat front lawns to where the hills rise roughly, white-streaked dun, toward the blue of the sky. It's the direction where the ranch is, where he was raised with his half-sister Fay, and his half-brothers, Barney and Wesley, and fought them, and left.

"Why did you leave me?" she asks him. After all these years — twenty — since he went away and never came back, after all the times she yearned to ask him by letter, by phone, in person, in her dreams and her nightmares, from Eastern Canada, from Africa, from Europe, and never has, never dared, they seem the easiest words she has ever uttered. She squats there in the wild grass watching an ant crawl over her grubby sneaker and listens to the echo of her own question.

"I couldn't look after you kids!" he says automatically, as if this is a question he has answered a thousand times already.

"Why did you never write or phone?"

He twists his head first one way and then the other. She looks up, just in time to see a look of — it's anger, she recognizes that, it seems to be the only reaction he knows how to have — but his face is also so twisted into bewilderment, that she sees she is witnessing an unresolved anguish she never guessed he had. She can feel colour flooding her face now, her bowels have clenched and her stomach goes queasy. Abruptly, she sits on the ground, crushing dusty weeds under her.

"How do you think I felt?" he asks her. She forces herself to look back at him, not blinking, not looking away. He drops his eyes finally. "I wasn't much of a husband," he says. "When she died, I just wanted to get the hell away from here — away from this — " He throws his arm out violently, indicating the house behind him, the street, the town. Coffee slops out of the mug onto his thigh and he rubs at his jeans roughly. "They all blamed me. I knew it." He says this abruptly, but in a quieter tone, as if he has given up his anger, and then he laughs, a quick, self-conscious snort, as if he has never told anybody this, and never thought he would.

"So you gave away your children," she says. "And you left."

They sit in silence while robins sing in the poplars that separate this lot from the next one and down at the end of the street somebody's dog barks steadily. She feels as if, for the first time in years, her head is clear. She is sitting in the grass looking at her father: her real father, her only father. And he is big and violent and confused and incapable of kindness. He is a bad father, a hopelessly bad father.

She can see too that he feared Iris even more than he feared his "good" brother Barney's censure. It was easier to forget his oldest daughter, easier not to think of her, than to keep coming back, having to face Iris and Barney's contempt every time. He had mistreated her mother, his wife, and everyone knew it. He had been unreliable, often drunk, always emotionally unpredictable. And now, she knows what she has to say to him. She opens her mouth but no sound comes out. She tries again, her jaw trembling with the effort to make the words. He glances at her. She tries once more, forcing the sound through a tightened throat, from between lips that tremble.

"You have destroyed my life," she tells him, as calmly as if she is remarking on the weather. She pulls herself to her knees, looking up into his weak, handsome, aging face. She can see the muscles in his upper arms bulging and wonders fleetingly if she should run. But no, he blinks rapidly, as if she has swung her fist at him, then his expression shuts down, stony. She thinks suddenly of all the men, total strangers, she picked up in bars and slept with, when she was an undergrad at university. She thinks of them without her usual horrified and sickened shame; she thinks of them instead as inevitable, as pathetic. "I have spent all these years wanting you to be my father, because I needed you so much. I couldn't see that it was no use at all."

Behind them the small, dilapidated house rises up in the morning sunshine, flecks of blue trim still hanging from its window ledges below the cracked panes. Inside her mother walked once, rocked her in her arms, in her high, sweet soprano sang her lullabies, fragments of which still enter her dreams, her mother's fine, red-gold hair sliding down over her eye so that she tossed it back with a quick flick of her head. Her blue-green eyes with the reddish lashes and eyebrows, her soft, narrow lips, pinkish and cracked, her pert nose, her bosom, high and small, her thin arms and legs with the delicate, slender ankles Lannie has inherited, her almost transparent fair skin with its covering of tiny, faint freckles.

"She died from meningitis," he says. She looks into his face and understands he has been seeing the same apparition she has. "It came on sudden — the doctor was away, nobody could do anything. By the time one came — three hours! — it was too late." He shifts and stands up slowly to his full height, towering over her, his shadow spreading darkness over the house behind him. "I was a bad husband. Maybe I been a lousy father too. But *I didn't kill her.*" He tosses the coffee from his mug off to one side, into what was once a flower bed under the window where gold and orange marigolds and zinnias once bloomed, and drops the empty mug with a thud at her feet.

Then he strides away, down the cracked cement of the narrow sidewalk, past his dead brother's truck to his own. He gets in, slamming the door hard, and drives away, gunning it so that the motor roars halfway down the block.

What she feels is such longing for her mother. It is as if all the years since her mother's death she has held her longing in a hard-shelled nut tight inside her, that she has been squeezing smaller and smaller with the years, and now — ever since she got on that plane in Addis Ababa to head back to Canada, a crack has been developing in its shell, first tinier than a hair, then widening and descending its length. Now she feels that nut crack apart with a soundless *boom* like the earth's layers shifting subterraneously, its contents spilling out and expanding. Her head is full of soundless roaring.

After long moments Lannie gets slowly to her feet. Staggering abruptly before she regains her balance, she walks the few feet to the stairs. They creak loudly as she goes up them and into the porch, past the sagging, cracked wooden outside door that sits half open, to the closed, locked door with the blue paint peeling from it that leads inside. She reaches into her shirt for the old-fashioned iron key she has hung on a cord around her neck. Fumbling, she lifts the cord over her head, weighs the key in her palm, grasps it and, her hand shaking so badly that the key chitters against the rusted metal plate, manages to insert it in the lock. It squeals, resisting her effort at first, before its voice lowers to a groan, and with a last rasp, clicks open.

"I didn't expect you back so early," Iris says, as Lannie comes into the kitchen. She glances at the clock — it's early afternoon — and then at Lannie who is grubby with dirt and grass stains on her jeans and shirt and her hair stringy with sweat. Iris looks into Lannie's face.

"How's the house coming?" she asks.

"I want to talk to you."

"Sure," Iris says carefully. "I made some iced tea. Let's take it outside." Lannie goes out onto the deck to the picnic table and benches. As she shuts the screen door behind her, she hears Iris opening and closing the fridge. When Iris comes out a moment later carrying a tray with a pitcher of iced tea on it and two tall glasses, Lannie is seated on the bench facing her.

"I don't need iced tea," she says, through clenched teeth. Iris's smile wavers slightly and is replaced by a frown that she also erases. "Iris," Lannie says. "For God's sake, sit down." Iris puts the tray down on the table and slides onto the bench across from her. Lannie can see her resisting her need to fill the glasses, and she reaches across the table and takes Iris's wrist firmly in her hand to prevent her. Iris flinches. "Listen to me."

"I *am* listening," Iris says in a clear, precise voice. Lannie withdraws her hand then, realizes she has been counting on Iris's weakness, and Iris's weakness isn't there any more. Both of them stare at the red mark that's fading from her wrist.

"I want to know about my mother," she says. "Tell me about my mother." Iris gazes out across the yard to the row of steel bins that shine in the sun. The faint roar of the combine Vance is driving floats across fields to them. She opens her mouth, but Lannie interrupts, "I want the truth."

"The truth!" Iris says then. "You think *I* know the truth?" There is such irony in this response that Lannie draws back. Then Iris lowers her head, embarrassed apparently, and says in a low voice, "I didn't know her well. You look exactly like her. She was very pretty, but she was — I think she was weak. Which you are not."

"Weak," Lannie repeats.

"She was raised in foster homes."

"I know that," Lannie says.

"Well, think about it!" Iris snaps. "What did she know about being a wife or a mother? Batted around the way she was from pillar to post when she was a girl. I suppose she thought Howard would save her — he was so big and strong — "

"Did she love me?" Lannie cries.

"She adored you."

"Adored me?" Lannie repeats uncertainly.

"Yes," Iris says firmly. "She told me herself that you were the best thing that ever happened to her. She couldn't get over how beautiful you were, or how smart. She had no time for Howard for a couple of years after you were born. I think that was part of the trouble between them, I mean, that she couldn't see Howard any more for this baby she had, that in some strange way I can't quite figure out but I see it now — "

"What!" Lannie cries.

"That mothering you was like *having* a mother — like it was filling up the emptiness from not being mothered herself — You were everything to her." Lannie has been leaning toward Iris, her back rigid, her eyes not leaving Iris's. Now, she relaxes a little.

"Dad was jealous?" she murmurs.

"Maybe, I don't know," Iris says. "But he was always rough and angry — you know that — and I don't think it could have worked out anyway. He was fighting with Luke, and he was jealous of Barney because Barney was Luke's real son and he wasn't. He took his anger out on Dorothy a lot, I think." Lannie winces at this, remembering his voice shattering her sleep. "Then Dillon came along, and then Misty, and by then Dorothy was getting worn out. She just seemed exhausted by it all. And I think she was depressed." She says this last sentence slowly, as if she's just becoming sure of what she has said.

"I remember her not getting up in the morning," Lannie says suddenly. "I remember getting breakfast for the three of us before Dill and I went to school. I don't know why Dad wasn't there."

"He'd drive up to the ranch early to work," Iris said. "Sometimes he wouldn't come home at night. After he quarrelled with Luke finally, he got a job near Medicine Hat and then he'd only come home on weekends. When your mother got sick — " Lannie's head goes up at this, to stare at Iris. "He took her straight to the hospital, but it was the weekend, the doctor had gone to Swift Current for the day and his replacement was busy with a heart attack over in Antelope. By the time he got back it was too late. She died within minutes."

"Were you there?" Iris shakes her head no.

"She was gone by the time I arrived. Howard was inconsolable."

"Where was I?" Lannie asks, then, "Inconsolable?"

"At home with Dillon and Misty. He'd phoned his mother to come and get you. Yes. Inconsolable."

"What do you mean?"

Iris sighs, passes her hand across her face, as if remembering all this wearies her. "He cried. He tried to pick Dorothy up and carry her away as if he thought he could bring her back to life. Or maybe, he just didn't want death to have her. The doctor stopped him. He broke the glass in the hospital door on his way out he banged it so hard."

"You saw this?"

"I was coming up the steps with Barney, but I don't think he even noticed us."

"I don't remember this."

"You weren't there. Mary Ann took you three home with her."

"Dad?"

"Nobody saw him again until the next day. Barney made the funeral arrangements. It was meningitis, they think." There is a long silence during which Lannie tries to take all of this in.

"Does he deserve," she hesitates, "some kind of — sympathy?"

"Don't we all?"

Lannie has turned sideways on the bench as if she plans to get up and walk away.

"Did he love us?" she asks. Iris is silent for a long moment and Lannie feels such a hard, sharp pain in the centre of her chest as she waits for the reply, thinking now that she already knows what it will be.

"I don't know, Lannie," Iris says. "I think he did in his way. I think he tried to love you — " She falls silent again. Then continues, in a voice so different that Lannie steals a glance at her. "His own father had rejected him. Mary Ann left him because he was violent and a drunk, and then she married Luke. Luke had trouble loving him, I think. Luke has trouble loving, period," she finishes. Lannie swings her other leg over the bench and sits for a moment with her back to Iris. Then she stands, slowly, not knowing where she's going. Iris says quickly,

"Lannie!" so she turns back to her questioningly. The words burst out of Iris, low, fast, as if she's been holding them back a long time.

"I was going to clear out your room — I went through your old book bag, from university, I mean, I found . . ." Iris stops, staring into Lannie's eyes.

"What," she says softly, involuntarily.

"I found some — notes. In the zipper compartment on the side."

"Notes?"

"From men — " Lannie takes a step backward away from her. "I put them away and forgot about them because I was sure there had to be some explanation — like, maybe, they weren't yours. But then, when I knew I would go to find you, I thought of them again. And now that you're back, I can't stop thinking about them." Iris waits, her eyes on Lannie's face.

"I have to go," Lannie says, but now Iris reaches out and catches her wrist, holding it tightly. Without letting go or taking her eyes away, she rises, comes around the table to Lannie's side, and stands, her back to the railing, facing Lannie, still holding her wrist.

"I want to know what that was all about."

"No. No you don't want to know."

"So, they *are* yours," Iris says, at last, and her cheeks flush with pink and her dark eyes take on a new light. Lannie lifts her head and meets Iris's gaze.

"You seemed to think I was full of virtue. As if losing your mother purified you — made you into a saint. Or else so exhausted you, you wouldn't have the energy for evil," she says, not looking at Iris. "I was angry with you for that, too," she mutters.

"Too?" Iris asks, and when Lannie merely glares at her, goes on. "Maybe I did think that. Maybe I was too . . . " Then softly, "What are you telling me?"

"Let go of me," Lannie cries. Iris releases her quickly; she seems to have forgotten she's holding her. "I am not a good person. If you could see inside me — "

"I can!" Iris cries. This silences Lannie and in the moment she is stilled, she looks into Iris's face and sees some new seriousness there that reminds her of Abubech.

"You'd see that I have failed to be — what you wanted me to be — I was never what you thought I was — "

"Lannie!" Iris cries. "It's all right! You don't have to tell me!"

But now she's started, she can't stop, she doesn't want to stop. "When I was at college? When you thought I was eating pizzas with my gang, going to dances and movies, playing cards in the student union lounge like you did. Well, I wasn't. I was going to bars and drinking and picking up men. Men I didn't know. Men I never saw again. I lied about my name, what I did, where I lived. I went to their rooms with them. I did what they wanted me to do. I — "

"All right," Iris says quietly. "That's enough, Lannie. You don't have to say any more. It's all right."

"You wanted to know," Lannie cries, and when she hears the ungovernable *pain* in her own voice, she tries to quiet herself. Iris puts her arms around her and pulls her close. Lannie, her face pressed against Iris's hair, doesn't move, although she finds now she yearns to collapse there, to give up all resistance. She struggles with herself, feeling Iris's fingers smoothing back her hair.

Now Iris stiffens and steps back, releasing Lannie.

"Your baby — you didn't know who the father was. It wasn't Tim. That's why you swallowed James Springer's pills. Isn't it?"

"Would you have wanted to live if you were me? Knowing what you know now?" she asks.

"And yet, you must have wanted that baby," Iris says. "You tried to kill yourself, and the baby, but, nonetheless, you've blamed me for making you have an abortion."

"I didn't!" Lannie denies, and then, "I did. It's true. I'm — sorry. I — " But what can she say to explain to Iris what she doesn't understand herself? "I haven't menstruated for years," she hears herself tell her, and recognizes consciously at last, the full implications of this devastating fact.

And her own anger confuses her. What genuine grievance has she against Iris who fed and clothed her when her parents left her, who mothered her as best she knew how? She feels herself whirling back through time: the day she left here ten years earlier, the day she understood Barney desired her although he would not, had never touched her; the day she knew Iris was having an affair with James Springer and had hated her for it and, wanting to die, although not solely because of their affair, she had swallowed his sleeping pills and only later, back from the dead, had forgiven Iris; the day her father brought her here; the day her mother died.

Grandma Mary Ann coming into the house, walking so quietly, her face soft and sort of hollow, holding Lannie pressed against her stomach while she smoothed back Lannie's hair and smoothed it back over and over again so that Lannie knew that her mother wouldn't be coming back.

She had screamed and hit Mary Ann. She had struggled and pulled away from that hand that was smoothing her hair and hit her over and over again, flailing with both fists against her grandmother's stomach and thighs and arms until Grandpa Luke had grabbed her, picked her up bodily, carried her out of the house, and put her in the truck beside him. After a moment Mary Ann had followed them, Dillon walking ahead of her, his eyes fixed on the sidewalk, Misty asleep in her arms.

Then, suddenly, she remembers the look on Iris's face when her father brought her here and said, "Look after her for me, Iris, will you?" In that expression Lannie saw Iris's refusal.

Barney broke in, "You know we will. Until you're ready to make a home for them again." And Iris still standing there. Lannie had seen all that through a sort of haze that for a long time had sat between herself and the rest of the world, a gauzy veil through which she saw everything happening as if her life were only a dream, and not real at all: Iris standing there looking at Lannie as if she were a worm, or a disease she was afraid of catching.

"You didn't want me," Lannie says, and hates herself.

Iris blanches, then colour comes rushing back and she says, "For about five minutes I didn't want you. I was selfish and childish and Howard took me completely by surprise. All I had to do was look at you for a minute and then I wanted you. And I have wanted you ever since." She turns away to look out over the railing at the caragana hedge and the ripe crop bending in the wind as it waits for the combine and the grid road to town beyond it. When she speaks, her voice is muffled. "You resisted me, you refused me, no matter what I said or did. You would not unbend and let me be your mother."

Lannie finds herself moving to Iris's side. The wind that buffeted them now and then has quietened, and overhead very high in the sky a jet stream arches silently. They stand quietly side by side, looking out over the countryside.

"How could I trust anyone?" Lannie asks. "If my mother and my father both could go away and leave me, how could I trust you and Barney not to do the same? How could I trust anyone or anything at all?" Now she realizes Iris has always known this, and not known what to do, beyond never leaving herself.

She finds herself thinking about Mariam, the little girl she loved so long ago, in the famine camp in Ethiopia. She'd be maybe sixteen now, she would have suffered the trauma of her ritual mutilation. If she had survived it, she might even be a mother herself. Mariam had lost everyone and still she had smiled at Lannie and held out her arms to her. But no, she can't weigh her own losses against Mariam's. She long ago gave up such foolish, pointless machinations, as if they might make any difference to the weight of her lot. Fate singled her out; fate chose her.

Now she remembers a long ago visit to the rock churches at Lalibela, a vacation she'd taken with some of the men and women she'd been working with after the crops had begun to grow again, the people had dispersed, and the camp had closed. The painting high on the wall, or perhaps it was the ceiling of one of the churches, of the Virgin Mary spinning as the angel Gabriel announces Mary's fate to her. She remembers that in the painting Mary is an Ethiopian woman; she gazes up mutely at the angel, who is not in the painting, her black eyes wide with wonder and fear, her left arm arrested high above her shoulder as she draws up the red spinning thread.

"Lannie?" Iris has been speaking to her. Lannie turns to her.

"Do you remember how in the story of the Garden of Eden Adam and Eve are driven out because Eve tempts him with the apple?"

"Of course I do," Iris says. "It was the fruit of the tree of the knowledge of good and evil, and when God comes, Eve blames it on the serpent, and Adam blames it on her. And then women have to bear children in sorrow, or something, ever since, as punishment."

"It's a dumb story," Lannie declares. "There's another one that's just as true. I'm beginning to think it's truer."

"Tell me," Iris asks softly.

Lannie tells her about the maiden Persephone, who had been stolen from her mother by Hades while she was gathering flowers in a meadow, and taken in his chariot down to his underworld kingdom. Her mother, Demeter, had gone to Zeus to beg him to intercede with Hades and return her daughter to her. Zeus agreed, but on the condition that she must not have eaten anything while she was below. But Hades had offered Persephone a pomegranate, and she had eaten some of it, and thus, the Fates decreed that she might return to her mother and the sunlit world of her girlhood for only half the year, while she must spend the other half below as Hades's sorrowful queen in the realms of the dead.

"Oh, I see," Iris says. "It's another kind of Fall — the Fall of maidens stolen from the safety and innocence of their mothers' world into the world of men."

"Something like that."

"I think it's true," Iris says. "So men accuse women of stealing their innocence and driving them out of the Garden of Eden, and women accuse men of the same."

"Only we don't beat and starve and rape and mutilate men," Lannie says. "We don't want to own all the land; we don't start wars; we don't — "

She's thinking of Ethiopia now, of all she was a witness to there, and of all she did. I was not just a voyeur of others' suffering; if I went there for the wrong reasons, I stayed and worked until I earned the right to be there. A burden she has been carrying lifts with this thought, leaving a strange pleasing lightness.

Iris is speaking. "I know that's all true, but it seems to me that it's not the whole truth about men and women. It seems to me the true story is bigger than that." She falls into a silence.

"What do you mean?" Lannie asks, puzzled. Then she thinks how all her life there has been nothing she wouldn't give to have had a mother.

The Garden of Eden

Down in this narrow valley there isn't a breath of wind, the tall pines stand motionless, the leaves of the few deciduous trees dotted among them now turned golden or red. The stream runs past quickly, a moving ribbon of sunlight, so shallow that with the window rolled down Iris hears its passage as a slight, tinkling song. The corrals are empty, there's not an animal in sight, but the small cabin looks exactly the same as that terrible day she came here through rain and mud with Luke. She shudders, but this is a journey she has to complete.

After the long, dry summer the stream is barely ten feet wide and at its deepest it's well below her boot-tops. She moves slowly, remembering crossing the swollen stream, a rope looped over her shoulder, falling, half drowning, pulling herself upright, gasping and choking while water coursed over her. As she moves up the slope toward the cabin, she feels a tightening at the bottom of her throat. The place is eery, the sun-and-shade dappling on the cabin walls, its very stillness in the warm fall light, seem to carry a message that she isn't sure she'd want to read if she could. She reaches the door, lifts the latch, and steps inside.

As before, her eyes need a moment to adjust to the shadowy interior. Clean coffee mugs stand neatly upside down on a spread tea towel beside the old blue granite basin and she thinks she detects the faint odour of brewed coffee. A neat pile of split wood rests on a square of linoleum beside the cookstove. Goose bumps jump up on her arms, a shiver rushes down her back, but then she realizes all of this must have been done by the Castles, who would need to use the cabin occasionally.

She walks into the living room. There she sees a neatly rolled and tied sleeping bag lying on the old sofa where she'd found Barney that day, and on the floor at the end closest to where she stands, there's an open sports bag out of which hangs the sleeve of what has to be a woman's blouse.

Have the Castles moved in here without asking her? Well, that's all right. Why not? She takes a step forward, thinking to walk through the room, to possess it as her own.

All Barney's treasures are gone from the walls, taken by Luke. Mary Ann said something about it to her in an apologetic way. And Luke loaded up Barney's horses and took them to the family ranch where he'd been born. There's nothing left of Barney here. Bitterness strikes, but she stifles it, and feels in its place sadness that she never managed to possess the Barney she'd been in love with as a girl — that cowboy part of him that he'd abandoned almost as soon as they were pronounced man and wife. And she had herself colluded in it, for how could he be at once both a copy of her phlegmatic farmer father and a wild, romantic cowboy?

She goes back into the kitchen with its freshly swept floor and its shiny coffeepot sitting empty on the cold stove. She means to walk through the corrals, something she has done only once, the day eighteen or so months ago when he'd brought her here and told her he was planning to buy this ranch. This will be the last time, she's thinking, when as she puts her hand out to open the door, it opens inward and she finds herself face to face with a woman. With her back to the light, the woman's features aren't clear. It takes Iris a second to recognize Daisy Castle.

"Oh!" they both say, and stare. Daisy's hair is blonde, cut short and straight, which suits her because she has such good bones. Iris sees that even without makeup or any gesture made toward her femininity, Daisy is beautiful. For an instant they stand motionless, assessing each other, then both speak at once.

"Come in," Iris says, because it is her house.

"I saw your car," Daisy says. The way she steps back she obviously wants Iris to come outside and just as suddenly Iris finds the cabin chilly and too dark, the ghost of Barney's body hovering back there behind her. She's grateful to go out into the warmth and light.

Daisy's saddle horse, a slender sorrel, is tied to a corral railing to Iris's left. Iris feels awkward, can't think what to say. Daisy is silent, walks to the sawed-off stump of a big tree in front of the small window to Iris's right. Iris says, "It was in the back of my mind for a long time to come out here, but I couldn't seem to — "

"I'm sorry about Barney," Daisy says rapidly, and lifts her chin to look away into the trees up the hill behind the cabin, as if she can't bring herself to look at Iris. "So, you've come to — what? Throw me out?"

"I didn't know you were here," Iris says, surprised. Daisy studies her, her blue eyes narrowed, a hard, impenetrable expression on her face. Iris stares back, confused. She remembers what she has heard about her, that she does what she wants, takes off on the spur of the moment, comes back as unexpectedly, that men want her, that she has always had any man she wants. The longer their eyes engage, the more something is slowly beginning to stir in Iris's bosom. Some funny feeling — some — At the same time she notices Daisy's expression is losing its hardness, her mouth softening. She looks away again, blinking, and in that gesture, Daisy's uncertainty, Iris's uneasiness, her sense of something strange going on here begins to form itself into a hint, then a notion, then a shattering certainty.

"You were having an affair with my husband," she says, and there are so many emotions rising in her at once: rage, hatred, loss, a sense of profound betrayal that knocks speech right out of her. She thinks of his corpse again, lying as if he were merely asleep, on the couch in the room behind her, then turns aside, runs a couple of steps away from Daisy, back to the house. Tears start to pour out, but this so humiliates her in front of this woman that she manages to stop. And besides, she's thinking for the first time: *I did the same thing — I had an affair with James*, and for the first time, she feels shame over it. But confusion overcomes her and she takes a minute, panting, breathing deeply, then turns back to Daisy.

Daisy is standing silently. She wears faded tight Levi's, scuffed brown riding boots, a denim shirt, a heavy silver and turquoise Indian bracelet on one tanned wrist, a man's wristwatch on the other, and her straw stetson dangles from her fingers. She's excruciatingly slender, and taller than Iris by at least six inches. She's younger too, Iris notices, although she's pleased to see apprehension in her face and, also, hints of the toll that hard living has taken.

"I thought you must know," Daisy says quietly. "Everybody else around here did, at least they suspected it." She shrugs. "They would have thought that about me no matter what."

"How would I know?" Iris spits out furiously. "I hardly saw him from the time he moved out here in the early spring." Then she thinks, Ramona and Vance — they must have known, and she sits down hard on the old railway ties that form the step into the cabin. "Why?" she asks, not really of Daisy. Daisy shrugs again.

"I was there," she says, "and you weren't." When Iris looks up at her, she's surprised to see that hard expression back. "Don't worry," Daisy says. "He loved you." Iris would like to tell her to shut up because she knows it isn't true, Barney had stopped loving her. But she doesn't, she's overcome with amazement at her own naivete, her stupidity. Small birds in the branches of a pine a few feet away from them have begun to quarrel noisily among themselves. Iris wants to tell them to shut up. Just shut up. She remembers now that she'd thought he couldn't be having an affair because there was no one to have it with. Now she knows he didn't want to make love to her any more because he was making love to Daisy. She sees the two of them in bed together and is sickened and humiliated. She looks up at Daisy and says with great bitterness, "I suppose he thought I'd never know."

"I don't blame you if you hate me."

"I do hate you," she says. "You smug bitch." She isn't even surprised to hear herself say this, nor sorry. She finds she'd like to walk across the few feet that separate them and slap this woman's face hard. Daisy flushes so slightly that Iris isn't sure she's not imagining it. "And him," she says, "That lying — " but words won't come for whatever it is Barney has done to her. Now she has had a minute to think about it, she isn't surprised after all. It's the logical thing, given how their marriage had gone. Resentment and anger is leaking slowly out of her, being replaced by a heavy, dragging regret, by sorrow over the whole business — their marriage, which started out so perfect, going so wrong. Surely her affair with James came out of whatever was wrong with it, that she'd not been able to see, and not out of — whatever she'd thought it was: her own benevolence in the face of James's flattering need for her, his amazing passion for her. "We should have had children," she says. Daisy goes rigid.

"What do you mean?" Daisy asks. "Adopt them?"

"No!" Iris says. "Have them, you know? Give birth?" This is a challenge, an insult. At least I could have had them if I'd wanted to, she thinks. Another thing everybody says about Daisy is that she can't have children and that's why she's always been so wild. Some childhood horse accident or something.

"If you think being a father will stop a man from being unfaithful, you're crazy." Then Daisy turns away as if she plans to go over to her horse, mount it, and ride away. But she stops abruptly in midstride, and turns back to Iris. "Are you telling me — " She hesitates. "Don't you know?"

The small birds in the pine behind Daisy gather themselves into a bunch and whirr up out of the tree and then down to vanish in the tall grass at the edge of the stream. A few yellow leaves float by them on the water.

"Know what?" she asks finally.

"That — " Daisy frowns as if she can't decide whether to go on or not. She lifts her eyes to Iris's and studies her across the distance between them. Iris would like to walk away across the stream, back to her car, but she stands slowly to face Daisy. "That Barney had himself tested and he couldn't have children either." Iris knows she means, *the same as me.* As if that gave them rights Iris doesn't have.

"Liar," she says. "You lie!" Daisy flushes, shakes her head slowly, adamantly, *no.* "How do you know that?"

"He told me, when I — when we talked about my not having any kids either. He said it didn't matter to you, because you didn't want children." She walks the rest of the way back to the tree stump and sits, her shoulders slumped, the straw stetson falling from her fingers to the ground. She may be crying. Iris is unmoved; she's thinking, This would explain why he finally stopped bothering me about children.

"He never told me," Iris says. "I didn't know. Why didn't he tell me? When did he have himself tested? Where?"

"I don't know," Daisy says. "Ten years or more ago, I think. I don't know where. Montana, I suppose." Then she straightens her back slowly, arching it a little, clenches one fist and presses it against her chest, and an expression of such pain crosses her face that Iris looks away.

"Why didn't he tell me?" she says again, plaintively.

"It isn't easy to admit that you're infertile," Daisy replies sadly. "You don't feel like a worthwhile person when you can't have children. A man — " she hesitates, "a man feels like he's not a man. That's why he could tell me and he couldn't tell you. I am famously infertile." She drawls this last, her voice filled with bitterness.

Iris doesn't know what she feels: Regret? Anger at herself? Sorrow at the loss of her unborn babies? She rubs her face with both hands, trying to think. Sweat has broken out again all over her body, and she's furious too at this annoyance, and then at the reminder that it's too late, it's too late, it's too late. *Barney, how could you do this to me?*

Daisy has been watching her apprehensively as if she thinks she might need to run from Iris, or maybe to rush to her aid should she faint or go crazy. But Iris is trying to figure out what really matters here, because she can't handle this confusion.

"Did he love you?" she asks Daisy finally. Daisy looks down at her scuffed boots and turns one ankle as if considering it.

"I don't think so," she says lightly. "Nope," she says. "No, he was going through something. I don't know what. He talked about you — Iris this, Iris that. Never anything important, just — " She shrugs. "What we had — " She falls silent, then goes on. "We had a good time." But the way she says it, Iris knows that it wasn't a good time at all, not for Daisy. Maybe not even for Barney. And knowing him as she does, far better than this woman could know him, she knows too with a frightening sadness that Barney had to have loved Daisy, and in ways Iris would have wanted for herself, but could never arouse in him in all those years together.

Passion, she supposes. Yes, everything about Daisy's history tells Iris that she's a passionate woman, and the truth is, as Iris has known since her affair with James Springer who was passion itself, that she is not a passionate person. She has something else, grace, maybe, or — she doesn't know what. But passion belongs to other people, not to her.

Then she remembers what happened to her in Lannie's apartment in Addis Ababa, when she beat her head against the floor, when she cried because she loved Jay and he didn't love her, and she could never have him. Even though she understands that her anguish was for Barney's loss and not for Jay's. During that endless time of Lannie's near-death she had found that thing in herself that had always been missing — her passion — that she thought she'd been born without and had been glad of. But no, she is just like everyone else after all — as capable of suffering and of joy — has always been like everyone else, only has refused to allow it.

How afraid she has been of suffering. She remembers an hour alone with Ramona in the hospital in Chinook. Ramona had just given birth to her second, or is it her third child. Iris sat in the visitor's chair beside her, leaning close to her, Ramona tired, her cheeks flushed with colour. "What is it like?" she asked. Or maybe she didn't ask, but Ramona told her, "It's pain and work and more pain until you think you can't endure it — You can't imagine how bad it is, Iris. It's like having your bones pulled apart. But then, at that moment when the baby slides at last out of you, what you feel is heat, and the gush of blood, it seems like the whole world is coloured with that blood, this whole ravishing world is made of women's blood."

And Iris refusing that female darkness. Not understanding then that it is the darkness that lights the world.

She glances at Daisy and finds she has stopped hating her.

"I could have had children, as far as I know, anyway, but I didn't want them." Daisy stares, wide-eyed into Iris's face as if she's seeing something there that surprises her. "What I've found out since Barney's death — about being human — that — that is what I tried so hard to escape knowing. I thought that if I had children, I would never again be safe." She presses her palms together in an unconscious gesture of prayer. "I didn't want to know that there is no safety, that no one can ever escape the lot that goes with being a human being. Maybe, in the end, I was just a coward."

She turns away from Daisy then, and walks to the water's edge, crosses, gets in her car, and starts it. As she manoeuvres the car into a turn to drive away, Iris sees Daisy still standing there across the water. She seems very small.

"I've come to take you home with me," Iris says to the figure sitting beside the low window, one arm resting on the sill next to a pink geranium, the legs hidden under an afghan. She hears a laugh, a light, musical sound that confuses her and, with the sunlight coming through the window casting the woman in shadow, she pauses, wondering for an instant if she has come to the wrong room.

She advances, and the shadowy figure sitting in the chaise longue acquires features, the mauve bedjacket with the frill at the neck, the narrow satin bow quivering against the drooping, puckered skin of the throat, the two gaunt, trembling hands resting now on the afghan, and the eyes, so blue, two beams of light in the dim old face surrounded by the thin cloud of white hair.

"Home?" her mother says, her voice quavering. "I've been here long enough to call this home." She closes her eyes and lets her head fall back to rest against the leather couch. Iris stoops to kiss her withered, powder-dry cheek, and sits.

"I should never have left you here," Iris says. "It was wrong of me. It was so wrong and I'm so terribly sorry. Forgive me, Mom." Lily opens her eyes. Their unseemly brightness today frightens Iris, it speaks to her of some otherworldliness creeping into this still living person. She is afraid, she finds, of what these old, wise eyes might see.

"Did I ever ask to come back to the farm?" her mother asks. Iris is taken aback. No, her mother had never asked to come home. "Do you think that because I'm old I have no sense of what my life should be?"

"It isn't that I think that exactly," she says. "But only that you aren't strong enough to do things without help, and so I thought maybe you haven't . . ." *Known*, she was about to say.

"I have thought it often," her mother says. "But I have known what must be given up." Iris sits back, recognizing that her mother has finally gone somewhere that Iris will not be able to follow.

And her eyes, so large and glittering, so unlike her mother's eyes. It's as if with them Lily is swallowing the whole earth and everything that's on it — all of us, Iris thinks, and our past together, and the barn and the rippling yellow grasses and the swallows and the radishes in her garden and the babies and the blue-checked apron she wore on Easter Sunday, and the tines of the fork she held in her hand when she ate, and the yellow cup her mother gave her to drink out of when she, Lily, was a child and that I, Iris, still have somewhere. She is eating the earth, my mother is, this life, she is going to digest it at last and then leave it behind. And I too am now no more than that yellow cup, so precious and so insignificant, or the tang of the earth in the spring, or the white stones on the prairie.

She would cry out, *Mother, do not leave me.* But the futility of this is clear. It is as if the earth has rumbled and split, opening a chasm between the two of them.

Her mother has always loomed so large in her life, an omnipresent, giant shadow in which Iris has walked. She has not remembered that her mother walked in her mother's shadow, and that mother in hers, and on and on, backwards into darkness. That her love and reverence for her mother are both necessary and over. That in some new and profound way she can barely imagine, she will have to cast off her daughterhood to achieve herself.

And, of course, she knows her mother will die soon, and that she, Iris, like every other child, will never cease to miss her and to mourn her. For a split second she holds both these worlds in her cupped hand and cannot tell which is the more true or the least true, which matters more and which less. And then she thinks, I will bear my grief in this knowledge; I will stop being the child in order to become the mother.

It is late afternoon, the days are growing shorter, and Iris is leaving the deck to go for a walk wanting to enjoy every moment of every day before the snow comes, the storms and blizzards, the shattering cold that is life on the Great Plains, that linger in back of the bright shadows of the hottest day. The caragana hedges are losing their leaves, and beyond them the harvested fields lie in shattered strips of brown or thin rows of gold where the crops have been taken. A good harvest, a good profit made. For the last time, she tells herself and feels excitement.

Then she hears a motor and lifts her head to see the Swans' red car putt-putting up the access road to the driveway where she stands. It halts a few feet from her, the driver's door opens and Jay Anselm emerges. For an instant her knees go weak before she steadies herself. He comes toward her slowly not quite frowning, his mouth wavering, his eyes troubled, glances off to the fields and then back to her as he reaches her. They stand facing each other, neither speaking for a long moment. He clears his throat, she moves her feet, they both speak at once, laugh, and Iris says, "You first," and when he seems to be having trouble finding something to say now she has given her permission, she says, "It's nice to see you, what are you doing here?"

"I've decided to stay in Chinook, at least for a while. The novel —" He shrugs, smiles at her, but when he bends his face close to kiss her, she turns her head so that his kiss lands on her cheek. "You're angry," he says. Now she's searching quickly through herself to find that centre so newly discovered, out of which truth flows. She steps back, away from him.

"I was about to go for a walk," she says. "Would you like to come?" They set out walking, squeezing through the hedge, rounding the yard, then moving side by side down the machinery trail that leads to the coulee where months ago he kissed her for the first time, where Barney came to help her on the day of his funeral, where her grandparents first settled when they came from the Old World to make a home in the new one. They don't speak as they walk; it is as if he can divine her need to be silent.

At the patch of prairie he goes immediately to the edge of the coulee and stands staring out over the immense view beyond the small curving river glinting softly in the fading golden light, toward the purple river cliffs and above them to the brilliant, deep blue of the late fall sky. She walks past the stone circles, past the depression that is all that's left of her grandparents' lives, past the hapless, decaying old barn. The grass is stiff and yellow and smells of dust.

"How beautiful it is here," he says, but she is looking at the earth.

"It's dry, there's been no rain, pray for snow this winter." And yet, there is such beauty in the brilliance of winter. And after it, comes spring.

"You're angry because I left you. I had to go, I had things to do — "

"I'm not angry," she says quietly. "I was hurt, I admit that, but if I'm angry with anyone, it's with myself. My fascination with you was very foolish. I thought you were something you were not — "

He turns back to her quickly. "What did you think I was?" The quickness of his question startles her.

"I thought you were my youth, I guess. For one crazy moment I thought I could have it back, as if all those years of Barney — all those years of *living* could be scrubbed away and I could start all over again." He's still staring at her, wants her to say something more, or something different. It makes her pause in surprise at what she sees now is his desperation. "It isn't your fault it's over, or at least not in any way you seem to be able to do anything about. I met this handsome, interesting young man and I went sailing off into never-never land. You're a figment of my imagination, Jay." She says this last softly, laughing a little at herself, then lifting her head to gaze around her at the prairie, at the fields of her farm, and back toward the house she has lived in nearly all her life. "I was lost," she says to him. "But now I'm found." He's moving toward her, she sees he wants to hold her and kiss her, to will her back into his spell, and she puts up her hand to stop him.

For when she looks at him she sees him clearly even though the sun is low on the horizon and all the shadows are growing long and crickets are lilting in the narrow slough below them. He is a handsome man, although not as beautiful as she once thought. Gazing at him she can see what a lot of trouble he is. At her age she hasn't the energy for a man like this. "You'd be better off with a woman your own age." He's silent, gazing at her.

Looking down at the circle of stones they've inadvertently stopped inside, he says, "Our lovemaking was no imaginary event. It was good — "

"Jay. I thought I was in love with you. It was foolish of me; it was wrong. Sometimes I can hardly believe what a fool I've been — " She tries again. "I was desperate — I couldn't see a future so I grabbed at a chance to go backwards, to be a girl again. As if anyone ever could. Life is a stream and it only runs in one direction."

"Iris," he says, moving toward her again. "I — "

"It runs to the sea, Jay," she tells him. "That's where it's going — to the sea."

Iris wakes suddenly as if someone has been calling her. It's four in the morning, but she's wholly awake and alert, knows she won't sleep again. She has only partly drawn the curtains and the moon is shining in across her bed, flooding the carpet and the mirrored wall with its white light. She listens. Is someone in the room with her? In the silvery shadows at the end of the bed a figure is taking shape, a dark robe or a cape, a head covered with a nun's veil or a *shamma*, a woman's face, the round cheek, the dark eyes gleaming in the moonlight. Then it's gone, melts slowly away into the shadows.

She listens again, but the house is silent, Lannie in her room sound asleep, and Misty in hers. How good it feels to have the house full.

The moonlight illumines the pages of the book she has left open on her new desk. She lies still musing about all the books and papers she still has to read. There's so much to learn that sometimes she thinks she will never be able to educate herself properly about the issues that she really cares deeply about: food for the hungry, crops, biodiversity, water supplies, the true nature of the grassland and its place in some not-yet-formulated system to provide food security.

She regrets deeply all the wasted years, the education she turned away from. Whenever she despairs, thinking herself too old to learn all she needs to, she forces herself to count the years ahead of her, to spread them out and see them as day after day, and then she knows that as long as she stops wasting time, she has enough left to find out what she needs to know, and to do what she wants to do.

She hopes in two years' time, with Lannie's, Vance's, and Ramona's help, maybe even Misty's too, to have found a legal way to establish people on her land, to have the capital in place to supply them with homes, equipment, and a living, to have recruited the first special few, and to have done enough research to know what seed she needs — the native seeds of the original short, mixed grass prairie, and from nearby — and to have purchased some to begin her reclamation project, to have built a greenhouse and started the plants herself so as to have more seed.

They have agreed to set the first people up on a plot adjacent to the mouth of the coulee because there is already a water supply there, and because it is still in native prairie. Already, she and Vance have begun to locate the few patches of native grass remaining in their area in order to get more seed most nearly indigenous to her fields. She sees a husband and wife hand-broadcasting the seed mixture from seeds, or using one of the grass seeders other prairie-restorationists have invented. It's an experiment, she says to herself, there may be a better way, and if there is, in time we'll find it.

She and Lannie have begun to search out the experts and to talk with them. Soon they'll travel to Arizona to see all the systems people there have developed to save precious water. She sees in the shadowed ceiling a council of all the people who'll come to help them, the farmers of the new millennium, deep in discussion about alternatives, exchanging ideas, arguing, shouting, laughing together. A thrill runs down her back. This will come, she's sure of it.

And, too, they've had their first confrontations with the doubters, telling them her dream. To start over again, here, on this land, first, to put it back the way it was, and then to find out what it was we should have done a hundred years ago. "We are not too old a country, we are not too overpopulated; we haven't yet done irrevocable damage. We can learn from the Native people. We will try to find a way for all of us to have a place of our own that will somehow provide for us." Their countering arguments are predictable, and are not without truth. But she can answer them.

A hundred years, she thinks to herself, pleased with the sound of it. It will take at least that long to set things on these thirteen and some sections to rights again. And when she thinks of the long struggle ahead, she finds she's not afraid of all those who say she's crazy, a dreamer and a fool.

She pushes back the covers, gets out of bed, finds her heavy dressing gown, and goes downstairs, thinking as she passes the dining room the carpenters will be back in three or four hours. They are cutting out a window in the wall facing the land where already she has had a section of the caragana hedge removed. They're building shelves for her new office too. She goes outside and onto the deck, where she leans on the frost-covered railing and stares out over the glinting silver that is the frozen lawn and the newly thin shadows that are leafless shrubs and trees.

The night is still beyond stillness, hushed beyond quiet. It is familiar to Iris, this magical time in the night, whose quality is different from any comparable hush of the daylight hours. She sees everything out there: the trees, the sky, the stars, the moon, the dormant grass below, the quicksilver air, as one whole, and something that lives. She conceives of all that as if that living presence is listening to her, waiting on her in some calm, eternal, and benevolent way.

An owl begins to call softly from the trees along the far side of the house. In their stark, uneven shadow she can't pick out the bird, but it sings on softly, as if it means to remind her of something she has forgotten, or to call up something in her spirit that has always been there, but buried under the rush and disorder of life: a link, her connection to this earth. She thinks of the woman she has just dreamt of, recalls the Madonna in the painting on the church wall in Lalibela.

In the clear light from the moon she sees that her hands resting on the railing are veined and rough, becoming the hands of an old woman. She had thought she and Barney would grow old together, and now, here she is, facing old age without him. She feels such yearning now for a man's love. It troubles her deeply, even though she knows now how much more there is to the world than the love of one man.

She straightens and lifts her eyes to the sky. She doesn't think she has ever seen so many stars, as if they've been multiplying while she has been occupied. They hang above her, the dazzling blooms of the cosmic tree. Somewhere, far out along the river's edge or at the mouth of the coulee coyotes are howling out their ancient grief —

or is it joy? She listens carefully. Their voices make her think of Ethiopia, of the people there who even now may be abandoning their huts, trekking miles across the barren, dusty countryside in search of food. The sound runs through her bones and muscles and blood with all of its primeval yearning. She could lift her head and howl along with them.

The coyotes fall silent and she listens, waiting for them to start up again, but there is no sound, no revelation rushing at her from the crystalline darkness of the centuries. She experiences a second's piercing loneliness, remembers the frightening dream she had of being cast out alone into the empty universe. It occurs to her now that maybe it was only a memory of her own birth, the inexorable rush from the safety of the womb into this care-laden world. But the dream of Eden, she thinks, it is just as real.

The owl flies up from the bushes, a rustling blur of white wings, an angel, departing suddenly for celestial realms.

Acknowledgements

In November 1995, at the invitation of the CEO, John Martin, and the Board of Directors of USC Canada, I went to Ethiopia to observe their "Seeds of Survival" program, a project which consists of scientists and farmers working together. I travelled to the plots of farmers using USC Canada's and the Ethiopian Biodiversity Institute's elite landraces (instead of hybrid seeds), and attended lectures about biodiversity with fellow students from all over the developing world, all of whom were involved in agriculture and the preservation of landraces, and thus biodiversity, in their home countries. John Martin and other members of the USC staff in Canada — Laura Breuer and Susan Fisher — and SoS/Ethiopia workers, field manager Hailu Getu, researchers Dr. Mara Tsega and Bayush Tsegaye, and the eminent plant breeders Dr. Melaku Worede and Dr. Tesfaye Tesemma were most generous in answering my endless questions.

Many people gave their time and their expert knowledge about aspects of this novel, in particular, about their experiences in Ethiopia, and about prairie restoration. I also wish to thank retired nurse Mary Howard; Verna Thompson, editor of the *Eston Press Review*, who sent me material about a controversial land deal in her area; Kathy Baylis of the National Farmers' Union, who sent me information about plant patenting legislation; John Morriss, editor of the *Manitoba Co-operator,* who sent me articles concerning food and food security; and Dan Patterson, manager of Saskatchewan's Farm Land Security Board, who talked with me in a general way about issues the board deals with. Gerald Schmitz, Research Branch,

Library of Parliament, took time from his busy schedule to read and comment on the manuscript.

I cannot thank nurse Beth Mathews of Perth, Ontario, enough for her help in describing the camp where she worked in Ethiopia during the Great Famine of 1984–1985, nor Tanys Hickerty Kush, formerly of Eastend, also a nurse, who allowed me to read her diary of the two years she spent mostly in Sidamo, Ethiopia, during the same time.

In a visit to Ottawa I spoke with Bon E. Cummings of CIDA, Gaetane Gascon and Mel Peters of Oxfam-Canada, Oxfam-Canada staff, and Alice Doell, all who worked in Ethiopia during the war and the famine, or are working there now. Major (retd.) Ted Itani showed me photos and explained to me how the food drops in 1988 and 1989, which he organized, were done and why. Blaine Marchand of CIDA and Ron Elliott of CUSO answered my questions over the phone, and Nancy Gordon of CARE talked with me in my kitchen one July day about her experiences in Kenya and Rwanda, and aid issues in general. Alison Hancock of the CBC was most helpful, as was Brian Stewart, who was kind enough to answer my questions and to show me videotape, some of which was not shown on television. His prizewinning documentary on Tigrayans during and after the famine and war is the most eloquent testament to the courage of Ethiopians.

Carol Shepstone spent hours digging out up-to-date information about Ethiopia, including the reports of the Ethiopian Human Rights Council (EHRCO), and an account of an October 1995 meeting of a group of American Ethiopianists with Prime Minister Meles, in Washington.

In the matter of prairie restoration, Peter Jonker of the University of Saskatchewan; Don Gayton, a range manager (and author) in British Columbia; the eminent plant geneticist, Wes Jackson of the Land Institute in Salina, Kansas; and a host of other range ecologists, biologists, neighbours, and just plain prairie-lovers put up with my questions. The distinguished and much-loved Professor Emeritus, University of Saskatchewan, J. Stan Rowe, was gracious beyond words, as was Dr. Zoheir Abouguendia of Saskatchewan's New Pastures and Grazing Project. Both of them, out of their extensive knowledge of prairie ecology and of restoration projects, helped me elaborate on my basic idea.

Others too numerous to name influenced and taught me. The first of these is always my husband Peter who taught me everything of importance that I know about this agricultural life. I am especially grateful to my editor and publisher, Phyllis Bruce, who believed in this book when I'd almost stopped believing in it, and who wouldn't let me quit too soon. Too often to mention she saved me from myself, and I am endlessly grateful for her wisdom. My agent, Jan Whitford, was encouraging and helpful. I could not have written this book without their help.

Nonetheless, all the views in this novel are my own and no one else's and I take full responsibility for them, and for any errors or omissions or misinterpretations. Nor are any of these characters or experiences taken directly from real life, but are my own invention.